Praise for John Franco[...]

'A taut and twisting plot gallops along all the way to the finish line' *Daily Express*

'The natural successor to Dick Francis' *Irish Times*

'Genuinely exhilarating descriptions of races that capture the tension and excitement . . . could be written only with a jockey's insight' *Daily Mail*

'The racing feel is authentic and it's a pacy, entertaining read' *Evening Standard*

'Francome has produced his best thriller by far. An action-packed storyline that gallops to a thrilling end' *Racing Post*

'Mr Francome is a natural storyteller' *New York Times*

'A murky brew that Francome keeps bubbling nicely . . . the background to the skulduggery is completely persuasive' *Good Book Guide*

'Look out, Dick Francis, here's Francome riding another winner' *Peterborough Evening Telegraph*

'Mr Francome adeptly teases to the very end and cleverly keeps a few twists up his sleeve until the closing chapters' *Country Life*

'Authentic, thrilling and compulsive' *Bookseller*

Also by John Francome and available from Headline

JOHN FRANCOME

Free Fall

headline

First published in 2006
by HEADLINE PUBLISHING GROUP

First published in paperback in 2007
by HEADLINE PUBLISHING GROUP

1

ISBN 978 0 7553 2695 2

Typeset in Veljovic by Avon DataSet Ltd,
Bidford on Avon, Warwickshire

Printed and bound in Great Britain by Clays Ltd, St Ives plc

Headline's policy is to use papers that are natural, renewable
and recyclable products and made from wood grown in
sustainable forests. The logging and manufacturing processes
are expected to conform to the environmental regulations
of the country of origin.

HEADLINE PUBLISHING GROUP
A division of Hachette Livre UK Ltd
338 Euston Road
London NW1 3BH

www.headline.co.uk
www. hodderheadline.com

Free Fall

Prologue

The house stood on its own, surrounded by three acres of land. It was going to be very beautiful when all the building work was finished – so he'd been told. All the original features would be restored inside: the grand staircase, the library panelling and the Victorian stained glass. In time the gardens, too, would be returned to their original glory – the lake would be dredged and the apple orchard replanted. It would be turned into a paradise.

But who for?

For *him* and *her*.

He couldn't bear the thought. He'd spoil it if he could.

The scaffolding on the back of the house went all the way up to the roof. It was a heck of a view from up here. Not that he cared about that. All he cared about was how hard the paving stones were below and what a mess a body would make when it went splat.

They could scrub all they liked but they'd never

get rid of the stain he'd leave behind in their paradise. Every day they'd look out of the window and see the spot where he'd died. On their sweet little trips to the orchard or carrying picnic baskets to the lake they'd have to sidestep his ghost.

He liked the thought of that.

But first of all, he had to have a witness. And there he was.

It would have been better if it was *her*. But now might be his only chance. If he didn't do it now he might never have the courage again. So Alex would have to do.

Alex had been shouting up at him ever since he'd got out of the car. He hadn't bothered to listen to what the man was saying – it was pretty obvious he'd start off by demanding what the effing hell he thought he was doing up there and ordering him to get down. But when Alex took in how he was standing, right on the top tier with his legs over the guard rail, he'd soon change his tune.

Like now. *Come down, you little fool. Don't do anything stupid.*

Couldn't he think of anything more original?

He wondered about the best way to do it. Not that it really mattered, the result must be pretty much the same whatever bit of you hit the ground first.

But to jump with style would be even more memorable. To pick a spot on the flags below and make a dive like off the top board at the swimming pool. That would make a statement.

He'd always liked heights. Like when Mum and Dad took him up Blackpool Tower when he was five. His sister had refused to go all the way to the top and she was older than him. Too scared. But not him. There'd be a heck of a splat if you fell off Blackpool Tower. A long time to think before you hit the ground.

This would have to do.

Where had Alex gone? He couldn't believe the man had turned his back. That would ruin it – his death had to be observed. That was the point.

Then he saw him, climbing up the ladder on to the first storey of the scaffold.

Just stay right where you are. Let's talk about this.

What a joke. Alex is coming to try and talk me down. Like the good guy does in the movies.

Pity the heroine isn't here to see it.

Alex was on the next ladder now, still reading from the Samaritan script.

How close shall I let him get?

Quite close. Close enough so he thinks he's going to pull off his mercy mission. Close enough to see all the grisly details.

Look at me. Stay calm. Take deep breaths.

The idiot thinks I'm freaking out. Can't he see how cool I am?

Now Alex was up on the same level. Still talking in that phoney tone of voice, like some TV doctor.

He's probably intending to make a grab, to pull me back from the brink.

Then he had his brainwave.

Suppose Alex takes the dive instead?

The hero goes splat – that would make a change.

And it would serve the heroine right.

He liked the sound of that.

OK, Alex, come a little closer.

Part One

Chapter One

When he was little, Pat's mam always said he was too clever by half. As the youngest of five, Pat had had to have his wits about him, especially since his four brothers were all strapping Munster lads with rugby players' appetites for a fight. Pat himself was out of a different mould – half their size and nimble, quick brain and quick fingers like his seamstress mam. He was no less keen on sport, though – which was how he'd ended up as a jockey, plying his trade in England. He'd got away from home as fast as he could, leaving the Fighting Vincents, as they were known, and their many troubles back in Ireland. He loved his brothers well enough, the drunken dimwits, but the bond was stronger at a distance. And they appreciated the money he sent them.

Pat was rarely nervous before a race but then it was only rarely he tried to fiddle the result. If his plans were discovered, the consequences didn't bear thinking about – he'd be warned off racing for the rest of his life, chucked out of the only business he knew. Who wouldn't be nervous in those circumstances?

But how could he be caught? The scam was too damn good, conceived in a flash of brilliance in response to the needs of his good mate Andy, not to mention his own hungry tribe of nephews and nieces back in Cork. The moment Pat had dreamed up the sting he knew he was bound to put it into practice. As his mam might say, why else had the Good Lord given him wits, if not to use them?

All the same, as Pat rode out of the parade ring at Bath he cast a swift look back at Joe Parkin, the lad who had just given him a leg-up into the saddle. For a crucial second or so, Pat's weight had been bearing down on Joe's hands and the lad's grin had frozen on his face. Had he noticed anything? Pat wouldn't put it past him, Joe was the yard's travelling head lad and nobody's fool.

But Joe just slapped the animal on the rump and said, 'Good luck, mate,' as he always did.

So, no worries. All he had to do now was lose the race.

Jack Lucas enjoyed watching his horses run at Bath racecourse for a number of reasons. For one thing, he'd achieved a degree of success there over the years he'd been training. Also, it was just seventy miles from his yard on the Somerset coast near

Kilve, which made Bath his local track. That's if you didn't count Taunton, which Jack didn't because Taunton was for jumpers and he was a Flat trainer, always had been. Apart from the convenience of the journey – he could be there in an hour and a half along the motorway – Jack liked the quirky little course, shaped like a bent sausage, situated on top of a hill overlooking the old Roman city. At nearly eight hundred feet above sea level, Bath was the highest Flat-racing course in the country. A man could breathe freely up here, horses too. When one of Jack's runners performed poorly, he always offered 'altitude sickness' as the cause – which amused him, even if some owners didn't find it funny. It was another reason he always enjoyed a trip to Bath.

At the moment, however, Jack wasn't cracking jokes. His weathered brow was furrowed in deep contemplation of the race about to take place. Away to the left from his vantage point in the stands, he could see the eye-catching shape of his runner, Pipsqueak, being loaded into the starting stalls. Jack was too long in the tooth to have favourites amongst the forty-odd horses in his yard, but he couldn't deny that he had a soft spot for this one. In his current crop of two-year-olds, Pipsqueak stood out for his Golden Syrup-coloured coat and white forelegs and for his speed on the gallops. Jack had never trained a Classic winner but he'd had several sprinters who'd gone on to win Group races and he prided himself on spotting quality horses early in their careers. After working closely since the winter with Pipsqueak, he had a good feeling about him. He'd not had such a likely prospect for years.

So far, or so he thought, Pipsqueak had not brought his gallops form to the racecourse. He'd run twice and both occasions had been a disappointment. Jack had dismissed his poor showing at Warwick on his debut as stage fright but coming in fifth at Windsor had not been so easy to rationalise. Today was another chance for the horse to show his true colours – and to prove to Jack that his judgement wasn't failing.

'Cheer up,' said the smartly dressed woman by his side. Pipsqueak's owner: Mrs Leopold. 'I'm not expecting miracles, you know.'

Ursula Leopold had kept horses at Jack's Beach Head stables since she'd been widowed a dozen years previously. Every season she acquired four or five promising yearlings and placed them in Jack's care. He hated to think how big a hole her passion for racing had made in the fortune her husband had left her. Not that she cared. 'I can't take it with me,' she often said. 'It's either horses or toy boys and I think horses are less risky in the long run, don't you?'

Jack thought that owners didn't come much better than Mrs Leopold. It was another reason why he hoped Pipsqueak would perform today.

He turned towards her. 'If he runs like the other morning he'll win this pulling up.'

Two days ago Ursula had stood with Jack on the seaside gallops watching Pipsqueak leave the rest of the novices in his wake as he flashed across the turf.

She nodded. 'Watching is the worst bit for you, isn't it, Jack?'

He forced a smile on to his face. The owner shouldn't be bucking the trainer's spirits up – it should be the other way round. But today was different. He had an emotional investment in Pipsqueak that wasn't wise. Perhaps his judgement wasn't what it once was.

How did a man know when it was time to pack it in?

'At least we've got a low draw.'

The sprint course at Bath had a distinct bend to the left before joining the home straight and it helped to be drawn close to the far rail. Fortunately, that's where Pipsqueak was placed.

'There's nothing you can do now, Jack. It's up to Pat.'

Pat Vincent had been Jack's stable jockey for the past three years and had ridden every one of Mrs Leopold's horses – she insisted on it.

The starting gates sprang open.

'Come on, Pat,' Ursula shouted at his side.

The horses hurtled towards them.

* * *

Pat was well acquainted with the Bath track. In his ten years as a jockey he had ridden it dozens of times and every kink, curve and sudden gradient was familiar to him. In a short race like this – a five-furlong dash for the line – his tactics were clear: hug the rail down the slope and get your horse set up for the left-hand bend. If you got it right, and having a low draw was a big help, you could shoot the horse out of the bend and into the straight with an advantage over the animals drawn outside. Then it was a question of galloping like hell on the uphill run-in to the stands and hoping the horse held on.

Pat had made up his mind to give Pipsqueak every chance to make up for his previous failures. If it went wrong again, he was determined no one would be pointing a finger at him.

There were eight runners in the race. All of them, like Pipsqueak, were real babies on the track; some of them had only run once before. But good horses learn quickly. The careers of Flat-racing horses are short and if they don't cotton on fast, their chances of making a mark are soon gone.

It was plain to Pat that Pipsqueak's previous appearances on the racecourse had not been wasted. The horse didn't react in the parade ring when one of the other runners began to act up and he stepped into his allotted starting stall without protest – unlike his first two races. And as they headed into the left-breaking elbow in the course, he held his position on the rail and accelerated out onto the straight at the first touch of Pat's stick.

Pat shared Jack's opinion of Pipsqueak. The animal had a lot of promise and was destined to win some decent races.

But not this one.

With half the race run, they were in prime position, ahead by half a length and Pipsqueak was lengthening his stride under instruction as he dug in up the hill.

It was looking good. Looking good was what counted.

Then the first horse overtook them.

Pat went for his whip and Pipsqueak responded.

A second horse went by.

Pat rode his mount as hard as he could. No one could say that he and the horse weren't giving everything they had.

They were in the last furlong now, lying third. Where were the others?

In the last fifty yards another horse came past, then another. Pipsqueak didn't want to let him but he'd given everything.

They finished fifth. Thank God for that. It would have been a nuisance if they'd come in fourth and Pat had had to sit on the scales for a second time. But they only weighed in the first four jockeys for a little race like this.

'Sorry, boss,' he said to Jack as the trainer laid a consoling hand on Pipsqueak's shoulder.

'It's OK, Pat. You gave him a great ride.'

That was true enough. Sometimes it was a damn sight harder to lose than to win.

The most difficult part of all, however, was seeing the disappointment on the faces of owner and trainer. There were punters out there, too, who had suffered but Pat didn't know them. It wasn't so easy to dismiss Mrs Leopold and Jack Lucas – and God forbid Zoe should ever find out. He was always trying to impress on her that he wasn't perfect but his adorable young girlfriend thought the sun shone out of his arse.

He'd just have to ensure she carried on thinking that way.

No worries. Pat was one of life's optimists.

Andy Burns had delayed taking the dog for his walk until the first race at Bath was over. Jasper didn't like it but that was too bad. In any case, it was for his own good. The silly mutt benefited from a happy home as much as anyone and Pipsqueak's fortunes at Bath had a direct bearing on domestic bliss, or lack of it, in the Burns' household.

The way Andy had it figured was that his wife, Harriet, would have more time and respect for a husband who owned his own business, as he had done when they had first met. Going back to work for someone else – even a first-rate fellow like Jack Lucas – had been a blow. And the gambling debts he had racked up in the subsequent years had further diminished him in his wife's eyes – which, of course, was why he couldn't now tell her he was on a guaranteed winning streak. If she found out he was betting again, he suspected that might be the last he saw of her. He'd sworn blind he'd never ever place another bet and he'd lied to her. He felt bad about that.

Mind you, she'd lied about certain matters too.

But he dismissed those matters from his mind as he watched Pipsqueak labour on the run-in and finish fifth. Andy greeted the defeat with the enthusiasm he'd once reserved for victory. If Jasper had understood horse-racing he'd have thought his master was bonkers.

Now the Jack Russell skipped happily ahead of him up the steep steps cut into the hill that led to the cliff path, their customary route.

Pat was touched with genius in Andy's book. There was an art to fixing races and getting away with it; Pat excelled at both.

But, as Pat often reminded him, they were a team and Andy's job was as important as Pat's. Not that he'd had anything to do today but next time Pipsqueak ran, Andy would have his hands full. Because next time Pipsqueak would be trying to win and Andy would have to get the money on.

That's how they'd worked it during the winter on the all-weather tracks. Pat laid the groundwork with losing runs and then, when the odds were at their most generous, Andy placed the bets – a task forbidden to jockeys. So far it had worked like a dream and the money was in Andy's account to prove it.

Soon he'd be back on his feet and not even Harriet could quibble about that.

Harriet – it never took long before his thoughts were back with his mercurial flame-haired wife. Pat was now shacked up with her younger sister, Zoe, and most of the lads at the yard thought he had the pick of the Morris sisters.

But, for all Zoe's blonde prettiness, Andy would never trade.

Maybe he shouldn't but he pulled his phone from his pocket and speed-dialled Harriet's number. He couldn't help himself.

Her mobile chimed just as Harriet noted that the fair-haired figure on the tennis court below had changed ends. It was a blessing and a curse that her station at the hair salon was next to the window with an uninterrupted view of the health centre courts below. It was only natural that her attention should stray in that direction from time to time. And when Martin, the new tennis coach, was at work, bending and stretching his athletic frame, gliding without effort next to the donkeys he taught, Harriet had to make an effort to keep her eyes on her customers' hair. And that had been before she started sleeping with him.

She checked the small screen of her phone –

Andy calling. Of course it was. It was tempting to ignore her husband but he deserved better than that.

'Hi, sweetheart. Everything OK?'

He was always concerned about her and sometimes she thought that was sweet. But at times like this, when her mind was full of Martin, it was an irritation – made worse by guilt.

She'd been surprised to discover Martin was younger than she was. He'd confessed to her after they'd made love for the first time – strictly speaking, the second time because he'd scarcely allowed her to draw breath between the two acts – and she'd been lying in his arms, heart still thumping, fingers tracing the golden skin of his chest, drinking in the unbelievable newness of him, listening to his life story. Not that there had been much of it but she'd never been in bed with a tennis champion before. Nor, for that matter, a graduate in economics from the LSE. A man, it turned out, of education and culture.

Even though he'd first caught her attention on the tennis court and, if asked, she might have agreed she fancied him in an abstract, what's-the-harm-in-dreaming sort of way, she'd never have approached him – or even considered it. She'd blotted her copybook once in her marriage and sworn, to herself most importantly, that it would never happen again.

One day three weeks earlier she'd been crossing the centre concourse when he'd rushed up to her.

'Hi, Mrs Thomson. Ken can't make it today. He's very sorry but I can take the lesson if that's OK.'

'You've got the wrong person,' she said.

'You're not Mrs Thomson?'

'No.'

'Oh.' He had blue eyes, as clear as a summer sky. Now they were clouded with confusion. 'Are you sure?'

She laughed and he coloured with embarrassment.

'I mean,' he said, 'the way Ken described her I was sure it had to be you. I mean,' he turned to look at the busy concourse, 'do you see any other Titian-haired beauties around here?'

She'd virtually run off at that point, the encounter was a bit too weird and overwhelming. But later she'd looked up Titian hair and discovered it was a fancy way of saying redhead. Beauty, though – there was no mystery about that. Had he been trying to pick her up?

Two days later, in the café, he'd discovered her in the queue and insisted on buying her coffee.

'Did you ever find her?' she asked.

'Find who?'

'Mrs Thomson.'

He'd given her a dazzling smile, all white sparkling teeth and laughing eyes. 'Who's Mrs Thomson?'

So it *had* been a ruse to pick her up but things had gone past the point where she wanted to be put down again.

'If you don't know who Titian is,' he said, 'I've got a fantastic book on Renaissance art.'

She'd accepted the invitation and its inevitable consequence. It was all pretty hackneyed really, except it was honeyed over with the gloss of a desire she had not been able to resist.

'Andy, I'd better go,' she said into the phone. 'Diane Connor's just turned up.'

That was true enough. The young woman in designer sweatpants was being led to the chair by the window. She waved a hello.

To be honest, Harriet had a good five minutes while one of the girls washed the woman's hair and rustled up a cappuccino.

'Is that the one whose husband owns a property company?'

'You've got a good memory.'

It was one of the things she'd always appreciated about Andy. She could come home from work, dump a whole day's worth of trivia on him and he'd remember it – not a skill that many husbands possessed, as far as she could tell. Though sometimes it could prove awkward. It had been responsible for Andy finding out about her fall from grace two years earlier. A lot of her husband's calls, she knew, were to check up on her whereabouts. Such as that occasion ten days ago.

'I'm in the car,' she'd told Andy. 'I had to dash out to Tesco's.'

She'd thought she'd got away with it even though

19

she was lying stark naked in Martin's arms on the cramped bed in his tiny loft room. Andy had seemed to accept what she said and was prattling on about some stupid horse when Martin's mobile had gone off on the other side of the room. Talk about bad timing.

'What was that?'

'Nothing,' she blurted as Martin scrambled to switch the bloody thing off. It wasn't an adequate response.

'That was a phone. Whose is it? Who's with you?'

'No one's with me.'

'Don't bullshit me, Harriet. You said you were in the car.'

His voice had gone hard. It was the tone he used when he was beyond outrage and panic. He'd gone straight to cold-blooded fury.

'I *am* in the car.' The panic was in her voice. 'I'm sitting in Tesco's car park.'

'Who's in the car with you?'

'No one, I swear. I've got the window open and someone's phone went off as they walked by.' She was recovering now. She'd slipped up but she knew how to make good her ground. 'God, Andy, you're such a suspicious bastard. Just because you're pissed off about some effing horse you think you can take it out on me.'

'What do you mean? I'm not talking about horses.'

It had been OK after that. Once she'd got him on

the back foot she knew how to broaden the argument and vent her frustrations about the narrowness of their lives – about his job and hers and the lack of money that tied them to the poxy little cottage that they didn't even own. It was all true enough, on one level anyway, but afterwards she felt bad about putting Andy through the wringer, because none of it was his fault.

Later he'd apologised for acting like a suspicious sod. He'd been out of order – could she forgive him? She found that she could, though she didn't feel great about it.

If only her feelings weren't so complicated.

Apologies or not, Andy was now in the habit of ringing her at work a couple of times a day, just to let her know he was thinking of her. She supposed that was considerate of him. It was also, sometimes, a bloody nuisance.

'I'm sorry, Andy,' she said now as she watched Diane, her hair freshly shampooed, being led to the chair by the window, 'but I must go.'

Thank God for that. She'd kept her insecure husband happy. This time anyway.

Andy put the phone back in his pocket. He shouldn't have called Harriet. He could tell from the frosty tone of her goodbye that he'd simply irritated her.

Jasper had charged along the cliff path while Andy made his call and was now no longer in view.

Andy didn't bother to summon him back; he knew Jasper was eager to get up to the top where his keen terrier eyesight might be rewarded. Jasper lived for hunting rabbits.

If the rabbits had any sense, the dog's arrival would not come as any surprise. Andy brought him up here six days a week, often seven, in his break from Beach Head stables where he worked as head lad. He'd leave Jack's yard at half twelve and be home within ten minutes. By the time he'd fixed some lunch and leafed through the racing paper, it would be a few minutes after two'clock and time to take Jasper for his walk. Maybe it was his army training, or the discipline of running a racing yard like Beach Head, but Andy believed in regular habits. For him, routine was not a dirty word.

It would have been a better routine if he'd been able to see more of his wife. Every day he was up at five to be in the yard by a quarter to six, while Harriet was just a bundle beneath the blankets and a copper-coloured cloud of hair across the pillow. Even if she were awake he'd get no civil words out of her at that hour. And when he came home for lunch, she was at work. Then it was back to the yard for four and he'd often not be home till half the evening had gone, especially on race days when horses were back late from meetings across the country.

It was worst of all in the Flat season, and that was eight months of the year. He'd be in the yard each

Saturday and Sundays too when race days choked up the calendar. Last summer, he reckoned he'd barely seen Harriet in the hours of daylight. Two weeks in Lanzarote in January was not long enough to keep a marriage shipshape and storm-proof.

Andy had never thought of himself as the jealous type. Before, back in his army days and when he'd first worked at Beach Head, he couldn't remember shedding any tears when a girlfriend decided she preferred someone else. But none of those girls had much mattered to him. Some had been brash and some needy but their company had been strictly for entertainment.

Harriet had been different. Reserved and pale, she appealed to him at first because she made so little effort to be appealing. And he recognised the protective wall she'd built around herself because he'd built one too. He'd needed it after he'd left home and gone into the army. They were at a party and she'd been cold-shouldering the boys who'd sauntered over to her. Andy had thought he'd try his luck too – there was something special about her.

'You're not enjoying this much, are you?' he'd said to her. 'Me neither,' and he'd given her a spiel about not being one of the crowd and making his own way in life. Not long afterwards, he'd discovered she'd only gone to the party to keep a discreet eye on her younger sister though she'd not introduced him that first night. Later, he'd asked her why.

'I wanted to hear what kind of bullshit you were going to come up with,' she replied. 'Anyhow, she's too cute to introduce to men I'm interested in.'

He'd laughed. There was no denying Zoe was pretty but the notion that he'd prefer her to Harriet was preposterous.

He'd probably never have broken down Harriet's barriers if it wasn't for her mother's death soon after he'd met her. But he'd been with her that night and so he'd driven her to the family home where Zoe had found the dying woman and he'd done his best to help, dealing with the paramedics and the hospital and, later, the undertakers. Harriet had needed him then and, by the time it was all over, there was cement in their partnership. At the time he'd been two years into training on his own account, running his own small yard on a shoestring, mortgaged up to the hilt but determined to make a go of it.

He remembered his reaction when Harriet told him she was pregnant. Not 'That's the last thing I need' – which was what she'd expected, he could tell. It had simply been 'Fantastic!' A response born of pure instinct. A baby with Harriet was the piece of the jigsaw that would complete his new life. By God, he'd make a success of his business if it was for a family of his own.

They'd been married within six weeks.

Then Harriet lost the baby on their honeymoon and his one decent owner blundered into an expensive divorce and had to get out of racing. With only half a dozen horses left in his yard and the bank breathing down his neck, Andy had grabbed a lifeline – his old job back at Jack's place. Jack was a great man, in Andy's book. He'd have been sunk without him.

The breeze on top of the cliff ballooned Andy's shirt outwards and rattled the gorse. Two fields inland he could see a brown and brindle blur as Jasper streaked after some prey, probably imaginary. Away to his left the water of the Bristol Channel was almost Mediterranean blue as it surged onto the cracked limestone of the beach below.

A perfect early summer day, Andy noted, but now it was spoiled.

He mulled over the conversation with Harriet. Whatever she said, she never sounded pleased to hear from him. As if she was putting on an act for his benefit. It reminded him of how she'd behaved when he'd caught her out last time – that's if you ever could catch Harriet out. The evidence then was circumstantial and there'd been no confession, but his was the only verdict that counted. And he'd been sure at the time that she was guilty.

He'd spent a couple of nights away when Jack had asked him to attend the Ebor Festival in York. They'd won a good race on the last day and he'd stayed on an extra night for the owner's party. He'd made an early start the next day and driven back in the early hours of a wet morning. The rain had stopped by the time he parked outside the cottage and the first thing he noticed was a car-shaped dry patch in the small driveway.

'What did you get up to last night?' he'd asked Harriet as they sat in the kitchen over breakfast.

'Nothing much,' she'd said. 'Just watched the box and went to bed. I was tired.'

'You didn't have company then?'

'No.'

'So whose car was parked here overnight? There's a dry spot outside.'

Her green eyes were unreadable as they met his accusing stare.

'Zoe stayed the night.'

'But you just said you were on your own.' His hands were trembling.

She rolled her eyes. 'No, Andy. You asked if I'd had company and my sister doesn't count as company.'

He'd felt impotent, as if she'd tricked him. For all her weaselling around, she'd lied to him. Hadn't she?

He'd run upstairs to the bedroom. The windows were open and the room was neat. Freshly tidied.

She watched without comment as he'd ripped the covers off the bed. The sheets were fresh, just changed. The sound of the washing machine echoed up the stairs.

'So?' she finally challenged him. 'Zoe slept in here with me. I thought you'd like to come home to clean sheets.'

He'd wanted to slap the superior expression off her two-timing face – but he couldn't be absolutely sure she was lying. So he'd gone in search of Zoe and found her mucking out in the yard. She'd only just started work as an apprentice, newly graduated from the Newmarket training academy; he had persuaded Jack to give her a job.

To her credit, she'd looked unhappy when he began to quiz her about the night before. Yes, she'd stayed over with Harriet and left early, she hoped he didn't mind. But she couldn't tell him what they'd been watching on the TV – 'Just the usual rubbish. We turned it off and talked.' Her voice was firm but she hadn't looked Andy in the eye when she said it. Harriet had got to her, Andy knew it.

Things had been bad after that. Circumstances he'd not thought twice about came back to haunt him. The nights Harriet had been home late because of a last-minute booking at the salon. Phone calls when the caller had hung up at the sound of his voice. The pair of size 12 trainers he'd found in the boot of her car – she said she'd given a customer and her boyfriend a lift home and they'd fallen out of his bag. He'd believed her at the time.

He started spying on her and monitoring her responses to him in bed. After the overnight incident, she'd become much more enthusiastic – but that's how she would behave, wouldn't she, if she had something to hide.

Eventually, his anger cooled and his suspicions dulled. They'd talked once more about having children and she'd been keen – at least he'd thought she had been. That was the problem with betrayal: like remission from cancer, you could never tell when the disease might come back.

But she'd not fallen pregnant yet. He'd assumed it would just happen naturally, like it had done before. He thought that, before long, they ought to talk to a doctor but he'd not dared raise the subject with Harriet. Suppose she told him she'd changed her mind?

Suppose she told him she was in love with someone else?

Jasper was back now, breathing heavily, his tongue lolling.

'Let's go,' Andy said but the dog was off again, shooting along the path that skirted the cliff edge ahead. Andy refrained from calling him back. At least one of them was enjoying himself out here.

If only they hadn't lost that baby. With a child on her hands Harriet wouldn't be out working, at least not full-time in that trendy new health complex where she could meet all kinds of sporty guys and thrusting office types. She and Andy would have been a proper team, building a home together and, maybe, they'd have managed to have more kids.

Well, they still might turn it around and have that family. Whatever his wife thought, Andy was not prepared to throw in the towel just yet. Harriet might think he was a financial screw-up, a wage slave with no ambition, but he was about to prove her wrong. When he was back training in his own right, with a yard full of potential Classic winners, let her look him in the face and say she didn't want him any more.

He glanced at his watch. Time to get back down. He whistled for Jasper but there was no pounding of doggy paws in response. He shouted. Still the animal did not appear.

What had the silly dog got up to? Andy strode down the path in the direction Jasper had taken. Fifty yards ahead, the small bank of grass and undergrowth that separated the footpath from the cliff edge had been eroded and Andy knew that, on the other side, there was a sheer drop to the beach a hundred feet below.

'Jasper!' he bellowed and broke into a run.

Chapter Two

Diane Connor had good hair, thick, lustrous and able to withstand most things fashion demanded – which was just as well, in Harriet's opinion. Diane was one of her best customers chiefly because she was always requesting some new colour or cut. Maybe it was because she used to be a model, but if I had her money, Harriet thought, I'd find better things to do than have my hair restyled every five minutes.

Diane was more than just a regular customer. At some point in the low period after the end of Harriet's affair, she'd become a friend. Or, at any rate, someone to confide in over a glass of wine on the nights Andy was working late at the yard. There were many advantages to her company, among them that Diane knew nothing about racehorses and cared less. Also, which was even more important, she knew no one connected with Andy or Beach Head yard.

'Oh, for God's sake,' she'd said at the end of Harriet's tense whispered confession about Andy virtually catching her in bed with Robin, 'you've got to stop beating yourself up. Don't tell me your Andy wouldn't jump on some horny little stable girl if he got the chance.'

'He wouldn't.' Harriet spoke with complete certainty.

'Lucky you. I'm never certain quite what Maurice gets up to when he's off on one of his trips.'

'Doesn't that worry you?'

'Up to a point. If I had proof he was cheating on me I'd cut his balls off.' Diane crunched into a peanut to emphasise her point. 'But I do think old married couples should give each other room to breathe.' And she'd smiled a sly grin which Harriet had taken to mean she wasn't the only sinner at the table.

Room to breathe – that had struck a chord and still did. Andy smothered her sometimes. She was committed to him for the long haul but didn't he realise that sometimes she needed room to breathe?

'I hope,' said Diane now, grinning at Harriet in the mirror, 'that I can rely on your full attention.'

'What do you mean?'

'You're like some kid drooling outside a sweet shop.' Diane cast her eyes sideways, indicating the window to her left and the spectacle of Martin.

The Cut Above hair salon was on the first floor of the complex, hence its name, which Harriet found cringeworthy. The view was useful, however. Apart from the tennis courts, she could keep an eye on the café concourse below and the car park. A couple of times she'd had an early sight of Andy's battered Escort nosing into a space. Not that she'd been doing anything she shouldn't but she didn't like to be taken unprepared. As she had been by Diane's remark.

'Is it that obvious?'

'Only to me. Because I know your guilty little secret.'

For a second Harriet wondered whether she should have confided in Diane but what was the point of a girlfriend like her if she didn't? Anyway, she was the only one who knew. Apart from Zoe, of course.

'I must say,' Diane continued, 'he does look rather fine on court, much sexier than cuddly Ken.'

Ken was the senior tennis coach. He gave Diane regular lessons which, according to her, made absolutely no difference to her ability. Harriet wondered why she bothered – until she reminded herself that Diane was in the business of filling up her leisure hours. It was all right for some.

'Did Martin ever try to make it as a professional?' Diane asked. 'I mean, is he actually any good?'

'He was in the final of Junior Wimbledon. Then he had knee trouble and decided to pack it in.'

Martin had told Harriet about it the first time

they lay squeezed together in his narrow bed, a shaft of spring sunshine from the high small windows falling across their bodies, an orchestra playing in the background – Brahms, Martin had told her; it was all very romantic. 'The doctors said I stood a risk of permanent damage,' he'd explained as she lovingly examined the swollen contours of his right kneecap. 'So you'd better be gentle with me.' She'd been more than that.

'Why is it, do you think,' Diane continued, 'that I only ever see him teaching girls?'

Really?

'He has lots of male pupils.'

'Like her down there in a pink skirt?'

Across the net from Martin on the court below was a lanky teenager.

'So what? I'm told he's a very good teacher,' Harriet said defensively. Diane was just teasing but, in her opinion, it was hardly a subject suitable for jokes.

Out on the court below the players were packing up. The girl in the pink skirt was bending over to pick up balls, revealing an enviable length of teenage leg. Was Martin enjoying the show? For a second Harriet's stomach lurched in panic, till she saw the blond figure below looking up in her direction. He often looked up at her window – thinking of her, he said, though she was hidden behind the blue-tinted glass. This time he held his racquet up in a salute.

Silly boy, she'd tell him that he really ought to be more discreet.

Zoe Morris drove back from Newmarket with the horses. It was a fair old ride from Suffolk to Somerset in the lorry and she didn't expect to be back much before ten. As a rule, when they were riding at the same meetings, she travelled with Pat and those journeys were one of the high points of the week. Pat drove his Audi like the wind and always knew some interesting spot to stop off, from rock-and-roll transport caffs to country-park hotels. He'd chauffeured her all through last summer – her first full season as an apprentice jockey – and by the end of it she was head over heels in love. By then, of course, the stopovers had turned into all-nighters, followed by a hectic dash in the small hours to get her to Beach Head stables on time to muck out. Not that Zoe cared about missing a few hours of sleep. She was twenty-one and out to make the most of it – she had the rest of her life to doze off.

Nowadays she and Pat didn't have to stop off anywhere to enjoy some time alone, not since his housemate had left and Zoe had moved in with him. It was only a few weeks ago but she felt like they were a proper couple, as good as married. Like Harriet and Andy – only, God forbid, not remotely like Harriet and Andy at all. She would never use Pat the way her sister used her husband. She had no idea if her romance with Pat would last – he was her first serious boyfriend – but she was determined to give it the best shot she could. And she'd certainly never look at another man while she was committed to him. It wouldn't be right.

That afternoon she'd turned down a lift from another jockey who'd said he was going to Taunton and offered to take a detour to drop her off. Zoe had a pretty good idea what kind of detour he had in mind and she'd not been impressed. She supposed she could have strung him along and got back to Somerset faster but it wasn't the kind of game she liked to play. So she'd opted for the horse box with old Ted at the wheel, who wasn't the world's greatest conversationalist. But she didn't mind. Nothing could spoil the glow of satisfaction that the afternoon's race meeting had given her.

A win at the headquarters of racing. Her first. If she had to give up tomorrow, no one could ever say she wasn't a decent rider. Look at the record book, she'd say. And there'd be a DVD of it too; Pat had promised to set the recorder.

Pat had been so generous to her since she'd gatecrashed his life. He'd not raised a murmur when she'd started rearranging his place. 'Just leave my study alone,' he'd said. Since the study was little more than a broom cupboard, with barely room for a chair, a computer and a pile of riding kit, she was happy to steer clear. She'd gone to town on the rest of the place, though, and he'd let her.

She thought he might object to the squashy pink cushions she'd bought for the bedroom but he'd just rolled his eyes and said that if they were what she wanted, he guessed he could live with them.

Since she'd moved in, Pat had been lovely to her in every way. The moment she'd left the changing room and turned her phone back on, Pat had been on the line saying how thrilled he was for her.

'You're a little star,' he said, sounding as happy as if he'd had a hatful of winners himself. 'I'll be down at the yard tonight – I can't wait to see you.'

'What did you make of Pipsqueak?' she asked.

'Just not good enough, I suppose.'

'I don't believe it, he's been going so well!'

'Yeah, I know. Maybe he needs more time. He'll be OK.'

How could he sound so upbeat about it? Poor Pat. It would have been great if they both could have won today. It rather took the gloss off her own victory.

Her phone rang above the drone of the engine and she grabbed it. She hoped it was Pat again for a bit of sweet talking, in which case she'd better be careful. Ted might not say much but there was nothing wrong with his hearing.

But it was Harriet and her heart sank, just a little. Zoe knew what her sister was after when she rang at the end of the afternoon.

Harriet launched straight into it. 'I know you're at Newmarket but if anyone asks, you and me are doing a bit of late-night shopping in Bridgwater, OK?'

'Anyone' meant Andy. It was awkward seeing him every day at the yard when she knew Harriet was cheating on him. Zoe hated lying to him and it was wrong of Harriet to ask her. But how could she not support her elder sister? On this occasion, however, Zoe couldn't help out.

'I can't. I'm coming back in the lorry and won't be back till late.'

'Does Andy know where you are?'

'Of course.'

'OK.' Harriet didn't sound happy. 'I'll think of something else.'

'Aren't you going to ask me how I got on? I had a winner. My first at Newmarket.'

'Really? Tell me about it tomorrow. I've got to go.'

Zoe put the phone away, glad that she wasn't going to be implicated in whatever Harriet was up to – a session with Martin no doubt. She wondered where it would end. She didn't know all the details of Harriet's love life but she knew enough. There'd been the affair with Robin two years ago and Andy had virtually caught them red-handed. That had been embarrassing because Harriet had dragged her into it and she'd had to lie to Andy. Harriet had sworn faithfully she'd never jeopardise her marriage like that again and Zoe had believed her. But now Harriet had fallen for a tennis coach – Martin. She'd wanted Zoe to meet him but Zoe wasn't having any of that. She just hoped Harriet got over him quickly before there was trouble.

Given her sister's tormented love life, Zoe wasn't surprised she hadn't been impressed by victory at Newmarket. Trust family to bring you down to earth and Harriet was the only family she'd got.

Just as well she loved her big sister.

Martin lived a mere ten-minutes' walk from the health centre. All the same, Harriet drove them there because, when you only had a few hours, time was precious. She parked her little blue Clio round the corner as a token precaution and turned off her mobile.

This was her third or fourth visit and she'd yet to see Martin's landlady who let him two rooms at the top of the house. He claimed old Emily was deaf and Harriet hoped that was the case as the ceilings were thin.

After Zoe said she couldn't cover for her, Harriet had been inclined to put Martin off. But his look of disappointment when she told him she couldn't make it forced her to relent. His blue eyes had clouded in pain and for a second she'd glimpsed a small boy in the man's face. He'd recovered quickly but that flash of hurt had got to her. He wanted her so badly.

So she told Chrissie on reception that if Andy should call, she'd be home late as she'd lost a filling and the dentist was staying open specially to fix it.

Chrissie probably didn't believe her but Harriet didn't give two hoots either way. She drove to Martin's place hot with anticipation, as eager for him now as he was for her. His long lean frame seemed to fill up the small car.

Being so close to him was intoxicating. She felt drunk with his presence. But there were things she had to say before she surrendered to him entirely.

'Have you just started teaching that girl in a pink skirt?' she said as they reached the top of the stairs.

'Young Haley? Yeah.'

'She looked old enough to me. Are you sure you wouldn't rather be bringing her back here?'

He had his arm round her waist, his eyes sparkling as he waltzed her through the door to his bedroom.

'A pretty little teenager who worships you,' she said, turning her head so that his mouth grazed her cheek. 'No strings. No sneaking around. Better than an old married lady.'

This time his lips found hers and he shut her up with a kiss. Delicious. But she couldn't give in just yet. She was still in control.

She pulled her head back.

'Well?'

'She's just a kid with braces and spots—'

'And legs that go up to her armpits.' His hold on her body was thrilling – the urgency in his grip, the heat of his breath on her face.

'I'm not interested in her, Harriet, I only want

39

you. Just you. You're the most fantastic woman I've ever met.'

Mmm. This was what she wanted. She let him pull her blouse from the waistband of her skirt and slip his big eager hands onto the bare skin of her waist.

They were kissing again now and this time, she knew, the words were over. The conversation she'd planned about being more discreet would have to wait. Right now all she wanted was for her athletic lover to pull her clothes off and throw her down on that silly little bed.

But before she had her wish, he surprised her. This time it was he who broke their kiss.

'I love you, Harriet,' he said.

She stared deep into his cloudless blue eyes looking for untruths.

There were none.

Andy took his phone from his pocket, then replaced it. He'd been repeating the action throughout the past ten minutes.

Harriet would be pissed off if he rang her again. Unless, of course, he had a good reason. Was the fact that Jasper had almost gone over the cliff good enough? The silly hound had gone too close to the edge, thundering after some rabbit no doubt, and had nearly come a complete cropper. Fortunately, a scrubby ledge just under the lip had prevented him tumbling all the way to the unforgiving rocks below. Andy had had to get down on his belly and inch himself over the edge to get a grip on the panicky animal's collar.

It had been a close call and both he and the dog had the scratches to prove it.

But was that sufficient grounds to ring his wife? Harriet wouldn't think so. She'd accuse him of checking up on her and maybe, if he were honest, she'd be right. And he'd get a lecture about not looking after Jasper properly. She never took the dog for walks on the cliff top because she claimed it made her nervous when he went close to the edge.

He'd already called the number at the cottage to remind her he was on late tonight but there'd been no reply. Still, it was only six thirty and the salon stayed open till eight most nights to cater for the after-work crowd. But Harriet hadn't said she was on the evening shift.

Sod it. He had a right to know where his wife was. He called her number. It rang a few times and transferred him to voicemail. She'd turned it off – why?

He rang the Cut Above reception.

'Hi. It's Andy, Harriet's husband. I was wondering—'

'She's not here.' He recognised the voice. He'd had similar conversations in the past. 'She went to the dentist to get a tooth fixed.'

He felt a stab of alarm. 'What happened? Is she all right?'

'She just said a filling came out. She didn't look in pain or anything so I wouldn't worry.'

So that explained it. Harriet must have turned the phone off when she was in the dentist's surgery.

He heard the sound of a car pulling up in the yard and put his phone away. He really had to get a grip. It was stupid to be paranoid about her every move. Especially when other things were going so well.

Outside, Jack was getting out of Pat's car.

'That flaming Pipsqueak,' the trainer said without preamble. 'He's a mystery wrapped up in a puzzle.'

Andy nodded, looking suitably grave.

Behind Jack, Pat looked Andy in the eye and winked.

'I swear,' Jack continued, 'he's one of the best two-year-olds I've ever had in my hands but he won't do it when it counts. I can't work him out.'

'If you can't, boss, then nobody can,' said Andy.

Jack didn't appear to hear. He shook his head, his face sombre, looking his age for once.

'Cheer up,' said Pat. 'He wasn't far off today. I've a feeling we'll crack it next time out.'

Andy and Pat watched as the older man made his way across the courtyard to the path that led to his house.

'Poor old boy, makes me feel like a right bastard,' Andy said when he was sure the trainer was out of earshot.

'Me, too.'

'Bollocks. You're loving this, aren't you? "I've a feeling we'll crack it next time."' Andy mimicked the jockey's faint Irish brogue.

'And so we will.' Pat's grin was wide – and infectious. Andy found himself smiling too. There was nothing like contemplating a life-changing pile of cash to lift a man's spirits.

'What's the joke, lads?'

Andy hadn't noticed the thin sandy-haired man standing just a few yards off. That was often the way with Joe Parkin, the travelling head lad. He cropped up where you didn't expect him.

'Why are you looking so cheerful?' he repeated.

Andy ignored the question and Pat walked back to his car with a hand raised in farewell. Joe regularly had the effect of sending people scurrying in the opposite direction.

'I didn't know you were back,' said Andy. Joe's job involved him going to meetings to supervise the care of the animals. He often travelled in the horse box though not today, obviously, for Pipsqueak was still on the road.

Joe ignored the remark. 'It's about Pipsqueak, isn't it?'

'What?'

'You heard.' A knowing smile fluttered along his thin lips. 'Pipsqueak should have strolled that race. He had nothing to beat but he could hardly drag himself across the line at the end.'

Andy wondered if Joe was simply being nosy or whether he'd had a bob or two on Pipsqueak. More likely, knowing Joe, he'd tipped the horse to a punter who'd watched his money go west.

'Look, Joe, there's plenty of horses who look good on the gallops and not all of them shape up when it counts.'

Joe shook his head. 'Not this one. I've sat on him and I know I'm not wrong. Jack's the best judge of a horse in the county and even he can't work it out.'

Andy shrugged. 'Don't look at me, mate. I wasn't even there.'

But Joe *was* looking at him, his pale boiled-sweet eyes glistening with an interest Andy could do without. 'This isn't the first time I've noticed you looking suspiciously cheerful. There's been hooky things going on here for months. What are you up to?'

Andy was getting annoyed. Time to pull rank. 'Watch your mouth, Parkin.' Andy had made sergeant in his military days and the knowledge came in handy. 'You're not so essential to this operation that you can go around making unfounded accusations.'

The pale eyes blinked but Joe stood his ground. He was a persistent little sod.

'Don't be like that, Andy. I'm just interested, that's all.'

'There's nothing to be interested in.'

'Course not, no. But we're mates, right?'

That's not how Andy would have described their relationship but he didn't want to make an enemy of him.

'Sure.'

'So, just give me the nod when Pipsqueak's really going to show, will you?'

'Joe, I haven't got a clue how he's going to perform.'

'If you say so. You're the head man.'

And finally, flashing his irritating grin, the lad lolloped off.

Andy watched him go, his earlier satisfaction now frayed at the edges. But there was no need to worry. Joe might be an annoying little toerag but he couldn't prove a thing.

Chapter Three

Zoe didn't think of herself as pretty, let alone beautiful. It was true there had always been plenty of boys after her but she'd thought that was because she laughed at their jokes and wasn't stand-offish like some girls. She'd grown up in the shadow of her sister who, in Zoe's opinion, was a genuine beauty with thick copper-red hair and commanding green eyes. It was only natural Pat should say she'd got it all wrong and that she was the real looker of the two sisters. Even if Zoe had a face like an old boot, Pat would be bound to pay her compliments – he was going out with her, not Harriet.

If she were honest, Zoe would concede that she was lucky with her clear hazel eyes and the fact that she found it easy to smile, so people thought her approachable and happy-go-lucky. Sunny and shallow, that's me, she said to herself, not dark and deep like Harriet. If she'd had the choice, Zoe wasn't sure which of the two personalities she would have opted for. But there was no choice and she didn't intend to spend time brooding on what couldn't be altered.

For all that, she'd like to have altered the gossip column in that day's *Racing Beacon*. She knew she had a large mouth but in the photo her grin was so wide her face looked all teeth and her eyes were screwed up, almost reduced to slits. The text beneath the picture read:

Distracting beauty saddles up at Nottingham
Racing's latest lovely, Beach Head yard's in-form apprentice Zoe Morris, takes over the reins of Pipsqueak at Nottingham this after-noon. So far the two-year-old has shown little on the course but perhaps the female touch can change his fortunes. Or maybe canny old Jack Lucas – who knows a good-looking filly when he sees one – is relying on his eye-catching jockey to distract the opposition.

Her heart had sunk the moment Andy had shown her the paper in the yard this morning. How embarrassing! How was she going to face the other jockeys? It was the last thing she needed on a day when she already felt under heavy pressure. Pat had been jocked off Pipsqueak in her favour and that was bad enough.

The decision had been made a few days after the race at Bath. Jack had called her into the office and told her.

'I couldn't do that to Pat,' she'd blurted out.

'Don't be daft, my lass. You'll do just what I tell you. If you want to be a proper jockey you'll grab your chances with both hands.'

'But how's Pat going to feel?'

Jack looked her squarely in the face. 'I've just spoken to him and he understands – he's a professional. He also understands that I'm at my wits' end with this horse so I'm trying a change of jockey. OK?'

'Yes, boss.' What else could she say?

Despite what Jack had said, Zoe had thought Pat might be a bit fed up but he'd brushed aside her apologies. He'd seemed more concerned to pass on his knowledge of how to ride Pipsqueak in the upcoming race – which was typical of him. He was riding for another trainer at Warwick today and she hoped he had some luck. She didn't expect any herself. If Pat couldn't get Pipsqueak into the winner's enclosure she didn't see how she was going to manage it.

She was greeted with wolf whistles the moment she stepped into the weighing room. Even the crustier old stewards seemed to have seen the article in the paper. 'Look lively, lads,' said one. 'Here comes Miss World.'

Her cheeks flamed crimson and she knew that silly grin was plastered all over her face. It was a reflex she couldn't help. At least she could hide in the female changing room till it was time for her race.

Ginger Weaver, an apprentice whom she considered a mate, stood in her way. 'Can I have your autograph?'

'Bog off, Ginger.'

'I'm serious.' He was holding a copy of the paper. 'Just sign it, will you, so I can prove to me brother that I know you.'

Oh heavens. Feeling utterly foolish, she scrawled her name and added a heart and a row of kisses. She might as well ham it up. Ginger held up the page so the other lads could see and she fled to the changing room with a chorus of cheers ringing in her ears. Trust those buggers to take the mickey out of her.

There was no laughter later when she came face to face with Pipsqueak's owner in the parade ring. She'd met Ursula Leopold before, when she was mucking out in the yard. This was a different set of circumstances. Jack had said Mrs Leopold was happy to see her on board Pipsqueak but she didn't look particularly thrilled about it. She'd always been loyal to Pat in the past and Zoe wondered how hard Jack had had to argue for his young apprentice to take her regular rider's place.

The first words she spoke did nothing to put Zoe at ease.

'I've never had a female jockey on one of my horses before,' she said, scrutinising Zoe without warmth. 'I'm of the old school.'

Zoe guessed that meant she would have preferred

a male rider. Well, she should have stuck with Pat. She didn't say that, however.

'I'll do my best, Mrs Leopold.'

'This lass knows the horse as well as anyone,' said Jack, stepping in to rescue her. 'Let's see if she can change our luck.'

Jack had talked the race through with her already and there was little left for him to say in the way of final instructions.

'You've got good instincts, young lady,' he said. 'Just follow them and we'll see what happens.'

He didn't sound optimistic.

'Take the little lane on the left as we go down the hill.'

Harriet did as she was told. This expedition had been Martin's idea and she was only the driver. She was entirely in his hands. She liked that.

He was a local lad and he'd been nagging her for weeks to take a trip out to where he grew up. It had been difficult to arrange – the demands of their clients always seemed to clash – but they'd finally managed to block out three hours when they could get clear of the health centre. As far as Andy was concerned, she had a lunchtime session with one of her private customers – a lady in her late seventies whom she visited at home. If he rang she'd accuse him of paranoia and say Mrs Dickinson didn't like her taking calls at her home. Then she'd cut him off. What could he do?

The road they were on was a twisting pot-holed track, shielded from the sun by high hedges.

'It used to be a bugger along here in the winter,' said Martin. 'The council were meant to keep it passable but it was usually down to us.'

'Is it much further?' Harriet had slowed to a crawl, worried she was going to damage the car.

'No, look, just here.'

A five-barred gate broke the wall of hedge on the right and she stepped on the brake. Suddenly the sun was on her face again and she found herself looking down a gently sloping pasture to a cluster of honey-coloured stone buildings. A line of trees marked the line of a substantial stream snaking across the valley.

'That's our old farm,' Martin said with satisfaction in his voice.

'And that's where you grew up?'

'I was born in the big house, the one with the clematis over the front door.'

'Gosh,' she murmured. She had spent her childhood in a poky terraced house in Bristol. The thought of living in those substantial buildings surrounded by a private expanse of meadow and sky was beyond comprehension. 'Lucky old you.'

'I know but I didn't think so at the time. It was bloody cold in the winter and hard work all the year round. There's always some crap job to do on a farm. I liked the animals though.'

'Have you got brothers and sisters?'

51

'No. There was just me – and Benson. My lurcher. We grew up together.'

'Where are your parents now?'

'They sold up and went to live in Spain. They said they were doing it to fund my tennis career – I went to a tennis academy out there – but I reckon it was just a good excuse to pack in farming.'

'Don't you miss living here?'

'Sure – some things anyway. Do you want to see more?'

Of course she did. She assumed he hadn't brought her all the way out here for one nice view. There were better things they could be doing with their time.

Zoe cleared her mind of distractions as she cantered Pipsqueak down to the start. He was a typical Beach Head inmate. He had perfect manners and enjoyed his job. Jack's analysis of the race was that although three of the horses had already won, the only horse they had to beat was Bold Venture, a newcomer from Cecil Clark's yard.

As she arrived at the starting gates Bold Venture pulled up alongside her. He was a well-made horse, sturdy, black and with a white blaze across his face. He was sweating up a bit and his tail swished in irritation but he was obviously powerful. If all that pent-up energy could be harnessed to good end – and he had an experienced rider on his back – Zoe imagined he would be the horse to beat. The racecourse punters obviously thought so too because he was the firm favourite.

Pipsqueak stepped into his stall like a veteran and ignored the protests around him as a couple of temperamental animals kicked up a fuss. Zoe could feel a tremor, like an electric pulse, running through him. It occurred to her that he, too, was keyed up for the race ahead.

She couldn't understand why Pipsqueak had caused them all such heartache. She'd ridden him at home almost every day and he'd given everything she'd asked of him and more. Yet he'd failed on the racecourse. She was as puzzled as everyone else.

Today it was her turn to see what he could really do. She found it hard to believe that he'd let her down. But if Pat couldn't get him to perform, what chance did she have?

Andy had trained himself not to bite his fingernails. He prided himself on self-discipline and the raw bitten fingers of his pre-army days were an embarrassing memory. But his fingers still found their way to his mouth in moments of high tension when instinct took over. Moments like this one.

He'd shut Jasper in the kitchen, where the dog whined and grumbled, unhappy that he was being deprived of his walk. Andy ignored the noise, in fact he scarcely heard it, so focused was his attention on the television screen. He'd justified the cable subscription to Harriet on the grounds that it was a professional requirement that he studied racing form. He'd told her nothing but the truth.

At first he'd been alarmed when Jack had informed him he was giving Zoe the ride on Pipsqueak. He'd assumed that the change of jockey had scuppered all their plans but Pat had put him straight.

'Don't worry, mate. Zoe won't muck it up.'

'But you've ridden him each time he's run.'

'I've done the hard part, you mean. All she's got to do is win. Anyhow, her riding will probably lengthen the odds and that's what we want.'

So Andy had calmed down – Pat was right. All the same, in Pat's shoes he wasn't sure he'd be taking it that well. If Zoe won on Pipsqueak it wouldn't reflect well on his previous jockey.

'You really love that girl, don't you?' he said.

Pat hadn't replied but the bashful grin that had crept over his features was answer enough. For a second, Andy envied the simple affection Pat and Zoe shared for each other. He loved Zoe's sister profoundly but their relationship was altogether more complex.

At the time of that conversation, Andy had had no doubt that Pipsqueak would breeze home to claim his first, long-delayed victory. But now, hunched in front of the television with the yowls of his unhappy hound echoing faintly through the walls, he wasn't so certain. It was a horse race, after all. Anything could happen.

He bit down on his fingernails, unaware of what he was doing.

He'd been a punter all his life and he'd enjoyed a few good wins. But he'd never stood to win eighty grand on one race before.

Jack had been right about Bold Venture. The black horse shot out of the stalls like a cork out of a champagne bottle and fizzed into the lead. He had two lengths on the rest of them by the time they'd gone half a furlong.

Zoe swore out loud, the word audible only to herself. It was just her luck that she should find herself up against a special horse on a day like today. That's if he really was special – she was determined to make him prove it.

'Come on, Pip!' she shouted into her horse's ear but he'd already found a rhythm and was matching the leader's stride.

By halfway they were still two lengths off Bold Venture who was now hugging the stand side rail. Zoe stole a quick peep over her shoulder. The rest of the field were well adrift, burned off by the pace that had been set.

It was getting to the stage of the race where in previous runs Pipsqueak had started to tire. Zoe was almost afraid to ask him for an effort but she had no choice.

She gave Pipsqueak a tap with the whip, and in an instant he took off, moving up a gear like a high-performance car. He passed Bold Venture as if the other horse were standing still. It seemed effortless.

Even when they were in the last furlong Zoe didn't ease up riding Pipsqueak out with hands and heels, determined not to be caught on the line, acting the perfect professional – which is what she aimed to be.

She knew Pipsqueak was a quality animal but she didn't know he could do *that* – switch on the afterburners like some jet-propelled wonder horse. And she'd thought Bold Venture was the special one. Once they were safely over the line, she looked behind to see the black horse a good five lengths down and the rest of the field so distant they could have been in another race.

She raised her arms in triumph.

Andy was transfixed by the image of Zoe standing up in the saddle as if she'd won a Group One race. But this was better.

When he and Pat had planned this coup, before Pipsqueak had run his first race, they were pretty sure the horse was good. But not this good. The way he'd surged past Bold Venture showed rare talent. On reflection, maybe he'd showed a bit too much. If Pat had been riding, Andy knew that the more experienced hand wouldn't have made the victory so spectacular. Zoe, of course, had not pulled her punches – and why should she? He'd not appreciated before quite how good a race rider she was becoming. Beneath that fragile exterior she was tough. But then, she was his wife's sister, after all.

His phone rang. Harriet? He'd been forbidden from ringing her because she was at some old biddy's house but he'd been hoping she might call. Now would be a good time – she could have whatever she wanted.

It was Pat.

'I just watched it,' he said. They both knew what 'it' was. 'I knew that horse would come good in the end.'

They'd agreed at the beginning, when they'd dreamed up the scheme, never to discuss it directly on the phone. You couldn't be too careful.

But today's triumph couldn't go unacknowledged.

'He did more than come good. Top class, I'd say.'

'You bet. Everything else go all right?' That was Pat asking about the business end of things – the placing of the bets.

'No problems.' Andy couldn't go into details. Later he'd give Pat a rundown of how he had placed ten thousand pounds through a variety of betting accounts, on and off line. He'd got a range of prices, all of them based on Pipsqueak's history of disappointing performances. That would change from now on. He'd never get the horse at 8–1 again in such a low-class race.

Andy and Pat had achieved their target amount of £80,000 to add to the pot they'd been building up on all-weather races throughout the winter. This was the largest amount they'd landed in one hit and took their winnings to over £200,000.

A sweet result all round.

The old barn smelled a bit so Martin spread his groundsheet outside in the sun. They were well shielded from the lane by a stand of beech trees and the farm buildings were a good mile off down the hill. Harriet reckoned there was little chance anyone would see what they were up to. Anyway, it had made it more exciting. It had been a long time since she'd made love in the open air.

She and Andy used to do it on a sunbed in the garden that went with his old yard. It had been more fun than inside the musty little house – and a sight sweeter smelling to be lying in the shade of a trellis covered by climbing roses. That had been at the beginning of their romance, before the wedding. Andy had got her pregnant in that garden and she'd never had sex outdoors since.

She banished thoughts of Andy.

'I'm going to burn,' she mumbled into Martin's chest. Unlike him, she was fair-skinned and there was still a lot of her exposed.

After they'd finished he pulled on his trousers and fetched their picnic from the car, parked fifty yards away up the hill. She stretched out in the sun, savouring the moment, and remained that way as he laid out the food. He enjoyed the sight of her. 'It's like that Manet painting of a picnic,' he said, 'where the men are dressed up and the girls have got their kit off. *Déjeuner sur l'herbe*. Of course,' he added as he offered a fat red strawberry to her lips, 'you're more of a Pre-Raphaelite type with that fantastic mane of red hair.'

She laughed to cover her confusion, because she didn't know what he was talking about. It must be another of his arty allusions – she had so much to learn. All the same, it thrilled her to hear him talk about her in this way. It was so romantic – and she knew what that meant, all right.

He reached for his shirt and arranged it over her shoulders with one hand, holding her close to him with the other arm. 'I don't want you to move,' he murmured in her ear.

Neither did she. She felt as if she belonged in his arms. She could stay here forever.

'Oy, you!' The voice came out of nowhere, angry and coarse. 'This is private property. Get off my land.'

The man was middle-aged and red-faced. He wore baggy cord trousers and a stained singlet over a bulging chest and bare tattooed arms. He glared at them from ten yards off.

Harriet yelped and pulled the shirt across her chest. Martin sat up, turning his body to shield her.

'You've got a bloody nerve,' the man shouted.

'I'm very sorry,' said Martin, 'but we're not doing any harm. I used to live here.'

'So bloody what? Get out of here before I fetch the dogs.'

'All right, we're going.' Martin's voice was firm. 'If you could just leave us for a moment to get dressed.'

But the man didn't move. 'I'm not going anywhere. Your little tart's not got anything I haven't seen before.'

Martin was on his feet now, standing between the man and Harriet. As she grabbed for her clothes, she was amazed to hear him say, 'Just because we're on your land doesn't give you the right to insult my wife.'

Oh no! Surely he wasn't going to upset this monster any further. She just wanted to escape with the minimum of embarrassment – and in one piece.

'I'll say what the hell I like. I reckon any woman who sneaks up here to drop her drawers is just a cheap whore and I won't have filth like that on my property.'

As Harriet scrambled into her jeans she heard a soft thud, like a hammer being driven into a sack of flour. She looked up to see the red-faced man bending forward, clutching his stomach. His face was even redder now.

As she watched, the man hurled himself forward, swinging a large bunched fist at Martin's head.

Martin only moved a fraction, shifting his neck so the blow whistled by his nose, then he stepped forward. Harriet wasn't certain she saw the punches – Martin didn't appear to move his hands far – but she saw their effect. The man fell heavily against the side of the barn and slumped to his knees. He stared at the pair of them in surprise.

Martin calmly folded the groundsheet and pushed their things into a rucksack.

The man coughed and cleared his throat. 'I'm getting the police on you,' he said. The words were faint.

Martin hoisted the pack onto his shoulder and said softly, 'If you do that, then my wife will say that I had to restrain you from assaulting her. You've obviously been spying on her like some peeping Tom.'

'That's a lie.' Some of the old fire was back in the voice but the man made no attempt to get to his feet.

Martin turned to Harriet and held out his hand. 'Shall we go, babe?'

She held on to him tightly as she stumbled up the path to the car.

Ursula Leopold was all smiles now as she rushed towards Zoe in the winner's enclosure. Funny how a person's opinion could be changed in such a short space of time – the race had taken little over a minute. Jack was looking pretty pleased with Zoe too, but he'd always known what she was capable of.

'I can't thank you enough,' said Mrs Leopold, throwing her arms round Zoe in a perfumed hug. 'You've worked a miracle.'

'I wouldn't say that.' Zoe extricated herself politely, wondering how much lipstick the delighted owner had planted on her face. 'There's a whole team back at the yard. I just got him to do what he does at home.'

'Exactly!' cried Ursula. 'And the only difference is that you were riding. Isn't that so, Jack?'

The trainer was looking as cheerful as the owner, but in the grin that wreathed his face Zoe could read relief – and confusion. Thank God Pipsqueak had finally shown his true worth, but what was the reason for it?

'I've got to hand it to you, lass. You made him look top class.' He chuckled and added, 'In this race anyway. Mind you, I didn't know he could quicken like that.'

Zoe hadn't been aware of that either. The truth was, Pipsqueak had done more than simply reproduce his good home form, he'd improved on it. At the sharp end of a race against good competition he'd put in a burst of speed that had left his rival for dead. At least that was what it had seemed like. She couldn't wait to see a recording and judge as an onlooker. For the moment, she was happy just to bask in the sunshine of their victory.

She guessed that Jack was also happy to leave the analysis for another day.

He put an arm round Zoe's shoulder. 'Let's just say the horse prefers a woman's touch. He won't be the first fellow who does.'

Harriet did not object when Martin took the car keys from her shaking fingers and eased himself behind the wheel of the Clio. She didn't think she was capable of driving anyway.

He seemed cool, focused only on getting them on their way safely. He made her stop and check her things before he turned the engine on.

'Just go!' she cried. 'He might come after us.'

'Forget about him. Have you got your bag? And your phone?'

'Yes! Please get me away from here, Martin.'

She could imagine their enemy charging out of the trees with a shotgun in his hand or – as the little car whipped down the narrow carriageway – blocking the lane ahead. But there was no sign of him and, within a few minutes, they were out on the main road, merging with the traffic around them. At last her heart rate began to slow and her breath came easier.

She looked across at Martin, who'd only murmured 'Don't worry, babe' a couple of times since they'd driven off. His teeth were bared in a grim smile as he concentrated on the road.

'What did you do to that man, Martin?'

'I just gave him a tap. He'll be fine now.'

'He went down as if you'd shot him.'

'I thumped him in the gut. Winded him, that's all.'

'But . . .' Harriet replayed the moment in her mind. For all his big belly, the man had been strong and solid – and angry. He hadn't looked like someone who'd be deterred by a 'tap'. Yet Martin had put him on his backside and placed a look of fear on his red face with the minimum of effort. Almost casually. 'Where did you learn to do that?' she said.

'I used to go to a boxing gym and spar a bit. I had a theory that hand speed and racquet speed were related.'

'Are they?'

He flashed her one of his boyish grins. 'I don't know. I quit before some bruiser decided to rearrange my face.'

It was true he didn't have the appearance of a boxer, not with those pretty-boy looks.

He took a hand from the steering wheel and reached for hers. 'Are you OK?'

'Yes,' she said firmly. But was she? She'd stopped shaking and the sunny clearing by the barn already seemed many miles off. The shock and fright at the landowner's interruption were being replaced by outrage and irritation. How dare he treat them like schoolkids caught trespassing? Even if he was within his rights to order them off his land, why did he have to be so rude and aggressive? Why should their presence have incensed him so much?

It was her nudity that appeared to have offended him. He'd called her a tart and a whore. It made her feel sick.

'Martin, do you think that man really was a peeping Tom?'

'No. I just said that to make him think twice about complaining to the police.'

'But what if he was?'

If he was, he could have seen them making love. It hadn't taken long – they'd been too hungry for each other to make it last – but it had been intense and passionate. A thrilling private act that had transported her, almost literally she'd thought afterwards, to a special place: this patch of sunlight beneath the trees under an open sky. For once a place worthy of their love, better than his poky attic bedroom or the back of her car or the other backstairs places they'd used for their stolen moments.

This was spoiled now, of course. That man must have stood in the wood and watched. Watched too while she stretched out on the ground to bask luxuriously in the sunlight, enjoying the memory of her lover's weight on her naked body.

It made her flesh creep to think what that man could have seen. And what he must have thought of her to work him up to such a rage.

Unaccountably – for she didn't do pathetic girly things – she began to weep.

Martin pulled the car over to the side of the road and put his arms round her. Then he listened intently while she told him what had upset her.

'Do you want me to go back there?' he said.

'What do you mean?'

'Well, I know where he lives. I could go back tonight and hit him a bit more.'

She stared into his innocent baby-blue eyes. They were cold.

'You only have to say so, Harriet.'

She said nothing, lost in confusion. This wasn't the toy-boy tennis coach she'd been dallying with for the past few weeks.

Suddenly he laughed, his eyes unfroze and he began to plant puppyish kisses on her cheeks.

'I had you there for a moment, didn't I?'

The breath she'd been holding escaped in a sigh of relief and she laughed too. But not because she found it funny.

Chapter Four

It was late when Joe Parkin finally got home, very late. The journey back in the horse box from Nottingham had taken an age and his frustration at being cooped up for so long had not been helped by having Zoe Morris for company. Sure, she was a right little cracker and nice with it, which wasn't always true of good-looking girls where he was concerned, but her bubbling euphoria had got on his nerves.

He knew one thing for sure, she hadn't been in on whatever trick had been pulled to allow Pipsqueak, finally, to run his race. The girl was too green. She still thought race riding was all about sporting glory and the best horse winning. She hadn't yet realised that the real sport was in making money.

Zoe wouldn't be asking herself how come Pipsqueak had suddenly run like a train after three duff outings. She'd probably just give herself the credit for bringing out the best in him whereas it was obvious to Joe that the horse had been stopped in his previous races. There were lots of ways to do that.

Joe had made a point of monitoring Pipsqueak's every moment on the course after his disappointing first run. So he knew that nobody had been slipping him things he shouldn't. And from his observation of the jockeys' performances – both Pat and Zoe's – he could swear that the horse had been ridden honestly on every occasion. So the fix must have been organised back at Beach Head – which was why he suspected Andy.

There was another reason. Andy was known to like a bet and he'd never been much cop at it. But Joe's gambler friend, Mr Harris, knew plenty of bookmakers and he'd found out Andy had been punting successfully over the winter. As far as Joe was concerned, that proved it.

A voice inside him wanted to shout out that he'd been right all along: Pipsqueak was the real thing, a sprinter with rockets in his feet and an animal to lump your money on. But this voice was drowned out by the moan of pain that came from the almost certain knowledge that, on this occasion, no money had been lumped at all.

With Zoe sitting next to him throughout the journey he couldn't make the call that would put him out of his misery. He listened out for his phone throughout the trip but he received no tone telling him of an arriving text. Mr Harris usually sent a text after one of his tips had come home. They didn't say much – 'Nice one' or 'Get in there' – something short like that. All the same, they meant plenty, confirmation that Mr Harris had gone large on the animal selected by Joe and that a tidy little present would soon be winging its way into his pocket.

The trouble was that he'd tipped Pipsqueak to Harris three times already this season and each time the horse had run like a three-legged donkey. The last occasion, at Bath, Joe had had to beg Harris to take him seriously.

'I don't know what's the matter with you, Joe. You've gone right off the boil recently,' he'd said.

It was true there'd been a few mishaps on the all-weather during the winter but Joe had his suspicions about those too. But he'd not gone into that, just urged Harris to take Pipsqueak seriously, and he had. 'Because you've been bloody good in the past, Joe. I'll give you that.'

Then Pipsqueak had performed like a no-hoper and Harris had taken it badly. So badly that when Joe had rung to say he was sure that today, at Nottingham, the horse would show for real, his benefactor treated him with barely concealed contempt. 'I might be a gambler, sonny, but I'm also a businessman. And no sensible businessman throws his money on the same fire four times in a row.'

So Joe had no reason to think that, on the day Pipsqueak had finally vindicated his judgement, he would profit from it.

Over the years, Joe had worked with several

'punters' – as enthusiastic gamblers like Mr Harris were termed. And Harris had been by far the most generous. Joe had come to rely on the bundles of ready cash that came his way. Not that he could retire on the proceeds but a regular handout of the odd grand, out of sight of the taxman, was the kind of perk only an idiot would turn down. And he'd earned it fair and square, through his own observation and knowledge of the animals in question. He had a pretty good eye for a horse and he kept his ears open too, so when people in the know like Jack rated an animal, Joe took note. But all of that carefully assembled knowledge went down the pan when someone was on the fiddle.

What really ate him up was that Andy hadn't given him the nod. It would have been no skin off his nose, would it?

He hoped for a message when he got in. A cheery verbal from Harris thanking him for finally bringing home the bacon. But there was nothing.

He knew he shouldn't but he rang Harris anyway. So what if the bugger was in bed with some bird, Joe had to know for sure. And he wouldn't say 'I told you so' – there wouldn't be any need.

'What do you want?'

Harris sounded half asleep. So there was no bird – just as well.

'It's Joe. Sorry to call so late but I wanted to know if you got a piece of Pipsqueak.'

'Don't talk to me about that carthorse.'

'Didn't you see him at Nottingham? He romped home. Like I said he would.'

Harris sighed heavily. 'Yeah, I read about it on Ceefax. It's no use to me if you can't say when he's going to be trying.'

'But I told you he'd come good.'

'Too bloody late, mate. Now, will you get off the phone? I need my beauty sleep.'

'Sorry. Catch you later, eh?'

'I don't think so, Joe. I'm not touching your yard with a bargepole after this.'

Joe crashed the phone down so hard he chipped the receiver. It just about topped off a bloody awful day.

As Ursula Leopold turned off the downstairs lights she considered the events of the afternoon – and the evening. Naturally Pipsqueak's performance brought her considerable satisfaction and she admonished herself for her past prejudice against female jockeys. Young Zoe's riding had been a revelation and, much as she liked the cheerful Irishman who had ridden for her over the past few seasons, Zoe would have to keep the berth on Pipsqueak – it was only fair.

However, she liked more about the girl than her riding ability. She'd invited Jack and Zoe back to her house for a celebratory supper, an off-the-cuff invitation which had worked out well, as impromptu events often did. Zoe had helped her in the kitchen and shown an interest in far more than horses.

Ursula had even found herself talking about Joel and life before widowhood had claimed her. By the time the evening was through, she had revealed far more than she had intended, digging out old photo albums to show her guests. It was plain to her now how much she had used horses to plug the hole left in her life by her husband's death. She guessed Joel wouldn't mind, though he'd never much cared for racing – his sport had been tennis, at which he'd shown more enthusiasm than skill.

Ursula pushed these thoughts away – getting misty-eyed over the past last thing at night was not a good idea. Instead she considered how she might help Zoe's career along. As an apprentice, there were weight advantages to putting her up on a horse. That was food for thought.

As she readied herself for bed, the phone rang. Clive, an old friend, worked for one of the national bookmaking chains and she'd spent many a happy afternoon in his employers' box at race meetings, rubbing shoulders over lunch with the firm's clients and shareholders.

So she listened carefully as he told her that a member of Jack's stable staff had won significant money on Pipsqueak's victory that afternoon.

'Who is it?'

'I'd rather not say – he *is* a client. Besides, we have high hopes of getting the money back and if I go spreading his name around he won't give us the opportunity.'

She was determined not to let this information spoil the glow of Pipsqueak's stirring performance but, given the nature of his previous attempts, it was hard not to conclude that someone at Beach Head was using her horse to land a touch. He'd been prevented from winning on his first three outings and today he'd been allowed to show his true ability. That would explain a lot.

Ursula was long enough in the tooth to know that these things happened in racing though they did not, thank God, involve her. She wasn't a gambler, she measured her satisfaction in the way her horses performed and not by how much they made her. Of course, she didn't need money, not with Joel's money in the bank. All the same, she didn't approve of anyone altering the basis of a fair contest. Just because she could afford to have scruples didn't mean she shouldn't act on them.

She considered her options. She could remove all her horses from Jack's yard or she could say nothing and opt for the quiet life. But she'd never been one to do that. And to take her horses away from Jack would surely be an overreaction. Apart from anything else, this was not Jack's fault and she had no desire to find another trainer.

On reflection, a middle course seemed the most sensible. She'd dump it in Jack's lap and let him sort it out. It was his yard.

She'd make the call first thing in the morning.

* * *

73

First lot pulled out at Beach Head at 7.45 a.m. on the dot. Although Pat was no longer expected to muck out, Zoe was, but it made sense for them to travel together. As usual they stopped in the village on the way to pick up the papers. Pat stared at the front page of the *Racing Beacon*. Then he burst out laughing and tossed the paper into Zoe's lap. 'You've not hired yourself a press agent, have you?'

Oh no, what had they printed this time?

She'd been embarrassed by yesterday's small head shot on the inside pages but today she was mortified. She could feel her cheeks glow crimson as she stared at the front of the paper. The photograph took up a quarter of the page and showed her sitting on Pipsqueak after yesterday's race, one fist held up in triumph. Her face – of course – was split in half by a melon-sized grin. Behind her, leaning over the white racecourse rail, a row of male onlookers applauded. The caption read: 'Fair maid of Nottingham – top apprentice Zoe Morris rides 8–1 outsider Pipsqueak to victory.'

It was as if someone at the paper had got it in for her. They probably thought she'd love the attention but it wasn't her kind of thing at all, especially the innuendos. She'd much rather they wrote about her ability as a jockey than keep going on about her being female.

If there was one thing she'd like to do in racing, it was change people's ideas of women jockeys.

There had been top female riders elsewhere – the fantastic Julie Krone in America, for one – and successful show-jumping girls were no surprise to anyone. She didn't see why a woman shouldn't make it as a Flat jockey in British racing as well – it was what was needed.

Maybe it was up to her.

'You know,' said Pat, slipping his arm round her shoulder, 'you take a decent photo for a mucky little stable lass.'

'Don't.' He was always teasing her about the way she looked.

'If the riding doesn't work out, I reckon you could give it a go as a model.'

'Don't patronise me.' She disentangled herself from him and threw the paper on the floor. Why did everyone go on about her appearance? She just wanted to be taken seriously as a jockey.

'I was only joking, sweetheart.'

He was still laughing as they pulled into the yard.

'So, mate, you had a good day yesterday, eh?'

Andy looked to his left and groaned inwardly when he saw the identity of the rider who'd come up alongside him on the narrow bridle path. He could have done without the tedious banter of Joe Parkin.

It was the end of second lot and the string were returning to the yard. They were just a hundred yards or so from the gate so at least he wouldn't have to put up with Joe's conversation for long. Andy was leading his horse and picking grass for him as he walked.

'Sure,' he said, when Joe repeated the remark. 'We all had a good day, didn't we?'

Joe laughed without mirth. 'Yeah, *very* good – thanks to you.' The sarcasm was thick.

Andy would have liked to ignore him but he knew Joe wouldn't be easily brushed off.

'What are you getting at, Joe?'

'You know.' Joe's pale face under his riding hat had lost all semblance of geniality. 'We had an agreement and you went back on it.'

What?

'I never had any agreement with you, Joe.'

'Yes, you did. You knew I was on to you. You knew you had to give me the nod on Pipsqueak and you didn't.'

They were at the rear of the string, separated from the other riders by some twenty yards. But Joe's nasal whine was raised above the steady thud of hooves and the rattle of tack.

'Keep your voice down, you fool.'

'Why should I? Afraid what I might say? Don't worry, no one's going to be surprised when it gets out what a hooky sod you are.'

'There is nothing to get out, Joe. So I suggest you keep your stupid mouth shut or I'll be having words with the governor about you.'

Andy quickened his stride to close the gap

between himself and the other riders ahead. He'd deal with Joe in private.

'That's right, run away to Uncle Jack.' Joe's voice rang out loudly behind him. 'You've got your nose so far up his arse it's turning brown.'

Andy brought his surprised horse to a sudden halt and turned to face Joe. 'That's it, you're history at this yard.'

'Yeah? You can't fire me.' The lad grinned, a loathsome smirk that deserved to be smacked off his face. 'The old boy will kick you out first when I tell him that you're on the fiddle.'

For a second Andy lost it. He punched Joe hard in the thigh, making certain his knuckles were well and truly buried into the muscle. Joe squealed in pain and outrage.

Andy didn't look back. He carried on walking through the gates and down the drive into the yard, trying to control his seething anger. His thoughts were in turmoil and he was scarcely aware of the other riders and their mounts as they milled around him.

The blow that knocked him to his knees took him completely by surprise. His head was suddenly wrapped in a circle of fire.

His hands flew to his face and came away covered in blood. Above him loomed the jeering face of Joe Parkin, his whip raised.

Despite the pain, Andy launched himself at him.

* * *

Zoe couldn't believe what she saw. A dozen people were shouting and jostling and horses whinnied and stamped. In the middle of the melee two men grappled with blood-slick hands.

Zoe had grown used to some strange sights in her short experience of racing but she'd never seen anything like this.

The lads had formed a circle to watch the fight – like in the school playground, she thought. The figures in the centre were rolling in the dirt, trying to get a hold on each other. The shorter, stronger one was on top. He lifted his face and, beneath the blood, she recognised Andy.

'Stop it, Andy!' she screamed. 'Stop it!'

No one took any notice of her but they did rush to pull the contestants apart when the office door opened and out rushed Jack.

Suddenly it was all over and, in an instant it seemed, order was restored. Lads rushed around the horses and the bloody evidence of conflict was washed away as the two protagonists were taken to separate quarters.

Not everyone was as alarmed as Zoe. Most of the staff were finding it hard to contain their amusement. 'It's not often you get the boss lads having a punch-up,' said Abbie, one of the stable grooms.

'But what was it all about?'

'Who cares? Best laugh we've had all year.'

But Zoe wasn't laughing. She'd seen Andy's bloody face through the office window. It looked dreadful.

* * *

Jack drove Andy to A&E in Taunton himself. In his opinion, it was more a precaution than anything else. The scarlet ridge across Andy's mouth and jaw looked spectacular at present but it would heal OK, provided it didn't get infected. Just as well the lad had been wearing his peaked riding hat which protected the upper half of the face. Jack didn't like to think of the outcome if the whip had fallen across Andy's eyes.

The trip gave Jack the opportunity to get Andy on his own. There were things on his mind.

He'd already dealt with Joe.

'Joe said you punched him.'

'He was being lippy. He deserved it.'

'What on earth were you arguing about anyway?'

'He challenged my authority, Jack. And he was rude about you – basically he was just being an annoying little toerag, as usual.'

'I still don't understand why you had to punch him in the first place.'

Andy stared straight ahead. He was obviously in pain. 'I'm sorry, boss. I apologise.'

An apology was OK, as far as it went.

'If it's any consolation,' Jack said, as they turned onto the main road, 'Joe won't be coming back. I don't know what started it between you two but I can't have my senior men assaulting each other.'

Andy grunted. It could have been a thank you.

The trainer wondered whether to tell him about

Ursula Leopold's call; he'd been on the phone to the owner just as the brawl started in the yard outside. Or the allegations Joe Parkin had made in the brief and bitter conversation they'd had.

'Andy Burns is the one you should be firing, not me.'

'You've done enough damage, Joe. Just pack your stuff and go.'

'But he's bent, guv'nor. I swear he's been fixing races.'

Jack had hoped these kinds of unpleasant scenes lay in his past. It seemed not.

'Have you got any evidence?'

'I know for sure he's been taking lumps off the bookies. And I bet he cleaned up on Pipsqueak yesterday.'

Jack sighed heavily. He disliked the betting culture that existed at Beach Head alongside all the hard work and clean effort to present horses in the best shape to win races fair and square. But it was the same in every yard he'd ever worked in. Racing and betting went hand in hand and always would do. The sport probably wouldn't exist without man's urge to wager. Though he might not bet himself, he could not deny another's man's right to do so. Andy, for instance.

He'd cut short Joe's complaints about his head lad. Joe had overstepped the mark by raising his whip. If Andy wanted, he could have called the police.

Now, as they neared the hospital, Jack weighed the whole business in his mind. Ursula had told him a member of his staff was winning serious money on her horses and Joe's allegations had backed up her information.

Jack wasn't a fool. He'd been aware for the past six months that some results didn't add up. Pipsqueak was only the latest and most obvious case. It galled him that he couldn't put his finger on how the fiddle – if it was a fiddle – was being conducted. In his time he'd seen most ways of stopping a horse but this situation had him foxed. The only thing he was sure of was that the jockeys were not involved. He could spot a bent jockey a mile off.

That left the other stable staff and here at last, in this afternoon's nasty altercation between his two senior lads, was a sign of the trouble brewing beneath the surface at the yard.

It seemed clear to Jack that they had fallen out over gambling. As travelling head lad, Joe was in charge of the horses at race meetings. He was in the best position to do something to an animal which would affect the result. Or maybe – it was unthinkable, surely – Andy fixed the horses at the yard.

In his younger days he might have sacked the pair of them – and half the stable staff too if he thought they were in on it, no matter the inconvenience. But he was older now and replacing people and rebuilding morale in the yard loomed as a large problem. Anyway, Andy wasn't just an employee to be replaced. He was more than that.

'Look, son,' he said softly as he parked outside the hospital. 'I don't know what's been going on but I know there's money been made off horses in the yard. Some of them are Ursula Leopold's and she's not happy. You may know about it or you may not and you don't have to say anything. But I want to make one thing clear – this has got to stop.'

Andy didn't speak, just stared at him, pressing the bloodied gauze bandage into his wound. 'I hear you,' he said eventually.

Jack turned off the engine. There was one more thing he had to say.

'I don't know how much longer I can keep going, Andy. The way I'm feeling, this could be my last season. I don't need to tell you it's as much in your interest as mine to stamp out this gambling culture right now. You understand what I'm saying?'

Andy nodded slowly. 'I think so, Jack.' He was on the brink of adding more but Jack stopped him.

'Just think on. Now let's get them to take a look at you, see if we're going to have to call you Scarface.'

Andy managed a bloody grin. 'You're a great guy, Jack.'

A silly old fool more like, the trainer thought, going soft in my old age. But he kept it to himself.

Chapter Five

On Thursdays and Fridays, the days Harriet worked late, she wasn't expected at the salon till mid-morning. She always took the opportunity to lie in. Early morning starts were not for her. She didn't understand how Andy could get up at dawn each day and be cheerful about it.

It was another reason not to work with horses, in her opinion. They were like big babies and those responsible for them were on call at all hours of the day and night. What's more, these babies never grew up. Andy was welcome to them.

Not that she minded her husband being up and away long before a civilised breakfast time. She liked having the cottage to herself. She could make a mess and leave the clearing up till later. She could play her choice of music loud and sing along. And she didn't have to watch her words in case she let something slip – like the other Sunday when Andy wasn't on early at the yard.

'How's your tooth?' he'd said to her as she crunched into a piece of toast.

'It had taken her by surprise. 'What tooth?' she'd said without thinking.

He'd lowered his coffee mug and given her that look, the one that made her feel about six inches tall. The wound on his face had scabbed over and the bruising had turned purple. It didn't improve his looks.

'Forgotten already?' he said. 'It can't have been such an emergency after all.'

Then it came back to her – the alibi she'd cooked up to cover sneaking off with Martin.

'Of course it was,' she said with as much confidence as she could muster. 'You can't go around with a hole in your teeth. I had to get it fixed at once.'

'Which one is it?'

'It's right at the back.' Help, he'd be asking her to open wide in a moment so he could have a look.

Fortunately he hadn't but she knew he'd have filed the incident away in his memory bank – under Harriet's Assorted Lies probably. And, God knows, there had been plenty of those.

The sound of the morning post hitting the hall floor brought her back to the present. Here was another advantage of a late start. As a rule she had left for work before the postman arrived and Andy got to it first when he came home for lunch – which had caused her some awkward moments in the past.

She'd never set out to be an unfaithful wife but then she'd not set out to be married in the first place. If she hadn't got pregnant maybe she'd not have found herself tied to Andy for the rest of her life. But if she'd not lost the baby maybe marriage would have fulfilled her. Who could say? She only knew she went to bed every night with a man who had stood by her side through the darkest hours of her life and who was committed to her without question. You didn't walk away from that lightly.

She'd come to realise this following her aborted fling with Robin. At the time she'd treated it as a game. She'd not kidded herself that she was Robin's only love interest, and that made it more permissible. She and Robin were only ever going to be in lust – that was a given. Letting Robin stay overnight when Andy was away in York had been a big mistake. She thought she'd covered her tracks but Andy had not been fooled, and she'd seen from the look on his face that it was no game as far as he was concerned.

After that Andy had turned into her jailer, clocking her in and out, looking over her shoulder – and reading her post. Stupidly, Robin had sent her a postcard which Andy had picked up before she got home. It just said: 'No hard feelings – Love, R' – referring to the fact that she'd chucked him in panic after the night at the cottage. Harriet had had to work hard to convince Andy that R was a female client she'd fallen out with.

In retrospect, Harriet doubted that Andy was convinced, any more than Robin was stupid. The bastard probably sent the card to make mischief.

She was more careful these days. She would never dream of bringing Martin back to the cottage. And her phone and credit card bills were sent to her work address. She didn't think Andy would have the nerve to deliberately open her post but 'accidents' could always happen. It was best to play it safe.

She turned the envelope over in her hand. The letters SPBS decorated the top left-hand corner: Somerset Providential Building Society. It was addressed to Andy.

She was confident this wasn't a circular. Over the winter she'd seen one or two similar letters arrive and Andy hadn't tossed them aside with the other junk mail. Why were the Somerset Providential writing to her husband? She wasn't aware he had an account with them. If he did, it would hardly be worth enough to cover the cost of postage. As ever, money was tight.

Sod it. She slid her thumbnail under the flap and ripped. Accidents could happen, all right.

The SPBS Bonus Saver statement was not hard to understand but it took Harriet some moments to absorb the information it contained. She took the single sheet of paper into the front room and sat down to read it through again. And again.

There were five columns – Date, Description,

Withdrawals, Receipts, Balance – and five lines of entries. On 31 May, £10,000 had been withdrawn. On 6 June, £45,000 had been transferred in, and on the 8th, cheques of £12,000, £15,000 and £18,000 had been deposited. On the 10th, £2,000 had been transferred to a bank in Cork. Nevertheless, together with a balance brought forward of £135,000, the total amounted to £223,000 plus a few pence.

No matter how many times Harriet read it over, she could not accept it as true. Her husband had almost a quarter of a million pounds sitting in a building society and, until this moment, she had known nothing about it.

She took the letter into the direct sunlight by the front window and held it in trembling hands. It looked genuine. The SPBS logo – white out lettering on a red oval – was not something that could be easily forged, surely? She retrieved the envelope from the hall and examined it with the same intensity. There was nothing fishy that she could detect.

But if it told the truth, how on earth had Andy got hold of so much money?

There was only one way to find out about this whole business for sure. She tucked the statement into the envelope and put it in her bag. She was running late for work; in the circumstances, that was no surprise. It was going to be hard but she'd have to contain her curiosity till the evening then she'd get to the bottom of this.

Andy was going to tell her all about his secret stash. As his wife, she had a right to know.

Jack picked up the phone before it had even completed the first ring. Ursula Leopold would be expecting him to be on stand-by in the yard office, waiting for her call. They knew each other pretty well after years of working together.

'It's a done deal,' she said without preamble. 'They'll send him over this afternoon and take Horatio back in the box. If that's OK with you.'

It was indeed. When Ursula bought and sold horses she was always aware of the logistics involved. This deal was particularly neat. She had arranged a swap with a horse stabled near Newbury. The box that arrived with her acquisition, Magnetic, would take Horatio off to his new home and Magnetic would inherit Horatio's old stall.

Jack would be sorry to see Horatio go but it was a feeling he was well accustomed to. In forty-odd years of training there had been hundreds of farewells. And, though two-year-old Horatio had won his maiden race last month, he'd not been in the yard long enough to make a significant mark.

The new horse, Magnetic, was a different proposition. He was a five-year-old sprinter with some decent wins under his belt, not a world-beater but a quality animal all the same. Ursula had plans for him.

'You wanted me, boss?' Zoe was standing in the office doorway. Though she didn't yet know it, the change in equine personnel was due to her. He knew she'd be upset about Horatio leaving because he was one of three horses she mucked out twice a day. He guessed that was the reason for the absence of her usual grin.

'Look here,' he said, 'I don't want any long faces. Animals come and go at every yard – it's the owner's business.'

'But he just won his maiden race and he's really good. Pat's going to be disappointed.'

Pat had been on board when Horatio won his first race.

'Magnetic's a good horse too. Tried and tested. He's entered for the Wokingham.'

The Wokingham Stakes was run on the last day of Royal Ascot. A cavalry charge over six furlongs, it usually attracted a field of two dozen or more and was one of the big betting races of the meeting.

Jack enjoyed watching the effect of his words on Zoe. It was like the sun coming out.

'So Pat will be riding him at Ascot?'

'No, Zoe. You're going to ride him. We are going to make good use of your allowance.'

As an apprentice who had yet to ride twenty career winners, Zoe was entitled to carry seven pounds less in weight when riding in any race except Listed or better. The Wokingham was a handicap, so that qualified. Once she reached twenty winners, her allowance would be cut to five pounds, after fifty it would be reduced to three and, after ninety-five winners, it would be removed altogether – but that day was a long way off.

'The handicapper has given him eight stone twelve but with your claim it comes down to eight five. That could make all the difference.'

'Thanks, boss.'

'Don't thank me, thank Mrs Leopold. It was her idea so you'd better make sure you do a good job.'

'I will, I promise. I'll do the absolute best I can.'

Jack had no doubts about Zoe – not any more. Originally, he'd taken her on as a favour to Andy. Though he'd been looking for a new apprentice, his inclination had been to sign up a boy. But he trusted Andy's judgement and to have gone against his head lad's recommendation would have been awkward. In the old days he'd not have cared about that and he'd have insisted on having his own way. It had taken him many years to learn to listen to those around him. And thank God he had, or else Zoe would have slipped through his fingers.

He thought he'd made a mistake with her at first. She was an open-hearted girl with a talent for riding, eager to please and get things right. But sometimes you can try too hard and she'd expended her energies in too many directions. There'd been a bit too much socialising and burning the late-night candle for Jack's taste. So he'd been pleased when she'd thrown in her lot with Pat

– an older, experienced hand was what she needed.

And so it had proved. This season she was beginning to ride to the best of her abilities and the winners were starting to come. She could have a big career ahead of her and Jack wasn't the only one to think so. The racing journalists didn't just have an eye on her because of her looks – though there was no doubt that helped. And now Ursula had been won over and had come up with the idea of buying Magnetic. The deal would not have gone ahead without the prospect of putting Zoe on his back at Ascot.

As she turned for the door, she said, 'I feel bad about Pat. He's lost Horatio and I've got the ride at Ascot.'

Jack just nodded and watched the girl go on her way. Maybe Pat had lost out in the shuffle but he had no doubt Zoe would find a way of making it up to him.

Andy wasn't surprised to see Pat on the bench on the cliff path. It was a great spot to take in the majesty of Bridgwater Bay. And it was a good spot to have a conversation that wouldn't be overheard.

'How's the injury?' asked the jockey as Andy sat down beside him.

'Getting better. It doesn't hurt any more but it's ruddy awkward.'

'Should help your chances with the ladies though. All the girls like a tough guy with a scar.'

Andy glared at him. 'What are you getting at?' He didn't give a stuff about impressing girls. He was a married man – didn't anyone appreciate that?

'Sorry, Andy. No offence.'

'None taken,' he said quickly. It was a sore point but there was no call to fall out with his best mate. For a moment he was tempted to confide in him about Harriet's recent behaviour – Pat had been a rock throughout their troubles a couple of years back – but he thought better of it. And there were more cheerful topics to discuss.

'We've got well over two hundred grand now,' he said. 'Around two twenty, I think.'

'Great.'

'What do you want to do?'

Pat grinned. 'I was thinking about that grey, Full Force. He's just getting fit, isn't he? I reckon we could work it with him.'

Andy shook his head. 'Not a good idea. Jack knows something's going on.'

'He knows it's you?'

'Joe made all sorts of accusations when Jack kicked him out. I don't think Jack believed him though. He just told me to make sure it stopped. He said Mrs Leopold was upset about it.'

Pat shrugged. 'I can live with that. Anyway, I'm the one who's taking all the risks, aren't I?'

Andy knew that was true. Provided no one made the money connection between them, he personally was safe. He'd done nothing to affect the way these horses ran, he'd just placed the bet. Of course, the Jockey Club might not see it like that.

'Let's cool it, Pat.'

The jockey reflected for a moment. 'All right then,' he said. 'If that's how you feel, we'd better lay off just for the moment.'

'Thanks.'

Jasper had had enough of hanging around the bench. It was obvious his master wasn't about to budge. Andy watched the dog plunge through the hedgerow to reappear in the field behind them. He was much happier when the animal stayed away from the cliff edge.

He turned to Pat. There was another matter. 'I've been thinking about the money.'

'Oh yes?'

At the start of their arrangement Andy had assumed that Pat would ask for his share to be paid over at once. But, apart from requesting some payments to be made to his family back in Ireland, he hadn't. 'Just sit on it for the moment,' he'd said, 'till I work something out.'

They'd both known that the riskiest part of their operation – short of Pat being caught red-handed – was paying the jockey his money. It would be naive in the extreme for Andy to simply transfer it into an account in Pat's name. They needed to create the kind of complex money trail used by characters in John Grisham novels – offshore bank accounts in the Bahamas or whatever. For that some legal expertise was required and who could they go to who wouldn't rip them off or turn them in?

So they'd ended up in this situation, with Andy sitting on over a hundred grand that belonged to Pat.

'We're practically brothers-in-law,' Pat had said. 'I trust you.'

Recently, as their winnings had grown, they had discussed going into business together. If Andy set up training again, it would be easy to include Pat as his partner and make over a portion of the business in lieu of Pat's share of the money. Since Pat's riding career was treading water these days, it looked like a solution to a number of problems.

So far, though, their discussions had been vague.

'Jack's talking about leaving the yard at the end of the season,' Andy said.

Pat gazed at Andy intently. He was listening.

'His daughter in the States is expecting a baby. He fancies spending time over there being a grandad.'

'You mean he's thinking of selling the yard? It's a bit out of our league, isn't it?'

Pat had a point. Beach Head with its house and outbuildings, fifty horse boxes, fifteen acres and a private gallop was worth a tidy sum. Even with a £200,000 deposit they'd be stretched to the limit to get a mortgage.

'That's what I said. He told me he wasn't

necessarily thinking of selling. He could put in a tenant and charge a rent for the premises. He'd give me a good deal too – on the basis he could stay in the back meadow cottage when he wasn't in the States.'

Pat nodded. Obviously working out the wrinkles. 'Give *you* a good deal,' he said. 'Where do I fit in?'

'Well, I'm the one with the trainer's licence so it's got to be in my name but as far as I'm concerned we're partners. You get half the profit from the business. With luck, we'll hang on to all Jack's owners so that should give us a start. And I was thinking about that gallop.'

Andy had often maintained that, by extending the length of the gallop from three to five furlongs, genuine Classic contenders could be trained at Beach Head. But Jack had always been reluctant to make the change.

Pat was grinning. 'You want to extend it, don't you?'

'We've got the money to do it. Give me a few decent prospects and a longer gallop and I guarantee we'll have a Group One winner in three years. The Guineas in five.'

'Whoa, Andy, don't get carried away.'

'Don't you believe me?'

'Actually, I think you might just manage it.'

Andy felt a rush of pleasure at his words. He was nowhere near as confident as he sounded but if you couldn't shoot the breeze with your best mate and business partner, who could you?

Not Harriet, unfortunately. But she'd appreciate moving into Jack's big house, seeing him become master of the yard, and if they ever did start producing contenders for the great races she'd be there by his side at Newmarket and Epsom, he was sure of it.

Magnetic looked about his stable with disdain – or so it seemed to Zoe. She could well believe that his new surroundings were not up to the standard he was accustomed to. He'd get used to it, though, horses were happy in the shabby but comfortable surroundings of Beach Head. Jack made sure of it.

She couldn't quite believe what the trainer had just told her. Mrs Leopold had gone out and bought this big beautiful horse on the assumption that she, Zoe, would ride him. Ride him, what's more, at Royal Ascot. She had only ever seen Ascot on television, when she'd laugh at the ponced-up toffs in the crowd, secretly nursing the hope that one day she might make it in person, dressed in riding silks. And now she was gong to do just that.

Zoe wasn't accustomed to her dreams coming true. Even when she'd been accepted into the racing school at Newmarket, or when Jack gave her a job at Beach Head, she'd not believed it would happen until she'd held the offer letters in her hand. But Jack had clearly promised her the ride on Magnetic in the Wokingham and told her it had been Mrs Leopold's idea. She had to believe it.

It was her mother who'd taught Zoe never to expect favours from the world. Elaine Morris had always expected life to kick her in the teeth and she'd rarely been disappointed.

Zoe had a dim memory – a feeling more than a picture – of her father as a warm and smiling man. Maybe he'd been the optimist in the family. In which case, his optimism had been misplaced as he'd died of lung cancer when Zoe was four. Elaine had carried her anger at being left to bring up two daughters on her own throughout the rest of her life. She'd directed much of it at Harriet and the two of them had battled all through Harriet's long adolescence, with Zoe caught in the middle.

Zoe had friends at school whose parents had split up and made new partnerships, with all sorts of uncomfortable results for their offspring. She used to listen to her best friend bitch about her mother's new husband and her insufferable new step-brothers. But Zoe wouldn't have minded changing places. At least a new man might cheer her mother up and other children around the place would provide new playmates. But her mother wasn't interested in finding a new man. Though her partner was dead, she remained married to his memory.

The Morris household was gloomy and quiet. Elaine worked nine to six in an accountant's office and the girls were left to get on with their after-school lives. Zoe made friends with a newsagent's daughter who was lucky enough to own a pony and the pair of them spent hours riding and grooming him. Harriet, five years her senior, simply stayed out as long as she could, doing God knows what with her disreputable friends and longing for the day when she could leave home for good. The summer she turned sixteen, she quit school and signed on at a hairdressing college in London.

'Why London?' said her mother to Zoe. 'She could go to college here, couldn't she?'

The reason was obvious to Zoe. Harriet simply wanted to get away from home and Zoe couldn't blame her. All the same, she resented her sister's desertion. Though the house was more peaceful, her mother was becoming strange, as if bit by bit she was withdrawing from life. 'You're so much easier to manage,' she'd say as Zoe was left to put some food on the table at supper time and run her own clothes through the washing machine. It soon became obvious to Zoe that her mother wasn't doing much managing at all. Some nights she'd come home from work and go straight to bed. At other times she'd sit in silence with an open book on her lap, but she scarcely turned a page.

Zoe nagged her to go to the doctor and things improved after she'd been prescribed a course of anti-depressants. But the improvement didn't last. Soon the pills were sitting untouched in the bathroom cabinet and Elaine was lying in bed all day. Her job had long gone.

When Harriet returned to Bristol on one of her

occasional visits, she was shocked. Within a week she'd moved back into the house and found a job at a swanky hairdressers in the city centre. Elaine didn't even seem to notice that her eldest daughter had come home.

Zoe could hardly believe that Harriet had returned to save her. They'd never been close. The age gap prevented them being proper playmates and Harriet had always bossed her little sister around. Sometimes it had been like having two mums – and no dad. Zoe had always resented the fact that Harriet had proper memories of their father whereas she just had an impression, like a distant tune in her head, which only emphasised the absence of a father in her life.

But the Harriet who returned was different, not so aggressive, happier in herself, less selfish. They made an unspoken pact to be friends.

So, when faced with her lousy GCSE results – inevitable in the circumstances – Zoe turned to her sister for advice. Should she give up the idea of A levels and try for the British Racing School in Newmarket instead? Harriet had encouraged her. She'd met Andy by then and thought the racing world was exciting.

It should have been Harriet who found Elaine. Zoe had arranged to stay overnight with a friend following a party but the friend had got off with a boy and, in order to avoid the unwanted attentions of his mate, Zoe had returned home. She'd thought the house was empty; certainly Harriet was out but her mother was lying in a profound sleep on the bathroom floor, surrounded by empty packets of pills. She died in hospital a day later, exactly a month after Zoe's sixteenth birthday.

She considered postponing her course at the racing school but what would have been the point of that? She needed to get away and throw herself into a new life. The last thing she wanted was to hang around the house where her mother had killed herself. Officially her death had been one of misadventure but neither Zoe nor Harriet had any doubt that Elaine had made a deliberate exit.

Zoe didn't often think about her past now, her present and future were too good. Harriet wasn't interested in talking about it either though it lay behind them like a journey through a dark tunnel they'd travelled together. Thank God they'd made it into the light.

Magnetic lifted his head from his feed bucket and deigned to give her a look. He was a sturdy, barrel-chested creature with none of the coltish grace of the two-year-olds like Pipsqueak. This was a mature horse, bristling with brute strength – and she was going to ride him in an important race. Would she have the strength? she wondered.

Maybe not the physical strength but she'd find a way. She'd overcome bigger obstacles than the racehorse in front of her.

'You don't scare me,' she told him. And he didn't.

* * *

Andy heard the sound of the front door opening with relief. He always worried when Harriet was working late; in the first years of their marriage because he was concerned for her safety but nowadays because he wondered what she might be up to.

She appeared in the doorway, holding up a large carrier bag. 'I've got Chinese – are you hungry?'

It was a silly question. After a day at the yard he was always hungry and the pizza he'd put away after work was now a distant memory.

He turned off the TV and helped her unpack tinfoil cartons from the bag. There were a lot of them, she'd obviously bought with more than herself in mind. She'd also brought home dishes he liked – crispy shredded beef and Singapore noodles – dishes he knew she didn't much care for.

She produced a Tiger beer and poured it for him and still he didn't smell a rat. Not until the meal was over and she reached for her handbag.

'Andy, we have to talk.'

The words had an ominous ring. On occasion, he'd wondered how she might go about telling him she was leaving him. Those imagined conversations always started with words like these.

But what she said next was nothing like he had imagined.

'I owe you an apology.' She took an envelope from her bag. 'This came this morning. I opened it by mistake.'

He recognised the building society letter at once. As he took it from her he hastily rearranged his thoughts. She was still explaining how she came to open his post but he wasn't interested in that.

The statement was in order, as he knew it would be. All the same, it was good to hold in his hand confirmation of the money he'd recently deposited in his account. He'd never laid claim to such a sum before. It looked like a small fortune – and it was.

She was looking at him expectantly. The apologies were over and now she wanted information. He could hardly blame her.

'Andy, is that correct? It's not a mistake?'

'No.'

'You've got almost a quarter of a million pounds?'

'Sure. As you can see.' He could feel the grin tugging at the corners of his mouth and he noted the way her green eyes sparkled despite the confusion on her face. This was as he'd imagined it would be. Large sums of money had an effect on people.

'But how, Andy? Where on earth did this money come from?'

He'd always known he would have to account to her one day, though this was earlier than he had intended. Still, he'd already rehearsed what he would say.

'I've had a good run on the horses recently.'

Her mouth tightened, her sinuous lips curling

into a familiar line of disdain. 'Are you saying you've made all this money gambling?'

'Yes.' It was the simple truth.

'I don't believe you.'

She had reason to be cynical. Up to now he hadn't had the best record with the bookmakers and it had been a contributing factor in the failure of his training business.

'But you promised me you wouldn't bet any more.' The green eyes were flashing with anger now.

For once, Andy wasn't bothered. The justification for his disobedience was in his hand.

'Sorry, sweetheart, but I broke my word. Aren't you glad I did?'

There was no answer to that. Harriet had had no objection to gambling in principle, just that Andy was lousy at it. Not any more, of course.

'But I still don't understand. How did you make such an enormous sum of money?'

He shrugged. 'I just built it up. I've been putting in the hours studying form and got a bit lucky at the beginning, so I had a stake to play with. I did most of it on the all-weather over the winter.'

He could see her turning the information over in her head. In these circumstances it was fortunate she had no interest in racing or she'd have started asking him which horses and when. That way she could have put a pattern together and seen the connection with Pat. Andy had to be careful there.

'So, can you swear to me that you have won all this legitimately?'

'Yes.'

'And you're not doing anything illegal?'

'Of course not, Harriet.' He managed to inject a note of indignation into his voice. Perish the thought that he would do anything illegal.

That was why it was important to keep Pat's name out of it. What Harriet didn't know couldn't hurt her, and she didn't need to know that Pat had supplied the seed money to begin betting. Left to his own devices, Andy wouldn't have been able to come up with much more than £500; Pat had kicked in £4,000 to get them started. And, of course, the whole thing had been Pat's idea in the first place.

Harriet didn't need to know any of it. Just that her husband was not the penniless loser she thought he was.

He drained his beer and smiled at her. She gazed back at him steadily, silent for the moment. He didn't think for a moment he'd satisfied all of her curiosity but he could swear she was looking at him with new respect.

Harriet took a long time to fall asleep – she had a lot to think about.

The origin of Andy's money still worried her. Though she had no knowledge or interest in betting, it perplexed her that her husband could suddenly be so successful at it. Only a year ago they'd had a stand-up row after he'd admitted to losing a couple of hundred in a can't-lose wager on one of the yard's most fancied animals.

She supposed it was just possible he was telling the truth. A gambler's luck did go in streaks, didn't it? Maybe Andy had used up all his bad luck and was now on a good run.

In which case, he had to stop right now. Quit while you're ahead – that's what she'd demanded of him. And he'd agreed, though what store she could set by it wasn't certain. He'd made the same promise before, and he'd been losing then. She couldn't imagine a gambler on a successful streak would pull the plug on his operation without a real incentive.

Andy's incentive, it seemed, was her. He'd told her the money was to finance a new life for the pair of them. He'd done it for her, he said, so they could start again.

Harriet had said little as he'd spoken of his plans, though she'd kept his glass topped up and made encouraging noises. It was essential to get everything out of him so she knew where she stood.

Now, she lay in the dark with her husband happily asleep by her side. He'd reached for her as she'd slipped into bed and she'd not resisted – how could she, in the circumstances? He'd made love to her with a confidence that recalled the early days of their marriage and she'd played her part too.

The money changed a lot of things, there was no denying that.

But the new life he'd outlined for the pair of them filled her with dread. He wanted to set up as a trainer again but who was to say that would work out any better than last time?

She'd listened to him enthuse about Jack's offer to install them at Beach Head as tenants. Admittedly, the thought of moving into Jack's house was appealing, though she'd want to make some radical alterations and would that be allowed? But the word 'tenant' nagged at her. And the notion of sinking the money into a couple of furlongs of racing ground sounded like madness to her. Would that really make any difference? All Andy's talk of winning big races sounded like hot air to her.

She'd rather they used this windfall to buy a house of their own. A two hundred grand deposit would get them nicely onto the property ladder – there were plenty of affordable places in the countryside nearby. And if they had a house of their own she might feel better about trying again for that family Andy was so keen on.

If necessary, of course, they could move out of the area. Andy would find work at another yard easily enough and she could find a job anywhere.

Not that she wanted to move far from the health centre. She didn't care all that much about the job itself; there were other attractions that kept her at the Cut Above.

She couldn't give Martin up just yet. The thought was like a fish-hook in her guts. On the other hand, the end of the season was half a year away and she might feel differently then. She'd not been brought up to burn bridges.

Andy or Martin – she would have to choose. But not yet.

Chapter Six

It wasn't easy to impress Diane Connor, not in Harriet's experience. Wherever you'd been, whoever you'd met, whatever you'd seen, Diane was guaranteed to have done it first. Seen it, bought it, got the T-shirt. You'd never win a game of one-upmanship with her. And, to be fair, with her indolent existence underwritten by her millionaire husband, all of life's little luxuries were at Diane's fingertips. Her cupboards had to be bulging with those sodding T-shirts.

But Diane *was* impressed to hear about Harriet's trip to Royal Ascot to watch Zoe ride Magnetic in the Wokingham Stakes.

'Oh wow,' she said. 'That's fantastic. I don't suppose you'll get to meet the Queen though, will you?'

Harriet said she didn't suppose she would. And Diane embarked on the story of how her father-in-law *had* met the Queen when she'd opened a new conference centre in Bristol where he was the director. Harriet kept her face straight as she trimmed Diane's thick chestnut hair. It scarcely needed her attention but Diane came in once a week, sometimes more. It was plain she had nothing better to do.

To Harriet's surprise, Diane returned to her visit to Ascot. It must have made a real impact on her.

'Your sister's riding, you say?'

'That's right.'

'I didn't realise she was that good.'

Harriet was stung. 'Zoe's brilliant. She's had twelve winners already this season. If she keeps going she could end up top apprentice.'

Diane pulled a face. 'What's an apprentice doing at Royal Ascot? Don't people want to watch proper jockeys?'

Harriet kept her exasperation in check. 'It just means she's new at the job. Once you've ridden enough winners, you're not an apprentice any more. The way she's going, it won't be long.'

If there was one aspect of racing for which Harriet could raise enthusiasm, it was her sister's career. She'd thought Zoe was potty when she'd announced she wanted to go to racing school and secretly she'd thought she'd be wasting her time. But Zoe had proved her wrong – not for the first time. Harriet knew that beneath her sister's naive exterior was a core of steel. If things got tough, Zoe wouldn't flinch and she wouldn't give up – she'd proved it in the past. Harriet was happy to talk about her little sister for as long as she was allowed.

But Diane had heard enough about Zoe. 'What is it your husband does exactly?'

'He's head lad at a trainer's near Kilve.'

Diane laughed. 'That sounds so funny. So a lad is taking you to Royal Ascot?'

'I can assure you he's a grown man. The job title's a bit of an old-fashioned thing. He's actually second-in-command.'

But Diane wasn't interested. She'd moved on to more important matters. 'What are you going to wear?'

Harriet was happy to tell her. For once, she had something to boast about because Andy had bought her a new dress for the occasion, jade green with a square-cut neck and a hat to match. She was going to look great.

If Harriet hadn't discovered the existence of that building society account, this would not be happening, she was sure of it. Now the cat was out of the bag and Andy was still feeling guilty about keeping it hidden in the first place, suddenly he was spending money on her. Apart from the trip to Ascot and the outfit, he'd bought her a new mobile phone with an assortment of high-tech features she wasn't sure she'd ever use.

She'd been surprised when Andy had offered to take her to the last day of Royal Ascot. Normally she avoided race meetings but she could see the appeal of this one and Zoe had been thrilled to hear her sister would be present. Harriet knew Zoe had been upset about the way she had dismissed her victory at Newmarket and this was going to make up for it. It was thoughtful of Andy to arrange it. Normally he'd be stuck at the yard but he'd taken a day off to be with her.

She *did* love Andy, though it was a different feeling to being in love with him, like she had been at first. But who was still giddy about their partner after five years? Time rubbed the gloss off all relationships and the new became old – it was only natural. But that didn't mean the tried and tested did not retain its value. She and Andy had weathered a fair number of storms together. She mustn't overlook his good points just because they had become too familiar.

She hadn't had her fill of Martin yet though. She had simply put the blond tennis coach on the back burner for this weekend. He'd been gratifyingly upset about it.

'Come on, Harriet,' he'd murmured into her ear when she'd told him of her plans. They were back in that little bed in his flat – at least no one would come barging in on them there. 'You keep telling me how much you hate racing. Let Andy bugger off to Ascot and we can spend some time together. I'll cancel my afternoon lessons.'

She explained to him about Zoe but it didn't make much of an impression.

'Watch her ride some other time.'

'You don't understand, Martin.' And he didn't.

Only Andy could appreciate the nuances of her relationship with her sister and how important it was to be there when Zoe rode the most important race of her career.

But that wasn't Martin's fault. She hadn't told him about the way they'd been brought up and their mother's depression and how Zoe had found her body. Harriet owed Zoe for that. Even if she explained it to Martin, poured her heart out about her childhood in the kind of tedious detail that only lovers should endure, he wouldn't really understand.

Andy, on the other hand, had been there at the time. He'd come with her to the house that night when Zoe rang in panic and dried the tears of both sisters in the days that followed. Andy had been by her side through everything.

Maybe Andy was meant always to be by her side. The Martins of this world might be thrilling for the moment but, when it counted, she needed Andy to lean on.

Maybe.

It was funny how matters of such importance could flash through her head while she was trimming a customer's hair and making small talk. As she reached for the hand mirror to show Diane the back of her head, Harriet had the feeling she'd come to a significant conclusion.

Compared to all she had invested in her marriage, the relationship with Martin was of little value.

She could walk away any time.

* * *

Zoe's brain was buzzing as she dressed for the race ahead. Someone, one of the many reporters milling around the entrance to the weighing room, had asked her if she was feeling the pressure. She'd smiled – it was a nervous reflex – and said, 'No more than usual,' but that hardly covered how she felt. To be honest, there was too much to remember to be nervous.

She'd walked the course with Jack earlier, long before the crowds had arrived, and been in awe of the place. The track was much broader than she'd imagined. There were twenty-nine runners in her race and holding a horse up for a late run was going to be extremely tricky. Especially as there appeared to be a strong bias towards the stands rail and the entire field was likely to stay on one side. Magnetic had been drawn in the middle.

'That's OK,' Jack had explained as they set off on their inspection. 'There might be a couple of outside draw horses who chance their luck and go for the far rail but I want you to miss the break and head over this way. Keep six yards off the rail. That's where the tractor goes every time it mows the grass so that's where the fastest ground is.'

She'd left it to him. He'd had winners at Royal Ascot before, one in this very race back in the eighties. 'A tidy little grey called Tropical. He was drawn on the inside and went up the stands rail like a rocket. It was a hot summer that year and the ground was baked hard no matter how much they watered. Thinking about it, that did for Tropical. It was the only race he ever won. We won't have that problem this year.'

For the past week there'd been plenty of soft summer rain. It had spoiled Ladies Day. Today, however, the clouds had been chased off by a stiff breeze and the sky was a clear summery blue. The sun was not hot, however, and the going was good.

They'd stood by the winning post, looking up at the vast new empty stand while he gave her his instructions for riding the race. 'It's going to be all over in seventy-odd seconds. People who don't know much about riding reckon that means you've got to bust a gut from start to finish. But you know better than that. You know how to sit still. That's a gift, you know, to be able to sit still on a horse and let him find his own pace. Then you can help him along. Some riders want to push their horses from start to finish. It can't be done. They think they've got to be seen to do something all the time they're in the saddle but not you. I don't know whether it's just instinct but you've worked out that sometimes less is more.' His piercing blue eyes bored into her from out of his weathered face. 'So when this race starts and all those other horses go flashing off like bullets out of a gun, I want you to do nothing.'

He took her by the arm and bent his head so it was close to hers. 'Promise me, you'll just sit on him and count to twenty. Then think about riding a race. There'll be a lot ahead of you but this is a strong horse and needs covering up. You don't want to get to the front too soon.'

Zoe had pondered these instructions while she changed into her riding clothes. Other thoughts crowded her mind, many of them pleasant – like how much she appreciated Harriet and Andy making a special trip to support her. Some were less comforting, such as the embarrassment of having to pull out of a ride the previous day.

Gavin Speedie, the trainer, had booked her weeks ago. He had been impressed by her victory on Pipsqueak and she'd been thrilled to catch his attention – his was a yard that regularly turned out top-class horses.

But once Mrs Leopold had bought Magnetic with the idea of Zoe riding him in the Wokingham, other matters took precedence. If Zoe had ridden a winner for Speedie, it would have taken her career victories over the limit and made her ineligible to claim the full allowance for her ride on Magnetic. In the circumstances she'd had no choice but to withdraw at the last minute. Speedie had not been understanding and had sworn he would never use her in the future.

She'd been upset by that but Pat had laughed when she'd told him.

'I know Gavin Speedie,' he'd said. 'He blows a lot of hot air but he'll cool off. If he thinks you can do a job for him, all this will be forgotten. Get out there and do your stuff and he'll be offering you rides within a couple of hours, guaranteed.'

That was one of the great things about Pat. He knew just how to cheer her up.

Sitting on the café terrace, Diane stirred the sludge of her peach and mango smoothie with a straw. Should she have another? It was pretty bland and, no matter how healthy, it was bound to contain unnecessary calories. She might be tempted if it contained alcohol but drinking in the middle of the afternoon was not a bright idea, not if a girl wanted to keep her looks. And Diane fully intended to keep hers, they were about the best thing she'd got – together with Maurice's money, of course. Though realistically the one depended on the other.

She pushed her glass to one side and leaned back in the chair in the sunshine. The terrace was on the same level as the hair salon and also afforded a good view of the tennis courts below where Martin was hitting with a trim brunette – another of his pupils, no doubt. He was a magnet for female attention, no matter what Harriet said. To Diane's appreciative eye, he could have stepped out of one of those West Coast TV dramas full of sleek and suntanned bodies of impossible perfection.

Was it naughty of her not to come clean with Harriet? She could have said, right when Harriet had first told her about Martin, something like, 'Oh

God, not you too?' and immediately spilled the beans about her couple of encounters with the new tennis coach. But the chance had been missed and the more Harriet had spoken about Martin, the plainer it had been that she wouldn't be able to shrug off the knowledge that Diane had been there before her. In Martin's grungy little bedroom, sampling what the blond body beautiful had to offer.

It hadn't been that fantastic, to be honest. Not a meeting of minds, at any rate, though she'd been miffed by his failure to follow up their last session and the way he'd avoided her ever since. It was funny how he was never around in the gym reception when she went for her lessons, and how he managed not to look at her if she and Ken ended up on the next court.

All in all, she'd consigned him to history and decided to pretend their afternoons together had never taken place. That's how he was playing it obviously. At any rate, it sounded like he had his hands full with Harriet.

But Harriet wasn't here this afternoon, she was at Ascot. And Maurice was in Eindhoven on business with his new French PA, Virginie.

Diane rather wished Harriet hadn't told her about Martin taking her to look at the farm where he'd grown up. The story came back to her now. Though the bit about being spied on by some farmer was pretty creepy, the thought of being passionately ravished in a sunlit meadow was hot in more ways than one. She might, after all, be persuaded to overlook Martin's recent boorish behaviour if it led to something memorable like that.

'Put your eyes back in, Diane. You're a married woman.'

Jenny Mills, a woman from her yoga class, was lowering her tea tray onto Diane's table. 'Don't mind if I park here, do you?'

It was too late even if she did but Diane didn't say so. She was embarrassed to be caught out ogling Martin, to Jenny's obvious amusement.

'He is a bit of a dish, isn't he? He made a big impression on the ladies of Spillbury Tennis Club even when he was a schoolboy.'

'You know Martin?'

'Sure. His mother was friends with mine before they went to live in Spain. Little Martin Christie, the great white hope of British tennis – I don't think.' The last three words were said with some emphasis.

Diane was genuinely intrigued now.

'I was told he used to be very good. He got to the final of Junior Wimbledon.'

'Says who?' Jenny stirred milk into her tea. 'He was OK at club level but hardly a world-beater. He was more successful with the women, according to Mum, even though he was just a kid.'

'Really?' Jenny had all of Diane's attention now.

Irritatingly she was waving at a woman in a lemon sundress who'd just walked onto the terrace.

'There's my friend Stella. Late as usual.'

'So Martin bedded all the little girls at the club, did he?'

Jenny laughed. 'It was the bigger girls he was interested in. He had a fling with a member's wife when he was still at school – bit of a scandal. Hi, Stella. Let me introduce you.'

Frankly, Diane could have done without the new arrival. She'd turned up just when things were getting interesting but there was no way she could yank the conversation back to Martin without it being obvious that she was interested in him. Which she wasn't, not really.

Her gaze returned to the tennis court.

Harriet was a bit tiddly already. Andy had been pressing food and drink on her from the moment they arrived and she'd not said no to the champagne. A little voice had whispered in her ear that her husband had probably blown a week's money on her already but then she remembered that the husband was a man of means these days and the voice fell silent.

Now she stood in the parade ring with all the other fancily dressed connections. It wasn't exactly a unique experience. In the early days with Andy, when he'd been sending out his own runners, she'd often taken her place beside the owners and jockeys and listened in on the last-minute banter and whispered instructions. But standing in the ring at Yarmouth or Folkestone on a damp Monday afternoon hardly compared to the sunshine of Ascot on the Saturday of the Royal meeting. For all she knew, her tipsy smile was being broadcast to the nation.

Maybe being broadcast to Martin. There was a thought. Might he be watching the racing somewhere in the hope of catching a glimpse of her? She hoped so.

'Are you all right?'

Andy was by her side, smartly turned out, though to be honest he could do with some new clothes. His suit of three years' vintage didn't exactly cut it in this company. She'd have to get him to spend some of that money on himself.

She smiled at him. 'I'm fine. Couldn't be better.'

She made an effort to dismiss Martin from her mind. She was here with Andy who was doing his best to make sure she had a good time, though she wished he wouldn't put his arm round her shoulders in such a proprietorial fashion. She eased out of his grip.

'Here comes Zoe.'

Harriet peered through the crowd to catch sight of her sister amongst the brightly coloured riders pouring into the ring to merge with the substantial crowd.

'I wish I'd brought my camera,' she said.

Andy laughed. 'You have, sweetheart.'

'No, I haven't. I meant to put it in my bag but I forgot.'

'You didn't forget your phone, did you?'

Then she realised what he was getting at. The new mobile he'd bought her could take pictures. She hadn't used the facility yet but now was the ideal time to try it out.

'Brilliant,' she said and, for the first time in ages, she gave her husband a spontaneous kiss on the lips.

That's a good omen, thought Zoe, as she finally wound her way through the crush in the parade ring and found Magnetic's connections. The sight of Harriet kissing Andy gladdened her heart, eclipsing for a moment the many other thoughts in her head. But only for a moment.

'Don't look so worried,' said Mrs Leopold as she bestowed a perfumed hug. 'Let's see that big smile.'

'Yes,' came her sister's voice as she aimed her new phone at them. 'Say cheese, Chipmunk.'

Chipmunk! That was an old and much loathed nickname.

'You cow,' she protested but she laughed all the same.

'You see,' said Harriet in triumph, holding out the phone so they could see Zoe's digital image. It seemed to Zoe that her grinning mouth took up half the little screen. 'That's why we used to call her Chipmunk,' Harriet added.

Thanks, sis. But Zoe didn't mind really. They were all laughing, she amongst them, and the churning feeling in her stomach had vanished.

Abbie, freshly promoted to travelling head girl following Joe's departure, legged Zoe up into the saddle and said, 'Go and do it for us women.'

Zoe hadn't thought of it like that but why not? There were twenty-eight other jockeys in the race and they were all male. It would be a laugh to put one over on them – they'd hate it.

Jack had his hand on the bridle, commanding her attention.

His final instructions were not prolonged. Just three words in total: 'Count to twenty.'

Then she was out of the ring, leaving her wellwishers behind her.

Martin didn't bother to shower when his lesson ended at three thirty – there was no time if he wanted to catch the three forty-five at Ascot. He'd already asked Debbie in the Sports Bar to make sure the TV was tuned to the racing and she placed a cold mineral water with lime twist in front of him as he slid onto a stool.

On screen, horses strode around the parade ring accompanied by a commentary on their chances in the forthcoming race. Martin didn't pay much attention to the words. He wanted to look at the crowd in the centre of the ring, to see if he could catch a glimpse of Harriet. But, as horse succeeded horse, it didn't look as if he would get the chance. How many runners were there in this race anyway?

The screen filled with the only female jockey in the race, Zoe Morris. That would be Harriet's sister. A pretty little thing, as far as he could tell with her face half hidden by that cap. Built like a stick, though, and not a patch on Harriet, in Martin's opinion.

Eventually, as the last horse left the ring, the camera pulled back to show the milling crowd. There, a green hat on a gleaming crown of copper – surely that was Harriet. The image was gone in a flash but there'd been a man in a suit by her side and they'd been laughing.

That would be Andy. He'd seen Andy a few times. Twice when Harriet's car was in the garage and her husband had come to pick her up.

He'd not spoken to him, though, and not been introduced. As far as Harriet's husband was concerned, Martin did not exist.

The majority of runners in the Wokingham Stakes were four years old and upwards, experienced campaigners. Nevertheless, it seemed to take forever to load all twenty-nine of them into the starting stalls. Magnetic stepped into his cage without a fuss but Zoe could feel the agitation building within him as some of his rivals proved to be less amenable. He knew what was coming and he wanted to get on with it.

As Magnetic itched and fretted, Zoe murmured into his ear in what she hoped was a soothing tone. It didn't have a noticeable effect. Not that it mattered much, provided they didn't have to wait too long; a docile horse wouldn't be much use for the task ahead. She'd been on Magnetic's back as often as she could since he'd been at Beach Head and fancied she'd got to know him. He was a whole-hearted beast who ran with fire in his belly and she loved him for it. All she had to do was make sure he expended that energy where it counted – in the race.

A bar clanged home, a shout went up and suddenly the gate sprang open. Zoe had never ridden in a race with so many runners and, as all twenty-nine of them lunged forward in the same instant, she felt as if she were a leaf on the surface of a fast-flowing river rushing down the track.

She sat high, balancing on Magnetic's shoulders as he plunged ahead, but Jack's words were in her head. As horses streamed by on either side of her she stayed still and counted.

It seemed to take an age to get to twenty. In that time the leaders had covered almost two furlongs, a third of the distance. Magnetic was travelling smoothly in a long-striding gallop. All the same, they were firmly at the rear of the field.

Following Jack's instructions, Zoe steered Magnetic to the left to the back of the bunch racing six yards off the rail.

If they stopped the race right now, she'd be dead last.

'I can't see her, Andy. I can't see her!' Harriet squirmed in agitation in the circle of her husband's arms as they stood in the crush.

Andy wasn't surprised she couldn't pick Zoe out through his binoculars as the runners in the Wokingham thundered straight at them from half a mile away. It was a sight easier to follow the race on the big screen.

'She's at the rear of the bunch,' he murmured into the copper curtain of her hair. 'Look out for the yellow hat.'

'I've got her. She's not doing well though, is she?'

'Too early to tell. But he's travelling nicely. She's going to need plenty of luck. Look, they're starting to move up.'

They were approaching halfway now and Magnetic was picking his way through.

'Come on, Zoe!' called Harriet, her shout adding to the mounting cries of encouragement all around. The Wokingham was one of the big betting races of the meeting.

Unusually for Andy, he did not have a wager on the race. Maybe his philosophy of gambling had changed; these days he was used to backing horses guaranteed to win.

He'd taken Harriet down to the rails bookies, however, and put £100 on Magnetic for her. It would be worth a few quid if the horse won but a bet that size seemed like small beer to him now.

'Don't lose it,' he'd said as he'd handed her the ticket and he'd made her tuck it carefully into a corner of her bag.

For once she'd not objected to his solicitous behaviour. She'd not accused him of being patronising or 'anal' – one of her favourite criticisms of his precise habits. Instead, she'd done as he'd said and thanked him with a kiss.

That made two kisses today and he was looking forward to more. He savoured the moment as Harriet leaned back against him, her whole body quivering with excitement. Of course he wanted Magnetic to win, for the good of the yard, for Zoe, but most of all to make his wife happy. Who said their marriage was failing? How could it be when there were afternoons like this?

Zoe wasn't holding anything back now. But there was no need for her to work like mad with her hands and heels or go crazy with the whip – like some around her. Magnetic was galloping like a true thoroughbred, an animal born to run with the pack – and to get to the head of it. All Zoe had to do was to help him weave a path through the horses still ahead.

It was like racing through a maze, trying to anticipate the best way forward, guessing which way the horses in front would be moving, not just laterally but backwards and forwards. Spotting the horses which were tiring was key.

They were past the point where the straight came into the shadow of the stand but Zoe wasn't thinking about it.

She picked a path between two runners and around another tight to the rail. Now there were only three horses racing abreast between her and the empty track ahead. Zoe could see the horse on the rail had just about given its all and wouldn't be able to hold a straight line for much longer. But time was running out fast. If she had to go around the runners ahead she needed to be on her way. Then, just as she was about to manoeuvre to her right, the horse in front faltered – not much but enough for Magnetic to see some daylight. Zoe forced him through and for the first time hit him with the whip.

Magnetic understood that all right. He lengthened his stride and plunged into the narrow channel ahead.

Their rivals resisted and, for a second or two, the three of them were glued flank to flank and stride to stride.

Then Magnetic thrust free into the daylight.

Harriet would never have believed she could care so much about the result of a horse race. But Magnetic's victory was different.

As they waited for the presentation she wrapped

her arms round Zoe and squeezed her tight.

'Wow,' said Zoe when Harriet finally relaxed her grip. 'Being hugged by you is more dangerous than riding the race.'

'I just want you to know how proud I am of you.'

'Oh.' Zoe's face flushed pink. To Harriet, her little sister looked about twelve years old.

'And,' Harriet whispered in Zoe's ear, 'Mum would have been proud of you too.'

Zoe pulled a face. 'I don't think it mattered much to her what I did.'

'That's only because she was sick. She cared passionately about you. That's why . . .' Harriet broke off quickly, aware she was heading down a path she shouldn't take.

But Zoe seized on the hesitation, her chin lifting in a familiar look of defiance. 'That's why she waited till I'd left school before she killed herself, you mean. She cared enough to do her duty by me, I suppose.'

'No!' They'd never talked about this and now was hardly the time. Dignitaries were mounting the rostrum and the crowd was swirling around. Harriet could see a man she recognised as a TV racing presenter hovering nearby, microphone at the ready. 'Believe me, Zoe, Mum would have been thrilled. She loved us both very much.'

Zoe looked earnestly into Harriet's eyes. 'Do you really think so?'

'I do.'

Then Zoe was pulled away to join Ursula and Jack at the prize-giving. Harriet applauded along with everyone else but inside she felt flat. It was probably just a reaction to the champagne-fuelled excitement of the last twenty minutes.

Who was she kidding? Her sister had put her finger on a point that was always sore, and would be for the rest of her life. She had lied to Zoe but she had no regrets about that. She must never admit to the conclusion she'd formed as a teenager, when she'd resolved to leave home as soon as she could. What Zoe had said had been correct: their mother hadn't loved either of them. But she'd never say so to Zoe. Harriet had run away as soon as she could, leaving her sister to bear the burden. She regretted that now but she could never put it right.

'How are you doing, sweetheart?'

It was Andy. She switched on a smile. She didn't want him probing her mood. In this state she might admit to something she shouldn't. 'I'm fine. Doing well.'

'How about you dig out your betting slip?'

She'd forgotten about the bet.

'How much will it be, Andy?'

'Sixteen hundred quid, I reckon.'

Good Lord. The smile on her face was now genuine. And she didn't push away the arm that snaked round her waist.

To think she had doubted his ability as a gambler. 'Oh, Andy!'

She kissed him again – it was becoming a bit of a habit.

Martin was watching the after-race shenanigans on the box, toffs and plebs united in the merry conspiracy of the sporting occasion. He could relate to that. The only pity was that he wasn't there by Harriet's side instead of that oaf she was married to. The sight of Andy Burns' sleek shaved head and thick neck earned Martin's contempt. And that crappy old suit – it looked a size too small across the chest. What on earth did Harriet see in him?

'Hello, Martin.'

Oh God, it was Diane Connor.

'Do you mind if I join you?'

She was about the last person he wanted wriggling onto the stool next to him but a man was supposed to be gracious to old girlfriends. If that's what she was.

'Of course not,' he said.

Her legs brushed against his, skin on skin, as she arranged herself. The faint musk of her perfume reminded him of occasions not too distant though they were pre-history to him now. That is to say, pre-Harriet. It was remarkable how he'd managed not to bump into Diane since then.

She laid a finger on his forearm. 'Can I get you a coffee or something?'

'No thanks.' He didn't do coffee or tea or any number of other things that most people found indispensable – like alcohol. But she knew that.

He watched her order a cappuccino without comment.

'So, how did she do?'

The question took Martin by surprise. He looked at her blankly.

'Harriet's sister?'

He played it by reflex. 'Who's Harriet?'

'Oh please, Martin. Harriet and I are friends, she's told me about you.'

Her big brown eyes bored into his, knowing and curious. He turned away, thoughts elbowing for attention.

How could Harriet have spoken about him? She was always nagging him to be discreet and yet she'd told Diane.

And how come Diane knew Harriet anyway? Was she one of Harriet's customers?

Most important of all, what had Diane said to Harriet about him?

She appeared to read his mind. 'Don't worry, I didn't mention our little fling. I wouldn't want to rain on her parade – she's nuts about you.'

That was something. He wasn't happy, though. He'd have to think it through, run some damage limitation maybe. On reflection it was probably a good thing he'd found out about Harriet and Diane's friendship this way.

'So, come on, Martin. Which one's Zoe? Or don't you know?'

As it happened, the television was showing a replay of the moments after Magnetic's victory and the girl was milking the applause of the crowd.

He nodded at the screen. 'That's her. She just won the last race.'

Diane peered at the screen. 'I don't see much of a resemblance, do you? Maybe in the chin and the wide-spaced eyes. What do you think?'

'I couldn't say.'

'Don't want to, you mean.' She spooned foam from her cup. Her lips were full and plush. Diane was undeniably attractive, in an air-brushed, plasticky kind of way. He couldn't think why he'd ever been tempted.

The television coverage had moved to the next race. There was no chance of catching a glimpse of Harriet now, which was probably just as well. Time to make a swift exit. Martin pushed his stool back from the counter and stood up.

'I hope I'm not driving you away,' she said.

'No, but I need to grab a shower.'

She gave him a slow-burn look, taking in his tight tennis shorts and the singlet which clung to his chest.

'You could come back and shower at my place,' she said. 'Maurice is away.'

It was hardly subtle.

'For old times' sake,' she added in case he'd missed the point.

'I don't think that would be a good idea.'

She stood up and took a step towards him. The musky perfume was in his nostrils and the swell of her breasts inches from his chest. 'Don't you fancy me any more then? I shan't tell Harriet, if that's what's worrying you.'

More things than that were worrying him. Her rich-bitch arrogance for one. The assumption that he was available to her like the over-priced coffee she'd left almost untouched – an indulgence for a woman with time on her hands and mischief in her heart. Her body might be tempting but her mind was a total turn-off.

But it was more than that. She'd claimed to be Harriet's friend. Some friend.

'So?' She was still staring at him as if she knew just what might tempt him to step out of line.

'No thank you, Diane.' He said it carefully, determined not to be rude though his fingers itched to slap that superior look off her face.

'Suit yourself.' She picked up her purse. 'Can I give you a bit of advice?'

'Go ahead.'

She intended to say her piece anyway, he could see that.

'Don't muck Harriet around. Find a girl who's not already spoken for.'

The nerve of her. But he held himself in check as she walked away.

Chapter Seven

Andy seized his chance to speak to Pat when Harriet went to help Zoe in the kitchen.

'Shall we back Full Force this week?'

Pat turned from the television which was showing the recording of the previous day's racing at Ascot. He shook his head. 'Not a great idea.'

So far, during their 'understanding' Andy had taken his cue from Pat, only wagering as the jockey suggested. To suggest a bet himself was a departure, but he had his reasons.

'He's back to his best, Pat. I've been watching him every day. He's working great and is shouting for his food every time I walk past his stable.'

Pat looked unimpressed. 'He won't win, I'm telling you.'

Andy suspected that although Pat had agreed to ease up on the cheating, he had changed his mind.

'I thought we'd agreed to drop it for the moment. Jack's on to us. But we can still make money. No one can complain if Full Force storms home tomorrow and I've got a few bob on him.'

On the TV, the horses were parading before the Wokingham for the third or fourth time. The girls had insisted on running and re-running the recording of the race and Pat had put it on again before they'd rushed off to fix the food.

Andy ignored the action on the screen; at least it was handy cover for their conversation.

Pat shook his head.

'But Full Force is flying.'

'And what odds will you get if he wins on Tuesday? Half the price if you wait a few weeks. Trust me.'

Andy understood that well enough. But it wasn't what he wanted to hear.

'I don't think it's sensible to rock the boat right now. Jack's got his eye on us.'

'Not on me, he hasn't.'

That was true. Like everyone else, Jack appeared convinced that Pat's riding had not been to blame when horses had raced badly. On the contrary, from the conspicuous effort Pat put in, it always looked as if he had the accelerator pressed to the floor. The horses lost all the same. That was the beauty of the scam.

But it wasn't the point at issue.

'Look, Full Force has got to run an honest race or Jack's going to get on my back. If there's no dodgy results now Joe's out of the way, Jack will think it was down to him all along.'

Pat grinned. 'Come on now, Andy. I don't know why you're making such a fuss. You said yourself Jack's looking for the quiet life these days. That's why he's handing the business over to you, isn't it?'

There was plenty Andy could have said in response to that. Such as, it was hardly a done deal that he would take over at Beach Head and that was why they had to play it straight for the moment. He could also have pointed out that they were in this together and they had to agree. But it was hard to get round the fact that Pat controlled their strategy. He was the one in the driving seat – literally – and if he was determined to stop a horse then there was nothing Andy could do.

Pat gripped his arm. 'Haven't we always said that Full Force is perfect for us? Let's not get cold feet now. Trust me.'

Just then the door opened and Zoe appeared with a large tray loaded with cutlery and glasses. Harriet walked behind her holding a steaming casserole dish in gloved hands.

'Ooh look,' said Zoe as she laid the table. 'I'm on the TV again.'

There she was on the small screen riding Magnetic home for the umpteenth time.

'You're so sweet,' she cried, grabbing Pat round the neck. 'You can't get enough of me, can you?'

'True enough,' he said and hugged her back. As he faced Andy over her shoulder he winked.

He was an irritating bugger sometimes but Andy

couldn't help smiling. Pat was guaranteed to get away with blue murder.

Harriet looked up at the ceiling, staring intently at the cheap paper lampshade and crumbling cornice. Mozart played softly through tinny speakers – Martin was still trying to convert her taste – and art books were jumbled up with men's health magazines in piles at the foot of the bed. Funny how all the things that had seemed scruffy and unimportant took on significance in moments like these. She consciously tried to commit the details to memory. This, she told herself, was the last time she would be lying here in Martin's bed.

Not that she had intended to return to Martin's bed at all. The weekend had convinced her that her future lay with her husband. What did it matter that Andy didn't excite her like he used to? Her history with Andy counted for much and he'd shown her a brilliant time for the past couple of days. Finally it seemed he might make something of himself – provided she was by his side to make sure he made the right financial decisions. Anyway, they were married for better or worse. She had taken the vow. Her recent discovery of his newly acquired riches had no fundamental bearing on the matter.

Harriet's plan had been to deliver the bad news to Martin in her car outside the health centre. There they could shed their tears in private – it

would be a regretful scene and she'd be as easy on
him as she could – and afterwards return to work.
But Martin had been late to their lunchtime
rendezvous and had hurled himself into the car
with the words, 'Quick, let's get going before she
sees us.'

'Before who sees us?' she'd said but she'd automatically turned the key in the engine all the
same.

'Diane Connor. I saw her coming out of the
swimming pool reception. Does she spend her
whole life hanging around here?'

Harriet had been intrigued. Maybe this wasn't
the moment to launch into her prepared speech
about how she'd been doing a lot of thinking and
concluded they were getting in too deep and as she
was a married woman it would be best, etc. That
would keep for the moment.

'I didn't know you even knew Diane.'

'She came up to me in the café on Saturday
claiming to be a mate of yours.'

'I do her hair.'

'I guessed as much. She virtually threw herself at
me.'

They had left the car park and Harriet was
driving aimlessly. 'What do you mean?'

'I mean she started insinuating things about me
and you. You don't discuss me with her, do you?'

'Well, I have mentioned you once or twice.' That
was trimming things a bit but what was the point

of getting into a discussion about it when they were
about to break up?

'Anyhow,' he continued, 'she suggested I went back
to her place for a shower. Her husband was off somewhere, so how about it? She was as brazen as that.'

Harriet felt sick. She squealed noisily to a halt at
a red light.

'What did you do?' she said.

'I told her to get lost, of course.'

'Did you honestly?' She stared intently into his
sky-blue eyes. It had never been so important to
her to be told the truth.

'Of course I bloody did.'

Thank God for that.

What a bitch Diane had turned out to be. She'd
never talk to her again.

Martin's hand covered her knee and remained
there. It felt good.

Behind her someone hooted impatiently. The
light had turned green without her registering. She
accelerated away and found herself turning into
Martin's road. She must have been on autopilot.
She parked outside his house.

'Why?' she asked.

He turned towards her, his hand still on her knee
– on the inside of her thigh, in fact. His lips were
inches from hers.

'Why what?'

'Why did you turn her down? Don't you find her
attractive?'

The sky-blue eyes darkened and his brow creased. 'Attractive's got nothing to do with it,' he hissed. 'She could be the most desirable woman in the world and she wouldn't interest me.'

Her heart was thumping as she held his gaze.

'Why's that?' She knew what the answer would be but she ached for him to say it.

'Because I'm in love with *you*. In comparison, she's nothing.' His fingers dug into her flesh and his voice was thick. 'You're the only woman I want, Harriet, now and forever. Believe me.'

And she did. As a consequence, here she was, once again lying naked in the crook of his arm, staring up at his shabby ceiling.

Trying to get up the courage to go through with her decision to finish it.

Jack had a familiar sinking feeling in the pit of his stomach, the one he'd had when Pipsqueak was making heavy weather of running at Bath. At least this time he didn't have Ursula Leopold standing by his side – he'd hate to let her down again. Laurence Daniels, the owner of Full Force, had been with Jack for a couple of years. So far, despite having had a total of five horses with him, Jack had not managed to train him a single winner. Laurence was not a lucky owner, his horses always seemed to pick up sprains and niggles and go down with mystery viruses just when they promised to hit form. On this running of Full Force at Salisbury it didn't look like Laurence was about to break his duck.

The nine runners in the five-furlong sprint were a furlong from home and Full Force was just about hanging on to fourth place.

'Now use your stick, Pat,' Jack bellowed, more to give the impression that the race was proceeding according to plan than anything else. There was no chance of Pat hearing him and, in any case, the jockey had gone for his whip already, riding the kind of dependable race he always did. He wasn't a great jockey – he seldom won a race that he shouldn't – but he could be relied on to give an honest account of himself and follow instructions. To be honest, even a world-beater wouldn't get a tune out of Full Force today.

Not even Zoe? The thought flashed through Jack's head. But he didn't see what his accomplished young apprentice could do in these circumstances. Full Force was toiling back in the pack, making heavy weather of his progress. Five horses in front of him would have to fall over for him to get a sniff of victory and that wasn't going to happen.

'It's a stiff course,' Jack said – he had to pass some kind of comment though the owner was probably well aware of Salisbury's demanding incline. 'And it was a bit soft for him – I don't think he liked the going.'

'I don't think he liked anything.' Laurence's

voice had the kind of resigned note that suggested he had been in this situation many times before – and so he had.

'I'm sorry, Laurence.' Jack always thought it best to come clean. 'He's been working so well at home I genuinely thought he would win. We'll crack it soon, I promise.'

Laurence raised a half-hearted smile but his grip on Jack's arm was firm. 'If you say so.'

His decency didn't make Jack feel any better, not least because he hadn't been entirely honest with the owner. He'd not thought the race was in the bag at all, not today at any rate.

Before he'd left the yard he'd made a point of having a word with Andy. 'How do you think Full Force is going to do?'

Andy had been watching the horse working alongside Jack. They'd both been encouraged by what they'd seen recently.

But Andy hadn't managed an encouraging reply. 'He should be all right if he can take his home form to the track.'

That was obvious. Jack wanted more.

'If you were a gambling man,' and Andy was just that, as Jack well knew, 'would you be having a punt on him today?'

Andy hadn't looked Jack in the eye. He'd pulled a face. 'It's only his second time back on the track after his injury, isn't it? I think I might keep my hand in my pocket for now.'

That was what had set Jack wondering and now, after Full Force had laboured home out of the money, he pondered the situation. He wasn't happy with Andy. Maybe he hadn't made himself clear to his head lad last time. He'd allowed himself to be sidetracked by the drama of the fight with Joe. In those circumstances it was easy to blame Joe and convince himself that he'd weeded out the bad apple. He'd said as much to Ursula and she'd been grateful for his swift action. Or maybe it was him. Maybe after a lifetime of training he was losing his touch. Maybe these days Andy knew more about the horses than he did.

Jack intended to have words. He passionately hoped his suspicions were off the mark. But just because he liked Andy didn't mean the lad wasn't up to pulling a fast one.

Harriet listened to Martin without fully committing her attention. He was telling her about his latest scheme to make money, as he often did in moments like this, after they'd made love and before they began again – in the interval, as she thought of it. She didn't mind. She'd always been flattered he sought her opinion, considering he was a university graduate and she only had three crap GCSEs and an NVQ in hairdressing. But he gave the impression he was really interested in her opinion. A few weeks ago, he'd had a plan to sell health supplements to gyms and before that an ambitious idea to build his own fitness centre, though he conceded that might be one for the back burner. Today, he'd moved on. He was intrigued by the student who'd made a million by renting advertising space in tiny plots on his website. Harriet didn't understand that one but it didn't matter. Her fingers were playing in the blond curls on the nape of his neck. The interval would soon be over.

She knew she was a coward but she'd now decided that this was not the time to put an end to their romance. Not after what they'd just done – and what they were about to do. He'd been so intense, so passionate in his need for her, so vitriolic in his denunciation of Diane and, by definition, all other women. Only she would do for him. It would be unfair of her to deny him at the moment.

And why should she? Her decision was made. Long-term she'd stay with Andy, so why not enjoy the short-term? Let the tears fall tomorrow, not today.

She leaned up on one elbow and stopped Martin's flow of words with her lips. His arm circled her body, holding her tight.

Curtain up.

A high-pitched trill interrupted them.

'What the hell's that?' he said.

She didn't know. Then she realised it was her new phone, jangling in an unfamiliar tone from her handbag on the floor. She'd forgotten to switch the stupid thing off.

He frowned as she reached across him.

'Do you have to?'

'Just let me see who it is.'

As she feared, the little display on the front was blinking 'Andy'.

'Ignore it,' he said.

'I can't. He'll start ringing the salon. Now, shh.' She put a finger to his lips as she flipped the phone on. 'Hi, Andy!' She injected as much brightness into her voice as she could. She had to get him off the line quickly – there were better things to do.

'Hello, sweetheart, what kept you?'

'I haven't got used to my new ringtone yet. I thought it was someone else's phone.'

'You dope. So where are you?'

'I'm at work.'

'Really? I've just had one of your girls on to me asking if I'd heard from you. She said you'd left because you weren't feeling well.'

Oh Christ! It was true she'd left the salon saying she wasn't sure when she'd be back because she had a stinking headache, but that had been to buy her some time with Martin. She hadn't intended to be gone long – after all, you didn't want to prolong giving someone the boot – but events had overtaken her. Damn.

'Yes, well, that's true, I had a headache and popped out for some fresh air. But I'm fine now. I'm just going back.' That should cover it.

'So you're outside the health centre?'

'Just about.' Be vague, it was always best.

'OK. I was just worried about you, that's all.'

'That's sweet of you, Andy.'

She rolled her eyes as she said it, which was mean of her really, but Martin's face was inches from hers. It was weird to be having this conversation with her husband while lying across her lover's chest. His hand was on her hip, holding her firmly. It would be exciting if it wasn't so nerve-racking.

'I suppose I'd better let you go,' he said.

Yes, please.

'I just wanted to hear your voice,' he continued.

Well, you've heard it now.

'Just send me a picture before you go.'

What?

'Sorry, Andy, I didn't catch that.'

'I want to see where you are. Take a picture and send it to me.'

'How am I expected to do that?'

'With your phone.'

Oh my God, of course. What on earth was she supposed to do? Take a photo of herself lying naked in bed with another man?

'I don't think I know how.'

'Of course you do. We went through it all at the races, didn't we? You can't have forgotten.'

He was sounding irritated. And suspicious.

'Just give me a moment,' she said, shutting the phone off and tearing herself from Martin's arms. 'Oh *shit*!'

'What's up?' he said as she scrabbled on the floor for her clothes.

'I've got to send him a sodding picture on my phone. I'll go outside.'

'Just send him a close-up of your face.'

'No. He'll be able to tell. He'll blow it up big and analyse it on his computer or something.' She was dressed now. 'I'm sorry, Martin.'

'Aren't you coming back?'

'No. I can't.'

He lunged for her and caught her in his arms, pressing her tight to his lean athlete's body. She allowed him a second's embrace, then broke away.

As she stood in the street outside and aimed the camera phone at her face, she wondered if her husband would be able to read the imprint of another man's lips on her mouth.

She wouldn't put it past him.

As Andy took Jasper for his evening constitutional along the cliff, he pondered what to say to Harriet. After the high of their weekend, her latest deception dragged him lower than he had ever been. How could she?

When he'd bought her the new phone he hadn't set out to trap her, not consciously anyway. The camera feature was standard on decent phones anyway – he had one on his and he'd never used it. But it had registered in his mind that, if necessary, he could ask Harriet to send him pictures. It might be fun – another way of staying in touch.

Another way of finding out if she was telling him the truth.

Well, she'd failed that test.

The moment Andy had taken the call from the salon that Harriet was missing, alarm bells had started to ring. He'd not been hasty though, reminding himself how well things had been going recently. He was convinced there'd been a change in her attitude towards him. It was plain she'd appreciated his attentions over the past few days. The contempt had gone from her eyes and she'd listened to him in the way she used to, as if she cared about what he had to say. And she'd been generous in other ways too. He'd forgotten how tender she could be in bed.

Surely this hadn't all come about because of the money?

Jasper was making his habitual inspection of the fields inland, cutting back periodically to the cliff top path. Andy strode on, brooding unhappily. For once, the stirring scenery left him cold. He scarcely registered the sky above and the sea below. It was the blurred image of his wife's face that dominated his thoughts.

She'd finally sent him a photograph, filling the tiny screen with as much of herself as possible, so close her features were out of register. She must have done it on purpose so he couldn't see where she was. But she'd misjudged the frame and past the curtain of hair to her left he'd made out a section of building – in focus, ironically. Andy had studied it closely. A section of terrace, shabby old brickwork and the edge of a sash window with peeling paint – an entirely unremarkable piece of urban scenery. Except it looked nothing like the landscape near the health centre, which was on the outskirts of the town bordered by parkland and a new housing development.

And another thing, before the photograph business, when he'd been speaking to her – and the significance had only struck him later – he'd heard faint music. They played music all the time at the health centre, bouncy pop mostly but all sorts, depending where you were. But if you were out on the street, making your way back to work as Harriet said she was doing, where would the music come from?

If you were in someone's bedroom – in a row of old terraced houses maybe – there might be music playing. Then when you were rung up by your husband, you might kill the call and rush into the street to supply the photo he had requested. That would account for the time it took to send the shot. After all, you'd have to put your clothes back on first.

Andy doubted he'd ever get the truth out of Harriet. He never did, she always found some loophole to wriggle through. And, once he started to quiz her, she'd go on the attack like she always did and find some argument to make him feel like he was in the wrong – when she was the one who was betraying him. Probably.

Perhaps he was just a suspicious, paranoid bastard. Why couldn't he let it go by? Concentrate on the positives. Allow her to have her mysteries.

Allow her to cheat on him.

So who was she screwing this time?

He didn't want to know. Once you started picturing your wife with another man, giving him a face, a personality, wondering what he had that you didn't – that kind of thing turned you crackers. Andy knew it all too well.

Jasper came bounding up, panting hard. Suddenly he froze, alert to some interesting scent or movement, then shot towards the cliff.

'No!' shouted Andy. Didn't the stupid dog ever learn?

Jasper halted right on the edge, his front paws on the rim of the drop. Andy grabbed him by the collar.

How far was it down to the rocky beach? A hundred feet? A hundred and fifty? Far enough for the impact to dash the life from the body of a dog. Or a man.

Suppose he just didn't go back tonight? What would Harriet think? Would she care that much?

One step forward right now and she'd have to live with the consequences of driving him to his death. First her mother, then her husband – not even Harriet would be tough enough to shrug that off.

He pulled Jasper back onto the path.

It would serve her right.

He walked back slowly. What on earth was he thinking of? He couldn't allow himself to become Harriet's next victim.

Maybe it was time to seriously think of divorce.

By the time Jack reached home, Andy had left the yard; the discussion about Full Force's disappointing performance would have to wait.

Jack supposed he could have ducked Laurence Daniels' suggestion of an early supper before he drove back but he felt he owed the unlucky owner for the afternoon's failure. To be honest, he was glad of a bit of company. The thought of returning to an empty house was not enticing. It wasn't so bad on these summer evenings when he could nurse a drink in the garden and watch the shadows lengthen across the lawn. But the winter had been bad, coming back to cold dark rooms and a microwaved dinner. He'd never been much of a cook, he'd never needed to be.

Now he walked straight through to the back parlour and poured himself a malt whisky. He threw open the french windows and sat on the bench outside. Swallows and house martins swooped in the lea of the old barn over the garden wall. Only the ticking of the grandfather clock from inside interrupted their twittering.

The clock had belonged to Elizabeth's mother and he kept it going for that reason. His wife had been dead for five years but he'd made no changes to the house. The rooms were laid out as they always had been and decorated in the style she had chosen. There had been a firm division of labour in their marriage. Inside was her territory and everything outside it was his. It had worked just fine for thirty years.

The phone jangled into life, an old-fashioned-sounding summons from inside.

'Jack?' He didn't recognise the voice until the caller declared himself. Ed Cooper, a young trainer from Taunton. Jack had met him a few times at meetings and, more recently, had sat next to him and his wife at a charity dinner.

'Sorry to bother you in the evening but I've had one of your lads on the phone asking for a job – Joe Parkin. What's he like?'

'He got into a scrap with my head lad. Wrapped his whip round his face, left him with a nasty weal.'

'I see.' Ed didn't sound too concerned. 'What's his work like?'

'He's a good horseman, conscientious, reliable, knows what he's doing.'

'But?' Ed had picked up on the reservation in Jack's tone.

'Like most travelling head lads he's got punters.'

There was a pause in the conversation.

'It's the way of the world, isn't it?'

Jack thought for a moment. He liked Ed and intended to be honest with him. He didn't want the younger man to be able to say he had withheld information should anything go wrong.

'Look, Ed, I sacked Joe because his assault was vicious and because I reckon they'd fallen out over gambling. I've not got to the bottom of it yet but I think between them they've been pulling one or two strokes. I'm telling you this in confidence, you understand.'

Ed paused, obviously considering the significance of what he'd heard. 'I can do without that.'

That was no surprise. They didn't prolong the conversation – it was obvious Ed had heard enough.

After the other man had rung off, Jack did not replace the receiver. He dialled a number he knew by heart. Ursula would help out. If she pressed her bookmaking contacts he was sure she could come up with more information. He needed better ammunition.

For once, Harriet was at a loss. Throughout her married life she'd always reckoned she knew how to handle Andy. Even when she lost one of the battles in their relationship, she knew she had the upper hand in the war. Tonight she could not be so certain.

She'd been expecting a hard time from Andy when she returned home. It was late because there'd been a panic at the salon, with customers ringing for last-minute appointments – which was why they'd been so anxious to get hold of her in the afternoon. So she'd stayed on well past her normal midweek finishing time. All the same, when she got back Andy wasn't home.

When she heard his key in the lock she steeled herself for an inquisition: where were you? Who were you with? All the usual third degree. It wouldn't be pleasant but she knew the way to handle it was to get her retaliation in first, launch an attack on her husband for spying on her and dragging her down to his level of petty suspicion. With luck she'd get him so wound up, the substance of his complaints would be lost in the storm. Then he'd be remorseful and they'd make up. And this time she would share his remorse. She would end it with Martin tomorrow, for certain. She'd been self-indulgent today and look at the trouble it had caused.

But Andy didn't start quizzing her. He didn't mention the phone call or the photo. He simply hung up the dog's lead, said 'Hi' in a flat voice and headed for the kitchen.

They took it in turns to cook and tonight was hers. She made him a baked potato in the micro-wave and opened a tin of beans – a pretty feeble effort. He made no comment, just forked a few mouthfuls and pushed the plate aside. She wasn't eating herself. She'd be sick. Instead she opened a bottle of wine.

'What's his name?' Andy asked.

Harriet sipped slowly.

'I'm sorry?'

'What's the name of this man you're sleeping with?'

'I'm not sleeping with any man, you fool.'

He grinned at her. It was unexpected. 'Woman, then.'

She threw the remains of her drink in his face.

He blinked, wiped the drops from his cheek with a big hand but the smile remained in place. 'OK. That would have surprised me. Just covering all angles.'

The bastard was making fun of her. She refilled her glass and drank half of it.

'It's not working out, is it, Harriet?'

'What isn't?'

'Us. Our marriage. I don't think we're doing each other any good.'

He seemed very calm. And cold. She didn't like the turn things were taking.

'It's not that bad, Andy. We had a good weekend, didn't we?'

'Sure, but a weekend is two days, right? That's not much.'

'But we've had lots of good times,' she protested.

'Not in the past two years.'

She offered him the bottle. He waved it away and she topped herself up messily. It was unlike her not to be in control.

'Look, Andy, all marriages have ups and downs. We've got something solid, I know it. And you've been really good to me.'

He considered her grimly. 'Is that the best you can do?' He looked like a different person.

She wanted to say that he was the most important man in her life and that she'd never betray him. But confession was a dangerous path to tread.

'I love you, Andy.' She covered his hand with hers. 'I couldn't manage without you.'

He removed his hand. 'Sorry, Harriet, but you might have to.' And he pushed his chair back from the table and left the room.

She listened to his footsteps on the stairs and the creaking of the ceiling as he got ready for bed. That was the one place where she might make everything all right.

But when she slipped upstairs she found the bed empty. He was in the spare room and he'd turned the key in the lock.

She found another bottle of wine in the fridge. She had a lot of thinking to do.

Chapter Eight

'Ouch.' Chrissie on reception winced as she took in Harriet's appearance. 'What happened to you?'

'Don't ask.'

Harriet wasn't in the mood for explanations. She rarely drank much and the ache of the hangover in her head – like a vice round her skull – was all she could concentrate on. Her preoccupation was only broken by the throbbing of a cut on her lip, which had swollen freakishly. She was running late for a variety of reasons but chiefly because she'd spent an age trying to camouflage the damage. Obviously she hadn't succeeded.

Fortunately her first client was a regular who'd plainly had a heavy night herself. 'Black coffee for both of us, eh?' she said to Harriet with a thin smile and that was the extent of their conversation.

Harriet wasn't used to feeling a fool but there was no denying that's how she felt. Why had she allowed Andy to get to her last night? After she'd finished the second bottle of wine, she'd ended up banging on his door in the middle of the night. How stupid. Andy was meant to come crawling after her, not the other way round. That's the way it had always been in their relationship. But last night he'd played her at her own game and she was the one who'd gone begging.

Andy had simply ignored her, left her weeping in the hall with bruised fists. And when she'd dragged herself into the bathroom to splash water on her face, she'd slipped and smashed her mouth against the sink. It hadn't bled much but all the same she'd cried out in pain and yelled, 'Andy, I'm hurt – I'm bleeding!' But the bastard had still not opened the door.

When did he get so tough?

Did he mean what he'd said about divorce?

She slipped off to the toilet between customers to freshen up. The band round her head was slackening, thank heavens, and some fresh make-up helped, though there was no disguising her thick lip. She straightened her shoulders and ran a brush through her lustrous hair. She told herself she could look worse. So what if Andy didn't want her – many men would.

It wasn't as if the divorce word had not crossed her mind many times. To be fair, she'd have agreed like a shot not so long ago. It was ironic that Andy should threaten her with it just at the point when she had decided to commit herself to him completely.

Chrissie appeared in the doorway. 'There's someone asking for you.'

'Mrs Friedal?' Her next customer – she always arrived early.

'No.' Chrissie smirked. 'Someone more interesting.'

Harriet strode past the little bitch – she wasn't in the mood for games – and walked straight into Martin.

Her first reaction was of fury. How many times had she told him never to come looking for her at her work? But the shock on his face as he looked at her froze the reproach in her throat.

'My God, Harriet, what happened?'

Suddenly she couldn't speak. If she did, she'd burst into tears and that couldn't happen here, in front of the entire salon. He seemed to realise the state she was in and propelled her towards the door.

'Mrs Friedal's waiting,' protested Chrissie.

'I'm just going to steal Harriet for a minute,' said Martin. 'Tell the customer she'll be with her very shortly.'

Harriet surrendered to his command. There was something so comforting about having his arms round her at that moment.

He led her to the side of the concourse, shielding her with his body from the gaze of the curious.

'Are you all right, babe?'

No, she was bloody awful but what could she say?

'I'm fine, Martin. I've got to go back.'

'In a moment. Did he hit you?'

What?

'Did Andy hit you?' he repeated.

'No.'

'He hit you, didn't he?'

'No!'

'What happened then?' He had her by the upper arms, gripping her tight.

'I can't tell you here. I've got to go.'

'Meet me at lunchtime. You're hurt and I want to know why.'

She couldn't say no to him. Anyway, it was obvious he wouldn't release her unless she agreed.

'OK, but we're not going back to your flat.'

'Deal,' he said.

'Will you let me go now?'

His hands relaxed their hold. 'If I must.'

He was smiling down at her. Automatically, it seemed, she lifted her face and his lips touched hers painlessly, as gentle as the brush of a butterfly wing. A surge of emotion rushed through her and she jammed her lips against his. For a second she thrilled to the hurt.

Sometimes she didn't even understand herself.

It had been a busy morning at Beach Head yard. One of the lads had not turned up, there was a scare about a horse who'd taken sick in the back pasture and the vet had been sent for, and there were five horses to be transported to three separate meetings. Andy had dealt with every crisis as it had arisen without losing his rag. It was his job to keep on top of things.

Last night had been a nightmare, both awake and asleep – not that there'd been much of that. He'd heard Harriet thumping on the door and her cries of pain when she'd fallen – that's what it sounded like – in the bathroom. He'd been determined, for once, to stick to his guns. The last thing he wanted was to break up with Harriet and the mention of divorce was born of desperation; he'd not known how else to react to this latest crisis. His tactics had worked, though, and that was gratifying. He was proud of himself for ignoring Harriet's pleas in the night. If he'd let her in he'd have been back to square one. He could win this – and keep his wife – if he was strong.

'Andy.' It was Jack, looking dour. The trainer had something on his mind and Andy had a pretty good idea what that would be. He'd barely had time to think what he would say if Jack had a go at him about Full Force. But there was no ducking the confrontation as Jack summoned him into the office.

The trainer got straight to the point. 'It's still happening, isn't it?'

'You mean Full Force?'

'He wasn't himself, Andy. By the time he got to

the last furlong he was running on empty. He was nothing like the horse I've seen working here for the past fortnight.'

'Maybe he just needs another race. He's been injured for a while and this is only his second run since.' Andy didn't think Jack would swallow it but this was the line he'd taken before – it was plausible.

Jack sighed heavily. 'I might agree with you if it wasn't for Pipsqueak. And Sage Brush and Sir Vincent,' he added, mentioning two horses who'd disappointed on the all-weather. Andy and Pat had made a tidy sum on both of them. 'This kind of thing can happen once or twice but it looks like there's a pattern here.'

'So you're saying Full Force was stopped?'

'You've seen as much of these horses as me, Andy. How else do you account for it?'

Andy shrugged. 'Could be any number of reasons. I only know I never fancied any of them on the occasions they didn't do so well.'

Jack's blue eyes pierced him. 'That's what's worrying me, Andy. You and I watched Full Force tear up the gallops all last week and yesterday, before we set off, you told me you didn't fancy him. And, lo and behold, you were right. Did you know something I didn't?'

'No, boss, honestly. I just thought he needed another run before he came good.'

'So you can guarantee he'll come good next time, can you?'

'Of course not. He's a horse, not a machine – anything can happen.'

Jack wasn't mollified and his gaze was no less sharp as he said, 'But you seem to have a good record in making predictions, don't you? It's been quite profitable for you, I imagine.'

'I've had a bit of luck with my hunches, yes.'

Jack took a slip of paper from his top pocket. 'You took four thousand eight hundred off Blackstone's for Sir Vincent, eight thousand five hundred for Sage Brush and fifteen thousand for Pipsqueak. That's more than a bit of luck, if you ask me. Especially if you took lumps out of other firms, too.'

Andy was shocked rigid. He'd tried to be as discreet as possible in placing his wagers but it was impossible to keep the lid shut tight on success. Bookies talked to one another and a winning gambler was soon a known quantity. He tried to brazen it out.

'That's rubbish. I never won anything like that.'

The trainer slammed the flat of his hand on his desk, rattling the pens and pencils stacked in an old mug and sending papers flying. It was not like him to lose his temper.

'Don't lie to me, lad. These figures come from Ursula Leopold so I know they're right. There's something funny going on with my horses and you're making serious money off them. And don't tell me it's just luck.'

It was time to backtrack, denying the figures had been a mistake.

'I'm sorry, boss. It's true I've been on a bit of a roll. But those are decent horses, I knew they had to win sometime.'

Jack didn't seem to have heard. He picked up a pencil, tapped it idly on his blotter. 'I thought when I sacked Joe that it would solve our problems here. Evidently not. I had the option of getting rid of you instead, but I didn't want to do that.'

His eyes were back on Andy's face but the anger had gone, replaced by something even harder to take. Reproach maybe. Andy guessed that the only thing stopping Jack from giving him the sack was the fact that none of the horses that had run badly had been laid to lose. If someone was stopping them, to line them up for a punt, it would be very unlikely that they wouldn't try and make money along the way.

'You know, Andy, I can't keep you on here if there's any suggestion you're on the fiddle.'

'I'm not on the fiddle, I swear.'

'The money you've won says the opposite, son. If you're not stopping those horses—'

'I'm not.'

'Then someone else is and he's tipping you.'

Andy was silent. Jack was getting uncomfortably close.

Jack leaned across his desk and pointed the pencil at Andy's face. 'I want to know who that person is.'

'There's no one, honestly.'

Jack ignored him. 'You've got twenty-four hours to come clean, Andy, or we've got to say goodbye. Understand?'

Andy said nothing. He understood.

What the hell was he going to do now? He didn't have a clue. There was a possibility that soon he'd be facing life without Harriet or Jack.

How was he going to cope with that?

The way she'd been feeling, Harriet hadn't imagined looking at food ever again. But as she sat under the trees in the park next to the health centre and watched Martin take a pack of sandwiches from a carrier bag, she felt a sudden lurch of hunger in her stomach. She ate with determination – it was what she needed. Martin watched her without touching his own.

'This is the picnic we never got round to that day,' he said.

She knew immediately what day he meant – when they'd made love in the shade of the old barn and the farmer had caught them. She felt a pang of nostalgia. It was extraordinary to think that their short-lived affair had already produced treasured memories. But she knew she only felt that way because she was about to end it.

'I should have brought more to eat,' he said as she finished. 'Have mine.'

'No, Martin.'

But she accepted half of his sandwich all the same when he insisted. She needed all the strength she could get.

He drank from a bottle of mineral water and passed it to her. She put her lips where his had been. It was their last unsullied moment of intimacy. She took a deep breath.

'We're going to have to stop this,' she said.

'You bet.' He laughed. 'Give me a decent restaurant any day.'

'No, Martin. Stop seeing each other altogether.'

The laughter was shut off like a tap. He looked at her with suspicion – already she was someone else.

'I'm sorry but this is too hard for me. I like you too much for it to go on.'

'You don't *like* me,' he said coldly. 'It's not about *liking*.'

'OK, whatever you want to call it then.'

'I want to call it love.' His hand gripped her by the wrist, encircling it tightly, like a shackle. 'I love you, Harriet. It's not a small thing you can just decide not to feel any more.'

Oh dear, this was going to be even harder than she'd thought.

'I know,' she said, 'and I'm sorry. But that's why we have to stop, don't you see? We're getting in too deep.'

'Not for me, we're not. I want to get in deep with you, Harriet. Leave your husband and come with me. Don't waste your life in a dead-end marriage with a man who beats you.'

'I told you, I fell. Andy didn't touch me.'

'Credit me with a bit more intelligence, Harriet. He caught you out after that farce with the phone yesterday and scared the hell out of you last night. Look,' his other arm went round her and his voice dropped, 'I can understand that you're frightened and breaking up a marriage is a big thing. But I'll take care of you. I'll do whatever it takes to get you out of it safely.'

Harriet felt a bubble of panic burst inside her, and one of irritation, too. He was wilfully misunderstanding her.

'Please believe me, Martin, I'm not frightened of Andy. He didn't hit me or anything like that. And though I'm not in love with him like I am with you, I *do* love him. We have a history together. You and I don't even know each other that well. Do you see?'

He didn't reply immediately. The sky-blue eyes were clouded with unhappiness. She felt dreadful but maybe at last she'd got through to him.

He moved away from her and she surreptitiously rubbed the ring of bruised flesh round her wrist.

'So that's your decision, you're going to stay with that loser? I thought you were smarter than that.'

'He's not a loser.'

'Yeah, I know, he's your soulmate from way back who you've got *history* with even though you've gone off him in bed. Get real, Harriet. He's a failed trainer who works all hours as a stableman and comes home smelling of horse shit.' Martin's face

167

was dark, no longer lovable but hard-lined and bitter. 'Now, listen to me, Harriet. I'm going to make something of my life. I'm going to make a pile of cash and that's more than he'll ever do.'

'That's not fair, Martin.'

'It's the truth.' The words came out in an arrogant sneer. 'If you want to waste your life on a loser like him, go ahead.'

'Don't call him that. Andy makes good money.'

'Really?' He seemed amused. 'That's not what you've told me before. I thought he chucked his dough away on three-legged horses.'

'Andy's changed.'

'Oh, please. It's one thing for you to stay with your beloved husband out of a misplaced sense of duty but don't kid yourself he's a reformed character.' He laughed, an unpleasant-sounding bray.

'Andy's made nearly a quarter of a million pounds on the horses this year.'

The laugh rose in volume. He was being deliberately provocative.

'That's what he told you, is it? I can't believe you'd fall for that, babe.'

'I've seen the building society statement. I know the money exists.'

'Really?' She'd got him thinking now. 'I don't suppose you considered the possibility he cooked it up. He could knock a phoney statement up on a computer – I could anyway.'

She shook her head. 'It's not like that. I opened a letter from the building society. He was pissed off about it but he's always snooping on me. He didn't want me to know about the money, it was a secret, but it's in the account, all right.'

'Good God.' He believed her now. The anger and arrogance had vanished. 'What did he say when you asked him about it?'

'That he'd won it gambling. That he'd been studying form and building up his winnings and he'd worked out how to beat the bookies. I didn't think it was possible but the money's there.'

'And so you've decided to stay with him. The virtuous wife.'

She opened her mouth to contradict him but thought better of it. If Martin wanted to believe she was a mercenary little cow then why not let him? It might make this whole break-up a little easier for him to handle.

'I think we should go back now,' she said.

He gave her a sad, soulful look. 'Is it just the money?'

'It's not the money at all.'

'So it's because you've got this history with him and for that you can ignore the magic we have together?'

Oh God, he was determined to make it difficult.

'It's because I'm married to Andy. I never intended to get so involved with you and it's got to end.'

'No it doesn't. He's your past but I can be your future. Please, Harriet.'

For God's sake, don't let him beg. That would be horrible.

'Stop it, Martin.'

He loomed over her, his face inches from hers as it had been so often in moments that had thrilled her. But there was no sweetness in this.

'So, basically, you're staying with him just because he exists.'

She held his gaze. 'Yes.' It took courage to say it.

He turned away and they walked back in silence, between them a distance that neither tried to bridge.

Andy was about to leave the cottage when he heard Harriet's car outside. He met her at the garden gate, Jasper frisking at his heels.

'Are you going out?' She sounded anxious and she looked it too. He'd been with Harriet at several bleak moments in her life, when her face became a bloodless mask in the frame of her flaming hair. She looked brittle, as if she might shatter into pieces at any moment.

'I'm meeting Pat.' Andy's voice was firm, neutral in tone. He resisted the impulse to put his arms round her. After last night he had the upper hand and he knew how important it was to keep it.

'Oh.' She looked crestfallen. 'I was going to make us some supper. I thought we should talk.'

'Sure.' Still non-committal. He opened the gate to

allow her through with her shopping bags. When she lifted her face to his he bussed her briefly on the cheek. Her lip was big and swollen, painful he imagined, but he made no comment.

'Where are you meeting Pat?'

'In the pub. Then I've got to take Jasper for his walk.'

'You won't be too long, will you?'

How satisfying to hear her anxious for his company. It made a bloody change.

'We'll see.'

'I really do need to talk to you, Andy. It's important.'

For a moment he was tempted to hear what she had to say. A confession, an apology – whatever it was, he was eager to hear it.

Unless – the thought leapt suddenly into his mind – she had come to a different conclusion. Suppose she called his bluff and said, 'I've decided that you're right, Andy. We ought to get a divorce.'

Well, if it came to that, he'd made his mind up what he would do. He only hoped he had the guts.

Jasper tugged impatiently on his lead.

'I'll try and be as quick as I can,' he said and turned up the road. When he reached the corner he looked back but she'd disappeared inside the house.

Martin packed in a hurry – it would save time later. He'd already got the flight to Barcelona sorted.

Ken had been most understanding – you couldn't fault the guy. Even though Martin had dropped him in it, his boss had taken it in his stride.

'Don't apologise,' he'd said when Martin had broken the news. 'I can get cover. I know a fellow who'll step in for a few days and take your pupils. If any of them kick up a stink I'll say you'll make it up to them when you get back.'

'I don't know how long I'll be.'

'Sure, I understand. Just give me a call when you've got a better idea how your dad is faring. It's good what you're doing. I'd like to think that my kids would drop everything and rush home if I got sick.'

Ken was a good guy. Martin felt bad about lying to him. But he could hardly say, 'The woman I love has just decided to stay with her husband and I've got to get out of here' – which was exactly how he felt. Much easier to explain his distress by saying he'd just had a panic call from his mother in Spain: his father had had a heart attack. Everybody understood an emergency like that.

He'd bring Ken back a big bottle of fancy Spanish booze.

After a week away, maybe ten days, he'd be able to face the world again.

Pat knew the moment Andy stepped through the pub door that something was troubling him.

Though he stood as parade-ground tall and smart as ever in a gleaming white shirt – how a guy who worked in a stable could always appear to be dressed in clean jeans was a mystery – the usual alertness was gone from his face. His thoughts were not on the here and now, Pat could tell. People were no different from horses in his opinion; just from looking at them you could judge whether they were up for it or not. And, for once, Andy did not look like he was at the races.

'Over here,' Pat called from the bar but it was Jasper who dragged Andy in the right direction.

'What are you drinking?' the jockey asked. 'Have a large Scotch, you look like you need one.'

Andy nodded. 'Thanks.' When it arrived he finished it in two gulps.

'Another?'

'I'm not drinking on my own.'

Pat considered his Diet Coke. He'd never been much of a boozer, he'd seen how it had cut down his big brothers, but Andy seemed a bit needy tonight. He ordered shorts for the pair of them, and a beer for Andy to follow.

'So what's up?' he said. No point in beating about the bush.

'Let's sit down, shall we?'

Pat pointed towards a table in the window then noticed who was sitting amongst a group nearby – Joe Parkin. It wouldn't be a bright idea to go anywhere near him.

They took their drinks outside, which was pleasanter and suited Jasper better too.

'So?' said Pat. He believed in letting a man get his troubles off his chest. He'd already formed an opinion of the shape Andy's troubles might take: Harriet shape.

Andy focused on him for about the first time. 'I'm thinking about getting a divorce.'

Oh boy. No wonder he was down in the dumps.

'Sounds a bit drastic.'

'There might not be any alternative. I don't think Harriet gives a stuff about our marriage. She doesn't give a stuff about me anyhow.'

'That's not how it looked on the weekend. The pair of you were getting on like a house on fire.'

'Yeah, well, Harriet's very good at playing games.' Andy was now drinking beer. He took a long pull at his pint. 'I think she's got some bloke on the go. Has Zoe mentioned anything to you?'

Pat didn't quite know where to look. He shook his head but he could feel his face colouring.

'You know something, don't you?'

Pat started to deny it but Andy could read him like a book.

Andy fixed him with a gaze like a laser beam. 'What's going on?'

'Well, it's probably nothing, but she's been seeing a bit of that tennis coach.'

Pat realised he'd put his foot in it the moment

the words were out of his mouth. He shouldn't have had that drink after all.

'Who?'

'Sorry, mate. Maybe I got the wrong end of the stick.'

'Just tell me who he is.'

Christ, didn't he know?

'His name's Martin. He gives lessons at the health club.'

Appalled, Pat watched Andy's face drain of colour as he absorbed the information. He could see the tension in Andy's muscular frame and the whiteness of his knuckles as he gripped the edge of the table. The jockey was acutely aware that Andy was bigger than him. The bearer of bad tidings was rarely seen in a favourable light.

Don't shoot the messenger, mate. It's not me who's screwing your missus.

But Andy did not lash out. 'How do you know that?' he said softly.

'Zoe. Harriet's always on the phone to her and it's hard not to overhear.'

In fact, Zoe had told Pat some weeks back and sworn him to secrecy. He'd not mentioned it to anyone till now – not that it helped.

'Why didn't you tell me?'

'Because I didn't think it was anything. He's just some university type doing tennis for the summer and he'll bugger off soon. There's no future in it, Andy. She's not going to leave you for him.'

'Maybe she should. Like I said, I'm thinking about divorce.'

'Come off it.' Pat forced some jollity into his voice. 'You and Harriet make a great couple. You belong together.'

'Not any more, it seems.'

'But you still love her, don't you?'

Andy glared at him. 'What good's that when it makes me feel like jumping off a sodding cliff?'

There was no answer to that.

'Look, whatever happens, I'm right behind you. If I can help, you know, just say the word.'

Andy's look turned to contempt. 'How on earth can you help when you're living with her sister? As long as you're shacked up with Zoe, you're on the other side.'

There was no answer to that either. If Harriet and Andy split up, Andy would be on his own.

For a moment they sat in silence and Jasper seized the opportunity to lay his head on his master's thigh. Automatically Andy stroked the dog's ears. 'Look, Jack's getting heavy with me about the way the horses are performing. I told you Full Force was a bad idea.'

Pat didn't respond. As far as he was concerned, Full Force's substandard outing at Salisbury was a very good idea indeed. The timing hadn't been great, though, coming on top of Andy's Harriet woes.

'He's going to sack me unless I tell him what's going on.'

'Nothing's going on.'

Andy looked at him in disbelief.

'As far as Jack's concerned,' Pat continued, 'his horses are doing the best they can.'

'But you're stopping them.'

'No, I'm not. I give them an honest ride every time.'

Andy wasn't amused, the remark didn't raise a smile. 'So you won't mind if I tell Jack that you've been giving me tips?'

'You wouldn't do that.'

He wouldn't, would he? Not unless he'd completely lost it.

'It's OK, Pat. I'm not that daft. I'll just tell him to piss off. The way things are, I don't care about the job anyway.' Andy drained his glass and got to his feet. 'I'll see you. Jasper needs his walk.'

Pat thought about going with him but decided against. There was only so much gloom a man could take.

Harriet fussed over preparing the supper. She hoped it would be a meal of reconciliation. Maybe not one to be savoured – that would be for carefree times further down the road – but special in its way nonetheless. She made a fresh salad with roasted pine nuts and avocado as well as all the usual stuff. She stuck a decent bottle of wine in the fridge – not that the thought of drinking it was enticing – and laid out the meats and cheeses she'd bought from the deli. She'd wait till Andy got back before warming the bread in the oven.

She rushed her bath because she didn't want to be caught unprepared when he returned and then found herself wandering aimlessly from living room to kitchen and back as she killed time. She could have had a long restorative soak after all.

Where was he?

He was deliberately making her suffer.

But that was OK, she deserved it.

The sun was setting over the sea like a giant orange by the time Andy turned back along the cliff and approached the steps cut into the hillside that led down to the lane. Much to Jasper's delight, it had been a lengthy excursion. There was a lot on Andy's mind.

A tennis coach called Martin. Young and athletic, no doubt. A pretty boy. Andy knew Harriet's taste. He wondered what she'd ever seen in himself. Maybe, on reflection, not all that much.

Now he could put a name to her latest lover, he could go and do something about it. He could find the boy at the health centre and make him less pretty.

But what good would that do? It wasn't Harriet's boyfriend who was significant, it was Harriet. Unless he could change her, then there was always the possibility of another pretty boy.

Andy knew there was no hope of changing her.

Divorce then? He'd be out in the cold again, looking for another woman.

He didn't want another woman, just the one he'd got. But she no longer wanted him.

Life was a bastard.

'Oy!' The shout came from the fringe of gorse ahead. He looked up to see a familiar figure striding along the path towards him. Possibly the person he least wanted to see ever again.

Joe Parkin's face was red, maybe from the effort of climbing up the hill or possibly from the booze he'd been putting away. As he got close Andy could smell the beer on his breath.

'I've been waiting for you.'

'I've got nothing to say to you, Joe.'

'You shafted me, you bastard. And I'm going to make you sorry.'

Joe was blocking the way, swaying slightly, his fists bunched. Andy realised he was working himself up for a fight. The thought did not disturb him. Beating the daylights out of someone would fit nicely into his agenda.

'What's your problem?'

'You got me sacked.'

'You got yourself sacked.'

'I had another job offer till the governor talked to Jack Lucas. You're his little bumboy, aren't you? He'll swallow anything that comes out of your mouth.'

Andy laughed. 'You're pathetic, Joe. I'm not surprised you're unemployable.'

Even though he was expecting the attack, the other man's assault took him by surprise. Instead of coming at him with flailing fists, Joe lowered his shoulder and barged into him.

Andy toppled backwards with Joe on top of him, the smell of stale alcohol overpowering.

They wrestled on the path for a few seconds, Andy gripping him round the waist, trying to turn him over. But Joe was heavier than he looked and, as Andy finally began to shift his weight, the other man rammed his forehead across the bridge of Andy's nose.

The pain was blinding.

'Get some of that,' Joe breathed into his ear. 'You deserve it. You're still pulling your dirty tricks, aren't you?'

An outraged growl sounded from the field with an urgent scrabbling of feet. Jasper hurtled out of the thickening light to throw himself on Andy's assailant.

Joe screamed with pain as the dog's jaw closed on some part of him and Andy rolled the pair of them off his body.

The taste of blood was in his mouth – he didn't know whose – as he landed his first proper blow.

At nine thirty Harriet rang Zoe.

'Hiya.' Her sister sounded cheerful – it was all right for some. 'You OK?'

'Sure.' She couldn't get into things with Zoe right now. 'I'm just waiting for certain people to get back from the pub. Like you, I imagine.'

'No. Pat's been home for ages, if that's what you mean.'

Harriet's stomach turned over. 'Let me have a word with him.'

Pat told her he'd said goodbye to Andy at about half past seven. 'He went off to walk the dog.'

'That wouldn't take him two hours.'

'You mean he's not back yet?' Pat sounded surprised.

Harriet put the phone down with a trembling hand. What if Andy had left her? Just walked out with the only thing he cared about – Jasper. It was the kind of gesture he might make.

Maybe he'd gone to the yard, she knew he kept odd clothes and things there. She could phone Jack and ask him.

But not yet. Andy might walk in at any moment and he'd be angry with her if he knew she'd involved Jack. She didn't want to make things worse than they were already.

So she sat in the gathering dark and did nothing.

Andy lay on his back, panting heavily, trying to regain his breath. Above him the sky was thickening to grey, streaked with purple and magenta fingers of light from the western horizon where the sun had disappeared. Somewhere in his mind he registered the beauty of the sight. He ought to come up here more often at this time.

A furry shape blocked out the sight and doggy breath filled his nostrils. He felt wet warmth on his cheek as Jasper licked him. What a noble companion. Jasper had fought by his side and now tended his wounds. If it all went belly up with Harriet he wouldn't be entirely on his own.

He'd get up in a moment and the pair of them would make their way downhill to face whatever painful music Harriet had in mind. But first he wanted to give Joe Parkin a proper head start, make sure there was no chance of running into the stupid bugger on the way home.

He didn't think Joe would be lying in wait for him to prolong their encounter. He was a threat with a whip in his hand but not in a fair fight. Andy's punches carried more weight and he'd not pulled any of them. He smiled up at the darkening sky. Basically he'd smacked the crap out of the little turd and it had felt good. Faithful old Jasper had made it an even more one-sided contest.

Andy climbed to his feet and brushed the dirt from his clothes. He ached in several areas of his anatomy but he didn't think any serious damage had been done. And Jasper, thankfully, was unharmed.

'Come on, my friend,' he said to the dog. 'Let's go home and get you a nice big supper. You deserve it.'

* * *

'Oh God.' Zoe sighed heavily. 'I hope everything's OK with Harriet and Andy.'

Pat said nothing. Harriet's phone call had set all sorts of alarm bells ringing.

'I thought they were getting on much better,' she said. 'Was Andy OK in the pub?'

Pat hadn't told Zoe about their conversation. He'd opened his mouth too wide with Andy and he wasn't going to do the same with Zoe. If her sister's marriage was definitely on the rocks, it would be better she heard it directly from Harriet. And, whatever happened, he'd rather not admit he'd told Andy about Martin.

He didn't answer Zoe immediately. Instead, he rummaged beneath the kitchen sink in search of his flashlight.

'What are you doing?'

He pulled on his jacket and hefted the heavy torch in his hand. 'I'm going to look for Andy.'

'Oh Pat.' He could see she was pleased. 'I'll come with you.'

'Best not. You never know, Andy might turn up here.' The last thing he needed was Zoe quizzing him about what had gone on in the pub. 'Don't worry, I'm sure it's just a false alarm.'

As he turned for the door she hugged him fiercely. 'Thanks for doing this, Pat. I really love you, you know.'

He squeezed her back and then slipped out of the door.

It was as well she didn't realise he was only trying to rectify the damage he'd done. The damage he might have done. Surely Andy had only been using a figure of speech back there in the pub? In his situation, a man was entitled to feel desperate but he couldn't believe Andy really would jump off a cliff.

But that's what he'd said.

Andy called to Jasper but he'd disappeared for one last sniff around. It wasn't worth waiting for him, the dog knew the way back home as surely as Andy did.

He was nearly at the steps now and already his mind was on the kind of reception he might receive at home. If it went wrong, if Harriet had decided against him and opted for this other guy, then this would be the last time he'd ever come home to his wife.

Jesus, to think it had come to this.

There was a rush of movement in the gloom. The thud of footsteps coming from behind. He swung round, cursing Joe – didn't that drunken idiot ever give up?

The thump came from nowhere, catching Andy round the waist, like a giant hand pushing him out into the air. Suddenly there was no ground beneath his feet and he was falling free, down to the jagged rocks below. His screams were lost against the noise of the ocean.

No ground, no wife, no nothing.

* * *

It was dark in the lane where Pat parked the car. There were no vehicles about, which was a pity. He'd been hoping to ask other dog-walkers if they'd seen Andy.

He began the long haul up to the cliff path. It wasn't the kind of exercise he enjoyed and Pat wondered how Andy could put up with it twice a day. There had to be friendlier places to walk the dog.

He had to admit, however, that the cliff top scene was magnificent. It might be dark down by the car but up here the summer night sky was luminous and a three-quarter moon cast a silvery light over the sea.

'Andy!' Pat called but his voice sounded small in this huge open space. He began to walk along the worn dirt track, acutely conscious of the cliff edge close by.

'Andy!' he called again. Still no response.

This was looking pretty futile. Perhaps he should ring in. Andy could easily have shown up by now and he didn't fancy tramping miles in the dark.

His torch beam picked out an object on the path ahead, reflecting off metal. Someone must have dropped something, a coin or a cigarette lighter.

It wasn't either of those things.

Pat's hand closed on leather and he held the dog lead close to the light. He knew this lead.

As if in a dream he stepped to the edge and

aimed the torch down to the unforgiving rocks of the beach below. It was just as well it was a powerful beam for it was a mighty long way down.

But there, just where the shaft of light dissolved into the grey of the rocks at the foot of the cliff, was a white rectangle. As Pat stared, unbelieving but somehow already convinced, the shadows around the rectangle arranged themselves into a shape that made sense: the body of a man in a white shirt.

Andy.

Pat pulled the phone from his pocket with trembling fingers.

Part Two

Chapter Nine

Zoe had ridden at Epsom once before, on August Bank Holiday the previous year. They called it Family Fun day but it hadn't been much fun for Zoe. Her horse had trailed in a distant last and one of the owners, a middle-aged investment banker, had turned to his wife and said, 'Let's stick to male jockeys in the future, eh?'

Today, however, was going to be different. She was on Marshmallow, a delightful four-year-old bay belonging to Mrs Leopold. The horse had been placed at Windsor last time out and expectations were high. It was also the first time Zoe had ridden for Ursula since Magnetic's win at Ascot and she was determined to stay in the owner's good books.

However, the most significant thing for Zoe was to be taking part in the meeting at all. The past week had been wiped of everything but Andy's death. Jack had excused her from her duties at the yard and she'd withdrawn from the rides she'd been offered so she could be by Harriet's side. There had been Pat to consider as well – he'd found Andy's body and the experience had knocked him for six.

It hadn't stopped him taking rides, however, and Zoe had secretly envied him as he'd set off for meetings over the past week. She missed race riding and she knew it would have helped her own feelings of shock and dismay and loss. Andy had always been good to her and losing him was like losing an elder brother. At work in the yard he could be an irritating taskmaster but his off-duty teasing made up for it. And she had him to thank for her job in the first place. It was unbelievable to think he'd just been snuffed out like a spent match. Zoe had cried a lot.

Harriet, on the hand, had shed no tears. Her reaction had been much more worrying. She'd simply retreated into herself, her face a dry-eyed mask, her lips scarcely moving when she chose to speak. It was as if her power had been dimmed and she was simply existing, with no energy to spare for anything else. Zoe had seen this reaction before, when their mother died, and she knew better than to make conversation unless it was important. She just made herself available to Harriet, providing food, staying overnight at the cottage and acting almost as her sister's interpreter with the rest of the world.

It made for some tedious days, just being with Harriet, who sat still and silent for hours on end. Most visitors thought she was in need of medical attention but Zoe knew better. Harriet had her own method of coping with traumatic events. She shut herself off from all outside distraction to try and make sense of them. Zoe fancied she could see her sister's mind working as she stared into the distance without seeing, a pulse beating in her temple, one hand compulsively twirling a strand of copper hair.

Harriet had told the police Andy was in the habit of walking the dog along the cliff path, often twice a day. It was a routine and Andy liked routines. So he would have been familiar with the hazards posed by the crumbling cliff edge.

One thing seemed significant.

'A month ago, the dog nearly fell off the cliff. Andy said he went over the edge but there was a ledge. He said he had to get down on his stomach and grab Jasper by the collar to get him back. That's what must have happened, don't you think?'

'Do you know the spot where this occurred?'

'It's up on the cliffs somewhere. I was at work when it happened.'

'Yes, but could you point the place out?'

'I never go up there. It'll be just above where you found him, won't it?'

Zoe remembered Andy telling her about Jasper nearly coming a cropper. It was ironic to think that the incident had been repeated with fatal consequences just a few weeks later.

The irony lay in the fact that Jasper had not died.

They'd found the dog still alive at the bottom of the cliffs. His body had been badly injured but, unlike poor Andy, he had not been killed.

Pat had been there when they'd discovered him, having run down to the beach to see if he could do anything for Andy. He'd told Zoe he'd assumed at the time that the dog would have to be put down but, miraculously, Jasper was now making a recovery from two broken legs and a smashed rib in the local animal hospital. And his prospects were good. The vet said there was no reason he shouldn't be as good as new.

Thank God for Jasper – his survival had been the one bright spot in some black days. Monitoring his progress had kept them all going. Frankly, travelling to and from the canine sickroom had given the sisters something to do; it was better than moping around the little cottage. They weren't the only visitors as Jasper had become a bit of a local celebrity. The question everyone asked was, how come a dog could survive a hundred-foot fall?

The vet had explained it, something to do with the animal being more relaxed on impact because it had no idea what was happening. It was plain to Zoe, though, that there was only one reason – Jasper was a damned lucky dog.

The days had merged together as the two sisters had tried to make sense of their lives in the aftermath of the death. There were letters to write and well-wishers to deal with. Andy's family were from Scotland, a remote collection of aunts and cousins who had long ago ceased to be a factor in his world. Zoe had made the calls, explaining that Harriet wasn't up to it – she'd never met them anyway.

The Scots voices down the phone had been rich with concern and with nostalgia for a past when the dead man was known as 'wee Andy'. And they all asked for the date of the funeral but Zoe couldn't tell them. The death had been referred to the coroner and the funeral would have to wait. As yet, there wasn't even a date for the inquest. It was a state of limbo not unfamiliar to the sisters – they'd been through the same thing with their mother.

Thankfully, a week into this strange existence, Harriet pulled herself together. 'I'm going back to work tomorrow,' she told Zoe. 'Thanks for staying with me but we'll go mad hanging around here.'

So Zoe was able to resume her racing life at Epsom. She felt as if she'd got out of jail – that wasn't disloyal to Andy's memory, was it?

The fact was that while she'd been doing her best for her sister, she'd been losing ground in her career. With twenty-three winners for the season to her name before her lay-off, she had been in touch with the contest for the season's champion apprentice. Now she found she was ten victories behind the leader, Ginger Weaver. It looked like a huge gulf.

When, she wondered, had these kind of things become important to her? Until a couple of months ago she'd just been happy to consider herself an apprentice professional jockey. Picking up regular rides had been enough. Not now, though. Along with the press coverage she'd earned for her looks, which she'd tried to ignore, had come references to her riding skill. Suddenly she was playing for bigger stakes. Maybe she had been all the time, but now she could acknowledge it to herself. She had a chance of becoming champion apprentice and she wanted it.

Face it, she just wanted to win, like every other jockey in the weighing room.

It was inevitable she'd be up against Ginger Weaver in her first race back. Here was an opportunity to get one over on her chief rival and announce her return to the fray.

The situation had not been lost on Ginger, who was quoted on their rivalry in the day's *Racing Beacon*. 'It's great to have Zoe back,' he'd said, 'but no girl's strong enough to put one over the blokes at the end of a mile and a half race. Especially not at Epsom.'

He'd greeted her with a big kiss and some sincerely meant words of condolence but Zoe couldn't get what he'd said in the paper out of her mind. If anything was calculated to make her try harder, it was the suggestion that she couldn't square up to the lads.

She was going to shove those words right back down Ginger's throat.

There was awkwardness at the salon at the beginning of the day. The other girls looked at Harriet with a mixture of pity and embarrassment, at a loss how to handle the situation. Harriet wasn't close to any of them but as work colleagues they rubbed along well enough until something like this upset the apple cart.

'You don't have to treat me with kid gloves,' she said to Chrissie when the receptionist brought her a second unsolicited cup of coffee within half an hour, at which the girl burst into tears. Harriet was flabbergasted but steered Chrissie out of sight of the customers and put her arms round her. How come other people could cry so easily?

'I'm sorry,' Chrissie sniffed. 'I just can't help thinking if that had happened to my Benji.'

Benji was her fiancé; the name was more suitable for a pet poodle, in Harriet's opinion, but she didn't say so.

'Well, if it did, you'd just have to get on with your life like me. I can't bring Andy back by moping so I've returned to work. The best thing you can do is treat me the way you always do.'

Chrissie's eyes bulged like gobstoppers at Harriet's brusque tone.

'I know you think I'm a bit of a bitch,' Harriet continued. 'That's fine by me. Tell me to eff off like you usually do.'

The girl's jaw dropped almost to the floor.

'I just want to carry on like normal. Got it?'

After that, people stopped gazing at her with teary sympathy. If anything, they gave her a wide berth and that suited Harriet just fine.

The thing was, she didn't know how to cope with this situation. She felt the way she had when her mother died – she just wanted to pull a blanket over her head and let the world carry on without her.

How could Andy be dead? It wasn't possible. He was such a practical man, and careful too. Then she'd remember that near-accident with Jasper. She'd never liked walking the dog up on the cliffs but Andy had dismissed her fears. It gave her no satisfaction to say 'I told you so' to a ghost. She said it all the same.

None of her regular customers were in, though she was gratified to see that a number had called and asked after her. She asked Chrissie to ring them and tell them she was back. She was available for all evening shifts. Frankly, she'd rather be doing something than stewing at home.

All day, as she cut and coloured and made the best small talk she could, she could not prevent herself glancing out of the window to the tennis courts. So far there'd been no sign of the tall blond-haired figure she was looking for.

That was good. She'd broken it off with Martin and it had been ugly. She had no intention of going back on her decision even in these changed circumstances. She'd told him to clear off out of her life and that was how it must be.

Besides, there was no certainty that he would want to come back.

She'd spent much of her time these last miserable few days thinking about Martin and the way things had gone with him. She hadn't intended it to be that way; it seemed like a further betrayal of Andy to be thinking about her lover. Her ex-lover.

You weren't so fussy about betraying him when he was alive, were you?

Epsom is not an easy course for a young rider. Zoe knew that well enough and her previous experience there underlined the fact. That race had been over six furlongs and although it gave her a first-hand look at the descent of Tattenham Corner and the right-to-left camber of the finishing straight, it was insufficient preparation for tackling the contest ahead. The race was to be run over a mile and a half, the full Derby course, and the thought filled Zoe with excitement – and fear.

Pat had ridden it many times, in the Derby itself on a couple of occasions. But though he was eager to help, this time his advice had not amounted to much. 'You've got to stay handy all the way round,' he said. Keep in touch with the leaders then – Zoe had worked that out for herself. 'There's only one real way to find out,' he added. 'That's to ride it a few times yourself.' Today, then, would be the beginning of her learning curve.

On this occasion Jack wasn't much use either. He'd walked the course with her, pointing out the bends and slopes and throwing in several stories of past races and great feats over the famous ground. It had been entertaining but tales of Sea Bird and The Minstrel made her ambitions seem pretentious and Jack's advice highlighted her lack of experience.

One thing he'd said, which was separately reinforced by Ursula, nagged at Zoe. 'I'm not expecting you to win.'

So what was the point of her taking part?

Sod the rest of them, *she* wanted to win. She had to pick up where she had left off if she wanted to get back into the race for champion apprentice.

And she wanted to wipe the patronising smile off Ginger's face.

Jack had told her about Lester Piggott landing his first Derby at the age of eighteen. Well, she was four years older than that and this was a Class F handicap not a Classic. Marshmallow would hardly be up against the leading thoroughbreds of his generation. So why not?

FREE FALL

* * *

By mid-afternoon Harriet realised she had not taken a break. She'd pushed herself all day so far, finding things to do in lulls between customers that weren't, strictly speaking, her job. Like checking on stocks of haircare products and cleaning out the cupboards in the poky kitchen. After days of being unproductive, any menial task felt good.

But keeping her body busy did not solve the problem of her mind. There were many things to think about, not least what she was going to do with her life now. Harriet had not planned to find herself a widow in her mid-twenties with – she couldn't deny it – money in the bank. She might not be Brain of Britain but she had transferable skills and she could get a job pretty much anywhere – anywhere she might like to live, at any rate. Throughout her marriage she'd been tied to the needs of Andy's work and the demanding schedule of the horse-training life. Now, she could up sticks and move. Provided she steered clear of the most expensive places – and she had no desire to return to London – she could buy a flat, get a job and live a more sophisticated urban life. She could admit it to herself, it was a relief to no longer be living with a partner who woke you up at five thirty every morning of the year.

Starting over was in the future, though, when the money came through. It was unbelievable to think that the quarter of a million pounds in Andy's

199

secret account was now hers. She'd dug the statement out on several occasions in the past week just
to reassure herself it existed. And it did. Her
husband had had some life insurance too and she'd
been informed by their solicitor that his estate
would probably amount to around £300,000, all of
which would come to her. She told herself she'd
happily do without that money if it would bring
Andy back to life. And she meant it.

She tried not to think about the money. It wasn't
hers yet anyway. The legal process of winding up
Andy's estate could not begin until a death
certificate was issued and that would be delayed
until after the inquest. For the moment, she must
continue without it, which was another reason to
keep on at the salon. Jack had promised her six
months of Andy's wages to tide her over and said
she could remain in the cottage for the moment.
'You can stay as long as you like,' he'd said. 'I don't
want you worrying about it.' That was kind of him
but the cottage went with the job and at some point
she would have to go.

These were some of the thoughts that preoccupied
her, together with the 'what ifs'. What if she'd
insisted that Andy listen to what she had to say that
evening before he went off? If she'd sworn her com-
mitment to him and begged for a new start, would
that have kept him behind? Or might he have set off
lighter in heart, knowing that she was going to try,
really try this time, to make their marriage work?

If she'd told him what was on her mind, he might have taken more care. Or maybe he'd have cut short the dog's walk and come home directly from his meeting with Pat in the pub.

She'd tried getting out of Pat what they discussed that night but he'd been evasive.

'It was just horse stuff, Harriet. You know, things going on at the yard. That's all.'

Harriet had the feeling he was keeping something back but how many times can you ask someone the same question?

She ought to get some food. It was easy to neglect yourself at times like this and then people started to fuss over you. Zoe had been on her back all last week about not eating.

She went down to the café and automatically took her tray to the corner where she used to sit with Martin. She tried to repress the pang of disappointment that he wasn't there today. If he had been, would she have had the guts to turn round and walk away?

But there had been no sign of him out on the tennis court. She'd even seen that skinny teenager Haley, one of Martin's regular pupils, working with another coach.

Maybe Martin had left for good. And maybe she was responsible.

He'd left her that day in a sullen sulky silence; a curt 'Goodbye then' was all she'd got. No last lingering kiss or tender words of farewell. His

201

resentful behaviour had made it easier for her to turn her back and stiffen her resolve to repair her marriage.

But suppose he really had been heartbroken? He'd said he loved her and had demanded she leave her husband to make a life with him. Suppose her rejection had shattered all his hopes?

In those circumstances, she could understand that he might have packed in his life here and gone away. There would be nothing to keep him any longer, not after she'd let him down.

Was there something about her that destroyed the people around her? First her mother, then poor Andy and now broken-hearted Martin. Was it her fault?

She pushed her half-eaten salad away and made her way through the concourse to the reception desk next to the gym. She recognised the well-preserved middle-aged man on the desk though she'd never spoken to him. Ken, the senior tennis coach.

His face lit up with a well-practised smile as she approached. 'May I help you?'

'I'm looking for Martin.'

'He's not here, my dear. Do you want to book a lesson?'

'No, that's all right.' Maybe she should go. She didn't really know what she was doing asking for him. But Martin would surely want to hear about the terrible thing that had happened to her. And she needed to know if she'd driven him away forever.

Before she could frame a suitable question, Ken said, 'Are you a friend of Martin's?'

'Yes.' That was true, wasn't it? He might despise her now but she'd always think of him as a friend.

'He's on compassionate leave.'

Oh God, it must be her fault. Maybe he'd had a breakdown when she'd called it off.

Or taken an overdose.

'Don't look so worried,' Ken continued. 'His father had a heart scare over in Spain so he dropped everything to get out there. He'll be back once his dad's out of hospital.'

He was OK then. Thank God.

'Can I tell him who's been inquiring after his whereabouts?'

'No. It's all right – I just wondered. Thanks very much.' She almost ran back to the salon.

So Martin had not gone for good. What a relief. Not that she intended to have anything to do with him, except maybe as a friend. She had resolved to respect Andy's memory. All the same it would be a comfort in the bleak weeks ahead to be able to watch Martin gliding across the tennis courts below.

She stopped by Chrissie's station when she returned to the salon. 'Thanks for taking care of me today,' she said and gave the receptionist a kiss on the cheek.

The girl was speechless.

* * *

There's a climb of 140 feet from the start of the Epsom mile-and-a-half course to the top of the downs just before the midway point of the race. Zoe's mount, Marshmallow, coped well with the gradient and the bends, gently first to the right and then much more sharply to the left. At the top of the hill, they were lying sixth out of thirteen runners. So far so good, thought Zoe; she was in touch with the leaders and her horse seemed to be coping well with the undulations.

The difficult part, however, lay ahead.

The field swooped round the curving left-hander then down into Tattenham Corner to join the home straight. Zoe knew that this was where she had to take care. If anything, Marshmallow had a tendency to hang to the right, which was not helpful. As they met the steepest part of the descent, she tried to hold him back but her prompting had no effect.

She was no longer worried about their position in relation to the other runners. What mattered was keeping her horse balanced and under control. He had a heavy front end and the sheer weight of his body was pulling him downhill almost faster than his legs could carry him. As they entered the bend, his momentum swung them out wide to the right.

Zoe screamed curses in her frustration. On their walk round, Jack had told her about Lyphard in the 1972 Derby who'd made just this mistake, one she'd been determined to avoid. But here was her horse careering off line, giving away lengths to the others. She pulled her whip through into her right hand and cracked Marshmallow hard down the shoulder, preventing him from running further off line but by the time they'd rounded the bend into the home straight, they'd lost their position. The leaders were ten lengths ahead hurtling towards the stands. At least Marshmallow had now regained his balance and was racing in the right direction. As if to make up for his earlier disobedience, he responded eagerly to Zoe's urgings. Within half a furlong he had steamed past the runners immediately ahead and begun to close the gap on the leading group.

By the two-furlong marker, Zoe had Marshmallow flying. It was an exhilarating feeling to be swooping past the packed stands on a legendary racecourse at the climax of a close-fought race. They overtook two horses on the far rail who appeared to be standing still. There was just one horse ahead of them. Zoe recognised the scarlet and yellow of Crazy Jethro, Ginger Weaver's mount. It was no surprise.

In the final furlong, Jethro was just two lengths ahead and tiring – Zoe could tell from the way he was edging across the camber of the track towards the far rail. Could she catch him?

Then Marshmallow hit the wall, like a long-distance runner. The strength seemed to leak from his body like air from a balloon and suddenly he was running on memory alone.

The pair of them passed the post with clear daylight between them. Zoe had nearly recovered from her error at Tattenham Corner in allowing her horse to run wide. Nearly overhauled her chief rival in the race for champion apprentice. Nearly wiped that smug grin from his face that now beamed at her as they cantered side by side beyond the winning post.

But nearly wasn't good enough.

Zoe returned Ginger's smile but inside she was seething. She hadn't been strong enough to keep Marshmallow from running off line going round Tattenham Corner and it had cost her the race. What Ginger had said to the paper had been right.

That really hurt.

Jack considered himself a hardbitten professional but he seemed to be going soft in his old age. Every time he watched Zoe race, his heart beat faster and his stomach fizzed with nerves. He'd even caught himself searching his pocket for his pipe – and he'd quit the habit ten years ago. He'd been a mentor to many inexperienced riders in his time but he'd never felt as close to his other protégés as he did to this particular young lady. Why was that?

Ursula was aware of his feelings and she patted his arm in reassurance as Marshmallow ran wide on the bend.

'She's blown it,' he muttered and Ursula said nothing, which he appreciated. Most owners would be squealing in frustration at seeing their horse's chance go out of the window.

Marshmallow's fightback along the straight, however, stirred the blood.

'It was my fault, Ursula,' he said when the race was over. 'I shouldn't have persuaded you to put her up.'

'I didn't need much persuading.'

'Pat would have won it for you. He'd have kept hold of the horse down the hill.'

'Maybe, but Zoe rode a fine finish. I'd have settled for second before the race.'

That was fair of her.

'Well,' he added, 'she'll be better for the experience, any road.'

They could both agree on that.

Zoe, though, was plainly unhappy about her second place and said so on the drive back in Jack's car.

'Listen to me, young lady,' he said as she began to apologise for the third or fourth time. 'How many races have you run over a mile and a half?'

'That was the first.'

'Right. It's a bit different to a six-furlong dash along the straight, isn't it? You've just ridden a tricky track up and down dale and going sideways. Even the best get caught out at Epsom the first time, you know.'

'But you walked it with me. You told me where I could go wrong and I still did.'

'Talking's different from doing.'

'I know but,' she turned sideways in the seat to face him, 'I couldn't hold him. I wasn't strong enough.'

He nodded. It was true and there was no getting round it.

'But I promise,' she continued, 'I'm going to work at it. I'm going down to the gym. I'll do weight training, whatever it takes, to get stronger. Don't laugh.'

He wasn't laughing, just smiling with pleasure because he'd now worked out why he was so fond of her. She didn't just have talent, she had the guts to make it count.

Pat had been riding at Windsor, but racing was not on his mind as he drove home.

The circumstances of Andy's death kept going round his head.

He'd played an important part in the events of that evening and his role had been reported in glowing terms. He'd set out along the cliffs to search for his friend and withstood the shock of discovering the body. He'd summoned the emergency services and gone down to the beach to see if he could help the fallen man. And he'd helped rescue the dog who had caused the tragedy. From being a journeyman jockey known only to racing people and trackside anoraks, Pat had become, if only briefly, a nationally known sportsman.

And in Zoe's eyes, he was a hero. He'd stood up when it counted to help her sister, and he'd been steadfast ever since even though it was obvious that Andy's death had shaken him to the core.

That part was true at least. Andy dying like that had well and truly kicked the props from beneath Pat's world.

The more he thought about their conversation in the pub, the more he was convinced that Andy's death had been no accident. Andy's drinking, his angry what-the-hell mood as he'd left, his despair over the failure of his marriage – it all added up to Andy deliberately killing himself.

He'd suspected as much from the first. It was the reason he'd rushed out to find Andy – to dispel his fears. But he'd only succeeded in proving those fears were justified.

'It makes me feel like jumping off a sodding cliff.' Those had been Andy's words. Andy had told him what he was going to do and he had allowed him to go ahead and do it. He should have gone with him. He was no hero. A thoughtless fool more like.

And then there was the reason why Andy had done it and that damned Pat further. It turned him from an unthinking bystander into an accomplice to suicide. Finding out about Martin must have been the blow that pushed Andy over the edge – literally.

The one thing that didn't add up was Jasper. Why had the dog fallen from the cliff? He supposed Andy could have taken Jasper with him when he jumped. Suicidal parents sometimes took their children's lives along with their own, didn't they? There was a similarity. And that might explain why the dog had survived. If Andy had been holding Jasper in his arms, his body would have cushioned the impact of the dog's fall.

Pat had another theory. It was more fanciful but he preferred it to the idea of Andy deliberately killing his dog. Jasper was devoted to Andy. Suppose, in some mad moment of canine loyalty, he had followed his master over the cliff? Pat had never heard of a dog committing suicide, but he might have thought Andy was playing a game or that he needed rescuing.

Whatever the reason and no matter the cost to poor Jasper, it had spread a helpful smokescreen over the whole question of Andy's death. Everyone believed he'd fallen trying to save the dog.

Only Pat knew the truth and it was eating him up. That and one other matter, the big issue that he'd been trying not to think about because he didn't want to deal with it just yet. He could live with being thought a hero and keeping his suspicions to himself but he didn't know how he was going to stand the loss of over a hundred thousand pounds.

Half of the money in Andy's building society

account was his. Now Andy was dead, it would soon belong to Harriet. He knew from Zoe that there was a will and Andy had left everything to her. 'Not that there'll be much,' Zoe had said in her ignorance.

How on earth was he going to get his share?

Chapter Ten

'Aren't we stopping at the pub?' David said.

DC Laura Hammond shook her head. 'I've got dinner in the oven and a bottle of Beaujolais at home – better than you'll get in there.'

All the same, David looked regretfully through the mullioned windows of the old stone building as they walked to the car and Laura suppressed the urge to give in to her partner. She'd spent enough time in the Beach Head Inn the other week when she and a fellow officer were interviewing the staff and customers about Andy Burns. The stable worker had spent over an hour there before walking up the coast path to the cliffs where he had met his death. The spot where Laura and her partner had just enjoyed an evening stroll.

David, a man more dedicated to the theory of exercise than its practice, had made heavy weather of the stiff climb up the steps of the hillside.

'Give over whingeing,' Laura had said as he had

finally reached the top, puffing like a steam train. 'The man whose body we found used to come up here twice a day.'

'Didn't do much for his health though, did it?'

Laura ignored the remark. No one with an eye for the sea and sky could object to Beach Head. She concentrated on the view as she faced the sea. The great grey limestone beach lay at her feet, while away to her right the coast path followed the line of the cliff top.

This was the third time she'd been up here. The first time in virtual darkness on the night of the accident, the second when she and Paul Copper, the local community policeman, had spent an evening intercepting dog walkers and ramblers to ask if they'd observed anything on the night of the incident. Nobody had.

She'd returned for a third time because something was nagging at her. She wanted another look at the spot where the unfortunate man had fallen to his death. And, apart from being the companion with whom she wanted to enjoy romantic evening walks, David was a useful sounding board.

'How high is it?' he said, peering down.

'I'm not certain. Well over a hundred foot along this section.'

'And he fell from here?'

'A bit further along.' She pointed down to the beach, where the lighter grey of the limestone was interspersed with shale and earth. 'He was lying just this side of that recent fall. All that came down a few months ago, apparently. It's a crumbly old cliff.'

David took a firm step backwards away from the edge. 'I've never much enjoyed heights.'

Laura couldn't agree. She loved climbing to the top of things and looking down. It was symbolic, really; you knew where you were in life when you had a good view all around.

'Did the cliff just collapse beneath him then?'

'Haven't you been reading the paper? We think his dog got stuck on a ledge and he went over trying to rescue it.'

'Any witnesses?'

She laughed. 'Anyone would think you're the policeman.'

'You've dragged me all the way up here. You might at least give me the gory details.'

That, of course, was the point of bringing him along. As the senior partner in a well-established solicitor's practice in Taunton, David's opinion was worth having.

'His dog got caught and nearly fell off a few weeks ago. He pulled it back to safety. The assumption is that the same thing happened, only this time he wasn't so lucky.'

'That's your assumption too?'

As a matter of fact, it wasn't. Not now she was standing here looking for a ledge where the animal could have been trapped. They'd walked along the path to the point directly above where the body was found. The cliff was sheer from the edge to the rocks below. There wasn't a ledge big enough for a seagull to perch on, let alone a dog.

David was giving her one of his beady-eyed looks, his spectacles magnifying the intensity of his gaze.

'So?' he challenged her.

'There's a ledge along there.' She pointed further on down the path where the cliff edge snaked towards the sea.

'But,' David was enjoying himself now, 'if he'd fallen over there he wouldn't have ended up down here, would he?'

So much was obvious and she didn't intend to debate the point.

'The dog could still have been responsible – gone too close to the edge maybe and Andy made a grab for him and missed.'

David laughed scornfully. 'What, a strapping fit fellow who worked with animals? Doesn't sound likely.'

'I never told you he worked with animals.'

'And I never said I hadn't read the paper. He was head lad at Jack Lucas's yard, wasn't he?'

Of course, David was a bit of a gambler and followed racing. A bit of a know-all in every sphere, truth be told. It was just as well she liked him.

'It doesn't matter how fit you are, you can still lose your balance. And he'd been in the pub, so maybe he was under the influence.'

'Do you know how much he'd been drinking?'

'We don't know exactly – the post mortem report's not in yet.'

'What about the people he was drinking with? What do they say?'

The truth was she'd not spoken to Pat Vincent since the night of the accident. As David drove her home to dinner and that bottle of Beaujolais, she decided another interview with the jockey was overdue.

'You're Zoe Morris, aren't you? The jockey?'

Zoe couldn't deny it but she was hardly capable of uttering a word at the moment. After her defeat on Marshmallow at Epsom, she had joined the gym at the health centre where Harriet worked, determined to work on her strength. After a weights session in the gym, she'd just followed up with a stiff half-hour on an exercise bike and she was blowing hard.

She'd noticed a toned woman in pink on a running machine on the other side of the room. Up close, the woman was immaculate, she didn't look as if she'd even raised a sweat.

'Hi, I'm Diane Connor. I'm a friend of Harriet's.'

'Pleased to meet you.' She was acutely conscious of how she must look, steaming and red-faced.

Diane seemed to notice her physical discomfort for the first time. 'Sorry to catch you when you're working out but I'm anxious about Harriet. I read about her husband's accident and left messages for her but I haven't heard from her.'

That wasn't a surprise to Zoe. She suspected Harriet hadn't even turned her phone on after Andy's death.

'Don't take it personally. She's barely spoken to anybody. It's been very hard.'

'I can imagine.'

Could she? Zoe wondered. Diane looked so pristine-pretty, togged up in designer exercise gear that was barely crumpled. One neat punctuation mark of concern creased her flawless brow.

'How do you know Harriet?'

'She's my hair stylist. I've been going to her for ages.'

That made sense. Harriet rarely mentioned her customers and Zoe had certainly never heard of Diane.

'Will you tell her I was asking after her? I've been very worried.'

'Sure but you can tell her yourself next time you get your hair done. She's just gone back to work.'

'Thanks, I will.' She lingered for a moment. 'Maybe next time I could buy you a coffee or something. So I can boast I know Harriet's famous sister.'

'I'm not famous.'

'Well, you beat all those men at Ascot, didn't you? I mean, I know nothing about racing but you've got to be doing something right.'

Zoe decided Diane was odd, but she liked her all the same.

* * *

Diane said goodbye to Zoe hoping she hadn't put her foot in it. But her inquiry had been perfectly reasonable surely. What was really worrying her was that she'd upset Harriet.

It had been stupid of her to make a pass at Martin that afternoon. She'd just been carried away by the sight of him and by the sexy story Harriet herself had put in her mind. And, she had to admit, by the feeling that she'd been there first with Martin and so had the right, if she wanted, to make him a naughty little proposal.

Face it, she'd been a complete clot. It had only occurred to her later that Martin might have told Harriet about it. Told her that and more – she had no doubt he was capable of it.

What Diane had said to Zoe contained an error of omission. She'd been ringing Harriet before her husband's accident as well as after. She didn't want to lose Harriet as a friend over a silly slip-up with Martin but she feared she might have done so.

All of which seemed a bit petty and selfish in the light of what had happened to Harriet. Diane's heart went out to her. Imagine if something like that happened to Maurice?

It was unthinkable.

Martin dumped his holdall in the bedroom and kicked his shoes off. He dialled a number as he sprawled across the bed.

'Hi, Ken. I'm back.'

'So, the traveller returns.' His boss sounded pleased to hear from him, which was gratifying. 'How's your dad?'

'Better. He's back home now and Mum's flapping around him like normal. I reckon I've done my duty.'

'When can we expect to see you?'

'Can you give me a couple more days?' Martin was embarrassed but he might as well come clean. 'The thing is, I've buggered up my racquet arm – gashed it on some barbed wire when I was out running. The doctor told me to lay off tennis for a few days.'

If Ken was fed up he put a decent gloss upon it. 'A couple more days won't make any difference, I suppose. How about Monday? I can handle the girls till then, I guess.'

'What girls?'

'Your pupils have missed you, son. And I had a mystery beauty in here the other afternoon asking after you. She wouldn't leave her name but I've seen her around the place.'

'What did she look like?'

'Red hair, green eyes, great figure. Very worried by your absence but I said you'd be back.'

Martin lay back on the bed, ignoring the ache in his injured arm. He'd been a bit worried about returning but now he knew he'd done the right thing.

'Harriet,' he murmured to himself. These days away hadn't changed how he felt about her one jot.

* * *

Harriet noticed the flowers almost before she saw who was carrying them – a spectacular bouquet of white roses.

'They're for you,' said Diane, waylaying her outside the door of the hair salon.

When Martin had told her of Diane's attempt to seduce him, Harriet had resolved to sever the friendship. She'd been outraged. But that had been before Andy's death, in a world that seemed as remote as last century. Things had been different then.

'I don't know if they're appropriate but I wanted to give you something. I've been worried about you.'

Harriet had the flowers in her hands, the summer garden perfume in her nostrils. Diane looked sincere. And anxious.

Harriet could throw the bouquet on the floor and trample over it as she stalked off. But she knew she wasn't going to do that. Just how many friends did she have anyway?

They ended up in the bar of the restaurant in the centre.

'You are OK, aren't you?' Diane said, after she'd ordered a bottle of wine and poured generously.

Harriet shrugged. What was she meant to say to that? 'I'm pretty good, thanks, considering my husband's just been killed.'

'I couldn't believe it when I heard.' Diane was doing most of the talking. 'What a dreadful thing!

If there's anything I can do, you've only got to say. Are you all right for money?'

That took Harriet by surprise. Most people could be free with their sympathy if it wasn't going to cost them anything.

'Don't look at me like that, I mean it. Maurice gives me far too much. If you're short, just say.'

It struck Harriet that this offer – and the flowers and the wine – were Diane's way of saying sorry about Martin. She could bring it out into the open now if she wanted to. Clear the air properly or have a fight about it. But maybe it was best left covered up. All that stuff with Martin was history anyway.

'Thank you, Diane, but I'm fine. Andy's employer has been very generous and, anyway, money won't be a problem.'

'Good. How about company? If you want a change, you come and stay with us. We've tons of room and, anyway, Maurice is never home.'

That was kind of her too – though Harriet couldn't imagine taking her up on it. In return, she gave Diane all the details of the night Andy died that she felt were fit for consumption. It was only fair. The woman was a nosy witch but an amusing one. Drinking with her was more entertaining than dragging herself home.

And Martin's name did not come up once.

Later, having manoeuvred the flowers into her car with some difficulty, Harriet found herself driving through town, down a familiar route, not one that took her home.

She parked in a scruffy street she'd told herself she'd never set foot in again.

On the top floor of the house across the road the windows were closed and net-curtained, courtesy of the landlady. It was impossible to see inside. No lights shone but it was a bright summer evening so that was of no significance.

Was Martin back yet?

Go and see – ring the bell.

No. She mustn't. If she found herself up there with him, where they'd enjoyed so many honeyed moments together, who knows what form his commiserations might take?

Why was she here? Did she have no will power?

It would be wrong, utterly wrong, to end up in bed with Martin when Andy hadn't even been dead a fortnight.

How long *would* be acceptable then?

Never.

Was this how alcoholics felt when they faced the fact that there must be no more drinks ever again?

Oh God, she'd never felt so desperate. She had to get home.

But first she did the one thing that had eluded her so far. She wept.

Jack wasn't surprised to see Ursula's car in the yard when he returned from third lot. She never bothered to announce her attendance in advance and he'd long ago got used to her habits, though other trainers might have resented the casual intrusion.

'Nothing better to do, eh?' he said to her by way of greeting.

'Happily, no. I just like to pop in – you don't mind, do you?'

'Would it make any difference if I did?'

He knew he sounded grumpy. He *was* grumpy, but it was nothing to do with her. He had the drive to Brighton ahead of him shortly and he wasn't in the mood for a long stint behind the wheel. The new head lad, Fergus, had already alienated half the staff in the yard – which was one of the problems of promoting from the ranks. And, well, there was another matter that continued to hang over him like a cloud though there was nothing he could do to shift it.

Ursula, naturally, was aware of it.

'You're brooding over Andy, aren't you?'

'I suppose you want some coffee.'

'Not particularly.'

'I can only give you ten minutes. I'm off to Brighton.'

'You're not responsible for his death, you know.'

Sometimes the woman was a flaming nuisance. She never took a hint if it didn't suit her. He wished he'd never told her about his last conversation with Andy. What a terrible way to end things.

'It was just a coincidence,' she said. 'The accident

couldn't have had anything to do with your ultimatum.'

Not rationally, it couldn't. All the same, he'd given Andy twenty-four hours to come clean or lose his job and that same night he lost his life. What malignant spirit ordered that state of affairs? He wasn't, couldn't in any way be to blame. So why did he feel like he was?

'Did I tell you Andy was going to take the yard over from me?'

'When?'

'I've been thinking of packing it in at the end of this season. He could have taken over next year.'

She looked at him gravely. 'So he'd have lost more than the job if you'd kicked him out?'

He nodded. 'Andy was always on at me to extend the gallop. He reckoned that if our gallop had been two furlongs longer we could have had more winners.'

'What do you think?'

'He could have been right but I didn't want to flash out on a new surface. Not at this stage of my life. But that could have been behind Andy punting so heavily, so he could invest in the yard. Not that it excuses him or anything.' He stared ruminatively at the ground.

'Suppose I drive you to Brighton,' said Ursula. 'Would that cheer you up?'

'I wouldn't bank on it.'

But he accepted the offer just the same.

* * *

Pat was surprised to get a call from the police-woman who was looking into Andy's death. He told her there wasn't much point in setting up a meeting but she wasn't to be fobbed off, so he arranged for her to call at the house when he knew Zoe would be at Harriet's. Not that he intended to say anything he didn't want Zoe to hear but it was best to be on the safe side.

He brooded on the interview ahead. He didn't intend to elaborate on his final conversation with Andy but he would have to come up with something.

The policewoman – 'Call me Laura,' she said – wrong-footed him from the start.

'How long were you both in the pub that night?'

Pat couldn't see the relevance. 'About three-quarters of an hour.'

'Can you tell me how much Andy drank in that time?'

He saw the relevance now. He supposed it might have a bearing on how Andy had come to fall.

'He had a couple of shorts and then a pint.'

'What shorts? Singles or doubles?'

There didn't seem much point in lying about it, so he told her: two double whiskies and a pint of beer. Not an enormous amount of alcohol when spread over an evening but heavy enough when consumed in forty-five minutes on an empty stomach.

Policewoman Laura pondered the information. 'Would you say the drinks affected him at all?'

'No.' They just turned him from depressed to suicidal but Pat wasn't going to mention that. Or that he had told Andy about his wife's lover.

'So that's the amount he'd normally consume?'

'I wouldn't know. I don't go to pubs much these days. I can't go drinking and make a riding weight, you see.'

He wasn't sure that she did but she didn't ask him to elaborate, which was a pity. He was keen to steer this conversation into non-controversial areas.

She was making notes of what he said. 'What did you talk about?'

He'd prepared the answer to that one. 'Full Force.'

She blinked, her big brown eyes confused. But her tone was sharp as she said, 'Meaning what?'

'Sorry, Full Force is a horse up at the yard. I rode him at Salisbury the day before and he ran badly. We were all fed up about it because we couldn't work out why.'

'And what conclusions did you come to?'

'He didn't like the going, it was too soft.'

'And it took you three-quarters of an hour to decide that?'

'We were just chatting. About what the owner said and how Jack, the boss, felt about it. You know, we just discussed what was going on at the yard and things.'

She seemed to accept this – and why wouldn't she? He wondered if the police were specially trained to know when you were telling the truth. Didn't they just assume that everyone lied all the time?

'And how did he seem to you?'

'I don't quite follow.' He followed but he'd have to be dragged by the nose.

'What kind of spirits was he in?'

'He seemed fine.'

'He didn't seem troubled by anything?'

'No.' He looked her in the eye as he said it.

'And no worse for the alcohol he'd drunk?'

'Not particularly. I mean, I wouldn't have been happy if he'd offered me a lift but he was only off to walk the dog.'

Pat was quite proud of that. It made sense to plant the idea that Andy could have been a bit wobbly up on the cliff though not so under the influence that he should have stopped him going up there.

'Such a bloody terrible accident,' he said and meant it.

She didn't contradict him.

Laura was irritated with David for being late for supper. But it was impossible to stay annoyed with him for long. He kissed her hungrily and poured them both a generous glass of wine.

'I tell you, darling, it's no fun spending time in a pub just pretending to drink.'

'Is that where you were?'

He grinned expansively. 'In the pub at Beach Head, doing your sleuthing for you. I'm intending to send Avon and Somerset Constabulary a bill.'

'What sleuthing? I didn't ask you to go nosing around.'

Her tone was sharp but she was more annoyed with herself. She'd been intending to go back to the pub but had been sidetracked by other priorities. She'd known there would be pub gossip to unearth about Andy Burns, she'd said as much to David. It seemed he'd taken it as permission to stick his oar in.

'Go on then,' she said. She might as well hear it.

'I had a game of pool with some of the locals. Fortunately they were happy to indulge a lonely divorcee who doesn't get to play with his sons like he used to.'

David was a father of two teenage lads, now living with their mother in Exeter – a sore point.

'Call it the fraternity of Fathers for Justice,' he added, but he was smiling.

'Come on, David, tell me what you found out.'

'About what?'

'Andy Burns. That's what we're talking about, isn't it?'

'Yes, officer.'

Now he was taking the piss. She reached for the notepad she used for making shopping lists. 'I'm listening.'

He placed a large hand on her arm. 'There's no need to turn this into a formal interview. Let me just give you a quick rundown and if you think it's worth the effort you'll have to get statements yourself.'

It was true she could be a bit fixated on her job, especially one like this. Most of her work was mundane: snatched handbags, drunken brawls, car theft. Here, someone had died.

'OK, David, but get on with it, please.'

'I spoke to two fellows, Jeff and Porky. One's a farm worker and the other claimed to be a professional gambler so I assume he's on benefit. Neither of them knew Andy Burns or the jockey well but they knew plenty about Beach Head stables where they worked. The lads from the yard go in sometimes. Before Andy died, they'd been gossiping about him being in a fight and getting one of the other employees sacked.'

'When was this?'

'A few weeks ago. After a race at Nottingham when one of the Beach Head horses pulled off an unexpected win. The rumour is that the horse was set up for it and the lad who got sacked was fed up because he wasn't tipped off.'

Laura felt herself slipping out of her depth. David might be familiar with horse-racing intricacies but she wasn't. 'Do you want to run that past me again?'

'All you need to know for now is that this fellow who got fired – his name's Joe Parkin – believed

Andy had done him out of some deal and attacked him in the yard with a whip. He cut him so badly that the trainer had to take him to hospital and Parkin got the sack.'

'Did he cut him across the face?'

David looked surprised. 'How do you know?'

'The post mortem report came back. It said death was due to multiple injuries, which is what you might expect. But it mentioned an earlier wound across the mouth and jaw.'

'Aha. Corroboration – that's good.' He looked pleased with himself.

'That's interesting background, David. Thanks.'

'I haven't finished yet.' His shrewd grey eyes twinkled behind the spectacles. He was having such a good time spinning it out that she wanted to shake him.

'Well?'

'Joe Parkin was in the pub the night Andy died.'

'Oh.'

'At the same time. They didn't speak but Joe saw him and bad-mouthed him to several people. Apparently, he'd just been turned down for another job and he blamed Andy for that too.'

'So you're suggesting . . . ?'

'I'm not suggesting anything. But everyone in the pub is convinced Joe got his courage up at the bar and went after Andy along the cliffs.'

It seemed to Laura that the small room closed in on her. Suddenly she felt claustrophobic.

'If there's any truth in this,' she said, 'it changes everything.'

Harriet had done her best to be reasonable company during supper at Zoe and Pat's. That is, she'd ducked any opportunity to discuss Andy or the inquest or what the hell she was going to do with her life – she'd already spent enough time chewing that over with her sister. Instead she'd encouraged the other two to chat about horses and who was getting on with whom at the yard – matters that interested them, not her. She didn't mind. It was kind of them to rescue her from another lonely evening. And, provided she kept her glass topped up, she could ignore the fact that she was playing gooseberry once more.

Was this how it was going to be from now on? Sitting sozzled on the sofa at every social occasion, watching others snuggle up? She and Andy might not have played at lovebirds recently but at least she'd been one of a couple when he was by her side.

She didn't intend to prolong the evening but the film on the television was mildly entertaining. It gave her a break from turning her troubles over and over in her mind. When it was finished she got sleepily to her feet and realised she was not exactly sober.

'You're not intending to drive home, are you?' said Zoe.

'Why not?' Harriet fished her keys from her bag

and promptly dropped them. 'It's only ten minutes.'

'You can't. Stay here tonight.'

What? On the bumpy old sofa, listening to the pair of them through the wall. No thanks. She'd done that the other night and didn't intend to repeat it in a hurry.

'I've got to get back. I've got an early start tomorrow.'

Pat got to his feet. 'I'll take you home.'

'But what about my car?' She needed that to get to work. 'I'm fine to drive.' And even if she wasn't, she didn't much care.

'I'll take you,' Pat repeated. 'And Zoe can follow in yours, OK?'

She supposed it was. Anyway, she didn't have the energy to argue about it. All she wanted to do was get to bed.

She almost dropped off in the front seat of Pat's car. It might be old but it was comfy. But she woke up fast enough when Pat spoke.

'Did you know that Andy was holding some money for me?'

'Sorry?' Maybe she'd misheard.

'Andy and I were in partnership. We were making a bit on the horses and he was keeping hold of the cash.'

'You mean Andy owed you money?'

'Yes. I couldn't bring myself to mention it before, in the circumstances. I know it's a bit awkward.'

'No, it's OK, Pat. If he owed you money then I'll pay you back. How much was it?'

She didn't know what she was expecting to hear. A couple of hundred pounds maybe, enough to make it worth the embarrassment of asking for it back.

'It's around a hundred and twenty thousand. Half of what he's got in his building society account.'

Good God. That cleared her head – as if Pat had dumped a bucket of water over her. 'But I don't understand. Andy never mentioned owing you money.'

'It's not exactly something we wanted to shout about. I'm sure you realise why we had to keep it quiet.'

'You mean you were on the fiddle?'

Pat pulled up outside the cottage. He spoke softly. 'Technically, I suppose. As a jockey I can't bet. Everyone else in the industry has a chance to make a bit on the side but not us jockeys. So Andy placed the bets and held the money. It was a fifty-fifty partnership.'

Lights filled the interior of the car as Zoe pulled up behind them. Pat's face was grim and so, Harriet imagined, was her own.

'Whichever way you put it, you're telling me that you and Andy were on the fiddle.'

Pat sighed. 'No, fiddling is cheating, we were just punting. He was doing it for you, you know. He was desperate to set up in business again and impress you. The idea was to take over from Jack at the end of the season – the pair of us.'

That had the ring of truth. She knew how much it had hurt Andy to lose his independence as a trainer and go back to work for Jack. And how she had pilloried him in the heat of argument for his failure.

It was a lot to think about.

'I knew nothing about any of this,' she said.

'Yeah, well, I'm sorry to be the one who tells you but it's the truth.'

The lights went out behind them and a car door opened. Footsteps sounded on the gravel.

'Does Zoe know about it?'

'God, no. Absolutely nothing – please don't tell her.'

That was something. At least the pair of them weren't ganging up on her.

In a moment her sister would be at the car door.

'I've got to think about this, Pat. You can't expect me to agree to anything right here – I'm not that drunk. Anyway, I don't have any of Andy's money yet, it's all tied up in his estate.' She opened her door. 'Thanks for the lift.'

He sat still in his seat, saying nothing.

Chapter Eleven

'Do you think she'll be all right?'

Pat was so lost in his own thoughts that Zoe's voice seemed to come from a long way off, though she was sitting next to him in the car as they returned from Harriet's place.

She repeated the question and added, 'I should have offered to stay the night.'

It was tempting to tell her to give it a rest about Harriet. She was sitting on a pile of his money and, from the tone of their recent conversation, was not immediately inclined to hand it back. But Zoe mustn't know about the money – or, more to the point, how he and Andy had earned it.

Of course, if things went sour and Harriet dug her heels in, maybe Zoe would be his best means of getting Harriet to pay him back.

But he was getting ahead of himself, Harriet hadn't actually said no.

'She was fine,' he said finally. 'She could have

stayed with us if she couldn't handle being on her own.'

'Did she talk about Andy?'

'Not really. She was a bit out of it. She'll have a sore head in the morning.'

He had one right now and he was as sober as he'd ever been in his life.

He'd misplayed it, obviously. Asking for his money last thing at night when Harriet was half pissed was not the best time. But when would be? He'd been waiting since Andy's death for the right moment to raise the subject and it had never arrived. He'd tried to be sensitive and respect her feelings but this evening he'd had the opportunity to put down his marker and he'd taken it. It hadn't been well received but what did he expect? Harriet was hardly going to whip out her chequebook on the spot. No one would, in these circumstances. It was going to be a long campaign to get what he was due.

He'd always been wary of Harriet. It was hard to believe that she was Zoe's sister, they were so different in looks and temperament. There was no doubt that he'd got the better of the two. Look what Harriet had done to Andy – driven the poor sod to suicide and come up holding a cheque. She'd as good as pushed him over the cliff herself.

No, that was harsh. He mustn't rush to condemn her. If they were at loggerheads he'd never see his money.

The truth was there was no way he could have foreseen this turn of events. What were the odds on Andy dying? People didn't suddenly up and die unless they were cruelly unlucky.

'Pat?'

'Yes, darling.' He knew she liked it when he called her that and he raised a smile for her benefit as he made the turn into their road.

'Would you mind if we scrubbed round Sunday?' They'd arranged to run up to Bristol for a romantic day out to celebrate the six-month anniversary of their first date. 'I don't think I ought to leave Harriet on her own at the moment.'

'Sure. If that's how you feel.' He parked the car. 'Even better, why don't you ask her if she'd like to come with us? It might do her good.'

He could see she liked that. She was smiling at him fondly in the dim light. 'Thanks, Pat. Are you sure you don't mind? It's meant to be our special day.'

'That's OK.' He slipped his arm round her shoulder and pulled her close. 'We'll have lots of other special days.'

She kissed him.

If only Harriet were more like her sister. He'd stand a better chance of claiming what was rightfully his.

Harriet hardly slept. It was the worst night so far of this horrible period in her life. Though her alcohol-infected body desperately craved rest, her raging thoughts would give her no peace – Pat had seen to that.

So that explained the money. She'd suspected all along that Andy wasn't smart enough to make a quarter of a million backing horses. She'd been right. He'd been working some kind of racket with a jockey, pulling a fast one over the bookies. As if that wasn't bad enough – though they couldn't prosecute him now he was dead, could they? – half the money wasn't his at all.

It followed, then, that it didn't belong to her either.

That money, the knowledge that it would be coming to her soon, had been her life raft in this storm. It was going to give her a fresh start, put her on the property ladder and give her time to plan her future. She'd already decided on one or two indulgences. She fancied a new car, for a start. And a decent holiday in a few months' time once the inquest was over. She'd been secretly planning a trip to the Caribbean; she hadn't asked her sister but if she offered to pay for Zoe, surely she'd come with her at the end of the Flat season.

But if she gave away half of the money she'd have to think again. Twenty thousand out of a quarter of a million didn't seem significant. The same sum out of £120,000 looked like imprudence.

Funny how quickly she'd got used to the idea of owning this amount of money. To some people –

Diane Connor's husband, for example – it would probably seem insignificant. And there were some women who inherited millions when their husbands died. But they lived in a different world. To Harriet, who relied on customers' tips to balance the books, a quarter of a million pounds was a fortune. And she wasn't about to lose half of it.

It would be different if Andy and Pat had been engaged in legitimate business and there were contracts and commitments in writing. But there wouldn't be anything like that, would there? Pat had not said so and surely he would have done. All he'd said was that he and Andy had to keep their business quiet. Because he was a jockey and wasn't allowed to bet. And Andy had held on to the money because it would have been incriminating for Pat to have it.

In the circumstances, Harriet didn't think there would be anything in writing to back up Pat's case. So she could keep the money and tell Pat to get lost. More to the point, she could get lost herself when Andy's estate was wound up. She could disappear to the other end of the country, or go abroad. She'd always fancied Australia and they'd be happy to let in a woman of means such as herself. That would be a brand new start.

Only it wasn't as simple as that. Zoe was in love with Pat. Harriet couldn't abandon Zoe to Pat's anger. More to the point, she couldn't abandon Zoe. She'd rediscovered her sister in recent years and she'd lose more than just her best friend if she took off to live on the other side of the world. Anyway, it would be futile. Pat would be able to locate her at any time through Zoe.

She would have to face Pat down. Say that she didn't believe him and he was just trying it on. And maybe he was. Andy had been dead for nearly two weeks and this was the first time Pat had told her he was in business with her dead husband. Or maybe Zoe knew about the windfall money in Andy's account – she might have seen the building society correspondence when she was looking for documents after Andy's death, in that period when she herself was drifting around like a zombie. Suppose Pat had found out about it from her and cooked up this claim?

It was possible and Harriet was prepared to argue the possibility. There would be recriminations, bitter no doubt, but what could Pat do? And in time, if he and Zoe became a permanent fixture, she'd find a way to forgive his opportunism.

All the same, a war with her sister's boyfriend was not what Harriet needed. It would drive a wedge between herself and Zoe, and Zoe was her rock in this crisis. She was feeling vulnerable enough as it was.

It was four in the morning and she gave up on sleep. As she sat in the kitchen over a cup of tea, the little house creaked in the wind. A storm was blowing up and she felt utterly alone.

Oh Andy, you bloody fool, why did you do this to me?

He'd not been the perfect husband but he'd have held her close on a night like this – if she'd let him. On reflection, she was the fool. If Andy were asleep in bed upstairs right now, all these troubles would vanish.

But Andy was not coming back. She was on her own in the storm.

Jack wasn't thrilled to get a call from some police-woman asking if it was convenient for her to pay a visit to the yard. He had a busy morning, with horses to get off to race meetings. But it was the height of the season and there wouldn't ever be a convenient time, so he invited her over with reluctance.

To be fair, he appreciated the courtesy of her call. Presumably she had the authority to turn up when-ever she pleased. And she was sensible enough to arrive in jeans and walking boots, a small brown-eyed woman with a pleasant manner, obviously prepared to get her hands dirty. It could have been worse. He invited her into the office.

'Why are you still busying yourselves over Andy's death?' he asked as he boiled a kettle for tea. 'It's obvious how the poor fellow died, isn't it?'

'We have a duty to investigate the circumstances thoroughly, Mr Lucas. Just so the coroner has all the facts at the inquest.'

Fair enough. 'Ask away then.' He didn't imagine it would take long.

She produced a notebook but did not refer to it as she spoke. 'I understand that Mr Burns was recently involved in a dispute here at the yard. Can you tell me about that, please?'

Jack almost poured boiling water over his hand. It was the last thing he had expected her to say.

'How on earth did you find out about that?'

'It appears to be common knowledge in the local community. We have several statements but I imagine you could give me a more reliable summary of events.'

Jack had no doubt about that. He took a moment to compose his thoughts as he mopped up the mess he'd made. There was no point in trying to obscure the facts but at least he could present them in a sober fashion.

'You've got to realise that tempers can get a bit frayed round here. We're in each other's pockets all day long at this time of the year and there's the odd punch-up. These fellows love horses but they're not necessarily the most sophisticated.'

'So there was a fight?'

He nodded. 'Andy and another lad had words and Andy got whacked around the face with a whip. I took him to casualty. I had to let the other lad go.'

'That would be Joe Parkin?'

'Yes.' She'd obviously done some digging. 'He was my travelling head lad.'

'Why did you fire him?'

'According to the other lads, it was a deliberate attack after they'd had words coming back into the yard from the gallops. Joe was on horseback and Andy wasn't even looking at him.'

'So this was worse than the usual punch-up?'

'Yes.'

'It sounds like a premeditated assault. Did you consider reporting it?'

'It wasn't as serious as that, officer. I reckon I dealt with it fairly.'

She considered him for a moment, her expression neutral. Did they teach police officers that deadpan look specially?

'Do you know what they were arguing about?'

'No. They were never the best of pals.'

'So you didn't try and find out?'

'Neither of them would tell me. I'd dealt with the situation so I left it at that.'

This time she couldn't keep the scepticism off her face. 'Would you be interested to know what other people think?'

'You mean the gossips in the pub? OK, I'm listening.'

'Our information is that they fell out over a bet. Mr Burns had won money on a horse and Mr Parkin believed he should have been tipped off.'

Jack shrugged. 'That's quite possible. Half my

lads bet. I wish they didn't but it's a fact of life.'

'Mr Lucas, the rumours are that Mr Burns had fixed the race and he knew that the horse,' she referred to her notes, 'Pipsqueak, was going to win but he didn't pass the information on to Mr Parkin.'

'That's not possible, officer. There's no certain winners in racing though there's never any shortage of people thinking the opposite.'

'So you don't think Burns was fixing races?'

He had no intention of lying to her but it wouldn't be right to sully the dead man's reputation. After all, he had no proof Andy had been behaving dishonestly.

'Andy Burns wasn't fixing anything, officer. His job was here in the yard. He didn't even travel to meetings. We had Pipsqueak thoroughly checked out after his races and he came up clean – no drugs, nothing. I've been in this game for fifty years and I can't tell you which horse is going to win for certain and Andy Burns couldn't either.'

She made no immediate response to this speech, just regarded him thoughtfully with those penetrating brown eyes. He concluded she didn't miss much.

'Do you mind if I have a word with other members of your staff while I'm here?'

'I'll introduce you to the lad who does Andy's old job, will that do?'

Fergus couldn't say anything more damaging than had already been said.

He stood up, hoping she'd take the hint, but she remained seated with her notebook open on the desk.

'Can I trouble you for one more thing?' she said. 'Mr Parkin's address.'

Jack's heart sank. God knows what Joe would tell her but he didn't imagine it would be flattering to Andy or himself.

He located the information in his battered old filing cabinet and scribbled it on a piece of paper.

'We didn't part on the best of terms,' he said as he handed it over. 'Don't believe everything he comes up with, eh?'

He regretted saying it and, anyway, it was unnecessary. He could tell that his visitor was only interested in drawing her own conclusions.

Martin was pleased with himself. He'd completed a run around the streets near his flat, moving as fluidly as normal. It was funny how hurting your arm could affect an activity that depended on your legs. His arm still felt a bit stiff and sore but at least he could run now without holding it clenched against his side. Provided he ducked challenges from the most aggressive of his pupils – and there were some strong players who relished taking him on – and didn't hit too hard, he should be OK for Monday.

He rounded the corner into his street and came to an abrupt halt. A blue Clio was parked opposite his flat.

The sight of it set his heart racing. He peered at the number plate, afraid to believe it was really Harriet's. But that was her registration, he was certain.

He'd come across an article in the local paper soon after he'd got back from Spain, about Jasper the miracle dog who had survived the fall off a cliff which had killed his owner, head lad at Beach Head yard, Andy Burns. He'd taken himself off to chat to old Emily downstairs and see if she knew anything about it – which she did. The accident had been on top of the local news for a couple of days after he'd left for Spain. What's more, she'd dug out newspapers from the week before so he could read up on events.

Poor old Andy – what a terrible way to go.

And poor Harriet.

He'd wondered whether he should get in touch and offer his condolences but decided against it. Given the way she had rejected him in the park that day, as if he were a lightweight who hadn't earned his place in her life, it was for her to take the next step.

And now here she was, parked opposite his flat.

Should he go straight past? Pretend he hadn't noticed her car?

He didn't want to do that, but if he stopped by the car he'd never know if she was intending to come to him of her own free will.

Then his dilemma was resolved.

* * *

Harriet had arrived at the salon early and thrown herself into a busy Saturday morning's work. Despite the lack of sleep, she did not feel tired, or even hungover. She must be operating on pure adrenaline.

Just after nine, she fielded the first call from Zoe who wanted to know how she was.

'Oh fine.' It wasn't that much of an effort to sound breezy. 'There's nothing like a good night's sleep.' She wasn't used to lying to her sister. It didn't feel right.

'Pat and I have had a great idea. Why don't you come with us to Bristol on Sunday?'

Harriet froze. The thought of going on a jolly threesome which included Pat made her feel sick.

'I don't think so, Zoe. That's your big day out. You don't want me along.'

Those words were a mistake. Zoe launched into a speech about how much they both desired her company and how good for her it would be to get out for the day, and so on.

In the end, Harriet became fed up. 'Got to go, Zoe, there's a client waiting. Look, it's kind of you to ask me on Sunday but count me out, OK?' She finished the call and turned off the phone.

Later, when she turned it back on, she saw that Zoe had phoned again and sent two texts. There was another missed call – from Pat.

What did he want to say to her this morning?

'Sorry about last night. It was just a joke – Andy doesn't owe me any money at all.' No chance. More likely he was aiming to disarm her by being nice, hence this invitation to go to Bristol with them. Zoe had as good as said so – 'It's as much Pat's idea as mine.' Well, the pair of them were out of luck.

The pair of them – that was the problem. It would be hard to cold-shoulder Pat without alienating Zoe, and Harriet needed Zoe. If she didn't have her sister, who could she rely on?

She'd pondered the question the whole morning at work. She needed somebody to talk to, and her mind kept turning to one person – which was why she was now sitting outside Martin's house.

According to the girl on the gym reception, Martin was due back at work on Monday. There was a good chance, then, that he'd returned from Spain.

She'd decided to go and find out. Get up off her backside and take action. The idea of returning home and allowing Zoe and Pat to take over her life was repugnant to her. Even if Martin didn't want to see her – and who could blame him after the way she'd treated him? – he ought to be told about Andy's death. Maybe she could also build a bridge to avoid any embarrassment when they bumped into each other at the centre.

Harriet used to think it wasn't possible to become friends with former lovers – she never had – but she was no longer so certain. On reflection, it was an immature point of view. She'd grown up a bit recently. Martin could be her friend, untainted by the horse-racing world of Zoe and Pat, able to give her impartial advice on how she should live this lonely new life of hers.

She opened the car door. Better get this over with before she lost her nerve.

She locked the car and rushed up the path to Martin's door. She pressed the top bell and heard it ring. Then she waited, her heart pumping.

Maybe this was a terrible mistake. There was still time to run away.

'Looking for me?'

The familiar voice was directly behind her. She turned and there he was, standing over her, looking just as she always pictured him – blond, athletic, golden.

'I'm sorry, Martin. You can tell me to go if you want.'

God, that sounded so weak but that's how she felt these days. Would he be angry with her? His mouth was smiling but his eyes were not.

'I just came to tell you,' she continued. 'Not that it affects anything between us but because maybe you don't know—'

He stopped her by placing a hand on her arm, above her elbow. The touch of his flesh on hers dried the words in her throat.

'I read about Andy in the paper,' he said. 'How are you doing, Harriet?'

'I'm . . .' She shook her head, trying to shake away the stinging in her eyes. 'I'm OK. Sort of.'

'I don't believe you,' he said and put his arm round her shoulder.

She buried her face in the cotton of his shirt. The smell of him was familiar and intoxicating.

Harriet never cried but now it was becoming a sodding habit.

Joe Parkin's digs were ten minutes from Beach Head yard by car, Laura reckoned, and probably a bit less to the pub on the coast. She found herself walking up a long gravel path bordered on either side by glistening green. The house was large and sprawling. A rustic timber sign in olde worlde lettering read 'Clara's Catterie – est. 1992'. The front door was opened by a woman of about her own age with cropped grey hair and a spreading figure loosely contained in a cerise jumpsuit.

Laura presented her credentials and asked for Mr Parkin.

'God knows where he is,' said the woman. 'He just buggered off.'

'He's moved out?'

'Scarpered when I was out the other week. He left me half the rent he owes me and I'm still waiting for the rest. He backed a van right up to the front door and scattered gravel all over the lawn, he drove off so fast. My neighbour saw it.'

That was interesting. She asked the woman –

Clara Curtis – if she minded answering a few questions in connection with an accident on the cliffs at Beach Head.

'No problem, love, but you'd better come in. I'm in the middle of feeding the mogs.'

They walked through the house into a back garden of considerable proportions full of wooden sheds. Through the metal grille nearest her, Laura glimpsed a large tabby shape curled up on a tartan rug. This really was a cats' home.

'How many animals do you have here?'

'Forty-four this morning and it'll be over fifty next week. We're right in the holiday season, see. People come from all over to leave their cats with me. Come back year after year.'

'And you take in lodgers as well?'

'Only one at a time. I've got a couple of rooms separate from the rest of the house. Got their own entrance so it's like a little flat. Mind you, I have more trouble with the humans staying here than the cats.'

Laura watched as she doled out dried pellets of cat food into an array of plastic bowls. This was her cue.

'Like Joe Parkin, you mean.'

'Cats don't run off owing rent, do they? Cat-owners pay fair and square because they know I look after their pets proper. Be a love and give me a hand with those trays, would you? They go bonkers if they don't get their grub on time.'

It was true that some of the cats were pacing their cages, glittering eyes fixed on the food bowls. But most of them lolled around in deep unconcern and some turned their backs in contempt as Clara opened the grille and slid food through the hatch. From Laura's observation, cats didn't do bonkers – they left that kind of behaviour to dogs.

When the feeding was over, Clara subsided onto a garden bench in the shade and motioned to the empty space beside her. Though she was anxious to get on, Laura accepted the invitation and sat.

'Can you tell me exactly when Mr Burns moved out?'

'Nearly two weeks ago. The day after you found the body of that fellow on the beach.'

Laura must have registered surprise at this statement for Clara continued, 'That's what you want to know, isn't it? I've been wondering how long it would take you lot to make the connection.'

'Why do you say that, Mrs Curtis?'

'It's Clara and I'm not Mrs, no bloody fear. Look, it's obvious. Joe hated Andy Burns after he'd got him sacked from the stables – you do know about that, don't you?'

Laura said she did.

'Then he got turned down for a job at another yard because Jack Lucas wouldn't vouch for him after what had happened.'

Laura made notes as Clara talked. Clara had chapter and verse on Joe's dispute with Andy – it seemed she'd been on reasonable terms with her lodger until his defection. Her account was useful verification of all that Laura had learned so far. But it turned out to be more than that.

'He had a black eye the morning after Andy Burns went over the cliff. Did you know that?'

No, Laura didn't. She pressed for more details

'I knocked on Joe's door to ask if he needed any laundry doing and he looked a right mess. He had a swollen eye and a nasty graze on his nose. He said he'd fallen off his bike.'

'Had he? Do you know if there was damage to the bike?'

Clara heaved herself to her feet. 'Come and look for yourself. The bike's round the back.'

'Didn't he take it with him?'

'It's not his to take, it's mine. Mind you, that wouldn't have stopped him. I reckon he couldn't fit it in the van.'

Clara led the way up the garden to the rear of the house. An old-fashioned bicycle with drop handlebars leaned against the wall. It wasn't a robust machine and, from the look of her, Laura imagined it hadn't carried Clara's bulk for some years. There was a bit of rust on the frame but the tyres looked new and the chain had been recently greased.

'It looks in good condition.'

'Joe got it up and running so he could cycle over to the yard. I should have charged him bike rent, he made that much use of it.'

'Was he riding the bike on the night of the twenty-eighth of June?'

'I imagine so. He rode over to the pub all the time. Besides, he told me he was and that he fell off it.'

Laura couldn't see any obvious damage to the machine but that didn't mean Joe wasn't telling the truth.

She looked Clara squarely in the eye. 'I don't suppose Joe left a forwarding address, did he?'

Clara snorted, as contemptuous as her cats. 'Of course not. I've got a mobile number for him but it's not working any longer.'

'So you don't know where he might have gone? Relatives? Friends?'

The big woman shook her head. 'I never knew any of them. He could be at any racing yard in the country. Or in any bookies.'

Laura reckoned she could have worked that out for herself.

She had one more question. 'You said you asked Joe if he had any laundry. Did he have?'

'Of course he did. A pile of dirty stuff like always—' She stopped abruptly, her mouth frozen half open as she realised where Laura was going. 'And I've still got it, haven't I?'

'Have you washed it?'

Clara shook her head. 'Not after he cleared off like that. I left it in a bag in the outhouse. You want it, don't you?'

Of course she did.

* * *

For the first time in an age, Harriet felt safe. Life remained uncertain, she was still adrift on a stormy sea, but she wasn't alone. She was back in Martin's bed, lying by his side and looking up at his wretched ceiling. Only now it didn't seem off-putting or seedy; the crumbling cornice and stained lampshade had the familiar shabbiness of old friends.

They hadn't rushed to bed in indecent haste though they had ended up there all the same. There'd been none of that furtive immaturity that had accompanied all her other visits to his flat. Lying here with him now felt different, as if they were aware they were building something together, making sure to lay proper foundations.

He'd offered to take her out to lunch because he didn't have much food in the place but she found the makings of a pasta meal in a cupboard and set to work. Not that she cared a fig for eating but it felt good to do something for someone else for a change.

While they ate, she picking and him devouring with an appetite, she told him what had happened to her world since their painful conversation in the park (though she made no reference to that occasion – neither of them had covered themselves in glory).

She dealt with the drama of Andy's disappear-ance, the trauma and the hassle that had followed the discovery of his body and her return to work. She didn't raise the big issues, such as what she should do with her life. Or how she was going to deal with a demand for half the money Andy had left her. Those things could keep for later.

She'd known from the moment Martin had put his arms round her on the doorstep that there would be a later.

He'd told her that the day she'd broken off with him he'd had an emergency call from Spain that his father had been taken ill. She knew as much already but he filled in the details for her. Then, when he'd got back, he'd heard the news of Andy's death and been thrown into a dilemma.

'I wanted to see you,' he said. 'Just as a friend. But I wasn't sure it would be appropriate. Maybe it was selfish, babe, but I couldn't face being rejected again.'

That made sense to her. After all, she'd told him he didn't have a place in her life and he'd respected that, even when he'd had a good excuse to seek her out.

Then he said, 'But I knew you'd come to me when the time was right.'

'You did?' She hadn't known that herself.

'It's fate.'

Was it? A fate that had ordained Andy's accident just at the point when she'd broken from Martin and decided to reinvest in her marriage. She supposed it could be so and part of her thrilled to the thought. But it was a cruel fate that robbed Andy of life to make her dreams come true. She didn't want to think about that. She only knew that she'd not been able to prevent herself returning to this flat and the handsome blond man who, in the silence that followed, had held out his hand to lead her to the bed where they now lay. There'd been no point in resisting.

Chapter Twelve

If he'd been asked to describe his personality, Pat would have come up with 'easy-going', 'happy-go-lucky', 'carefree', and other such expressions. And he guessed that most people would have gone along with that. On balance, he was about the last person prone to depression.

But as he prepared for the third race at Chepstow, Pat felt far from sunny. Everyone was entitled to have a down day and this was his. Even the prospect of the race ahead filled him with gloom. When he'd started out riding – all of ten years ago, though it seemed like a century – he'd been as starry-eyed as the next budding jockey. This would be his route to riches. And even if he never made it to the very top, he'd be doing something he loved, playing a part on the sporting stage he'd followed from the moment he'd been aware that men ráced horses for a living.

Well, today the stuff of youthful dreams seemed

like a con. Most racehorses were useless lumps and the famed camaraderie among jockeys was simply a smokescreen that barely covered each man's naked self-interest. And that, he'd concluded, was fair enough. In the trenches of the weighing room, it was every man for himself, just like it was in life. It was a foolish man who trusted his fellows with anything of importance.

But that's just what he'd done. He'd trusted Andy and the stupid sod had killed himself with no thought for the mess he'd be leaving behind. That was one of the things that was eating Pat up. He'd devised a daring way of making money out of racing and he'd played his part, and then Andy, God rest his soul, had screwed it all up.

The trouble was, to be effective, his brilliant scheme required assistance from another person, someone who knew how to work the betting exchanges. Apart from his particular problem as a jockey of collecting on bets, placing them to best advantage wasn't easy if he was riding in the race. The days when there was a gamble to be landed, Andy would sit at the computer monitoring betting sites, placing a selection of wagers in response to the market. Very often the best prices occurred just before the off, when Pat was already out on the track.

It wasn't just a question of slapping down twenty grand – no online mug would take that kind of money; you had to trickle it on gradually right up to race time so as not to frighten people off. And

Andy had been damned good at it. So good that over one hundred thousand pounds of Pat's money was about to be handed over to Harriet.

That was enough to bring any man down but the morning's phone call from his eldest brother's wife, Eileen, had set the seal on his mood. Pat had been surprised to hear from her. As a rule his brother Ronan, next to him in age, supplied the news from over the water. So he knew something must be seriously amiss when Eileen's soft lilt came down the line.

She asked conscientiously after Zoe and Harriet, neither of whom she'd met, and how he was doing on the horses, a subject of which she was ignorant. Plainly she was not ringing to trade family chit-chat but, unlike some of his brothers' women, Eileen set store by social politeness. It had to be bad news.

'It's Ronan,' she said finally.

'I've not heard from him.' Which was odd, come to think of it.

'He got arrested. The boys didn't want you to know about it.'

The boys were his brothers. The reason they wouldn't want him to know was that Ronan was meant to have left that kind of trouble behind him.

Pat had sworn with some feeling then listened to the grisly details. Ronan had been charged with handling stolen goods and was facing an uphill fight to keep himself at liberty. For the moment, however, he needed to raise bail. Eileen didn't spell out the consequences for Ronan's wife, Bernie, and her three small children if he couldn't resume work.

Pat had called Bernie, then wired the bail money – 10,000 euros, almost £7,000 – which had plunged his current account well into the red. It would be refunded eventually but, barring miracles, Ronan and Bernie were going to need more than that. Pat didn't set any store by miracles. Bernie had not bothered to protest Ronan's innocence. It looked like her husband was heading back inside.

A few weeks ago, Ronan's needs would have been less of a burden. Pat might have resented the erosion of his nest egg, but it would have been easy to instruct Andy and arrange for more money to flow to Ireland. What's more, he could have set about making up the shortfall. Without Andy to place bets, that was no longer possible.

Or was it? He had set Full Force up for a punt. Done the risky part. There had to be a way that he could take advantage. Obviously, he could phone up a couple of punters but the reason he had thought up the scam in the first place was so that he could do away with them. They were parasites in Pat's book. All punters did was leech information from people in the know and then tell every Tom, Dick or Harry so that by the time your money was down, the price had gone.

There was one thing in his favour. His bank account might be cleaned out but he had a reserve of readies because Andy made cash bets as well and slipped Pat the proceeds to keep him going. But how was he going to place the bet without exposing himself? Having been so careful up to this point, he'd be mad to start punting on his own account.

These matters ate away at Pat as he changed into his silks and weighed out. He was riding a horse for Ed Cooper. The offer had come out of the blue through his agent, though Pat suspected he had Jack to thank for it.

He walked into the paddock and hoisted a pre-race smile for the owner's benefit and listened politely to Ed's last-minute instructions – it was all for form's sake. Then, as he left the paddock he saw a familiar figure leaning on the rail. The sight wiped all other preoccupations from his mind.

Though she knew it was unreasonable of her, Zoe was irritated. After she and Pat had come up with the idea of inviting Harriet along on their Bristol trip, her sister had turned them down. Zoe was sure Harriet was just being polite but she was a hard woman to persuade. And now she'd turned her phone off and wasn't even replying to messages.

Zoe wasn't riding today. Saturday afternoon and no racing – it was a whole other source of irritation. Ginger Weaver had three rides at Sandown. He was currently seven ahead of her for the season. Not that she was counting.

But a blank afternoon need not be a wasted

afternoon. She spent it at the gym. When she arrived at the centre she'd seen that Harriet was busy, so she'd left a message with Chrissie to say she'd be back after her session. The pair of them could go over to the vets' and see how Jasper was getting on. Soon the dog would be fit enough to leave. And while they were driving over, she could have another stab at getting Harriet to agree to come to Bristol.

But when Zoe had returned after a three-star workout, Harriet had left.

'She said she was sorry she'd missed you,' said Chrissie. 'She left about half an hour ago.'

Zoe reached for her phone and called Harriet again. She was referred to voicemail and left a message – she was off to see Jasper, why didn't Harriet meet her there? Or, at any rate, call her back. She tried not to sound at all fed up.

But there was no word from Harriet while she was at the vets' and no one at the cottage when Zoe called by on her way home.

It was silly to wonder where Harriet had got to. She'd been at work a couple of hours ago so she was hardly missing. And, knowing her sister, Harriet probably just didn't want to discuss the Bristol thing.

But it bugged Zoe all the same. Maybe she was being over-protective but she'd feel a lot happier if she knew where Harriet was.

* * *

Ed Cooper seemed happy with Pat's performance on Barnstormer and Pat accepted the praise for finishing a close second. Privately, he admonished himself for mistiming his challenge. He'd left it too late to catch the winner. Ed had noticed, as any good trainer would, but had chosen to take the blame himself.

'I should have told you to go for him sooner. We'll get it right next time.'

Pat hadn't been paying that much attention to Ed's precise instructions, his mind had been elsewhere – not that he was going to say so. And Ed was going to use him again. All in all, not a bad outcome.

And it might turn out even better if he could locate a certain person, the skinny figure he'd spotted outside the parade ring before the race. He imagined he'd have to go looking for him. Though he'd never fallen out with Joe Parkin himself, there was no doubt where his loyalties had lain in the lad's dispute with Andy. But Andy was no longer among the living and that changed everything.

He caught Joe heading for the rails bookies.

'Hello there. How are you doing?'

If Joe could have avoided him he would have done. He looked a bit rough, with a scab on his nose and a purple bruise under one eye.

'Pat.' The voice was non-committal and the handshake perfunctory. The lad bristled with suspicion.

'Don't look so worried, mate. I'm not going to

take a pop at you. It looks like someone's done that already.'

'Look, Pat, I've got to get on.'

'Sure. Let's meet up later.'

Suspicion was joined by astonishment in Joe's eyes.

'What for?'

'To catch up. Come on, Joe, I'm just being friendly.'

'What do you want?'

'Look, you had a beef with Andy, not me. A lot of us miss your miserable face around the yard.' That was stretching it a bit but Pat could see that it went down well. 'If you've not got transport, why don't I give you a lift home? I'll wait for you in the car park.'

'I suppose I could. I'm staying the other side of Bath though.'

'No problem. I'll drop you.'

Pat left Joe no longer suspicious but surprised.

Harriet had never been alone in Martin's flat before. It felt strange but, at the same time, right. Although she'd only been back in his company for a matter of hours, it was clear they'd passed into a new stage of their relationship. It was goodbye to those snatched and hasty assignations when they'd be undressing as they rushed up the stairs, just to give themselves a couple more minutes in each other's arms. Such sweet intensity. Was it guilt that had made it that way?

Already she'd spent more time in these two rooms than she'd ever spent before. For the first time she'd slept by Martin's side and she'd be sleeping here tonight, it was understood. Things had moved on now that there was no Andy to make demands on her presence. She was no longer compelled to go home and play-act the dutiful wife. What a relief that was.

But Andy still cast a shadow. Her jailer might have gone but she could hardly step merrily out of prison with a new lover on her arm. Her husband had only been dead a couple of weeks. There hadn't even been a funeral.

She and Martin would have to take it easy. Fortunately, he seemed to understand without her spelling it out.

'Why don't we just hole up here for the weekend?' he'd suggested. 'I'll go out and buy food and we can stay in. Unless there's things you've got to do.'

No, there was nothing. At least, nothing she wanted to do.

The phone on the bedside table burst into life, its unfamiliar ring catching her by surprise.

She hesitated to answer but it rang on. Suppose it was Martin calling for her? Her own phone, she remembered, was switched off, as it often was these days.

'Martin's phone,' she said into the mouthpiece, as if she were some office lackey.

'Is Martin there?' said a woman's voice, middle-aged and rich in tone.

'He's just popped out. Can I take a message?'

'You can tell him his mother is wondering how he is. He hasn't rung since he left and I'm a little concerned.'

'I'll get him to call you the moment he gets back.'

'That's very kind. And you are?'

'Harriet. I'm just a friend.'

'Oh really.' The woman's voice was full of innuendo. 'I could tell there was a new girlfriend in the offing and I suppose that must be you.'

Harriet supposed it was. The thought gave her a warm and naughty glow as the woman's voice continued.

'Well, Harriet, you sound a most capable girl so look after him for me. He was in such a state when he turned up here the other week. Even though he swore he wasn't in pain I could tell that he was. His sister's just the same. Believe me, a mother knows – as I'm sure you'll discover for yourself one day.'

As she rang off Harriet congratulated herself for making a reasonable impression. It would be useful to make an ally of Martin's mother. She was obviously a perceptive woman, discerning Martin's heartbreak even at a time when the family must all have been upset.

Damn, she should have asked after Martin's father and earned even more Brownie points. Too late now.

The call reminded her to switch her phone back

on. More messages from Zoe. For God's sake, couldn't her own kid sister give her a break?

That was unfair. Zoe was only hassling her because she cared.

But she'd have to get her off her back – and kill off the Bristol invitation at the same time.

She rang Zoe, praying that she'd be switched to the answerphone. No such luck.

'Harriet, I've been trying to get hold of you.'

'There's no need to worry, I'm fine.'

'But where are you?'

'I'm round at Diane's. The girl you bumped into the other day in the gym. She's invited me for the weekend so you don't need to worry about me being on my own tomorrow. You and Pat go and have a great time.'

Zoe wasn't entirely happy, Harriet could tell, but she didn't make an issue of it. Harriet finished the call with relief. She was used to concealing her movements but she didn't like lying to her sister.

She dialled another number, one she'd only recently added to her phone book memory.

'Hi, Harriet. Great to hear from you.' Harriet had never called Diane Connor on a Saturday afternoon before but the woman sounded thrilled. 'How are things going?'

'I'm OK. I wonder if you could do me a favour.'

'Sure. Maurice is off playing sodding golf and I'm bored out of my mind. Why don't you come over?'

'That's very kind but I really can't face seeing anyone at the moment.'

'Thanks a lot.'

'I'm sorry, that came out wrong. But I just want to be left alone and I've got my sister nagging me to go off with her to Bristol tomorrow.'

'So what's the favour?'

'I was hoping that, if you bump into my sister at the gym, you could say I spent the weekend with you.'

'But Harriet, why don't you? You can come over here and please yourself, Maurice and I won't bother you. You can sit all day by the pool with a gin and tonic, if you like.'

Oh God, this wasn't what she wanted. Diane sounded genuinely concerned.

'That sounds very tempting but in fact I do have plans.'

'What are you up to?'

'I'd rather not say.'

'How mysterious. You can tell me, surely. If you're asking me to back you up.'

The nosy cow – but she needed her help. 'It's just that I have to spend time with another friend and it's a bit awkward with Zoe.'

'OK then. I'll perjure myself for you.'

Relief washed over Harriet. 'Thanks, Diane. You're a pal.'

'Just tell me, is this friend male or female?'

Harriet didn't reply. She just muttered a quick

goodbye and put the phone down as Martin came through the door, plastic bags hanging from his good hand.

'Who were you talking to?' he asked.

'Zoe. I was just wishing her a good day out tomorrow.'

He grinned as he began to stow food from the deli in the fridge. 'I guarantee we're going to have a good day in.'

As she watched him unpack, Harriet reflected that she had spoken to three people in the last ten minutes and lied to every one.

'Your mother rang earlier. You've got to call her back.'

At least that was the truth.

'I've got to be honest and I know you were his friend, but I couldn't stick Andy Burns.'

Pat had barely negotiated his way onto the road outside the racecourse when Joe had launched into a speech about Andy. It was obviously prepared. Pat listened in silence, happy to let his passenger get it off his chest.

'That bloke went around the yard with a broom up his arse. What got me was his sheer hypocrisy. If you moved a step out of line he'd scream blue murder but he was on the fiddle himself. I knew it and I told Jack Lucas but I couldn't prove it.' Joe was getting excited, deviating from his script no doubt, and he halted in mid-flow. 'The thing is, whatever I thought about him, I get no pleasure out of him being dead. He was no mate of mine but it was terrible what happened to him.'

There was no arguing with that. Pat gave Joe points for not skating over his antipathy to Andy and he believed what Joe had said about his death. God knows, there had been plenty of blokes Pat would have liked to have thumped but it didn't mean he wanted them six foot under.

He bided his time on the journey back, letting Joe whinge on about being out of work. He was tapping up everyone he could but having no luck. Did Pat know anyone who was looking for staff? He'd take anything, he was so skint.

That was the best opening Pat was going to get.

'You could always help me out.'

'Oh yes?' Joe tried to sound casual but Pat wasn't fooled.

'Would you be interested in investing some money for me?'

'I might.'

Of course he might.

'There's a horse I fancy running on Monday.'

Joe thought for a moment. 'And you're looking for someone to place a bet?'

Pat didn't need to spell it out. Joe was a lad who'd been in this position before.

There was no one else Pat could turn to, not at short notice at any rate. He'd thought it through and Joe fitted the bill. He'd know how to spread a few grand around without attracting attention. The only question was, could he trust him? Pat thought he could and, in any case, what alternative did he have? He'd put a lot of work into setting up Full Force and he was damned if he was going to let it go to waste.

More to the point, his brother and his wife were relying on him.

Joe was sniggering away to himself.

'What's so funny?'

'You. I thought it was Andy pulling a stroke with Jack's horses but it was you all the time, wasn't it?'

'Don't be daft. I just know this horse has come right.'

Joe continued to snigger, plainly unconvinced. 'And when you had hunches before, did Andy get the money on for you?'

Pat didn't argue, what was the point?

'Bloody hell,' Joe breathed softly. 'So now I'm in Andy's shoes.'

Pat said nothing. The irony wasn't lost on him either.

DC Laura Hammond had become involved in Andy Burns' death by virtue of being the only CID officer on late on the night in question. From the first it had looked like a tragic accident, the section of cliff from which he'd fallen being notoriously unstable. The local council had done their best with warning notices and railings along sections of the path but, basically, you had to watch your step while walking near the edge. It was common sense, after all.

PC Paul Copper had given her a call from the scene, for form's sake, and she'd attended in the same spirit. Though due processes had to be set in train – an autopsy and an inquest with its attendant inquiries – Mr Burns' unfortunate death had not looked suspicious. DCI Dick Lane, with whom she had discussed the matter, had effectively told her to get on with it by herself because the department was up to its eyeballs.

But now matters had taken a different turn.

'Bloody hell, Laura,' Lane had said when she reported her suspicions about Joe Parkin. 'Are you sure you're not getting carried away?'

'If Andy was in a fight on the cliff top it might explain how he came to fall.'

'I thought you told me he'd been drinking.'

'He'd had a bit but he knew the path well, he was up there every day of his life.'

'He got careless. Booze can make you over-confident – look what happens at our Christmas party.' Dick Lane thought he was a bit of a wag. 'Anyhow, all this is entirely circumstantial. You've got pub gossips and a landlady with an axe to grind. I'll take it more seriously when there's a witnesses to this punch-up and a statement from Mr Parkin.'

Laura was well aware of these holes in her case

and had been doing her best to plug them when time allowed. She'd gone back over the statements that had been obtained from the pub regulars and local dog walkers. Though Parkin's animosity to the dead man was well attested, nobody had seen them even talk to one another, let alone get into a fight.

As for the search for Joe Parkin, as his landlady had said, his mobile number was no longer working. He'd probably changed it. Laura thought her best bet was to find him through the racing fraternity and she'd spent a few hours on the phone to training yards and other likely horsey establishments throughout the county – so far, without success. She'd also gone back to Jack Lucas's yard and talked to more of the lads. None of them appeared to have been that close to him though she'd learned he had a sister near Bath. She could enlist the help of the local papers, of course, but she'd rather track the man down without alarming him. The last thing she needed was for him to discover he was wanted and to scarper out of her reach.

She recounted all this to David as they drove to the coast. It was unprofessional of her, probably, but she didn't care. He made a more sympathetic audience than DCI Lane.

Anyway, David was eager to hear of her progress and she was happy to please him. In a funny way this incident was helping to glue them together. He'd been only too happy to accompany her back to Beach Head this evening.

The pair of them laced on their walking boots in the pub car park. David had come round to the idea of a brisk walk to justify the liquid intake and even refrained from moaning till he was halfway up the steep cliff steps.

The view, Laura had decided, was of the kind that never let you down. Only in a swirling mist, she supposed, would it be less than captivating. Tonight the sky was lagged with grey cotton wool but the sea still heaved on the rocks beneath, moody and threatening. Even at the height of summer this spot was touched with menace. Just ask Andy Burns – if only I could, she thought.

'I'm pinning my hopes on forensics,' she told David. She'd sent Joe Parkin's laundry to the lab for testing, together with the clothes Andy Burns had been wearing the night he died. That had entailed a visit to his widow, for his personal effects had already been given back to her.

'I bet that was tough,' said David. 'It must be bad enough having your loved one's things returned without some copper pitching up and asking for them back.'

'It was a mistake. They shouldn't have been handed over in the first place.'

Not that it had appeared to bother Harriet Burns. She'd simply gone upstairs and retrieved a plastic bag. Laura could see the clothes were in the same condition in which they'd been given back – which was to the good from Laura's point of view.

'I promise they'll be returned to you,' Laura had said.

'Don't bother. I've kept his wallet and his watch.'

The widow struck Laura as a cold fish but people had different ways of coping with grief.

After their walk, Laura left David to get the drinks in at the Coach and Horses and strode fifty yards up the lane to the first cottage in the row. She'd talked to the occupant, a lady of some seniority, during the house-to-house inquiries and this second visit was the real purpose of the evening's outing.

Mrs Perceval had been walking her trio of short-haired terriers on the night in question. 'I took the boys across the fields to the river,' she'd said. 'I don't like to go on the cliffs once it starts to get dark. I've got three dogs to look out for and I'm not as sharp-eyed as I once was – look what happened to that poor man.' She'd gone on to complain about a cyclist who had nearly run her over. It hadn't seemed significant at the time.

The old lady was delighted to see the police-woman standing on her doorstep. It made a change.

Laura declined the offer of a cup of tea. 'I've just got a couple more questions, Mrs Perceval. What time did you see the cyclist on the evening of the accident?'

'Between about half past nine and a quarter to ten. It was quite dark really and he was travelling up the lane just as we were getting to the front gate.'

'Can you describe the person on the bike?'

'Not very well because he came at us – whoosh! – out of the gloom. It took all four of us by surprise.'

'But it was a man.'

'Oh yes. A tall thin man with one of those T-shirts with slogans on. I'm sorry but I couldn't read it. And he wasn't wearing a helmet – isn't that against the Highway Code? He had blood on his face. I really think you ought to track him down, don't you?'

Laura did indeed, though for different reasons. In point of fact she could have told her new witness that the slogan on the rider's T-shirt read 'Glastonbury Festival 2005' – that's if the cyclist was wearing the same shirt as she'd retrieved from Clara Curtis's laundry.

Not that she was jumping to conclusions or anything.

Diane thought it was a pity Harriet hadn't accepted her invitation to come over for the weekend. It was all very well being married to a successful man who was generous with everything except his time. Right now Maurice was on the golf course, a more tedious location Diane could not imagine, and she craved some company. Harriet's would have been ideal.

Some of Diane's friends would have been a bit snotty about her being pally with a hairdresser. But those women had always had comfortable homes and men with six-figure salaries paying for their indulgences. They took their fathers and husbands for granted and looked down on women who'd started from scratch.

Diane had started from scratch, picked out on an Essex street by a photographer looking for fresh teenage faces. If she hadn't gone into modelling she'd have trained as a beauty consultant – or a hairdresser. She and Harriet had a lot in common. More than she did with the wives of Maurice's golfing cronies, that was certain.

So who was this mysterious friend Harriet was seeing today? Diane's antennae were bristling with suspicion. Obviously it was a man, otherwise Harriet would have said so. So what man would Harriet's innocent little sister Zoe disapprove of?

There was one obvious candidate.

Diane picked her car keys off the hall table and headed for the door. Harriet had involved her in this subterfuge so she was entitled to confirm her suspicions.

It was better than dying of boredom.

Like most long-awaited occasions, Zoe's romantic day out in Bristol with Pat did not live up to expectations. Even the summer splendour of the downs above the suspension bridge and the Georgian charm of Clifton could not lift the gloom that enveloped her companion. It was rare for Pat to go all moody on her, so why did he have to pick one of their few holiday afternoons in the long Flat-racing season?

To be fair, she could guess why he was out of sorts. He was missing Andy. She felt a pang of jealousy but ignored it. Pat and Andy used to spend many hours in each other's company. It was only natural that Andy would leave a hole in Pat's life.

And then there was the drama with his family in Ireland. She'd not got to the bottom of it because he refused to give her any details. It was the one area of Pat's life that he guarded from her and she guessed he was somehow ashamed of his background. But there'd been several phone calls back and forth over the past few days and she knew there were problems. While she was doing some clearing up, she'd discovered a sheet of paper scrawled with figures and phone numbers. She guessed that the calls from Ireland were about money and Pat had been calculating how to come up with it.

She'd made the mistake that morning of offering to help.

'I've got some savings,' she'd said to him after he'd finished a call with one of his brothers. 'It's not a lot but I could lend it to you. Would five hundred pounds be any good?'

He'd fixed her with an unfriendly stare. 'Thank you, Zoe, but I'd rather you minded your own business.' It was unlike him to be rude and his words had stung.

Now, she tried again. One subject may be off limits but maybe not the other.

'You really miss Andy, don't you, Pat?'

He sighed heavily. 'Drop it, Zoe. Andy's not coming back so there's no point in going on about him. Let the poor bloke rest in peace.'

Zoe tried to swallow her irritation at this typical male response. Got an emotional problem? Shove it in a cupboard in your head and lock the door. Then pray your skeletons never get loose. Pat could behave like a real stereotype sometimes.

She slipped her hand into his as they strolled across the bridge and he squeezed her fingers, so that was OK. Maybe it wasn't the right time for him to talk about Andy. Finding the body of your best friend must take some getting over. It was probably a bit glib of her to expect him to offer up his feelings on a plate.

They were returning back across the bridge and Zoe's mind turned to the mundane. Her needs were simpler than those of her boyfriend.

'Let's find somewhere to eat,' she said. 'I could murder a cream cake.'

Pat looked at her without expression. 'OK.'

Here was a case in point – he'd agreed to her suggestion without endorsing it. And was that a trace of scorn in his voice? If so, she knew why. She shouldn't have said that about wanting the cake because he couldn't, he was riding tomorrow and had to watch his weight. She had a ride too but she could pretty much eat what she liked.

Well, too bad. She wasn't going to start monitoring feelings that were expressed in all innocence.

So far on this outing she'd told Pat exactly how she felt about Harriet's defection to her new friend Diane (miffed and pleased in equal measure), she'd aired her frustration about Ginger Weaver landing two winners at Sandown the day before, and she'd grumbled about the weight-training regime she'd started at the gym (her shoulders *ached*). And Pat had said precious little in return, just glowered in the sunshine and made her feel like it – whatever *it* was – was all her fault.

What the hell. Maybe she'd have two cream cakes.

Diane was excited. If she'd had someone else to play with on a Sunday afternoon she wouldn't have bothered snooping around like this. But Maurice and Harriet had let her down and she had nothing better to do.

She had a little trouble finding Martin's street – on the occasions she'd visited before, she'd been following Martin's whispered directions and her mind had been on other things. This was it, though, she recognised the scruffy newsagent on the corner.

She also recognised the navy blue Clio parked halfway along the road – at least, she thought she did. She'd only seen Harriet's car on one occasion, the night the pair of them had shared a bottle and she'd given Harriet flowers. Given the state she'd been in, she could easily have been mistaken.

But there it was. Outside number fifteen which,

now she thought about it, was Martin's address. She parked next to it and got out to have a closer look. Diane would have expected a practised cheater like Harriet to take a few more precautions. She could at least have parked in the next street.

Then Diane remembered that Harriet had no cause for subterfuge. With her husband dead, she wouldn't be cheating at all.

'What the hell do you think you're doing?'

The voice made her jump. Martin was standing right behind her.

'Martin, hi.' She smiled defiantly – she didn't see why she should be made to feel guilty.

'Why are you nosing around here?' His eyes were like small blue chips of ice and his voice was cold. 'Are you spying on me?'

'Don't be daft. I was passing and saw Harriet's car. Is she here?'

'No.'

'But this is her car.'

'Don't be pathetic, Diane. You've come here because of me but I'm not interested. Got that?'

The arrogance of him, to make out that she was after him like that. And she didn't believe him about the car.

'OK.' She smiled lazily. Then, just to irritate him, added, 'Are you still entertaining your women in that crappy little bed? Harriet deserves better than that after all she's been through.'

A big hand closed round her forearm.

'Let go of me,' she hissed and tried to pull free.

'In a moment,' he said. 'Listen to me first.'

Diane looked around. The street had been busy just a moment ago but now it was empty. His fingers round her arm were like a band of steel.

'Well?' she said.

'I want you to stop poking your nose in where it does not belong. From now on, you don't know me or Harriet. Find yourself another hairdresser. Got that?'

She was tempted to argue. He couldn't just order her out of another person's life, it was outrageous. But, looking into those cold blue eyes, she had no desire to debate the point.

'Have you finished?' she said.

'Sure.' He relaxed his grip and flashed his trademark smile, regular white teeth and dimples. She'd once thought it rather charming.

Still smiling, he twisted her arm.

The pain lanced through her body like a lick of fire and she yelped out loud; she couldn't help herself.

'Get the picture, Diane?' he murmured as he let her go.

As she walked back to her car she resisted the urge to run.

Chapter Thirteen

Pat hadn't been back to Bath racecourse since riding Pipsqueak. That had been a good day's work though he was the only person alive who was aware of it. Sometimes success had to look like failure to succeed. The thought amused him.

He was feeling in better cheer today. And so he should be, he told himself. Full Force was in tip-top shape, just like he'd been for his last two outings. But this time Pat was going to allow him to bring home the bacon. He said as much to the owner in the parade ring.

'He's going to do you proud today, Mr Daniels, I promise you.'

Daniels had looked at him wearily, as if he'd heard such sentiments before and been disappointed – which he had and Pat had been the cause of his disappointment. Well, he'd make it up to the fellow today. It would be nice to put a smile on the man's face for once; he always looked such a sad sack.

By his side, Jack wasn't looking any more cheerful. The old boy had taken Andy's death hard. As had they all.

He'd had a crisis of confidence about Joe over the weekend. Could he really trust him not to waltz off into the sunset with his cash?

In the end, he'd concluded he didn't have all that much to lose. He'd never considered Joe a dishonest lad, just a bit of a toerag and too keen to be your pal – that was always off-putting.

Pat had counted up his available cash, which came to around £3,500, and kept back a grand because he didn't like to be without any money at all. Would Joe dare walk off with £2,500? He couldn't be certain.

In any case, the way Pat had put it to Joe in the car on the way here – he'd given him a lift to the course – the pair of them stood to make much more in the long run. He'd promised Joe ten per cent of whatever they won. Full Force was quoted at 12–1 in that morning's *Racing Beacon* and, if all went well, this could be the start of a profitable relationship.

'Full Force in the fifth,' he'd told Joe.

'I reckon I could have worked that out for myself.'

Pat had considered that but he had four rides on the card and a couple of them would have looked like possible candidates. Besides, he'd just provided Joe with the money to gamble.

He left the paddock and set Full Force off down the course, one of fourteen runners in a five-furlong handicap. He was confident Joe was out there doing his stuff.

All he had to do now was win.

Laura thought that DCI Lane was looking a bit rough. His big square handsome face was baggy under the eyes and his shirt had the appearance of having been slept in. Rumour had it that his marriage was a bit of a battleground and it certainly looked like a few blows had been landed over the weekend. Laura felt sorry for him. She'd been there.

So she forgave the abruptness in his tone when he barked, 'Just spit it out – I'm running late.'

'It's only an update on Burns. We've got two witness statements from drinkers in the pub that Joe Parkin left at around nine. He said he was going for a walk to clear his head and was seen joining the track that led to the coast path, the way Andy would have gone.'

Lane was on his feet now, collecting papers from the chaos on his desk. He was clearly a man in transit to a more important location.

'Go on,' he said. 'I'm listening.'

'I've got another witness who saw a man on a bicycle travelling up the road away from the pub at about half past nine. He was wearing a T-shirt similar to that worn by Parkin that night.'

Lane stopped hunting through his documents for a second. 'Who's this witness?'

'Mrs Perceval, a lady of seventy-nine. She was walking her dogs inland and saw the cyclist just as she got home. She lives about fifty yards along from the pub.'

'Why didn't you mention this before?'

'It didn't seem significant before. At the time we were just looking for witnesses to an accident.'

'Huh. An old bird pushing eighty with a dodgy memory. Doesn't sound very reliable.'

'Actually, I think she'd come over very well on the stand.'

Lane barked a mirthless laugh. 'Don't get ahead of yourself, darling. What's Joe Parkin got to say about all this?'

'We're still looking for him.'

Lane had now gathered all his papers and yanked the office door open with his free hand. He spoke wearily.

'Come back when you've found him, Laura. And make it this side of Christmas, eh?'

Full Force was drawn on the stand side, on the farthest right of the runners. Considering the left-hand kink to the course, this was the least advant-ageous draw and Pat was eager to get off to a flyer. Unfortunately, the grey horse was disturbed by the animal beside him, who was reluctant to load and had to be manhandled into the starting gates. Pat was amused to see that the rider swearing at his obstinate mount was Ginger Weaver. He was less amused when a distracted Full Force was slow to react when the gate sprang open, leaving them last as the rest of the runners thundered off down the course.

Pat had aimed to shoot to the front and get far enough ahead in the opening furlong to cross to the far rail as they descended to the left-hand turn. If he timed it right he'd have been in prime position for the uphill gallop to the stands.

But that plan had gone out of the window and he had to work hard to stay in touch with the rest of the field. Full Force was taking his time to find his feet and Pat was impatient with him. He had to yank hard on the reins to bear left at the bend and use his stick even at this stage of the race.

As they rounded the curve and started up the incline to the finishing post, Full Force was at last coming to terms with the race. The pair of them began to work their way through the field, picking off their rivals one by one. Pat just hoped they hadn't lost too much time at the start. A five-furlong sprint like this was over in a minute.

Not that it would matter much to anyone apart from himself and Joe if they failed to win the race. After recent outings, neither Jack Lucas nor Mr Daniels would have expected anything else.

They were at the stage where, on another day, Full Force would have found the going too tough.

But today wasn't one of those days. On this occasion, the sleek grey horse had licence to fly.

As they entered the last furlong, there was only one animal ahead of them, Masterpiece, Ginger Weaver's horse. Pat went for his stick and felt Full Force stretch under him. They surged alongside but Ginger's horse fought back, finding something extra under his young jockey.

The pair of them seemed glued together for the last 150 yards, with Masterpiece half a length in the lead.

Visions of failure flashed through Pat's head. He envisaged the look of chagrin on Zoe's face if he failed to beat Ginger, the weary acceptance of defeat on Laurence Daniels', the resignation in his brother Ronan's voice when he told him he had no money left to send him.

There was a cry from his left, a shout of anguish, and Pat saw Ginger's whip flip out of his grasp. For a split second, Masterpiece faltered and in that moment Full Force was past him.

A photo was called for but Pat wasn't worried. He'd won by a short head.

Pat couldn't remember when he'd last been so pleased at landing a victory. At a stroke he'd put himself back in Zoe's good books by stopping her rival going further ahead in the race for champion apprentice. He'd finally put a smile on the face of the horse's owner. And he'd be able to keep up his end of the silent bargain he'd made with his brother. All in all, it was most satisfying.

When a local reporter asked how he felt about the win, Pat took the opportunity to dedicate it to Andy. It seemed appropriate.

Jack had never seen Laurence Daniels so animated.

'I don't believe it,' the owner exclaimed. 'We bloody won!'

'Not before time, Laurence. You deserve it.'

'Not me. Us. We. We're a team.' Daniels was twitching with excitement as he fumbled for his phone. 'Wait till I tell my wife. She thinks I'm bad luck, you know. Whenever I go to see one of my horses run, they always get beaten. I tell you, I thought I was a goner when they called a photo. I've never won one of those. I don't know how to thank you, Jack.'

Jack tried not to listen as Daniels jabbered down the phone to his wife. He couldn't believe what he'd just seen either. Not because of the horse's fine performance, but because of what it told him.

The deception that had plagued his yard all winter was still being worked. Andy's death had changed nothing. And the genuine pleasure he felt at finally providing Laurence Daniels with a victory was just the silver lining to a large black cloud.

He kept a smile on his face for his owner's sake,

though he refused all offers to join Daniels and his wife for a celebratory dinner. Celebrating was the last thing on his mind as he drove home, back to his empty house.

It was time he faced up to the truth – he was past it. He could no longer police his yard effectively, people were taking advantage of him and he no longer trusted his own judgement.

How could he have suspected Andy Burns, a man who'd worked by his side for years and whom he'd envisaged running Beach Head on his retirement? Today's result was proof that Andy had not been responsible for fixing his horses. Yet Andy had died thinking that he suspected him of being a cheat and a crook on the strength of a few successful bets.

Jack didn't bother with supper, just fixed himself a drink and took his habitual seat on the bench outside. Tonight even the tranquillity of the garden and the antics of the birds did not soothe his spirit. He'd made a decision.

This would be his last season. A younger man would root out the bad apple at his yard but he no longer had the spirit for the fight. Time to pack in the training life for good.

'You don't like to make it look easy, do you?' Joe complained to Pat as he took a seat in the jockey's car.

Pat shrugged. He might have just got out of jail but he wasn't going to admit it.

Joe shook his head in grudging admiration. 'I always reckoned you were a cool bugger. I nearly had a heart attack while I was waiting for the photo.'

'So how much did we make then?' Pat had had enough of discussing the race – what was the point?

While Pat negotiated the traffic, Joe spent a few minutes scribbling on a scrap of paper, calculating the bets he'd placed. It was hard for Pat to keep his attention on the road when Joe started pulling banknotes from his pockets. Lots of banknotes.

Eventually his passenger said, 'I've got twenty-eight thousand five hundred pounds here. That includes the two and a half you gave me to put on.'

So the gamble had paid off. Not on the scale of the Pipsqueak touch maybe, but the way things had turned out, who was to say this wasn't better? A bird in the hand and all that. At least a man knew where he stood when he had a pocket – several pockets – full of used banknotes. And this money wouldn't be finding its way into the hands of Harriet Burns.

Pat parked around the corner from Joe's place which, as Pat had learned on the journey, was really Joe's sister's place; he was staying with his sister and her husband while he sorted out new accommodation.

Pat divvied up the cash and passed Joe his share. He had done a good job and, with luck, they'd be teaming up again. Maybe this was a better way to operate. Keep the wagers down and deal in cash only. It was certainly simpler.

'Thanks, mate,' Joe said as he squirrelled the notes away. 'I can't say I was thrilled to see you the other day. I reckoned you were after something but I'm bloody glad you were.'

They shook hands. As Joe reached for the door handle, Pat said, 'So what did happen to your face?' So far Joe had been reluctant to say.

Joe looked uncomfortable. 'I fell off a bike. Had a bit too much to drink. You know.'

Pat couldn't say he did.

'I'd forget bikes if I were you. You can afford to get yourself a car now.'

Joe brightened. 'I suppose I can.'

As Pat drove away he chuckled to himself. Fancy Joe falling off a bike at his age. That's something Andy would never have done.

It felt strange driving back to the cottage. Harriet had spent Saturday and Sunday nights at Martin's and the temptation to drive round to his place after work was strong. But they'd agreed it wouldn't look good for them to start living together so soon. Although – and the thought shimmered on the edge of her thoughts like a welcoming light – they would be together once this was all over. They'd decided last night, while they were lying together spoon fashion, her with her back nestling against his chest and him with his arms wrapped round her – well, one arm anyway. He tried to keep the one he'd gashed on barbed wire out of the way.

'Bring some of your things with you next time,' he'd said. 'Leave some clothes here.'

'You've got no room. Your wardrobe's bursting already.'

'I'll chuck some stuff out. I don't need much.'

'You could have fooled me.' His breath was hot on her cheek.

'Oh, I need a lot of you. I mean I don't need things that don't matter.'

They lay together in silence. She knew that he, like her, was savouring the magic of the moment. The knowledge that no clock was counting down the minutes of their time. She didn't have to get up and go to some other place and some other man. It was terrible of her but she couldn't deny the exhilaration of being free from Andy. Free to give herself wholeheartedly to Martin.

'I love you,' he whispered.

She kept her response trapped in her throat. It was too soon to let the words escape her lips but they were there in her head and she could not unthink them. She'd tell him she loved him too when the funeral and the inquest were over. When they were able to live together openly without causing offence.

'It won't be long,' he said, reading her thoughts. 'We can wait.'

Now, in the musty little cottage where she'd lived

so many unhappy moments with Andy, she wasn't sure she could wait.

Although she'd nipped back the day before for a change of clothes, it seemed as if she'd been away an age. The milk in the fridge smelt fishy and the bread in the bin was spotted with mould. She found a cold can of Diet Coke and picked through the pile of post, looking for anything of significance in the junk. Most of it was addressed to Andy and it dawned on her that this was another way in which he would haunt her. As long as she remained here, a never-ending stream of catalogues addressed to Andrew Burns would pour through the letterbox.

Among the pile was a letter from Charles Butler, her solicitor, saying that the coroner had agreed to issue 'an interim certificate of fact of death' so that the firm could proceed in the administration of Andy's estate. That was progress, at any rate. The sooner they started, the sooner it would be over and she could begin life as an independent woman.

She had to keep this to herself, however – well, she might tell one person. But that person could not be her sister. She wasn't sure yet how to deal with Pat's demand for money but it seemed logical to play for time. As far as he knew, it would be ages before Andy's estate was settled and that suited her fine.

It was hard but she had to face facts. She couldn't afford to tell Zoe anything she didn't want Pat to know about. With things as they were, there was plenty she'd have to keep secret from her sister.

Thank God for Martin. It might not be prudent for her to spend all her time with him just yet but no one was monitoring her calls any more. She reached for the phone.

Finally Laura got the breakthrough she'd been looking for – a call from Clara Curtis.

'I thought you'd like to know that I've just had a visit from Joe Parkin.'

Really?

'I've got to admit that some of the things I said about him were wrong. He paid me the rest of the cash he owed me and said he was sorry for running off the way he did.'

'Did he say why he went?'

'Not really. He said he'd been bashed up in his bicycle accident and his sister had been looking after him. But I'd have looked after him. It's only common decency, isn't it? Anyhow, I thought you ought to know he's not a bad lad after all. And I wouldn't mind having his laundry back.'

'Did you tell him you'd given it to the police?'

'Oh no. I didn't want him to think I'd been going behind his back. I said I must have chucked it out but I could always find it again, couldn't I?'

Laura ignored the question. The woman was on her own planet in some respects.

'Has Joe got a car?'

'Not yet. He said he was looking out for one.'

'How did he travel to your place then?'

'His brother-in-law brought him in his van.'

'Can you describe the van?'

Since Joe was staying with his sister, if Laura could trace the brother-in-law's vehicle then she'd as good as have Joe in her grasp.

'I didn't get the registration if that's what you mean.'

'Can you tell me the make or the colour?'

'White, apart from the lettering – that's red.'

'What lettering?'

'On the side. It says Brodie's Furniture Repairs. That's his brother-in-law, Pete.'

It had taken a while but they'd got there in the end.

Then to cap it all, Laura received another call which sent her scurrying off to find DCI Lane. She didn't care how harassed he was or how crumpled, he'd bloody well pay attention to her now. And he did.

It was one of the good days for a change.

Diane sat at the desk in the study and contemplated her arm – the one Martin had held the day before in a grip she could not break. She could see a faint pink bracelet of raised flesh. The lance of pain that had exploded through her nerves was fresh in her mind, as was the icy gaze that had accompanied it.

To think she'd lain naked in that man's arms and entrusted herself to him in the most fundamental way a woman could. How repulsive that seemed now.

She knew she'd been right about Harriet's car. She'd recognised the denim jacket on the back seat of the Clio. Harriet had bought it on a trip to Exeter a few months back.

Diane wasn't judgemental about other people's relationships. But if she were in Harriet's shoes, she hoped she would keep her lover at arm's length for longer than a fortnight. Though who could say how anyone might react in those terrible circumstances?

One thing was plain, from the way Harriet had spoken about Martin and how even now she couldn't stay away from him, she must be besotted. So deeply captivated by him that she couldn't help herself.

Diane might not judge Harriet, but others would be only too quick to do so. It didn't look good, taking up with Martin again so soon. No wonder Harriet didn't want her sister to find out.

Perhaps she should tell her? No, that would be a betrayal of Harriet's trust and Harriet hadn't monstered her in the street like her boyfriend. Though she'd put on a brave face, Diane had been scared. She still was. If she never ran into Martin again she wouldn't lose any sleep.

She turned on the computer and waited

impatiently for it to boot up. Scared though she was, she was also furious. Martin thought he could treat her like dirt and get away with it. That wasn't so. Harriet ought to know exactly who she was getting into bed with.

The moment Joe saw the look on his sister's face he knew something was wrong. Rachel was five years older than him and, at times like this, she wore the same kind of anxious expression as their mum.

'There's a couple of gents here for you,' she said. 'From the police.'

Joe could see that for himself. Over her shoulder he had spotted a uniform.

'I told them I didn't have a clue when you'd be back,' Rachel added, 'but they insisted on waiting.'

Her voice contained disappointment and concern in equal measure. He could see she'd made the obvious connection between his appearance the night before loaded with cash and the sudden desire of the authorities to 'have a word'. But he knew it was more than a racing matter, otherwise the Jockey Club would be on his back, not the police.

He put as brave a face on it as he could, since turning round and running like hell would be a futile exercise. The two officers were polite enough – full of Rachel's tea and biscuits no doubt – but there was no arguing with them as they ushered him towards their car outside.

'What's this about?' he asked. Maybe there was a way he could talk himself out of it. Or perhaps they'd made a mistake.

'Sorry, sir, we're just the taxi service,' said one. 'Avon and Somerset CID want you over in Bridgwater.'

No mistake then. They'd come for him about Andy. His stomach turned over.

Poor Rachel was in for a bit of a shock.

There was no time to put her fears at ease, even if he'd known how to do that. Instead he called from the back seat of the car, 'Rache, can you sort me out a solicitor?'

She burst into tears, unable to speak, but nodded her head vigorously. He didn't tell her not to worry – there was no point.

Chapter Fourteen

There was one thing Joe could say for the solicitor his sister found for him, the fellow was keen.

The journey down to Bridgwater had taken an age, mostly because he'd been left to stew at a police station in Bath until some plods from Somerset arrived to ferry him south. At least that meant they could get on with it when he arrived. It turned out that Simon Clifford, the solicitor, had been waiting for him for half an hour.

Simon looked young, which struck Joe as peculiar – he'd expected a bit of middle-aged authority – but he spoke like a solicitor should do, in an upper-class bray that would normally have got straight up Joe's nose. But right now he wasn't fussy. The bloke was here and he was on his side. They had a few minutes alone before his interview.

To Joe's surprise, the solicitor launched into a speech which justified his attendance, saying that his firm acted for several local trainers and horse facilities in the county. He confided that his uncle, the senior partner, owned several promising animals himself. Rachel must have appealed to the racing grapevine and the firm of Clifford & Menzies had been the obvious response. There was something comforting about being supported by a horse-mad representative but what did this little plummy-voiced fellow know about standing up to a murder charge?

Simon didn't mention the word 'murder'. He simply said the police were keen to ask Joe what he knew about the death of Andrew Burns. In particular, they were interested in the rumours of bad blood between the two of them and Joe's hasty departure the day after the accident.

Joe gave him a quick rundown of the situation – as much, that is, as he was prepared to admit. He'd already decided where to draw the line. Nobody had seen him and Andy having a tussle up on the hill and he'd be a bloody fool to admit it, given what had happened afterwards. In no way was he responsible for Andy going over the edge but he'd have a hard job of convincing some steely-eyed copper of his innocence if he told the complete truth. And he didn't tell Simon the solicitor about it either – he wasn't that naive.

When it came down to it, the two detectives who took their seats across the table from him in the interview room were not what he expected. For a start, neither of them was steely-eyed and one of them was a woman. That caught him off balance straight away. She was probably old enough to be his mum but, in other circumstances, he'd have classified her as a bit of all right. She had soft pretty features, framed by wavy chestnut hair and her eyes were a warm trusting brown. Bloody hell, he'd have to be careful with her.

The other one, the man, looked like he'd been on a twenty-four-hour bender. His face was saggy with fatigue and his hair stood up like a bogbrush. He was a big bloke, the kind whose pint you'd be careful not to spill if you were standing next to him at a bar – which, from his general demeanour, was where you were likely to find him.

They started off nicely enough, the big bloke almost apologising for dragging him all the way down here to help them out. It seemed he was the senior one, some kind of inspector. The inspector appreciated the inconvenience he had caused and was most grateful for his, Joe's, cooperation.

It was all most ominous.

Then the woman started off in a low voice, very soothing, asking him to tell them about his activities on the evening of 28 June. In his own time, no rush.

There was no point in Joe pretending that he didn't know which evening they were talking about. Besides, there wasn't much to tell. He'd been in the pub down at Beach Head. He'd seen Pat Vincent at the bar and Andy Burns had turned up with his dog. Then the pair of them had gone to drink outside. He hadn't gone over to say hello because he was pissed off with Andy after he'd got him sacked from Jack Lucas's yard.

Would he like to tell them more about their disagreement?

They'd fallen out over a bet. It was common knowledge that both he and Andy liked a gamble and he thought they had an agreement to tip each other off when one of Jack's horses was likely to win.

What did he mean by 'likely to win'?

Just that a horse was hitting good form. There was nothing fishy about it.

But if Andy had an idea a horse would win, surely Joe would know too? Weren't they both privy to the same information?

Joe denied it: things didn't work like that in a racing yard with nearly fifty animals to worry about. You got to know some better than others and, anyway, they were up one minute and down the next. That was horses for you.

Simon Clifford butted in to vouch for this point of view. He'd have gone on to give examples of contrary performances from his uncle's string if the bogbrush policeman hadn't muttered a 'Thank you, Mr Clifford' which plainly translated as 'Belt up'.

They moved on from the cause of Joe's antipathy to the consequences. There had been angry words coming off the gallops one day and they'd both boiled over. Joe regretted it but Andy was such an annoying bastard, striding around the yard like he owned the place, always threatening to go to Jack and get people booted out – which is exactly what he'd done. Admittedly, there'd been a bit of a bundle in the yard.

A bit of a bundle? Hadn't he assaulted Andy so severely with a whip that Jack Lucas had been forced to take him to casualty?

Joe agreed but Andy had punched him in the first place, which was out of order. In any case, the wound looked worse than it was. He'd been whacked over the face himself with a whip. These things happened, it was all part of the rough and tumble of life in a training yard, which wasn't for sissies.

But Jack Lucas, a man of great experience, had taken such a dim view of Joe's conduct that he'd sacked him as a result.

Joe agreed that he'd been sacked though he reckoned it was down to Andy putting the poison in, as much as anything else. Andy spent his life brown-nosing Jack. Anyhow, they were the two senior lads and Jack must have decided one of them had to go. Joe didn't blame Mr Lucas.

They returned to the evening in the pub. Joe was put out to discover that they'd obviously been talking to his former drinking buddies. You'd think that a couple of years of standing his round would buy him a bit more loyalty. These were guys he'd tipped the wink to when he was sure of a horse, and sat next to on quiz night. Not to mention lending the odd tenner and talking them out of driving when they were too pissed and, even, ringing the wife or girlfriend to say they were off to play cards at closing time when completely different games were afoot. He'd thought of that lot as mates. More bloody fool him.

So the coppers knew exactly how much he'd been drinking that night and precisely what he'd said he would like to do to Andy effing Burns who'd not only lost him his job but was making sure he couldn't get another – yes, they knew all about the Ed Cooper business too. And then, when he was really pumped up and belligerent, he'd seen Andy and his smelly hound heading off towards the coast path. He'd pointed it out to his dear friend Porky, combined, apparently, with the observation that he hoped the two-faced cee blank blank blank would take a running jump off the cliff. A sentiment which he had no memory of expressing but which had stuck in the mind of those who heard it on account of it coming true.

Joe was beginning to feel a bit punch-drunk at this point and solicitor Simon wasn't any help. He just sat there with his mouth open drinking it all in. Joe played for time and asked for a glass of water which the woman fetched for him. When she returned she was carrying a large brown Jiffy bag which she placed beneath the table. Joe registered the action but he had other things to worry about.

They switched the recorder back on and started on him once again. It was all coming from the woman, with the occasional interjection from the inspector. Joe reckoned the bloke would probably understand how he'd felt about Andy – he looked like a guy who could harbour a grudge – and Joe wished the two of them were sharing a pint right now. He couldn't imagine sharing anything with the woman, who was coming over like some soft-voiced shrink, insinuating herself into his head and making him say things he'd rather not. Wasn't the female meant to be the good cop and the man the bad one? They'd got it all arse about face.

Would he like to tell them when he had left the pub?

Probably about nine, he couldn't be sure.

How long was that after Andy Burns had left?

God knows.

But we're asking you.

Half an hour, maybe more. He wasn't looking at his watch.

And where did he go when he left the pub?

Home, of course. He'd had a skinful.

So he didn't go up the path after Andy?

No. Well – he was wising up now, Porky and the others had obviously spilled their guts – he had started off that way to get a bit of air but when he got to the steps up the hill he'd turned back. They were too bloody steep for a man who was a bit worse for wear. So he'd come back and got on his bike which he'd left in the pub car park.

What time would that be?

He didn't know for sure. Ten past, quarter past nine maybe.

Then what happened?

He rode home. Back to old Clara's and fell asleep in front of the telly. The next morning he felt terrible and decided he'd better get a grip. So he phoned his sister and she said he could stay with her and look for work around Bath. His brother-in-law picked him up that same morning. Admittedly he'd left without saying goodbye to Mrs Curtis but he felt bad about not being able to pay his back rent. However, he'd squared her off now and didn't owe her anything. And he'd been in complete ignorance about Andy's death till he heard it on the news that evening. It had shaken him up. Frankly, even though he didn't like the bloke, nobody deserved to die like that. Those cliffs were dangerous. Just as well he hadn't gone up there in the state he'd been in that night.

A small silence followed this speech. Joe reckoned it had gone down well. That's what had happened and nobody could say otherwise. Nobody who was alive, at any rate.

They'd have to let him go soon, now he'd told them all there was to know.

But the woman had a few more questions – just

to clarify things. Did anything happen on the bicycle ride back to his digs?

No.

Did he meet anyone on the way?

No.

What about an elderly lady with her dogs going into a house further down the lane from the pub?

The old bird – he'd forgotten about her. He'd nearly run over one of her yappy hounds. He conceded the omission – yes, he'd encountered a lady ushering her dogs through her front garden gate. That would be about ten minutes, a quarter of an hour after he left the boozer.

Mrs Perceval put the time at between half past nine and a quarter to ten.

So? The times were near enough, weren't they? Given that he was drunk and she was cracking on a bit. It could be somewhere in between, couldn't it?

The man nodded, it obviously seemed reasonable to him. The woman, whose eyes no longer seemed warm but calculating and intrusive, leaned forward.

Mrs Perceval had remarked on his appearance. The blood on his face, for example.

Oh right – hadn't he mentioned that? He'd fallen off his bike when he was leaving the pub car park. Served him right riding while he was pissed. And if they wanted to do him for being drunk in charge of a bicycle he'd put his hand up. It was a fair cop.

More silence.

Could he go now?

The woman said, 'Stop mucking us about, Joe. Tell us what happened when you caught up with Andy on top of the cliff.'

'I told you, I didn't go up on the cliff.'

'I think you went after him. You were drunk and angry. You wanted revenge for the way he had treated you – that's what you'd been telling everybody. When you found him on the cliff top you had an argument and got into a fight, with the result that Andy fell to his death. I'm not saying you deliberately murdered him but I have no doubt we could make a solid case for it in court.'

'Come on, son,' the man butted in. 'Just tell us the truth about what went on up there. It'll go easier for you if you get it off your chest.'

Joe took a deep breath. They were bluffing. Nobody had seen him and they couldn't prove anything. He just had to stand firm. 'I've told you the truth. I wasn't on the cliff top. I didn't even speak to Andy that night and there was no fight. I never saw him again after he left the pub. Whatever happened to him has nothing to do with me. I just rode home and went to bed.'

There. He'd drawn a line in the sand. They'd never make him cross it.

The woman pulled the Jiffy bag from beneath the desk.

Harriet had never been the kind of hair stylist who made inane chatter for the sake of it. She imagined she'd lost some clients because of her natural reserve. But if those customers wanted an upbeat motormouth then they had plenty of choice elsewhere and, in her opinion, they were welcome to exercise it. For the most part, her regulars returned to her not only because they liked her work but because she left them in peace. And, of course, most of them knew what had happened to Andy and respected her silence.

Today she was particularly grateful she was not required to make small talk. Last night, after a long phone call with Martin which had lifted her spirits, she'd had a visitor. She'd been half expecting Zoe to turn up on her doorstep but not Pat.

'Hi,' he said. 'Can I come in?'

She couldn't refuse though she'd dearly wanted to. They ought to try and resolve the money business though quite how that was to be done was a mystery.

As she made tea they talked of matters they could agree on – Zoe, in other words: her chances in the race for champion apprentice and how seriously she was taking her regime at the gym to build up her strength. Neutral ground.

Harriet waited for him to broach the subject of money. He began with an apology.

'I'm sorry about the other night. I shouldn't have sprung that stuff about me and Andy on you like that. I guess there's no easy way of breaking that kind of news.'

She told him she could understand that and made other conciliatory remarks, even when he began to repeat his claim on Andy's money. Part of her was tempted to simply tell him to get lost but she wasn't prepared to fall out with her sister. Although – and the prospect was chilling – she realised it might come to that.

'Look, Pat, I've taken advice' – she hadn't yet but it sounded good – 'and my solicitor says that unless there is proper documentation of your business with Andy then there is no proof of the debt.'

'I can assure you I'm telling the truth.'

'I didn't say you weren't but you can't expect me to give away half of what I have without something in writing. I'm a widow and this money is all I've got for my future.'

Pat was beginning to lose his cool. 'It's a damn sight more than most of us have got. And there's his life insurance coming too, isn't there?'

How did he know about that? Silly question – she'd told Zoe about it.

'It's my money, Pat. Unless you can prove otherwise, of course. That's what my solicitor says and I'd be a fool to go against his advice, wouldn't I?'

He took a deep breath and Harriet could see he was making a conscious effort to keep calm. 'I explained to you before why this isn't all signed and sealed in some legal document.'

Because it was illegal, that's why. But she didn't say that.

'OK,' he said, suddenly reaching into his jacket pocket, 'you want something in writing and I'm going to give it to you.'

She watched with curiosity and alarm as he began to scribble on a scrap of paper. What kind of trick was this?

He pushed the paper across the table towards her. She saw six rows of two words each.

'What's this?'

'Andy used to bet on the internet. Those are the sites he used and next to them I've put his passwords.'

She read down the list – they were just the kind of passwords Andy might use.

'Check them out, Harriet. Get on his computer and go to these sites. You'll be able to read a history of his betting.'

'What does that prove? He told me he made the money gambling.'

'But he couldn't have made it without me. That's why I know how to get into these sites. He gave me the passwords so I could monitor what was going on with our money.' He put an angry emphasis on *our*.

'Also,' he added, 'if you go back over Andy's building society records you'll see payments to the Bank of Ireland. They were on my behalf – for my family. When you settle up, you want to take that into account.'

Harriet had noticed payments to Ireland and puzzled over them. But was there a catch? Could he be conning her somehow? She was having to fight hard not to be convinced.

She put his paper in her purse. 'OK, Pat, let me check these details and get back to my solicitor. You do know the money is not mine yet, don't you? It's going to take a while.'

'Sure.' He gave her a tight smile. 'I can wait.'

At that point, thank God, Zoe had arrived and nothing more was said about it.

But throughout the day, as Harriet worked in silence, she'd turned it over and over in her head. After Pat and Zoe had left she'd gone to the computer and turned it on for the first time since Andy had died. She'd never spent much time online but she knew how to find the betting sites. She'd entered all of them without difficulty, using the passwords Pat had given her.

And Andy's building society records showed the details of payments to Ireland amounting to £7,500 over the last nine months. It all proved that Pat had not been lying but she'd never seriously thought he had been.

All the same, there had to be a way of hanging on to the money.

The woman detective removed a large plastic envelope from the Jiffy bag. Inside was an item of clothing which looked familiar to Joe. That was not surprising. He'd worn his Glastonbury 2005 T-shirt like a badge of honour since last summer.

'Do you recognise this shirt?'

'Sure, I've got one like it.'

'No, Joe. This one *is* yours. It's one of the items you gave to Clara Curtis for her to wash the morning after the night at the pub.'

Oh Christ. That hadn't been one of his brightest moves. But, of course, he hadn't known about Andy at the time.

He had a horrible feeling he knew where this interrogation was heading. But he'd drawn his line in the sand. He clung to the thought.

'So, Joe, can you confirm that you were wearing this shirt on the night of twenty-eight June?'

He could hardly deny it. They'd have a dozen statements saying what he was wearing that night.

'Yeah, OK. If it's my shirt, then I was wearing it.'

'Well done, son.' The male detective was smiling. 'It's nice to get a straight answer out of you. Must be his first,' he added for his colleague's benefit.

The woman took no notice, just tapped the clear plastic coating that covered the garment. 'See that,' she said. Beneath her finger a brown stain marred the olive-green material and overlapped the psychedelic red, yellow and blue roundel that provided the background to lettering which read 'Glastonbury Festival 2005'. 'That's blood,' she said. She pointed to other brown spots. 'It's all over the shirt.'

Joe shrugged. 'I told you, I fell off my bike. I was bleeding.'

She nodded. 'Yes, you were. The thing is, it's not

just your blood that's on this shirt. Would you like to tell us how Andy's blood comes to be on your clothes as well?'

The line in the sand was obliterated. So he told them.

But, just as he'd feared, telling the truth did not work to his advantage.

'Go on, Laura,' said the male policeman to his colleague. 'You do the honours.'

Joe listened in a state of frozen horror, his mind numb, hardly able to follow the details of what she said to him.

He knew what it all added up to, however. She was charging him with Andy's murder.

It wasn't until the interview was over that Laura allowed herself to feel any emotion. She'd finally done it, nailed the slippery little bastard and backed him into a corner from which he couldn't wriggle out, no matter how plausible he sounded or how inventive his excuses.

Naturally, Joe Parkin had admitted nothing, his type never did, but his final story was so flimsy it was practically transparent.

'OK, I admit I did go after Andy.'

At last.

'It was seeing him sitting there with Pat. He didn't even have the guts to come up to me and say sorry for the shit he'd dumped me in. So I went up the hill to have it out with him.'

'Have it out with him in what way?'

'To thump him one, I suppose. I wasn't thinking straight because I was pissed.'

'So what happened?'

'I got up to the top and saw him coming towards me. When he got up close we had a few words and then, well, we got into a bit of a fight. He hit me and I hit him. That's how his blood got on my shirt. To be honest, he gave me a bit of a working over. He must have had a couple of stone on me. You can see what he did to my face and I've still got bruises all over.'

Laura had made a note to have him examined and his injuries photographed. It was all looking good. It would have been too much, however, to expect Parkin to come right out and confess.

'He was alive when I left him, I swear. I'd got in a few punches and we'd rolled around on the ground but there was nothing wrong with him. And his bloody dog went after me and all. So I just scarpered down the hill, got on the bike and went home to bed. I gave my dirty things to old Clara next morning. Then my sister came on the phone and asked about this bloke Andy Burns who'd gone over the cliff. I couldn't believe it. Then I realised that it was going to look bad if it got out I'd been up there scrapping with him, so I panicked. I rang Rachel back and asked if I could stay with her for a bit and she sent Pete over with the van. And that's the God's honest truth.'

Laura had to hand it to him, he'd sounded plausible. Especially when he added, 'Look, it couldn't have been me. Anyone who knows me would tell you I could never chuck a dog over a cliff.'

That had been a nice touch but Laura didn't believe a word of it. If Joe could push Andy over then he could make sure the dog went after him, to make it look like an accident. She'd put it to Joe that he'd heard Andy mention his cliff top scrape with the dog a few weeks previously.

'No, he never told me that. Not as I remember anyway.'

But Laura wasn't convinced. She had statements from workers at Beach Head yard saying that Andy had told anyone who cared to listen that his ruddy dog had nearly dragged the pair of them over the edge of the coast path.

They had Joe Parkin bang to rights, she was sure of it.

DCI Lane was sure too. For the first time in weeks there was a smile on his weary face. 'How about a drink, Laura?' he said. 'You deserve a large one.'

She'd have liked to sit down with him and chew over the whole thing but there was something important that couldn't be deferred.

'Can we do it another day? I've just got time to get to the hairdresser's in the new health centre.'

His expression was a picture. 'You've got a bloody hair appointment?'

'No, sir. That's where Andy's widow works.'

The outrage vanished from his face. He understood.

Harriet was so far into her own thoughts that for a moment she didn't recognise the woman waiting for her in reception. Harriet's first impression was that her visitor's helmet of flyaway chestnut waves certainly needed attention. Then she realised she was looking at the policewoman who had informed her of Andy's death and subsequently interviewed her over tea in the cottage. Laura, that was her name. There was concern in her eyes.

'I'm sorry to disturb you at work, Mrs Burns. Can you spare me a few minutes?'

They went down to the café – fortunately, Harriet had twenty minutes before her next customer. But by the time she had absorbed what the policewoman told her, all thoughts of returning to the salon had vanished.

Oh God. Andy's death had been deliberate. She couldn't believe what she had just been told. Why would anyone do that?

Poor Andy, what must he have gone through? She couldn't bear to think of it.

And what did this mean for her?

It was hard to take in.

'There's a press release going out,' Laura said. 'I wanted you to hear about this before anyone gets on to you. I expect there will be quite a lot of media interest.'

Harriet knew she was right. There had been widespread coverage of the accident and now that it wasn't an accident at all, the whole thing would start up again – and it would be worse.

Laura went on to say that the police would appoint a family liaison officer to help her deal with the press and provide information about the investigation but Harriet was hardly listening. She got to her feet. She wanted to stop this conversation and leave.

The policewoman was concerned. Did Harriet have somewhere to go and people who would support her at the moment?

Yes, yes. 'There's my sister,' she said. The woman had met Zoe so that ought to satisfy her.

Laura was scribbling numbers for her to take – Victim Support and her own contact details. Harriet took the paper, steaming with impatience, and barely managed a civil goodbye. As she rushed for the door, she could feel the woman's soulful brown eyes burning into her back.

God, she hated being pitied.

She rushed to the reception desk in the gym. It was breaking all her rules to ask for Martin so openly but right now she cared nothing for rules. Was he on court?

He'd gone home early, she was told. His arm was playing up.

She ran to the car park and drove in a fury of impatience to his flat.

He'd better be in. She didn't know what she'd do if Martin wasn't there.

Could Joe Parkin really have murdered Andy? It seemed ridiculous. But the policewoman had said the case against Joe was strong.

She knew Joe Parkin, she'd danced with him at the Christmas party. A harmless lad, pipecleaner-thin. She couldn't imagine him throwing Andy over a cliff but he must have done. Of course – there'd been the incident with the whip. Her head was dazed but she supposed it made a kind of sense.

Oh Andy, how on earth could you let a silly little boy like Joe get the better of you? How did it happen? And how am I going to cope now?

But her husband couldn't help her any more. It was selfish but she'd only just come to terms with the idea of Andy dying as he tried to rescue Jasper. Murder was going to take some getting used to. Especially since she'd just begun to see a way forward for herself. But if Andy had been murdered then the past was under renewed scrutiny and nothing was certain. The whole mess would blow up worse than before and never go away. There'd be a trial carried out in full public gaze – much worse than an inquest and she'd forever be the widow of a murdered man.

It was a nightmare.

The door opened and Martin, her bright new future, stood there looking puzzled but pleased to see her. Before he could ask what she was doing, she flung herself into his arms.

Martin was surprised to find Harriet on his doorstep. They'd agreed to stay away from each other for a few days, to play it cool for the sake of what others might think. To Martin, that was pretty much bullshit. He didn't care what other people thought, though he respected Harriet's delicate situation.

For him, though, he couldn't get enough of his red-haired beauty. If he had his way he'd keep her by his side all the time – he'd told her that and she'd laughed. He had a feeling she'd not taken him seriously.

But here she was, in tears and needing him, just as it should be. He listened closely as she spilled it all out.

The police had arrested some stable worker for Andy's murder and they had some solid forensic evidence to hold against him. That was a shock.

Naturally Harriet was upset. Not least by the notion of a trial and all the publicity that would accompany it. He didn't like the thought of it either.

But there was a silver lining – Harriet would need him more than ever.

'God, Martin,' Harriet was clinging to him as they sat side by side on the sofa, her weight on his bad arm though he tried to ignore it. 'I don't know how I'm going to get through all this. The newspapers and the police. It'll be ages before a trial, won't it?'

'You've just got to tough it out, babe. In a year's time it'll be history.'

'A year!'

'It could be. But I'll be with you all the way.'

She rested her head on his shoulder. He knew she was thinking that this put back the time when they could openly be together. He didn't like that either but if he had to wait, then he would. He'd prove that nobody was as steadfast as he was.

'And there's your sister,' he added. 'Zoe will look after you.'

'Yes and no. She's with Pat.'

'What's wrong with Pat?' He knew the jockey was Zoe's live-in partner but he'd not got wind of any problems.

Harriet sighed heavily. 'You know that money Andy made on betting? Pat says half of it belongs to him. It turns out he was tipping Andy off about what horses were going to win.'

'Is he telling the truth?'

'He gave me Andy's passwords to get onto the betting sites he used. And there's a record of payments Andy made to Pat's family in Ireland. I knew it was too good to be true, Andy winning all that money.'

This was interesting. As far as he knew, jockeys weren't allowed to bet.

'Can he prove the money's his?'

'No.'

'Well, then he hasn't got any legal entitlement, has he?' Even as he said it, Martin realised things weren't that easy. 'I suppose you're worried about your sister.'

'Yes. And now it turns out that Joe killed Andy. Suppose the police think there might be more to it than Joe wanting revenge for losing his job? Andy told me Joe was pissed off with him for not letting him in on a bet. Suppose Joe knew what Andy was up to with Pat and wanted a share? I don't want the police raking over all that. What would happen to the money then?'

Martin didn't know but he didn't like the sound of it.

They sat in silence while Martin's arm throbbed, the pain slowly capturing his attention. He turned his body and pulled her across his chest. She met his hungry kiss with a hunger of her own.

'There's one thing, babe,' he murmured as he stroked her flowing hair. 'You can be sure of me.'

'Thank God,' she said. That was better – she almost managed a smile.

Part Three

Chapter Fifteen

Harriet found that Jack was reluctant to accept the keys to the cottage.

'I hope you're not moving out on my account,' he said. 'You know you can stay as long as you like.'

She was touched. Most people in his circumstances might say one thing but they would certainly mean another. Not Jack.

'Where are you off to?' he asked.

'I've found a flat in Bridgwater. It's handy for work.'

It was also handy for Martin, just a ten-minute bike ride from his place. The rent was pretty steep but the bank had fronted up once they'd looked into her situation. She couldn't see how being the widow of a murder victim would influence a balance sheet but all the personnel involved – solicitors, bank officers and estate agents – had bent over backwards to be sympathetic.

Now the removal van – only half full, for she

didn't have all that much stuff – was on its way to Bridgwater and she was saying goodbye to Beach Head. Thank God for that, she couldn't wait to get away from the place.

Jack looked regretful as if he were aware his yard would always be among her unhappy memories. At least she had one bit of news to cheer him up.

'They've let Jasper out.'

'Have they?' Jack's round face lit up. The dog had spent plenty of time in the yard and they were old friends. 'How's he doing?'

Jasper was managing as well as a dog with two legs in plaster could be expected.

'He can't exactly run around but he's got a spark back in his eye. And his tail hasn't stopped wagging.'

Jack smiled, which was more like it, and Harriet gave him a fierce hug before heading for her car. She couldn't wait to get to her new home.

In many ways, it was Jasper she had to thank for it. The dog had been discharged ten days ago and looking after him had proved difficult. Harriet had been reluctant to leave him on his own all day at the cottage while she was at work. Zoe had volunteered to take care of him but she, too, was busy and there had been a lot of driving backwards and forwards. Even Pat had lent a hand. The one person who hadn't been so keen to pitch in was Martin.

'This isn't going to work,' he'd said almost the moment Harriet had appeared on his doorstep clutching Jasper. 'How's it going to get upstairs?'

'We'll carry him,' she said but it was plain from the first that Martin was not going to do the carrying. He'd brought up the dog's bed and other stuff but left Harriet to take Jasper.

'I'm sorry,' he said, 'but I'm not much of a dog person.'

But she distinctly remembered a conversation from that day he'd taken her on a picnic to the farm where he'd grown up. On the drive there he'd told her about his boyhood dog – she couldn't remember its name. They'd been inseparable, so he'd said.

'What about your lurcher?'

'Yeah, well, that was a long time ago.'

It didn't make much sense to Harriet; once a dog lover, always a dog lover, surely?

But Martin did have a point about his place being unsuitable. Apart from all those flights of stairs, Emily, his landlady, had a strict 'no pets' rule. There were disadvantages to living in an environment that was kept so rigorously spotless.

The upshot was that Harriet had found a flat with a big, well-fenced garden and she knew it was the best thing that had happened to her since – well, since Martin.

He and Jasper would soon make friends, she was sure of it.

Since the news of Joe's arrest, Pat had been in a state of shock. His own involvement in Andy's death had been enough of a burden but he'd been able to justify keeping quiet about what he knew. After all, what good would it do anyone if he came out with his conviction that Andy had killed himself? It was better all round that people thought it was an accident. But it seemed not everyone was of that opinion. The police had suddenly decided it was murder, and that Joe, a former workmate and a guy who in the end had proved to be a reliable partner, was responsible.

Pat could see that, on the face of it, there was a case for Joe to answer. He'd had a public beef with Andy and he'd whacked him with a whip. And he'd been boozing in the pub the night Andy died. Suppose he'd got into a fight with Andy on the cliff and Andy had gone over? It was possible, wasn't it?

Bollocks to that. First off, if there'd been a punch-up Joe would have come off worse, in Pat's opinion. Andy was compact and muscular, army-hardened, more than a match for a streak of piss like Joe.

Second, though Joe had made no secret of disliking Andy, Pat believed he was genuinely shocked Andy was dead.

All of which Pat said to Joe's sister, Rachel.

He'd received a tearful phone call from her and agreed to drop in on his way to ride at Newmarket.

To his surprise, he recognised the tall girl who opened the door of a neat semi on a new estate five miles off the M4.

'I know you,' he said.

She explained she'd worked in racing until she

got married eighteen months back. Pat had ridden a couple of horses that she had looked after.

But he wasn't here to chew over old times.

'Look, I'm stone cold certain they've made a terrible mistake,' he told her. 'Joe could be a bit of an idiot sometimes but he's never a murderer. Never in a million years.'

He could see his words were what she needed to hear, though they were of limited use in the circumstances.

'How's he bearing up?' he asked. All he knew was what she'd told him on the phone. Joe was being held on remand and she was visiting as often as she could. Fortunately he was in Bristol so it wasn't too difficult.

To begin with she was tearful and he couldn't get much out of her. Then she became embarrassed and insisted on serving up coffee and cake, which was exactly what he didn't need with eight stone ten to do that afternoon. Finally she calmed down.

First off, Joe had sworn blind to her that he was innocent and she believed him. However, she could tell that others who'd heard the case against him – like Pete, her husband – weren't so sure.

'It's such a relief to talk to you,' she said, clutching Pat's hand. 'I thought I was on my own.'

'What have they got against him then?' Pat wanted the details and she supplied them, based on what her brother had told her.

As he listened, Pat had to admit that the lad had made a complete pig's ear of the whole thing.

He wondered if the fight with Joe had been the final straw for Andy. Would something as stupid as that make a man want to give up on life? He put the thought out of his mind for the moment.

Rachel was looking at him anxiously, plainly worried that he, too, was about to lose faith in her brother.

'Joe couldn't have made a bigger cock-up of the whole thing if he'd tried,' he said. 'But he still didn't do it. Do the police reckon he chucked the dog off the cliff as well?'

'Joe would never do that. He's always been mad about animals.'

'I know.' Pat had seen Joe around horses.

They both sat in silence for a moment, Rachel no doubt reflecting on the preposterous nature of the allegations against her brother, Pat thinking about the dog and his idea that Andy had taken Jasper with him over the edge.

But he wasn't about to share his suicide theory.

'What do his lawyers say?'

'They say they might be able to get the charge reduced to manslaughter. That would still mean a long time in prison though, wouldn't it?'

Of course it would. It wasn't a happy prospect.

Pat got to his feet and made his excuses. He didn't like to leave Joe's sister like this but he still had a long drive ahead of him to Newmarket. Why was it he felt like a complete shit?

Harriet was woken by the sun shining directly onto her pillow. The curtains, like a great deal in the new flat, didn't function as they should and a ten-inch gap between them allowed in an early morning shaft of light. She didn't mind. It was fantastic to wake up in a different place. She rolled towards the middle of the big old bed and met the solid warmth of another body. Fantastic, too, to wake up next to the man she loved.

Martin, it seemed, had been awake for some time.

'I've been watching the sunlight on your hair,' he said. 'My Pre-Raphaelite princess.'

She knew what this meant now – he'd shown her pictures from his art books. She wasn't entirely flattered, some of those women were a bit heavy round the jaw, but if it pleased him she was happy to let the comparison stand.

He kissed her forehead.

'I've been thinking,' she said. 'I want Zoe to come for dinner.'

He nuzzled her cheek.

'I was wondering if you'd come over too.'

His hand found her breast. 'I was hoping to have you all to myself for a bit.'

'I know but she's my sister and the two of you have got to meet sometime.'

'OK.' His hand crept down to her hip.

'She might bring Pat.'

His hand froze and his head pulled back. 'The bastard who's trying to steal your money?'

'What can I do? If I want to see her I can't avoid him, can I?'

Martin's eyes narrowed. 'Don't see her then,' he said.

For a moment Harriet was shocked then she spotted the upwards flicker of his mouth. 'You're joking, aren't you?'

'If you say so.'

He kissed her with purpose and she realised they wouldn't be getting up just yet.

A distant yowl broke her concentration. It was followed by another. Jasper.

She broke off their kiss. 'Go and let poor old Jasper out.'

'Let him wait.'

The dog howled louder this time, as if on cue.

'Just let him into the garden and come back.'

'He's your dog.'

'So if you want me, you should go and let him out.'

From the expression on his face, she thought he was going to refuse. Instead he released her and strode from the room. She heard a scrabbling of paws from behind the kitchen door and yips of anticipation which turned into a deep throaty growling. It seemed the antipathy between Martin and Jasper was mutual.

He strode back into the room, his face drawn and breathing heavily. His intensity was frightening. Thrilling, too, as he suddenly yanked the bedclothes from the bed and gazed like a hungry man at her naked body.

'OK,' he said. 'Get your sister and the jockey over. I'll have a private word with him.'

She would have asked him what he meant by that but he covered her body with his own and stopped her mouth with the kind of passion that could not be denied.

And when he'd finished with her, all thoughts of Jasper and Pat and Zoe had been driven from her mind. She lay there wrung out, surprised and thrilled by the way she felt. It was as if he were a drug she could not do without. So there was only one reply she could make when he asked her to marry him.

'It's fantastic, Harriet. I really like it.'

'You do?'

Actually, Zoe wasn't much taken with her sister's new home but she was determined to be positive. The flat was poky and badly decorated, though the garden was a saving grace.

The thing was, she didn't like the idea of Harriet moving at all. Her sister could have wound up in a luxury apartment with the best of views and swankiest of fittings and Zoe would have found fault.

Harriet was moving away from her in many ways. After that period following Andy's death when they'd been together night and day, a wall had gone up between them, and it hadn't been Zoe who'd erected it. It was as if her sister had made a conscious decision to cut her out of her life. And now she'd moved away physically as well. It was a half-hour drive to this new place instead of five minutes. That was significant – everything to do with Harriet was significant at the moment.

What she couldn't understand was Harriet cutting her out just when things must have been at rock bottom. She'd found out from the local radio station that Andy's death was now being treated as murder. And when she'd rung Harriet about it she'd had the impression the whole business was a nuisance rather than the emotional body blow it must surely be. Harriet had seemed more worried about the arrangements for looking after Jasper than the implications of her husband having been murdered.

Zoe had begged Harriet to come and stay with her and Pat but Harriet had flatly refused. So she had been relieved when Harriet had invited her and Pat round to look over the new flat. They'd arrived with wine and flowers and said how much they loved the place. What else could they say?

While they were milling around the tiny kitchen, trying not to step on Jasper or each other, the doorbell rang.

A tall blond man stepped into the room, shrinking the space still further, dazzling them with his lazy smile and sky-blue eyes.

'This is Martin,' said Harriet but even before she'd spoken his name Zoe had slotted the jigsaw piece into place. She'd seen this man at the health centre when she visited the gym. He was the tennis coach Harriet had been seeing before Andy's death.

'Martin gave me a hand moving out of the cottage,' Harriet was saying.

'I thought I'd just pop by and see if everything was OK,' he added.

Zoe knew it was rehearsed. She could tell from the way her sister was deliberately not looking at him that they knew each other intimately. It explained a lot.

This impossibly handsome, smiling man was the wall that stood between Harriet and the rest of the world. Zoe supposed she should be happy for her.

Jasper began to growl, the kind of noise he made when he saw something he wanted to sink his teeth into – like a cat.

'I don't think your dog likes me,' said Martin.

Jasper wasn't the only one, thought Zoe.

'I love him,' Harriet admitted. 'I know it's bad timing but I can't help it.'

Zoe was sitting next to her sister on a bench at the end of the garden, Jasper sprawling on the lawn by their feet. From the open back door to the kitchen came the faint clink of cutlery being loaded into the dishwasher as the men cleared up after supper.

Their tête-à-tête had been engineered by Harriet. The purpose of the evening was now clear to Zoe. It wasn't for Harriet to show off her new flat but to show off her new man.

'Must you look like you've got a bad smell up your nose, Zoe? Martin's wonderful. He's what I need.'

'I didn't realise it was serious with Martin. When you were seeing him before, I mean.'

Harriet thought for a moment. 'I didn't think it was. I'd broken it off with Martin just before Andy died. But when Andy wasn't there any more . . .' she tailed off, obviously picking her words carefully. 'It was like some force pulling me back to Martin. It just seemed natural for us to get together again.'

'But Andy hasn't been dead a month.'

Harriet's green eyes filled with reproach. 'You had to say that, didn't you?'

'It's what everybody's going to think.'

The reproach was replaced by a flash of anger. 'They're not in my position, are they?' Harriet's face softened. 'What happened to Andy was terrible but, to be honest, our relationship was over. I wasn't in love with him any longer.'

Zoe said nothing for the moment and forced herself to look on the positive side. It wasn't her place to judge her sister and much of what she said was true. Her marriage to Andy probably had run its course. Was it fair to blame her for falling in love just at the time of Andy's death?

Some people would blame her.

Zoe took Harriet's hand. 'I'm sorry. I only want you to be happy. But I'm worried how this will look.'

'I know. We're going to play it cool for the moment. Only a few people will know, like you. And, anyway, it's going to be ages before this horrible trial. I can't be expected to live like a nun for nine months, can I?'

Yes, was the answer to that question but Zoe knew it was not what Harriet wanted to hear.

Pat peered at the controls on the dishwasher. It was an old model and the layout was confusing.

'Here,' said Martin and twitched the dial round to some indecipherable symbol. The machine grumbled into life. He'd obviously had dealings with it before.

In fact, Martin seemed pretty much at home. As he made coffee he said, 'I understand you were big mates with Andy.'

'Sure. We worked up at Beach Head yard together.'

'And you found his body?'

'Yes.' Pat didn't particularly want to get into the grisly details. He wasn't yet sure what he thought of

Martin, beyond the fact that his size made him conscious of his own modest stature. The tennis coach was about a foot taller and probably weighed an extra five stone.

'So what do you reckon on this Joe Parkin fellow? Did he do it, do you think?'

During supper, so it had seemed to Pat, they'd been at pains not to talk of Andy's death or Joe's arrest. But, like the elephant in the corner of the room, it was the unspoken topic that overshadowed all else. So it was no surprise Martin was picking his brains now that Harriet was out of the room.

'Joe can be a bit of an idiot but I don't believe he killed Andy.'

'Why not? He attacked him with a whip, didn't he? Because he thought Andy had got him sacked.'

Martin seemed pretty well informed. But why wouldn't he be? He was shagging the merry widow so he'd be bound to be up to speed.

'Even if he did get into a fight with Andy on the cliff,' Pat said, 'I don't see him shoving him over the edge, not unless Andy didn't see him coming. For a start, Joe's just a long drink of water and Andy was all muscle.'

Martin gazed at him intently, as if making a note of his words. He's just a lad really, Pat mused, probably five years younger than I am. It was weird to think Harriet had replaced Andy with a toy boy.

Martin wouldn't let the subject drop. 'So how do you think Andy died?'

'I reckon it was an accident. It's probably Jasper's fault, the daft mutt.' Pat wasn't going to tell Martin what he really thought. *I think he topped himself because of you, mate.*

The lad didn't deserve that.

Martin brought them some coffee but did not join them. Zoe noted the look of longing in Harriet's eyes as her lover strolled back up the garden path. She looked as if she could hardly believe her luck.

Harriet put her cup down. 'How's it going with Pat?'

'Oh, fine.'

'He's not doing very well at the moment, is he?'

What an odd thing to say.

'How do you mean?'

'Well, he doesn't ride many winners, does he? Not compared to you, anyway. Don't look so surprised, I do follow your career, you know.'

Zoe felt irrationally pleased. Sometimes she wasn't sure.

'Anyway,' her sister continued, 'what's Pat thinking of doing when he stops riding?'

'I don't know. Why don't you ask him?'

'He's not thinking of rejoining the Fighting Vincents back in Cork, is he?'

Pat had confided in Zoe about his reprobate brothers in the early days of their relationship and she'd told some of it to her sister. She was shocked to have it dragged up at this moment, however.

'What's this about, Harriet? Why are you having a go at Pat?'

'Because you could do much better. With what you've got going for you, Zoe, you can have any man you want. Don't get lumbered with Pat like I was with Andy.'

Lumbered with Andy? Zoe couldn't believe she was hearing this but it was typical of Harriet – she could be brutal when she chose.

'Has Pat asked you to marry him yet?' Harriet continued.

'It's not something we've talked about.'

'Really? You've been living together for six months.'

'I don't want to get married.'

'Perhaps you shouldn't be so exclusive then. You want to be careful you're not stuck in a dead-end relationship with a guy who's just taking you for granted.'

This would be laughable but Zoe could see that her sister was deadly serious. Why on earth was she banging on about marriage? She hadn't exactly cherished the institution herself.

Then a thought struck her. 'You're not thinking of marrying Martin, are you?'

The green eyes now turned on Zoe were brimming with excitement. 'How did you guess?'

'You mean you've discussed it with him?'

'Better than that, he's proposed.'

'But you can't! What would people say?'

All merriment vanished from Harriet's face. 'Yeah, I know.'

Zoe felt a stab of guilt, as if she'd snatched an ice cream from a child. 'It's far too soon, you must see that.'

'Oh I do.' Harriet caught a strand of her hair and twined it round her finger, an anxiety reflex that was all too familiar to Zoe. 'It's just nice to think of good times ahead – when all this is over.'

She meant the murder trial and all the public exposure that would bring her.

Zoe imagined that if Martin stuck by her through the painful months ahead then maybe Harriet might find happiness with him. But it was a long way off.

She took her sister's hand from her hair, stopping that nervous twirling like she used to do when they were young.

'Don't worry, we'll get through it. I'm glad you've found someone. Just promise me you won't rush off and do anything daft.'

'Sure.' Harriet gave her a sad grin and squeezed her hand.

Zoe supposed that was good enough.

'Let's leave the girls to it, shall we?' Martin stood in the kitchen doorway. 'Come next door, there's something I want to show you.'

Pat followed him into the living room. The patterned carpet screamed a bit but the sofa looked cosy and at least the walls weren't covered in tasteless junk. In Pat's opinion, the place could be made pretty comfortable, though he suspected from the significant glances Zoe had aimed at him that she might not agree.

'Why don't you put your coffee down?' Martin said, which struck Pat as a pretty odd remark. Was he some kind of closet domestic freak? However, Pat did as he was told, placing the cup on the mantelpiece next to Martin's own.

'What do you want to show me then?' he asked.

'Just this.' Martin grinned affably as he stepped forward and thumped Pat in the stomach.

The wind shot from his lungs as he doubled over in soundless pain and profound shock. Before Pat had time to react, Martin cuffed him on the side of the head and then on the other side, as if to even things up.

Pat's bones turned to jelly and he fell to the carpet. His mouth flapped but no sound emerged, only blood-streaked spittle which vanished into the maroon swirls on the floor. His skull rang like a bell and his vision was blurred. He'd come off a thoroughbred once at thirty miles an hour and landed on his head. The sensation was much the same.

Martin yanked him off the floor by the shirt and dumped him on the sofa.

'Sorry about that,' he said in a soft voice, 'but I want you to remember what I'm going to say.'

'You're crazy!' It hurt to speak.

'Just a little maybe. So I wouldn't make an issue out of this. Just listen carefully.'

Pat wasn't capable of doing anything else. He'd have run but he knew his legs wouldn't support him.

Martin gave him the benefit of his friendly smile once more and spoke gently. 'Harriet tells me you've been pestering her for money.'

So that was it. The fellow had knocked the wits out of him or he'd have got there sooner.

'Andy was holding it for me,' he began but Martin held up his hand, the one that had done the damage. Pat shut up.

'Maybe he was,' Martin said, 'and maybe he wasn't. But Andy is no longer with us and my information is that you don't have any legal entitlement to the assets of his estate.'

Pat found his voice. 'I've got nothing in writing – of course I haven't.'

'Because what you were doing is illegal.'

'It's still my money. Andy wouldn't have earned tuppence if it wasn't for me. I've got a moral right.' His own belligerence astounded Pat but he was outraged.

'Keep your voice down. Let's just keep this between ourselves.'

'What? It's between me and Harriet and she owes me. The fact that you're shagging her has got nothing to do with it.'

It was a stupid thing to say but he wasn't going to just roll over for some muscle-bound kid. There was a principle at stake here besides the money.

He didn't see the blow coming, a back-handed flick that rattled his teeth and filled his vision with floating stars.

As Pat lurched to his feet – he had to try and get out of reach – his legs were knocked from under him. He found himself lying face down, being pressed into the noxious floor by an immovable weight. It felt like the bastard was kneeling on top of him. A precise, singing pain soared above all the other hurts that lit up his body and he realised his arm was twisted up behind his back, held on the cusp of fracture. He couldn't move or speak.

'Now,' Martin's voice was still soft but had lost all trace of amiability, 'let me tell you what's going to happen.' He paused and it struck Pat that the fellow was taking indecent pleasure from this. 'Absolutely nothing. I'm going to let you up and we're going to join the others and we're going to say nothing about it. And from now on, you're going to say nothing about Andy's money. Nothing to Harriet and nothing to anyone else. That money is not yours, legally or in any practical sense. There is nothing coming to you from Andy's estate. Do you understand?'

Pat lay immobile and helpless, unable to respond. Then the note of pain in his arm was raised another octave, obliterating all other hurts.

'Understand?'

Pat managed a nod. The pain eased its grip.

'Good. Because I know where you live and I know where you work. If you mention this conversation to anyone then I'm going to find you. I could break your arm or your leg. Dislocate your shoulder maybe. There's any number of nasty things I could do to a little runt like you and they'd all keep you from riding horses. And they'd hurt.'

Pat realised Martin was waiting for a sign from him. 'OK,' he managed. 'I won't say anything. I swear.' He'd swear to anything if only this monster would let him go in one piece.

The pressure on his arm faded and the weight lifted from his back. There were still stars in his vision as he squinted along the floor across the rucked-up rug tufted with dog hair towards Martin standing by the fireplace.

From far off he heard the chink of cup on saucer and the other man's cheerful voice. 'On your feet, mate, and drink your coffee.'

Trembling, Pat did as he was told.

Chapter Sixteen

'Thank God that's over,' Zoe murmured as she followed Pat to the car. The evening had been a disaster. Harriet had been so weird, the way she'd gone on about Pat. And the way he'd been behaving for the last hour hadn't exactly helped. He'd barely said a word as the four of them sat in the front room and chatted pointlessly. That bloody carpet had given her a headache.

'Honestly, Pat,' she said as they reached the vehicle, 'you could have made an effort.'

He looked at her without expression, his thin face pale in the dim street light. 'You drive,' he said, holding out the keys. 'I don't feel great.'

She snatched the keys from his hand. 'What's the matter with you? You were fine during supper.'

He opened his mouth to reply then shut it again, as if he was too weary to even attempt a reply. Perhaps Harriet had a point. He just took her for granted, like ordering her to drive. She might cook and clean around the home but she was nobody's servant.

They reached home without exchanging another word. Pat followed her into the house and went straight to bed. She had no idea what he was sulking about but she was damned if she was going to ask.

She brooded about the scene all through the next day. She even took her gloom into the weighing room at Leicester.

'What's up, gorgeous?' a voice murmured in her ear as she got off the scales. It was Ginger Weaver, looking irritatingly sunny.

'Mind your own business,' she spat at him and strode past, catching the look of dismay on his face as she went.

What was the matter with her? She wasn't angry with Ginger; her problems were nothing to do with him. She turned round to apologise but he'd vanished. Too bad.

This was Pat's fault, dragging her down to his level.

She rode her race with fierce intensity, commanding her mount by force of will – and bodily strength too. There was no doubt that her visits to the gym had added a new dimension to her riding. He was a comfortable winner half a furlong out but she rode him to the line as if the pack were breathing down her neck and won by six lengths. Even that didn't lighten her mood.

Her sister was no great judge of relationships. She was jumping without pause from a marriage she'd wrecked into another with a man nobody even knew. How stupid could you get – and she had the nerve to criticise her.

The clouds lifted a fraction as Zoe changed. At least she'd now recognised the real cause of her bad humour. Not Pat, nor Ginger but her own sister. Zoe was convinced Harriet was about to make the biggest mistake of her life but she didn't have a clue what to do about it.

Pat read the letter for the third time. Joe wasn't much of a speller and Pat guessed his written communications were usually restricted to text messages and filling in bookies' slips. Until now, of course. There probably wasn't much for a man to do while banged up in a cell. It could drive him to rediscover the dying art of letter-writing.

Joe said he'd heard from Rachel of Pat's belief in his innocence. That kind of support meant a lot to him.

And, he said, Rachel had been very pleased to meet Pat as, these days, she didn't get much of a chance to chat about racing like she used to. Joe had learned a lot about horses from her. She had an eye and it was a pity she was sitting around at home these days because Pete, who was a great fellow in every respect, didn't want her working all hours at some stables.

Jesus, the bloody letter hardly improved Pat's mood. If he were a braver man he'd visit Joe himself and look his mate in the eye while he said all this stuff. But the thought of stepping inside a prison gave him the creeps.

And if he were a braver man he'd find a way of getting even with that lunatic who'd almost pulled his arm off last night. Thank God he wasn't riding today; he still had a ringing in his head and his body felt as if it had been twisted and stretched on some medieval instrument of torture. He'd intended to ride work for Jack but he'd cried off and gone back to bed.

He lay there dozing and indulging a fantasy. He didn't own a shotgun but he knew men who did. He could borrow one and take a ride into Bridgwater, to the health centre. Martin would be on the tennis court, all blond and bronzed like some poster-boy athlete, posing and preening for that red-headed bitch in the hair salon upstairs. He imagined how she might feel if he turned up with a gun and turned her blue-eyed lover boy's face into a bloody pin cushion. He'd bet she'd write him a cheque damn quick in those circumstances.

It was a childish daydream. He wasn't going to get the better of the pair of them like that.

But there had to be a way. He might not be brawny but he was smart. There had to be something he could do.

He got up and turned on the television – it was time for Zoe's race. He knew he was in her bad books but he'd not been capable of explaining himself last night. He didn't want her to know about the money. But, as he watched her ride a brilliant clinical victory, he realised that she was his one hope of redeeming himself.

Diane finally cornered Harriet by waylaying her at the end of the day. Even so, she had to work hard to manoeuvre her into the wine bar.

'Just one drink,' Harriet said. 'I've got tons of stuff to do at the flat.'

It was the excuse she'd been using to duck Diane's previous attempts to get her face to face. What the hell – she was here now.

Diane rushed through the polite catch-up stuff – the move, the dog's health, all that. There was only one topic on her agenda – no, that wasn't strictly true.

'Any more news from the police?'

'I had to make another statement, about Joe Parkin and Andy's bust-up with him. Though, to be honest, Andy didn't tell me much about it.'

'And how are you feeling?'

That was an interesting question. Come on, Harriet, how does it feel to learn your husband has been murdered over some petty argument at work? Diane felt like a ghoul for asking but she was intrigued all the same.

Harriet shrugged. 'It's like I'm in a dream. It's not real somehow.' She finished her wine and Diane poured more. 'To be honest, I try not to think about it all. I just keep myself busy.'

Diane seized her chance.

'So how are things going with Martin?'

Harriet's eyes flashed with suspicion. She didn't reply, just reached for her glass.

'I know you're still seeing him. Do you really think that's wise in the circumstances?'

'Are you giving me a lecture, Diane?'

'Of course not. I just think you should be very careful at the moment. I'm not judging you but other people will if it gets out that you were sleeping with Martin before Andy died and you're still doing it.'

Harriet's face was like stone. 'Anything else?'

'Yes, as it happens. Martin is not worthy of you. He's a liar. He never played in the finals of Junior Wimbledon – I looked it up. And he told you he had an economics degree from the LSE – well, he told me he'd studied history of art at Edinburgh. He can't have done both. And you might be interested to know he told me that while he was in bed with me approximately two weeks before he started screwing you.'

Harriet stared at her, her face blank with shock. 'I don't believe you.'

'I'm sorry, I should have told you before but I didn't realise what a dangerous creep he was until he nearly pulled my arm off the other day.'

'You bitch.' Harriet got to her feet. 'I knew you wanted him, Diane, but I never thought you'd stoop this low.'

353

Diane watched her go. She wasn't altogether surprised her efforts had fallen on deaf ears. But, though Martin had truly scared her, she couldn't in all conscience have walked away without trying to get through to Harriet.

She set about finishing the bottle with a heavy heart. She'd better find herself another hairdresser.

Jack drove Zoe back from Leicester. As a rule she lifted his spirits and shortened the chore of yet another car journey. Today, however, the conversation did not flow.

Zoe obviously had things on her mind and, poor kid, there was plenty for her to brood on, with her sister in such a pickle. He imagined that Harriet moving further away would only have added to the burden. You'd want your nearest and dearest close at hand at a time like this. Things had been bad enough before the prospect of a murder trial, now the whole business of Andy's death would drag on in the light of grisly public interest. How was Harriet going to cope with all that? In Zoe's place, he'd be worried sick.

But he wasn't going to raise the matter. She knew she could come to him for advice any time and not just about racing.

Before she'd moved in with Pat she'd asked his opinion – was she doing the right thing? He'd been flattered to be asked. There's only one way to really find out how you feel about someone, he'd said, and that was to live with them all round the clock. If you're serious about him, why not give it a try? And if it doesn't work out, he'd added, you can always have Geraldine's old room in my house. It had been a bit of a joke but she'd not laughed, she'd hugged him and said, 'You really miss her, don't you?'

Zoe was a great girl and Jack hated to see her down in the dumps.

Harriet was sitting in the garden. She ought to be inside being busy, like Martin. He was fixing up Andy's computer. She should be cleaning the kitchen cupboards or unpacking her books but the confrontation with Diane had made those things unimportant. What a traitor Diane had turned out to be. She'd sworn once to cut the woman out of her life and she should have stuck to it.

Jasper, who'd been snoozing beneath the bench, suddenly growled. She knew what that meant. Sure enough, Martin appeared in the kitchen doorway. Harriet was disappointed that the dog was not warming to Martin as she'd expected. What was wrong with the stupid animal? She'd tried getting Martin to feed Jasper tit-bits, but even that had failed to do the trick.

As Martin strode across the lawn towards her seat, Jasper climbed painfully to his feet and slunk away. The pair of them spent their time avoiding one another. It was odd.

'Drink?' he asked, wine bottle in hand.

She shook her head, she'd had enough already.

'I saw Diane Connor after work. She says she had an affair with you before you met me.'

He stared at her blankly. 'What?' Surely no one could manufacture such a look of incomprehension.

She repeated her words and he sat down next to her.

'I can't believe that woman,' he said.

Harriet didn't believe her either but she wanted to hear his denial first-hand.

'She's lying,' he said finally.

Thank God.

'She made a pass at me once and I turned her down – I told you.'

'It's OK, Martin. I never believed her for an instant.' She found his hand with hers. 'And I'm never going to talk to her again.'

'Not on my account, I hope.'

'Yours and mine.'

He said nothing but began to massage the nape of her neck the way she liked. That was nice. She felt the tension begin to ebb away.

'I had a chat with Pat last night,' he said.

She'd wondered what they'd talked about while she and Zoe were in the garden.

'I don't think he'll be bothering you any more,' he added.

'Really?' That was fantastic. This man – her man – was a miracle worker. 'Tell me what happened.'

'Nothing much.' He gave her the benefit of his lazy smile. She loved the way his eyes sparkled when he was pleased about something, like he was now. 'We had a discussion about the matter and he agreed to drop it.'

'But how?' It didn't sound like the Pat she knew. And who would say goodbye to a hundred and twenty thousand pounds without a fight?

'I explained that he had no legal entitlement and that he stood a good chance of creating a severe rift in the family if he persisted in making a nuisance of himself.'

She liked the comforting sound of the word 'family'. She'd never really felt she had one, certainly not with her mother dead – she and Zoe didn't really comprise a proper family unit – and Andy had only ever used the word in connection with her having his children. But Martin made the word sound comforting, as if it were a sacred connection between them and Zoe and, maybe – if this trouble could be resolved – Pat.

'I told him,' Martin continued, 'that if he really loved Zoe he shouldn't make a fuss about money. People matter more than money.'

'And he said he'd let it go?'

Martin didn't answer immediately. Instead he increased the pressure on her neck and bent his lips to hers. 'You taste of wine. Very light on the palate.'

'Don't tease. Tell me what Pat said.'

'He didn't say much actually, not once I'd presented my argument. In the circumstances, he's prepared to forget the whole thing. And I suggest you do too. If he ever mentions it, tell me. From now on, it's my affair not yours.'

She could hardly believe it. But she did believe it. She was fast learning that if Martin said a problem was solved, then it was.

'I think we ought to celebrate,' he said.

She put her hand on his thigh and squeezed. 'Sure thing.'

He covered her hand with his. 'How about a trip.'

'OK.' She was game for a day out or a night away maybe. 'How about London? I haven't been for ages.'

'I was thinking of somewhere a little further off. Like America.'

America? She'd never been there and she'd love to go but . . .

Before she could start outlining the obvious objections, he said, 'Let's go to Las Vegas.'

She laughed. 'Why? Don't tell me you're a secret gambler.'

'There's other things in Las Vegas apart from casinos.'

She was puzzled. 'What are you getting at, Martin?'

'We could get married there. Do it quick. No fuss, no gossip, no hangers-on, just you and me.'

She gaped at him. The notion was too extraordinary to take in. She'd only just got used to the idea of them getting married but the event itself was far off in her mind's eye – after months had gone by and she was allowed to be happy again.

Martin appeared to be reading her mind. 'Listen to me a moment. We don't have to tell anyone, not even Zoe. Let's just keep it between you and me. I've just checked it out on the internet. All we've got to do is turn up and apply for a licence.'

Good God, was it that simple?

'We've got to prove neither of us is already married but you've got that interim death certificate for Andy, haven't you? Think how great it will be to be together properly. Otherwise we're just stuck in limbo until after the trial, aren't we?'

That was true. It would be difficult to have a wedding here before the trial – some people would be bound to disapprove.

'But what's it going to cost?'

He shrugged. 'A few thousand. We'll need a bit of a honeymoon afterwards.'

'But we haven't got a few thousand to blow on something like this.'

His face grew earnest. 'Our getting married is more important than anything else in our lives.'

'OK, that's true. All the same—'

'All the same what? Thanks to me, babe, you've just saved one hundred and twenty thousand pounds. What's a few grand on a wedding?'

Put in that light it was hard to argue. All the

same, it was a big decision and not one to be rushed.

'I need time to think about this, Martin.'

He glanced at his watch. 'How about five minutes?'

She laughed though he didn't. Sometimes she was aware of the four-year age gap between them. He was so earnest. She could see he was intoxicated by this idea and she had to admit the notion was appealing. But she couldn't afford to throw herself into a mad elopement without thinking things through. Surely he could see that.

'It's a lovely romantic idea – just give me a couple of days.'

'OK.' He pulled away from her. 'Tell me tomorrow at work.'

'Where are you going?'

Martin was now on his feet.

'I'm off home.'

'But I thought you were going to stay tonight.' There was panic in her voice. She knew she sounded feeble but she couldn't help it.

'Best not, babe. It'll give you a chance to think things over.'

She caught his hand. 'You don't have to go just yet.'

'I don't want to crowd you.' He disengaged his fingers. 'I can understand if you're not as committed as I am to us being together. We'll talk tomorrow.' And he walked down the garden path and into the house without looking back.

Harriet remained where she was, anchored by pride. She would not run after him. But inside she felt like a lovelorn teenager – bereft.

Zoe lingered in the yard after she returned. Though her riding was going well she still had horses to do as part of her duties and sometimes she resented it. Not this evening, however. She found herself spinning out the task of feeding the horses she looked after. For once, she wasn't much looking forward to going home and seeing Pat – he'd seemed so out of sorts when she'd left that morning, lying in bed like a corpse, not even saying goodbye.

When she got back it was obvious he'd done nothing all day. The place had a musty, unaired smell as if he hadn't even been bothered to open the windows. It seemed he'd spent most of the day in bed – it smelled like it. And the place was a mess, with dirty washing in the sink and papers scattered over the sitting-room floor.

She found him in the kitchen, putting ready meals in the microwave.

'Brilliant ride, sweetheart,' he said. 'You could have eased up on the poor bugger though, there was no one within miles of you.'

She was well aware of that, thank you, and she felt bad enough about it without him rubbing it in.

'What's the matter, Pat? Are you ill?' He looked a bit sallow but otherwise he seemed all right. 'If you're not well you should have said, I'd have got supper.'

He flashed a grin that was gone all too soon. 'Too late for that.'

'So what's up?' she said as she picked at the rubbery food he'd put in front of her.

He didn't reply and she wondered if he'd heard her; he was engaged in a hunt for the tomato ketchup.

'What do you think of Martin?' he said finally.

'I don't like him much.'

He looked at her, relief on his face. 'Me neither. What on earth is your sister doing with him?'

She didn't know what to say to that. She rarely criticised Harriet, though God knows her sister often gave her cause. And she'd promised Harriet to keep the marriage talk to herself. Frankly, she hoped that her sister would come to her senses and she'd never have to tell anyone.

Pat laughed nastily and answered his own question. 'I can imagine what she's doing with him, just the same as she was doing behind poor old Andy's back.'

'She's in love with him.' It was the best defence she could muster for Harriet.

He chewed with distaste. 'You want to know why I was out of sorts last night? That bastard beat me up.'

Had she heard correctly? 'What do you mean?'

'What do you think I mean? While you were in the garden we went into the front room and he beat the crap out of me.'

She put down her fork. 'Are you serious? You don't look like you've been beaten up.'

'He punched me in the stomach and hit me round the head. There's nothing to see but it hurt, I tell you. Then he twisted my arm up my back. I thought he was going to break it.'

She pushed her plate away. This was incredible. She might not have taken to Martin but he'd been perfectly polite and civilised throughout the evening. Though if Pat had been assaulted, it would explain his strange behaviour.

'But why would he do that to you? It makes no sense.'

Pat sighed heavily. He'd given up on his supper too. He picked up their plates and scraped the remains into the bin. It was plain he was playing for time.

'If you want me to believe you, Pat, you're going to have to tell me.'

He sat down heavily across the table and reached for her hand. His face was weary and his eyes pleaded for her sympathy. But she wasn't prepared to give it just yet.

'Look,' he said, 'I'm going to tell you something that's for your ears only. OK?'

'It depends what it is.' What on earth was he about to confess?

'It's nothing terrible, honestly. I could get into a bit of trouble if it got out, that's all.'

She removed her hand. 'Spit it out, Pat.'

For a moment she thought he was going to refuse, then he began. 'When I started racing I thought I was going to be the next Lester Piggott. I thought I'd be riding Group One winners and lining up at Newmarket on Guineas day – all of that. You have those dreams too, don't you?'

She nodded. 'They're good dreams to have.'

'Sure but you'll soon learn that dreams are all they are. This business is sewn up, unless you're one of the privileged few at the top yards and in with the richest owners. You've got no chance because you're a girl and you ride for an old maverick like Jack Lucas.'

Zoe couldn't deny there might be something in what he said though she was damned if she'd let him destroy her hopes. Anyway, she wanted him to stick to the point.

'You see what I'm getting at, don't you?' he said. 'The penny dropped with me last summer when I realised that I was never going to make it to the top of the tree. I'm at the peak of my ability and all I can expect is a few more years of plugging away. And what's going to happen in the future? There are guys who started after me who are coining it. Ride a Classic winner and you've got money pouring in – presents from the happy owner, a slice of the stud fees for years to come. I'd like a pension plan too, you know.'

'Get on with it, Pat.' She didn't like the sound of this.

'Me and Andy got talking about him setting up as a trainer again and how we might go into business together. Then I thought how I could do much more for my folks if there was a bit more money floating around. The long and short of it is that I started punting. I've a fair idea what's going to win, better than most jockeys, I reckon. It's a skill and I don't see why I shouldn't use it to my advantage. So I got Andy to put the bets on.'

'Which horses?' she asked, thinking rapidly. 'Ones you were riding?'

'Well, yeah.'

'Like Pipsqueak and Full Force?'

'Does it matter?'

Zoe thought it did but she just said, 'Go on.'

'Anyhow, it went pretty well and we made some cash. Then Andy died.' He paused, staring into her eyes, beseeching her to understand his predicament. 'Do you see the problem?'

'No.' She could guess but she wanted him to spell it out.

'Andy was holding the money. It would have looked fishy if I had it. We were going to go into business together and share it that way. But now he's dead the money's part of his estate and it goes to Harriet. I've asked her for it and she won't give it to me. She says there's nothing in writing.'

'What you were doing was illegal, wasn't it?'

'Well . . . technically. But morally half that money is mine.'

It was a funny use of the word 'morally'.

'How much money are we talking about?'

He named a figure. She sat frozen in shock. Harriet had told her Andy had some savings in a building society. She'd never realised it was that much.

'That's why Martin was working me over. He threatened to bust me up so I couldn't ride if I mentioned it to Harriet again. He would too. He's a lunatic.'

Zoe was consciously trying to control her breathing. She must think this through. One thing struck her immediately – Pat wasn't telling her the whole truth. He and Andy had not just been placing bets. Their record of picking winners was no better than any other jockey she had ever met. She'd been with Pat when friends had asked for tips and she'd noticed they rarely came back for more. To win hundreds of thousands of pounds Pat must have been up to something. Jack had quizzed her to find out who was cheating. Now she knew.

She had little sympathy for Pat and his lost cash. He'd been cheating and that went against everything she believed in. She herself had been riding Pipsqueak when he came home for his big win at Nottingham. Did that mean she was implicated in this too?

'You've got to help me, Zoe.'

'Me?' The last thing she wanted was to become further embroiled in this sleazy mess.

'Go to Harriet and ask her for the money. You're the only person she'll listen to.'

'No.'

'But you've got to! You can't just let them walk away with a hundred grand. It's money for us, sweetheart. Get her to pay it to you.'

She was on her feet, heading for the bedroom. It wouldn't take a minute to grab the things she needed.

'What are you doing?' He'd come after her.

'Packing.'

'What do you mean?'

'I'm leaving, Pat. It's all over between us.'

'You can't be serious. I love you.'

'Not as much as you love yourself, obviously. You're a thief, Pat, just like your brothers.'

She stuffed clothes into a holdall. He followed her as she stalked into the bathroom for her toilet things.

'Zoe, sweetheart, you can't just go. Let's talk it over. Please.'

'No.' She was heading down the hall for the door. He stood in front of her.

'Get out of my way, Pat, or I'll hurt you worse than Martin ever did.'

Maybe there was something in her eyes, something wild and crazy, but he stood aside.

As she opened the door, he said, 'You can keep half the money, I promise.'

She shut the door in his face.

* * *

Unless there was a programme of particular interest on the television, Jack was usually in bed by half past nine. The days when he would sit up late were long gone. Of course, in those days he'd had his wife to keep him company.

Tonight there was no TV programme of interest – there rarely was. He feared that this was his fault rather than the television programmers. His world was shrinking along with his curiosity.

One thing that still satisfied him, however, was his horses. There was always a reason why he should visit the yard and check on one animal or another. Listening to them chew their hay at the end of the day when they were settled and everyone else had gone home was one of the greatest perks of his job. Sometimes he didn't need an excuse and he went anyway. Like tonight.

To his surprise he found there was a vehicle still in the car park. He recognised the old orange Mini. What was Zoe still doing here? He thought she'd gone home hours ago.

He found Zoe in Magnetic's box. She'd been partial to the animal ever since their triumph at Ascot.

'What are you up to?' he called. 'I don't pay overtime, you know.'

But he saw at once she was in no mood for banter. Even in the dim light of the stall he could see moisture on her cheeks.

'I was just passing and . . .' She stopped, her voice petering out. 'I'm sorry, boss.'

'Come on out of there,' he said firmly. 'What's the matter?'

She let herself out of the stall, a tiny hunched figure. Jack wanted to put his arm round her but perhaps it wasn't appropriate and he didn't want to upset her further.

'Now, why aren't you off celebrating your fine ride this afternoon? Or tucked up at home with that young man of yours?'

The tears began to flow freely now and Jack made the connection. Boyfriend trouble. He'd lived through the years of his daughter's romantic ups and downs so it wasn't too difficult to hazard a guess at what had been going on.

'You'd better come up to the house,' he said.

She found her voice. 'Oh no, I don't want to upset your plans.'

He laughed. 'There's nothing to upset, my dear. I don't have plans – except to make a pot of tea. You'd better come and have some.'

Zoe wondered whether she'd subconsciously intended this to happen, to wind up in Jack's lovely old home where the grandfather clock ticked like a timeless heartbeat and every ornament and bookshelf spoke of a treasured past. She'd have liked to have grown up in a house like this.

She'd walked out on Pat on impulse, without

thinking where she would go. Her sister's flat was the obvious bolt-hole but the thought of playing gooseberry to Harriet and Martin turned her stomach. She'd ended up in the yard because it was the only other place she could think of.

But here she was in a first-floor room of Jack's big old house, contemplating a wall covered in posters, photographs of school hockey teams and numerous pictures of horses. The shelves were full of well-thumbed books and girlish knick-knacks. The CD rack was bulging with someone's dusty old favourites. This was Geraldine Lucas's old bedroom, lovingly preserved by her doting father who obviously couldn't bear to draw a line under the past.

Jack had not been intrusive – they'd discussed horses over tea – but he'd said, 'There's a bed in Geraldine's old room if you want to stop the night,' and he'd pointed her in the right direction and told her where to find clean sheets. It had been easy just to go along with his suggestion.

The bed was soft and she was tired but she didn't know if she could sleep.

Damn Pat. She thought they had something special but now she could see she'd been kidding herself. She'd almost rather he'd betrayed her with another girl. Some people wouldn't agree but this was as bad. He'd become cynical and corrupted and wanted to drag her into his dishonesty.

So maybe she was naive and stupid – he hadn't

said so but it was plain that's what he thought – but at least she was honest. It mattered to her. Was that wrong? It mattered like her dreams of being a successful jockey mattered. It was what she strove to be and if she went along with Pat, all that would be spoiled. Just because his dreams were tarnished didn't mean that hers must be too.

But if she was to keep herself honest she could have no more to do with Pat. She wouldn't shop him, that would be a personal betrayal, but she'd walk the other way if she saw him coming.

It would hurt, but that's the way it would have to be.

Chapter Seventeen

Jack thought hard before he made the call. It was a cardinal rule not to interfere in the personal affairs of his staff. But this was different.

Pat had sounded a bit ropey on the phone yesterday and he didn't sound much better today.

'How are you?' Jack asked.

'I'm fine. I've got a couple of rides at Newbury this afternoon for Ed Cooper.'

'Well, listen, I'm going to suggest that we put our understanding on hold for a few weeks.'

'Why's that?'

'Tell me it's none of my business but when I find my apprentice in tears in the yard at nine in the evening with nowhere to stay then I reckon it is.'

There was a pause. 'You're right, guv'nor, it isn't your business. Zoe and I had a row and she walked out but she's welcome back anytime. I've been trying to get hold of her.'

Jack ploughed on. 'Whatever the rights and

wrongs, she's staying in my house for the moment. If she wants to go back to your place then it's up to her but right now I'd rather you stay away. I don't want any domestic troubles interrupting the yard. Also, I reckon the pair of you could do with a cooling-off period.'

'You're booting me out?'

'I'm putting you on temporary hold. You won't be short of work, Pat. I'll put in a few calls on your behalf.'

'Jesus, I don't know what to say. I love Zoe. I didn't want it to come to this.'

He sounded like he meant it and Jack felt for him. But the yard wasn't big enough for the pair of them at present and he knew where his sympathies lay.

Harriet switched on her phone with fumbling fingers. She wasn't her usual collected self this morning. She'd nearly made a mess of a customer's highlights and had knocked over the milk in the salon's little kitchen.

She had two missed calls and a text from Zoe: 'Call me – urgent.' She ignored it, she couldn't get her head around anybody's issues but her own at the moment.

She'd tried ringing Martin, last night and this morning, but had been repeatedly referred to voicemail. She had to speak to him – didn't he realise the agony he was putting her through?

373

The answer to that was probably yes. She was getting to realise how strong he was – in every sense. He still wore a bandage on his arm but he wouldn't let her look at it and refused even to admit it bothered him – which it clearly did, especially if she banged against it in bed.

She thought with a pang of how lonely she had been in that big bed on her own last night. He should have been by her side but he'd deliberately walked out on her, as a punishment. She knew he'd have missed her too but he was harder than she was. He could take the pain.

Her phone beeped. Thank God, Martin had sent her a text. 'Can u make caff in half hour?' It might mean rushing her next client – just a quick wash and dry fortunately – but she'd make it all right.

In the event she was late because guilt got the better of her and she rang Zoe. She took in the news that Zoe had broken it off with Pat with some amazement. What a relief. Now she wouldn't have to pretend she liked him. And since she'd spent ten minutes the other night urging her sister to dump him she felt vindicated.

Quite why Zoe had done so was more mystifying. She wasn't exactly coherent about it. But Harriet didn't have time to get drawn into her sister's drama. She promised to call her later and rang off.

All the same, she ended up late for Martin. Just ten minutes, but would he wait that long? she wondered as she fled the salon. She couldn't be sure he wouldn't take it as a deliberate snub and those sky-blue eyes would turn wintry and cold. She couldn't bear that.

She forced herself to slow down and take a calming breath before she entered the café. She had her pride, after all.

He was in the far corner, at the table they'd used before in the distant past when Andy was alive and they were just conducting a naughty little affair. All of six weeks ago.

'Sorry I'm late,' she said and regretted the way her voice revealed her anxiety. To her relief, the eyes he turned on her were summer bright and free from reproach. He insisted on buying her a coffee and took his time flirting with the girl at the counter. Harriet knew he was doing it deliberately. He'd said he had no interest in other women but her and she believed him. It was part of what made his disapproval so hard to bear. As his goddess, she wasn't allowed to let him down.

'Well,' he said as he finally took his seat opposite, 'what's it to be?'

The way he said it, she knew this wasn't an invitation to debate the when and where of their future marriage. It was a yes or no – agree with me or feel my wrath. Might he walk out on her for good if she didn't say yes to his plans?

She only knew she couldn't live with the idea of him abandoning her. His love for her might be hard and implacable but it was the only thing that mattered to her in the chaos of her life at present.

'I printed out all that stuff about Las Vegas,' she said, pulling the pages from her bag. 'When do you want to go?'

Pat was still smarting over Jack's phone call as he barged through the doors of the gym reception area. To be booted out of Beach Head was a sickener, no matter how Jack had dressed it up. More than that, it had thrown his plan to find Zoe at the yard and plead his case. Sure, he'd been a flaming eejit and it had been wrong of him to stop a few horses but he'd had cause and he was prepared to do anything to get her back. If he could get Zoe to return he'd never, ever go off the rails again. He wanted to look into her big hazel eyes and tell her so.

But he couldn't show up at the yard after Jack's call – he didn't want to be banned for good. So he'd driven into Bridgwater to plead his case with Harriet. She might not like him but if he made his peace with her by relinquishing all claim on Andy's money, surely she would appeal to Zoe on his behalf.

He headed upstairs to the hair salon but the girl on reception told him Harriet was on a break.

'You could try the café,' she said with a smirk that Pat had no time to interpret. He didn't have long, he had to get on the road to Newbury shortly.

He froze in the café doorway at the sight of two

familiar figures at a table in the far corner: a woman with a crown of copper-coloured hair and a sprawling athletic figure in shorts. Harriet was with Martin, his least favourite person in the world.

As he stood there, Martin stood up.

Pat retreated as fast as he could. He had no desire to come face to face with his tormentor. He moved swiftly down the corridor and through the door of the Gents, though he didn't close it completely. He looked back through the crack. Which way was the big fellow going? If Martin headed his way, Pat reckoned he could hide in a toilet stall.

But Martin turned the other way, back in the direction of the gym and the tennis courts. Back to work, no doubt.

So was Harriet still in the café?

She was. He caught her trying to cram a wodge of folded paper into her handbag.

'Hello, Harriet.'

She looked at him as if she'd never seen him before in her life. 'Oh, hi.' She wore the kind of blissed-out expression that went with high-strength anti-depressants.

'Have you heard?' he demanded. 'Zoe's walked out on me.'

A slow smile spread across her face. 'I'm sorry, Pat. I'm sure you'll get over it.' She plainly couldn't give a hoot.

'You can help me,' he blurted. 'It's all a

misunderstanding. Tell her I love her and get her to talk to me at least. Please.'

The smile was replaced by astonishment. 'Why on earth should I do that?'

'If you get her to come back to me I'll forget all about that money. You can keep it – or give it away. I don't want it. I want Zoe, do you understand?' He realised he meant every word.

She shrugged. 'Martin tells me you've already agreed the money's not yours.'

'Your boyfriend's a psychopath. He ought to be locked up.'

'Bad-mouthing Martin's not going to get me on your side, Pat.' Harriet stood, slipping the loop of her bag over her shoulder. 'In any case, I think Zoe can do better than you.'

She turned to leave and he grabbed her arm. 'Please, Harriet!'

'Let go of me,' she hissed.

The people at a nearby table were staring at them and a waiter had stopped in the act of clearing cups.

Pat removed his hand.

'Goodbye, Pat,' Harriet said and walked off.

He stood there for a moment, no doubt looking like a complete clot.

He *was* a complete clot, he'd made a real fool of himself. But women did that to you.

He sat down to clear his head.

On the table top was a sheet of paper, like those

Harriet had been shoving into her bag as he approached. It was blank. Or almost. On the top of the page was a line of print, some web address and a small logo next to the words 'Las Vegas Chamber of Commerce'.

He thought nothing of it.

Diane put her foot down as she drove to Beach Head yard. She was in good spirits, better than she'd felt for days. She had just one more chore to complete then she was off for a week in Rome with her friend Trish, followed by three weeks in Majorca with Maurice. She couldn't wait to get away.

The week in Rome had been hastily arranged. The whole business with Harriet and Martin had got her down. She was never going to set foot in that health centre again. When she came back, she'd find something more constructive to do with her time – some charity work maybe. There was a gym at a new hotel on the road to Weston that was meant to be terrific. And, though she didn't like to count her chickens, maybe having Maurice to herself in Majorca would bear fruit. She'd binned her birth control pills. It seemed like good timing.

She pulled off the road and parked next to a jumble of distinctly shabby vehicles in the shade of an ivy-covered wall. Beyond, a solid double-fronted house and a clutch of outbuildings sprawled in the sunshine. House martins and swallows perched on the telephone wires and a clop of horse's hooves sounded from within. Beach Head yard wore a friendly air. She hoped she wasn't going to spoil it.

Zoe was waiting for her by the gate. Diane had rung ahead to make sure she wasn't setting out on a fool's errand and learned when Zoe was expected down off the gallops. Plainly the news of her visit had been passed on.

Diane didn't waste any time. She just wanted to deliver her message and get home to focus on more cheerful things, like the prospect of clothes shopping on the Via del Corso.

'Do you know your sister is involved with a guy called Martin?'

Zoe's smile was replaced by a frown. 'Yes.'

Diane plunged on. 'He's bad news. He's a liar and a creep and just the worst kind of person for Harriet to be mixed up with. I've said this to her but she doesn't care.'

'So now you're telling me?'

'She might listen to you.'

Zoe pulled a face – she plainly doubted it.

'Look, I wouldn't have come to see you if I didn't feel strongly about it. Martin's dangerous. He threatened me.'

'What do you mean?'

'I discovered Harriet's car parked outside his house and he came out. He wouldn't let me see her. Basically he told me never to talk to Harriet again. And he held my arm tight, like he was showing me how strong he was. I couldn't move. He didn't say he'd hurt me if I didn't do what he said but he didn't have to. I was scared.'

'But you went ahead and spoke to Harriet?'

'I felt I had to. But she thinks I'm jealous and I'm not. I did once like Martin but not any more. I know more about him now. He's told Harriet and me different stories about himself. And there's something in his past I can't get to the bottom of.'

'Such as?'

'When he was a schoolboy he ran off with a married woman. They both played tennis at the same club. Then there was a scandal. That's all I know.'

'What's the name of the club?'

Diane took a slip of paper from her bag. 'I wrote it down for you.'

She pressed it into Zoe's hand with a profound sense of relief.

Pat chucked his bag on the sofa and kicked off his shoes. The bag bounced off a cushion and rolled onto the floor. A shoe landed on the coffee table. He left them where they fell. There was nobody around this evening to nag him for his slovenly ways.

Looked at dispassionately, this had been one of the worst days he could remember. Zoe had left him and, from the short phone conversation he'd had with her, would not be coming back. The most honest, loving, best-looking woman he'd ever been involved with had dumped him. He'd been too honest, that was the problem. He should never have told her about the money.

The nest egg he'd been building for himself and his family was now out of his grasp, the property of a conniving bitch who had hopped into bed with a psycho capable of breaking his bones into matchsticks. He'd lost his job, booted out by an ageing trainer who was doubtless about to pass all his rides over to his ex-girlfriend. And he'd ridden two losers that afternoon – though one of them was a small cause for satisfaction. If he'd lost Zoe anyway, he might as well lay the groundwork for another gamble. The way things were, he'd be needing the money.

'I don't know what happened there, guv'nor,' he said to Ed Cooper after his horse had trailed in well down the field in the fifth race at Newbury.

'Me neither.' The trainer had looked as if he'd taken a kick in the teeth. 'I thought he was better than that. Don't blame yourself, Pat, you gave him a bloody good ride.'

And that he had. Anyone watching would have testified to his effort, which was how it should be. There'd been a bit of a fright after the race; all the riders were asked to weigh in for once and he'd had to be a bit nimble there.

So there was some cause for satisfaction amidst current disasters. The bastards hadn't ground all the life out of him just yet.

'We live to fight another day,' he muttered to himself, a well-known cliché in racing circles. Funny how many situations it applied to.

The doorbell rang. Surely it couldn't be Zoe? Maybe she'd come to her senses.

No such luck.

It was a woman, attractive in her way, but not one he wished to see. That bloody policewoman Laura Hammond.

Laura was not unsympathetic to Pat Vincent. He had been Andy's closest friend and was out at the pub with him just before the tragedy. He'd gone to search for Andy when Harriet had raised the alarm and, what's more, he'd found him. Laura had talked to Pat that night and subsequently. There was no doubt in her mind that he was genuinely upset by all that had taken place.

So she didn't share DCI Lane's opinion that Pat ought to be hauled in for a formal interview and quizzed about the possibility of Andy and Joe fixing horse races. However, she did agree with Lane that there might be more to Joe Parkin shoving Andy off the cliff than simple animosity. A fall-out over a betting scam might provide a stronger motive.

It was her superior's opinion that most racing people were bent. 'It stands to reason. They control the animals and all the inside information, and let's face it, there's a ton of money to be made.' But it was nigh on impossible to prove. Laura agreed with him there. There were regular police round-ups of trainers and riders, incurring vast expense in time and resources and creating banner headlines in the national press. But successful prosecutions of race-fixing were as rare as hen's teeth.

Pat didn't look overjoyed to see her but agreed to give her a few minutes. She noted that the house was far less tidy than before and that there was no sign of Harriet's sister, who had provided cups of tea during her last visit. Pat did not offer her refreshment but bundled a pile of newspapers and other obstacles out of the way so she could take a seat.

Laura began by asking questions about Andy and Joe at Beach Head yard, the nature of their working relationship and whether, as betting men, they traded information between themselves. His answers were not revealing but she plugged on, to his obvious irritation, until he finally said, 'You're barking up the wrong tree with Joe, you know. He didn't kill Andy. Andy killed himself – and his wife drove him to it.'

Laura tried not to show her surprise. She would have asked Pat to explain but he needed no prompting.

'The whole effing disaster is down to Harriet. She was having an affair and Andy thought she was going to leave him. So he jumped off the cliff. He as good as told me he was going to do it.'

* * *

The moment it was out of his mouth Pat felt a hundred per cent better. He'd been sitting on the truth about Andy for too long. It felt great to let it out.

He'd not had time to think everything through but the events of the past twenty-four hours had changed his situation. Now it was open warfare – him against Harriet and her personal hitman, Martin. The major obstacle to him speaking his mind had now, sadly, been removed. If Zoe was no longer to be part of his life, he didn't have to keep his mouth shut about the behaviour of her sister.

There were other advantages to him speaking out. First, of course, that he could now stand up for Joe. He'd been feeling such a heel about not doing his bit to save the lad. He'd written a clumsy reply to Joe's letter telling him to keep his chin up and that justice would be done – which he didn't believe for one moment. And there'd also been a couple of tearful phone conversations with Joe's sister. He felt bloody awful on her account too.

Second of all, he wasn't happy about the cops earmarking Andy's betting as a motive for their supposed murder. That was too damned close to home for his liking. Not to mention a red herring as far as Andy's death was concerned.

'Look,' he said, 'I know maybe I should have said this before but suicide's a terrible thing, isn't it?'

DC Hammond considered him sternly. He chose his words with care.

'When I met Andy that night in the pub, he was in a bit of state. He said he was convinced Harriet was cheating on him. She'd done it once before, though he'd not been able to prove it.'

She waited for him to go on and he obliged.

'Anyhow, that night Andy was particularly cut up because he'd thought things were going better with Harriet and then suddenly he'd found they weren't. He'd caught her out and he told me he was thinking he should get a divorce.'

'He had proof of her infidelity?'

'Something to do with a camera phone. You know, she's in bed with a bloke and Andy rings and asks her to send him a photo of where she is.'

'Is that what happened?'

'Yeah, so he said. She didn't send a photo of the guy's bedroom, of course, but pretended she didn't know how then sent him one ten minutes later when she'd put her clothes on – something like that. Whatever, it was pretty fishy.'

'And you're saying that because of this he decided to kill himself?'

'Not entirely. I'm afraid I put my foot in it.' This was the awkward part. Pat didn't know how to make his gaffe sound any better but it was what had happened. 'He said something along the lines of "I think she's got another bloke" and without thinking I let slip about her friend the tennis coach.

Only Pat didn't know who it was till I said that. I felt bad about it. I still do.'

'How did you know who it was?'

'Through Zoe. Harriet used to ring her up and sometimes I'd overhear things. Not on purpose but it's not exactly a big place, is it? Anyway, I could see that knocked old Andy for six. I suppose it was just having actual proof of who was misbehaving with his wife. He got very low, I can tell you. He loved Harriet and he'd never ever look at another woman. He wanted kids with her and everything but I don't think she was all that bothered. He said what good was she to him when she made him feel like throwing himself off a cliff.'

Laura looked at him suspiciously.

'Yeah, I know it sounds a bit neat but that's what he actually said. I didn't think anything of it at the time, I could understand he might be feeling that way, but when I went out to look for him that night it was going through my head, I can tell you. So I feel like shit about the whole thing. I've been blaming myself because he told me what he was going to do then bloody well went off and did it. I shouldn't have let him go.'

There was silence for a moment. 'You've kept quiet up to this point. Why are you telling me this now?'

'Well, you lot suddenly putting Andy's death on Joe changes things.' Pat contemplated the mess around the place, the empty bedroom next door

387

and the empty spaces in the cupboards – Zoe had returned while he was at Newbury and cleared out her things. He might as well come completely clean. 'Anyway, Zoe and I have split up. You could say I haven't got anyone's reputation to protect any more.'

Laura nodded. He could see her working it out.

He made a final plea on Joe's behalf – it was about the only aspect of this conversation that showed him in a decent light. 'Joe never killed anyone. He might have got into a fight with Andy but I bet he came off worse.'

Though she smiled sympathetically he could tell he hadn't convinced her.

'There's just one more thing,' she said. 'Can you tell me the name of the tennis coach who is friendly with Harriet Burns?'

Pat could. He did so with pleasure.

Zoe considered the small blue-lined slip of paper that Diane had given her. On it was written, in looping ballpoint, 'Spillbury Tennis Club', followed by an address and phone number.

She didn't know what to make of Diane's visit. She suspected the woman had some hidden agenda to do with the handsome tennis coach. Had Harriet stolen Martin from her? Diane had virtually said as much.

But she'd also said that Martin laid a hand on her and physically intimidated her. That tied in with what Pat had said – and she'd not believed him. It had seemed so incredible.

She'd found herself softening towards Pat. Clearing her clothes out of the house had been painful but she'd forced herself to do it. Now she wondered if she hadn't been too hard on him.

Suppose he'd been telling the truth about Martin? And suppose Diane was genuinely fearful for Harriet and trying to do her a good turn?

Zoe sighed as she put the paper away. She wasn't looking forward to her next conversation with her sister.

The policewoman was in reception again. Harriet could see her sitting patiently on the sofa flicking through a magazine while she put the finishing touches to her client's hair. For a second Harriet felt a stab of panic. What was it this time? The police never showed up with good news.

Then she turned back to what she was doing. She wouldn't let anything intrude on her newfound happiness. Whatever unpleasantness the policewoman was about to deliver, she wouldn't let it spoil the way she had been feeling since she'd submitted to Martin's will yesterday. Why had she ever thought to oppose him? They would be married soon and face the world together. All she had to do before then was stay true to that thought.

'I'm sorry to disturb you again at your work.'

Before her new understanding with Martin, this

policewoman would have irritated the hell out of Harriet. She put herself across as so understanding and sympathetic but there was always another agenda.

'I've just got a couple of questions,' the woman said. 'Do you have a moment?'

'I'm booked solid, I'm sorry.' She wasn't and Laura could probably tell from the way she said it. Too bad. Harriet smiled serenely. Go away, you tedious little woman, stop dragging me down.

On second thoughts, she didn't want her turning up at the end of the day or coming round to the flat. 'However, if it really is just a couple of questions, go ahead.'

Laura glanced around. There was no one close enough to overhear.

'The last time you saw your husband, how would you describe his mood?'

'He seemed fine. We just passed each other at the gate as he went out.'

'And how was he in the days before that?'

'The same as always. Certainly not depressed.' They'd been over this ground way back at the beginning. Naturally the police had looked at the suicide angle but it was rubbish.

'And how would you say the pair of you had been getting on?'

'We'd been getting on very well actually.' Harriet couldn't believe she'd been interrupted for this.

The woman was just being tiresome. 'That's three questions so far – are there many more?'

'Just one really. Can you confirm you are acquainted with Martin Christie?'

Martin.

The name broke open her cocoon of comfort. Though she'd known Laura would come up with something to throw her off course and she'd tried to prepare for it, she'd failed.

'Confirm you are acquainted.' What kind of language was that?

'Yes. I know Martin,' she said. 'He's a friend.'

'How long have you been friendly?'

'A few months. Why are you asking?'

Laura ignored her question. 'Did your husband know of your friendship with Mr Christie?'

She made the word 'friendship' sound so incriminating.

'He may have done, he may not. I have lots of acquaintances here but I didn't necessarily discuss them with Andy. What are you getting at?'

'People gossip, Mrs Burns, and considering the circumstances of your husband's death I am bound to listen to what they say. Don't be offended, it's not my job to make judgements.'

Harriet didn't believe that for a moment. She could tell this prissy cow had branded her in her mind as an adulterer. She had to set the record straight.

'Look, Laura, I don't deny that I know Martin,

why should I? There was absolutely nothing improper about our relationship before Andy died, if that's what you're implying. Since then he's been very supportive,' Laura would like that word, 'and I can't deny that we've become closer. But I don't see that it's anyone's business but our own. Do you understand?'

The policewoman nodded. She'd understood all right but what she would make of it, Harriet had no idea. She only knew that Laura had shattered her equanimity.

The detective turned to go. 'Thank you for your time, Mrs Burns. I'd better let you get on.'

'Wait. I've got a right to know who's gossiping about me. Who told you about Martin?'

Laura hesitated. 'It's just information that's come up in our inquiries.'

Harriet worked it out. It had to be Pat or Diane. Probably Pat. Now he was no longer with Zoe he'd be only too thrilled to put the boot in.

She laughed scornfully. 'I wouldn't believe a word Pat Vincent tells you. Do you know he's just broken up with my sister? He just wants to get back at her by upsetting me.'

And he'd succeeded. Thank God her next client only required a wash and blow dry. It was an hour before she could trust herself to pick up a pair of scissors.

Chapter Eighteen

'Quick!' Harriet seized Martin and dragged him into the hallway of her flat. She half expected the policewoman to be standing across the street observing his arrival.

'Steady on, babe.' His face was tense and she realised she'd grabbed him by his injured arm. It worried her that it was so slow to heal but he refused to discuss it with her.

'Oh God, I'm so sorry, Martin.'

'It's OK.' He held her at bay with the other hand. 'Just be more careful in future.'

'I'm sorry. I didn't think. I didn't do it on purpose, honestly.'

She'd discovered that he treasured apologies. Not that she minded grovelling in this instance.

'So why the drama?'

She'd not been all that coherent when she'd phoned him but she'd got over the main points. Pat had accosted her in the café and then she'd had a visit from DC Hammond. Pat had told the police about their affair.

She stood before Martin, not daring to touch him. 'I just can't bear the thought of you being dragged into all this mess about Andy. People are going to start talking and they'll bring it up at the trial and it'll get into the press.'

She heard her voice quiver and realised she was on the verge of tears. What was happening to her?

Martin put his arms round her and pulled her into his body. Oh, that felt good. Gradually she stopped trembling. She was safe in his embrace.

'None of that is going to happen,' he said. 'I'll have a word with Pat.'

'Why should he take any notice? Not now Zoe's broken off with him.'

Martin laughed and she relished the feeling as it rippled through his body. 'Don't you believe all that stuff about jockeys being tough. Pat's going to shit himself when I drop in on him.'

'But the damage has been done,' she protested.

'No, it hasn't. You and I had feelings for each other before Andy's death but we kept them under control. Then after his death you needed someone to lean on and things developed from there. The timing might be inconvenient but we can't help that.'

That was true.

He kissed the top of her head. 'Besides, it will be

much harder for them to criticise us when we're an old married couple.'

'When will that be?' Suddenly she couldn't wait.

'I'll turn on the computer and you get your credit card,' he said. 'We're going to book the flight right now.'

It was surprisingly easy. Martin had already done some homework and found a Continental Airlines flight to Las Vegas, leaving from Bristol at ten fifty the morning after next. There was a stopover in Newark, which made for almost sixteen hours' journey time, but Harriet didn't care about that. Once they were in the air she'd feel a hundred per cent better she was sure. Besides, travelling from Bristol saved them lots of time, the airport was only forty minutes away.

Just a day and a half and she would be out of all this hassle. Starting a new life with Martin.

They'd only just finished the booking when Zoe turned up at the door, which was a close shave. Martin had made Harriet promise not to tell anyone about the plan, not even her sister. It was really very romantic. Like planning an old-fashioned elopement.

Actually, she might let Zoe in on the secret. After all, Zoe knew that she was thinking of marrying Martin at some point. And though she'd promised, sort of, to go slow on the idea, Zoe would have to realise things had changed. Anyhow, it was her life. But she couldn't tell Zoe with Martin around.

Martin, however, took one look at Zoe and announced, 'Sorry, girls, but I've got to make tracks.' As he opened the door, he winked at Harriet. 'Lots of stuff to sort out.'

That was OK. He wasn't angry therefore she didn't mind him leaving.

Zoe wasn't looking her usual sunny self and, for a second, Harriet wondered why. Then she remembered – she'd just broken up with Pat, which would explain it. She supposed she was going to have to listen to the latest developments in the tale.

But Zoe took her by surprise.

'Did you know that Martin beat Pat up the night we came round here?'

Harriet laughed.

'I'm serious.' Her sister's face was drawn and pale.

'Is that what Pat told you?'

'Yes.'

'But we were both here. If there was a fight, we'd have known about it.'

'There wasn't a fight. Martin hit him and twisted his arm. He's about twice Pat's size.'

So that's how Martin had got Pat to agree about the money. It had been thoughtful of him to spare her the details.

'Why on earth should you believe Pat?' she said. 'He's just trying to make trouble – and gain your sympathy, I suppose. I wouldn't take any notice of him.'

'He says you're hanging on to money of his that was in Andy's building society.'

She supposed it was no surprise that Pat had told Zoe, but irritating all the same.

'That's ridiculous, Pat's just trying it on. Andy never said anything to me about owing him money. Frankly, I feel like I'm being blackmailed. I'm not surprised Martin gave him short shrift. He was only looking after my interests.'

'And was Martin just looking after your interests when he threatened Diane Connor?'

Harriet couldn't believe it, everyone seemed to be ganging up on her and Martin. 'For God's sake, Zoe, Diane has been throwing herself at Martin for months. She'll say anything to split us up.'

Zoe looked at her, seemingly stuck for words. She cut a small, miserable figure and Harriet felt a surge of affection for her sister. She held out her arms.

'Cheer up, Chipmunk. You've had a horrible few days but you'll get over it.'

Zoe returned her hug with warmth. 'Just promise me you'll take things slowly with Martin. It's going to take time for us all to get used to him.'

'Sure.' That was non-committal enough. She couldn't tell Zoe about the wedding now.

'And this money thing with Pat . . .' Zoe sounded hesitant.

'If he can prove Andy owed him money then he'll get it. I've already spoken to the solicitor who's dealing with the estate.' This was a white lie but permissible in the circumstances. Once Zoe had a chance to reflect, surely she'd see that it wasn't in the interests of either of them for her to give away thousands of pounds.

'Actually, I don't want to know about any money, it makes me sick.'

That was all right then. Harriet had always admired Zoe's scruples.

'All I care about,' Zoe continued, 'is you. I don't know Martin and I don't trust him. And I'm worried that, with Andy dying so recently and everything, you're not thinking straight.' She gripped Harriet by the shoulders and stared intently into her eyes. 'I need you and you need me and there's so much horrible stuff going on, we've got to stick together, haven't we?'

'Yes.' Harriet pulled her close. It felt good to hug her little sister. She stroked her thick spiky mop of hair. 'There's one thing you could do for me, Chipmunk.'

'What is it?'

'Take care of Jasper for the weekend. Martin and I are going to London.'

Zoe pulled away. Harriet could see she wasn't thrilled by the thought.

'Unless you don't think I should go,' she added.

It was a relief to see a smile back on Zoe's face.

'Of course you should go. And I'd love to take care of Jasper.'

So it worked out quite well in the end, all things considered.

Another night in Jack's house and Zoe found sleep hard to come by. The charm of the little room with its mementos of Jack's daughter's childhood all around was no longer seductive. Geraldine Lucas had shed her adolescent skin and gone on to have an adult life with marriage and, soon, a baby. Zoe yielded to a jolt of envy. It felt wrong to be lying here in a schoolgirl's narrow bed, as if she was going backwards in life.

Face it, she was missing Pat. Her heart pined for him.

But her head told her to be strong. It would be easy to fall back into his arms but would it be the right thing to do? To align herself with a race-fixer?

She couldn't stomach the thought.

But concern for her sister put her own miseries in the shade. She'd left Harriet's flat in a happier frame of mind but, lying awake in the small hours, her doubts returned. Reflecting on their conversation, she realised her sister had barely listened to her worries about Martin, she'd just pushed them aside as if they were irrelevant. It was hurtful to think that her own fears had been shoved into the same category as Diane's, whom Harriet now appeared to regard with contempt. Zoe felt she'd been fobbed off.

Harriet had always been able to get the better of

her in an argument. Once her big sister put her arms round her, granting her a rare moment of physical closeness, Zoe always gave in. It was funny how she'd never noticed that before.

God, she wanted someone to hold her now, in the dark, in this strange room.

Not just someone – she wanted Pat.

Time had gone by and Laura had not cashed in her rain check with DCI Lane. Now seemed a good moment. It was the end of a long morning and Lane was alone in his office.

'How about that drink, sir?'

Lane looked with longing at the bound folder on his desk, which he was annotating. He seemed wedded to his work. From the latest gossip Laura had heard, it would soon be the only thing he *was* wedded to.

'Yeah, OK, but it had better be quick. And I'm off alcohol.'

They settled for coffee and a sandwich in the café round the corner.

'Pat Vincent doesn't think Joe killed Andy. He says it was suicide.'

Lane was not impressed. 'It's because Pat and Joe are mates. They've probably fiddled a few horse races together.'

'Pat says Andy was talking about jumping off the cliff just before he went up there with his dog.'

'Why would he do that?'

'Because Harriet was seeing another man and he was depressed about it. He was thinking of getting a divorce.'

Lane shot her a poisonous look, as if she'd mentioned the word deliberately to upset him. 'Suicide might be preferable, I agree,' he said. 'But how would you explain the bloodstains on their clothes?'

'Joe and Andy had a fight but Joe didn't push him over. Once Joe had gone, Andy took the plunge.'

'With the dog?'

'Yes. Jasper's a child substitute. Andy was dead keen to have a family but she wasn't. He took his child with him.'

Lane snorted. 'God, I wish we'd gone to the pub after all.'

'Well?'

'I don't buy it. What's the story on the wife's lover?'

'Martin Christie. A tennis coach at the health centre where Harriet works. She says they were just good friends till Andy died. But now they've got closer.'

Lane regarded her balefully. 'Surprise, surprise. She hasn't let the grass grow, has she?'

Laura wished she didn't have to have this conversation. Everything she said seemed to hit home with her companion – it was embarrassing.

'The other thing is that Harriet's sister has

broken up with Pat so Harriet says he's coming out with this stuff to get back at Zoe through her.'

Laura watched Lane working this out. He wasn't as familiar with the relationships as she was. 'Sounds plausible,' he said finally.

'So I should just forget about the suicide and Harriet having a lover?'

'I didn't say that. We should check everything out.'

'We?'

'You. In the copious time available. And not forgetting that we already have a suspect in custody who has an excellent case to answer.'

In other words, cover our arses but don't waste too much time.

'I see.'

'Good. Now, I've got a nasty taste in my mouth. In the absence of a decent drink, how about a large espresso?'

Why not indeed?

Zoe's eyes were on the road ahead but her mind was on what she'd learned from the morning paper. Pat had a ride in the last at Salisbury that afternoon, and so did she. She'd known it was bound to happen sooner or later, but later would have been preferable.

The last race was her only ride, the longest on the card over a mile and six furlongs. She was on Soul Mate, an ironic name considering the encounter with Pat – a man who could no longer fit that bill.

Jack was at the wheel, geeing her up. 'Pat's just another rider when you're on the track,' he said. 'You've got enough to worry about with that Soul Mate. I reckon he's the laziest horse I've ever trained. Too lazy to keep himself warm most of the time.'

Zoe smiled; Jack had a way of cheering her up.

He caught her eye and began to chuckle.

'What's up?'

'Did you see the name of the horse Pat's riding?'

Despite herself, Zoe joined in the laughter.

Pat's horse was called Slippery Customer.

The one mile six furlong course at Salisbury begins with the runners heading away from the stand downhill to a dog-leg spur which swings round in a loop to bring them back onto the straight. From there it's some six and a half furlongs back up the hill to the winning post.

Over such a long and testing trip Pat imagined he'd have no trouble in putting up a decent show on Slippery Customer without coming home in the first three. Fourth or fifth out of the field of ten would suit him fine. He reckoned that Ed Cooper wouldn't be too disappointed though he couldn't answer for the owner, a sharp-suited Irishman who'd arrived by helicopter. Still, if it all worked out, Mr O'Neil's day would come – and soon, Pat hoped. He was going to need money. Bernie had been on the phone that morning – the Garda had interviewed Ronan about an attempted armed robbery on a security van. Ronan had sworn on his life that he wasn't involved but the possibility of further charges was worrying, not to mention the length of any likely sentence. Pat had promised Bernie he'd get his brother the best lawyers in Ireland, if necessary. And so he would, but they wouldn't come cheap.

All of which left him wondering how to cash in on the likes of Slippery Customer. If the police failed to come to their senses and Joe remained locked up, he'd have to find someone else to punt for him.

Rain was falling as they set off. For the moment summer was in abeyance. Pat didn't mind the wet, which always made the Salisbury course tricky – it would give him another excuse for his horse's poor showing. He was more concerned that Zoe was in the race. He'd tried to talk to her in the weighing room but she'd barely acknowledged him. The situation was killing him. Was there really no way back for him?

Slippery Customer appeared to like the rain. He was barrelling into the squall, enjoying the feeling of give beneath his feet. Pat was happy to give him his head for the moment. There would come a time when the animal wouldn't find things quite so easy. He rehearsed what he might say in the unsaddling enclosure. 'I had him in a perfect position but when I asked him to go, there was nothing left in the tank.' Or something like that, depending on the circumstances. It was too early to write the script when you didn't know the ending.

Zoe couldn't remember being more nervous about a race, which was silly. Royal Ascot, for example, had been a more important meeting, with her every move under scrutiny and much more hanging on her performance.

She'd had the whole afternoon to brood on the contest, which didn't help. Nor did the fact that Ginger Weaver had already ridden two winners that afternoon. He was eight ahead of her in the battle for champion apprentice and though the other contenders seemed stuck in the mud, leaving her in second place, she wondered if she'd ever catch up. The final race would be a good place to start but Ginger was on the favourite.

But it was the presence of Pat that was really putting her out. No matter how hard you steel yourself, there are some encounters that are bound to knock you for six. Coming face to face for the first time with a former lover is one of them. And Pat wasn't just an old boyfriend, he'd been her first serious partner, the man she'd lived with for the past few months, the man she pined for in the small hours. Suppose he'd asked her to marry him? Just a week ago, she would have said yes. Like a shot.

She'd steeled herself to walk straight past him in the weighing room. He'd smiled and begun to speak but she'd fled. Run away like a frightened rabbit. She hoped she wouldn't have to face him at the end of the race but who knew what would happen? Suppose they were in a tight finish together and he got home just ahead of her? Sportsmanship would require that she congratulate him. As Jack had pointed out, people would be watching. She didn't know how she'd handle it.

Soul Mate had eased himself into the race. The conditions had put him off at first but now, as they bore left into the loop, he appeared to have got used to the rain and soft going. She could feel him eager to stretch out and allowed him to close the gap that lay between them and the leading bunch.

They were approaching the sharp bend to the right which would take them back down to the straight and the ride for home. Suddenly Zoe felt good about the race. They were over halfway and her horse was full of running, unlike some of those around her.

But she was hemmed in, unable to break away from animals who were starting to make heavy weather of things. She looked for a passage up the rail but a green and gold jacket ahead blocked her way. It belonged to Pat.

Her instinct was to give him a shout and ask him to let her through. Sometimes riders played ball. If they were on a tiring horse and you were coming up like a train, they might take pity on you. Or they might not. She didn't think there was a hope in hell that Pat would do her a favour and she didn't want to ask. But this was business. And she had Ginger to try and beat. Already she could see him on Scarecrow, up front and starting to get away from her.

Don't take your personal life onto the course, that's what Jack had told her.

'Pat,' she screamed, 'let me through.'

Pat heard Zoe shout behind him and looked over his shoulder. She had some nerve asking him to get out of her way. His racing instinct was to keep her bottled up.

But he didn't want to win. And this was Zoe who was asking.

Letting another competitor up your inside was just about the worst sin a jockey could commit. Most trainers would never use a jockey again if they let it happen at all, never mind do it deliberately. But Pat knew that on this part of the course he could always blame the horse. 'He was hanging, guv'nor, I just couldn't keep him straight.' He could already hear himself offering the excuse. After all, it was Zoe.

In the split second they entered the sharp downhill bend he pulled his horse away from the white railing that was guiding his path. In a flash Zoe was through and he thought he heard a shouted

'Thanks' swirling on the rain-drenched breeze but it was lost as the horse beneath him missed his footing.

Maybe I shouldn't have done that, thought Pat as his mount slithered on the greasy surface and suddenly he was pitched forward out of the saddle into the path of the pounding runners coming from behind.

Zoe was elated as Soul Mate tackled the gruelling run-in up the incline towards the stands and the winning post. Pat had let her through and she owed him a big hug of thanks. Suddenly the thought of confronting him didn't seem so hard – she'd be allowed to embrace him in these circumstances, surely?

But right now she had more pressing things to worry about. Scarecrow was five lengths ahead. Could she catch him? She urged Soul Mate on. He was a lazy animal all right but each time Zoe drove him forward he responded. They closed to within a length.

Though the pair of them were well clear of the rest of the field, it was suddenly impossible to make further inroads on Scarecrow's lead. The weather had worsened and they were now riding into the teeth of the wet wind. Zoe felt a change in the horse beneath her, suddenly Soul Mate was no longer full of running.

'No, you don't,' she shouted, urging the horse on with her entire body.

Soul Mate rallied again. By their side Ginger was working just as hard but was beginning to tread water.

They were in front of the stands now and the race was going by in slow motion. It seemed to Zoe that she was watching from above as the two utterly exhausted horses stumbled towards a finishing line that never got any closer.

But Soul Mate had his nose ahead. Every part of Zoe was hurting from her efforts, but she wouldn't give in and her time at the gym was paying dividends. She felt as if she had bodily lifted the animal over the line.

As they plodded slowly back to the unsaddling enclosure, Ginger came up alongside, steam rising from his exhausted horse in a cloud. He held out his hand and patted her back in congratulation.

'Great finish,' he gasped.

'That's one for the girls,' she said.

He didn't have an answer to that.

She was smiling as Jack came towards her.

'Well done, lass,' he said but there was no triumph in his eyes.

'What's up?'

'Pat's copped a bad one. He's still on the ground.'

'I didn't see anything.'

'He pulled his horse off the rail to let you through and took a tumble.'

Oh God. It was because of her.

* * *

Zoe rushed back to the weighing room with Jack, barely able to acknowledge the shouts of congratulation from one or two happy punters. She weighed in, her mind in turmoil. What if it was serious with Pat? And all because he'd let her through. Her resolve to stay away from him had dissolved in an instant. She just wanted to be bathed in the warmth of his smile and to look into his laughing eyes – and to know he was OK. She wouldn't forgive herself if he wasn't.

They bumped into Ed Cooper outside the ambulance room. He took in their concern at a glance.

'He's come round,' he said.

Zoe's heart was hammering in her chest and she couldn't speak.

'The doctor wants to pack him off to hospital,' Ed continued, 'but Pat's objecting. He says he wants to drive home but the doc won't let him.'

'I'll drive him,' said Zoe firmly.

She saw the look pass between the two men, as if they were going to object.

'Don't argue with me,' she snapped.

'Wouldn't dream of it,' Ed murmured as she pushed past them to open the door.

The room was small but well equipped. Pat was propped up on a bed against a bank of pillows, a blanket covering his legs. A tall fellow in a white coat – the doctor, Zoe assumed – was sitting on an office chair by a small table, his long legs taking up most of the available space. On a bracket on the wall a television picture flickered soundlessly.

Whatever conversation they were engaged in was interrupted by her arrival. She wanted to throw herself into Pat's arms but managed to restrain herself – it would hardly be sensible, for more than one reason. Instead, ignoring the doctor, she fell to her knees by the bed and gripped Pat's hand.

'Are you all right?'

He was smiling at her just as she'd wanted. 'I'm tip-top, don't worry, sweetheart.'

'He's bruised and concussed,' said the doctor. 'I'm suggesting he should spend the night in hospital here as a precaution. He's in no condition to drive.'

She turned towards him. 'Don't worry, I'm driving. I'll get him straight home and into bed the moment you say he can leave.'

Pat's face was a picture of surprise and delight. 'Just when I was thinking it was a terrible mistake to let your horse go by.'

'What happened?'

'He slipped up. Dumped me in the traffic – but I've had worse.'

She stroked his forehead. 'I'm sorry.'

'At least you won. And you're here now.' He squeezed her hand.

The doctor was regarding them with some amusement. 'Well, he does seem to have regained his colour since you arrived. Come back in half an hour and I might let you have him.'

411

At the moment, for all her resolve of the past few days, she couldn't think of anything nicer.

Zoe enjoyed sitting behind the wheel of Pat's car; there was something comforting about it. The last time she'd driven it, she remembered, had been the night they'd returned from Harriet's when scarcely a word had been spoken. Not that Pat was saying much now as he lolled back in his seat, a dreamy look on his face. The doctor had doped him up, she guessed.

It was a point in his favour that he never made a fuss when he was in pain, unlike some men she had known.

'I'm sorry I didn't believe you about Martin,' she said. 'About him hitting you that night.'

'He hurt me a sight worse than falling off a horse.'

She laid her hand on his thigh for a brief moment. 'Sorry,' she repeated.

'So what changed your mind?'

'One of Harriet's friends came to see me. She said he'd threatened her too and told her to get out of Harriet's life.'

'Why?'

'Diane had been trying to put Harriet off him.'

'Good for her. The sooner Harriet realises what a nutter he is, the better.'

How true.

'I don't think she's going to,' Zoe said. 'I told her

what Martin did to you and she refused to believe me. She won't hear a word against him. I think she's completely under his spell.'

'God help her,' murmured Pat.

Zoe drove on in sober silence. The elation of Pat's recovery and their sort-of reunion – and her victory too – had worn off with the remembrance of Harriet's infatuation with Martin. He was more than unpleasant. Diane wouldn't have taken the trouble to warn her like that if there wasn't something truly dangerous about him.

'Do you know where Spillbury is?' she asked.

He chuckled. 'That's quite a change of subject. I thought I was the one who'd had a bang on the head.'

'Actually, it's relevant. Diane says Martin is a compulsive liar and has been in plenty of trouble before. Apparently he ran off with a married woman when he was still at school.'

'That must be a while ago. And you want to dig up the dirt?'

'I want to prevent Harriet making a horrible mistake. I'll try anything.'

Pat pulled a road atlas from off the back seat. 'It's not that far from Bridgwater, near where Mrs Leopold lives.'

Near Ursula – that was good news.

'Fantastic,' she said and laughed. She could feel the gloom lifting.

'Do you want to explain?' he said, as he observed her glee.

'You don't know? You've obviously never been to dinner with the yard's most important owner and reminisced about her past.'

'No, Zoe, I haven't.' Suddenly he sounded weary.

She took pity on him, he wasn't in any condition to be teased but she couldn't help it.

'Ursula's late husband didn't care much for horses. She's been making up for lost time since he died. Guess what his sport was?'

If it was a test of his wits, he passed it. 'Tennis, by any chance?'

'Exactly. I bet she'll know about the Spillbury Tennis Club. I'll call her.'

Zoe felt odd parking the car outside Pat's house. Odd because it seemed such a natural thing to be doing yet it was the last place she could have imagined ending up only half a dozen hours previously.

Pat opened his eyes – he'd been dozing in the front seat for the past fifteen minutes.

'We're home,' she said without thinking.

'Home?' A sleepy grin stole across his face as he reached for her hand. 'You'll stay, won't you?'

'We'll see.' She hadn't thought further ahead than getting Pat back in one piece.

She helped him out of the car though he waved away her assistance and insisted on carrying his bag. Indoors, she thought of running him a bath but then caution prevailed. She didn't want to end up towelling his naked body. She might not be able to resist cuddling up next to him in bed. Wounded though he may be, she wouldn't put it past him to try on a reunion seduction.

Well, not now – if at all.

She made him tea and toast while he got into bed but when she carried it through he was already asleep. She turned out the bedroom light and closed the door. The toast wouldn't go to waste at any rate – she was ravenous.

She stepped round his bag which he'd dumped in the middle of the hall. The place was a mess but that wasn't her responsibility any more, at least not one she was rushing to reclaim.

But she returned to the bag because she'd seen Pat shove some of the pills the doctor had given him inside. The state he was in, he might not know where to look for them, and putting out his medicine came within her remit as his temporary nurse.

She couldn't find the bottle, it must have slipped underneath everything else. She began to pull his racing gear out onto the kitchen table. She was curious, the bag contained two body protectors. Why would he need two?

But, as she lifted the second vest, understanding arrived in a flash.

Like every item of a jockey's clothing, body protectors are super light. Made from strong but featherweight artificial material, they incorporate tiny hinged sections of foam to help cushion the impact of a fall. Typically, they weigh under a pound.

But this vest weighed more than that – much more. She allowed the navy blue laminated material to fall onto the table top with a soft thump.

Zoe peered closely and saw that the lines of stitching, though neat, were not machine-made. And at the waist was a square of Velcro. She tugged and a small square of material lifted up. Hundreds of tiny grey balls rolled out onto the table top. She recognised them at once. Lead shot, the kind sportsmen used in shotgun cartridges. At a guess the vest weighed at least a stone – an extra fourteen pounds. More than enough to slow any horse.

So that was how Pat and Andy had managed to amass the money that had been in Andy's account. Well, she knew Pat had been fixing races but it didn't make her feel any better to be faced with the evidence of his crime.

She wondered if she would have the nerve to do what Pat had done. Presumably he weighed out at the correct weight, then changed body protectors. As a rule, only the first four finishers in a race would be weighed in afterwards and that would be unlikely to include the horses Pat had burdened with extra weight. But sometimes the whole field was required to weigh in. What would Pat do then?

The answer was staring her in the face. All he had to do was pull open the Velcro tab and let all the shot run out onto the course. Simple and clever.

And crooked. This was the reason Zoe couldn't happily slide back into bed with Pat, no matter how much she loved him.

She didn't know how things were going to be between them in the future but right now she had to get away. She'd done her Florence Nightingale act and delivered him home safe and sound, as she'd promised the doctor.

She put Pat's car keys on the table next to his pills and that incriminating vest. Then she called for a taxi.

Chapter Nineteen

'We're not going to be long here, are we?' DC Pete Pugh was peering at his surroundings with distaste.

Laura smiled. Pete was a good bloke, a middle-aged father of three and a reassuring figure to have by your side if you ended up in the St Paul's area of Bristol on a Saturday night. But the glass and pine interior of a health club was not his preferred environment.

They were on their way to a car dealership on the other side of Bridgwater to talk to the manager about a series of thefts – much more Pete's cup of tea. Laura had persuaded him to stop here on the way to check out Martin Christie.

'Twenty minutes, Pete,' she promised. 'Half an hour tops.'

But they ended up sitting by the side of the tennis courts watching the object of their attentions bash a ball around with an energetic teenager.

The guy in charge, Ken, had told them the lesson would be over in five minutes and Laura had settled for that, though Pete, bristling with impatience, had marched off, muttering, 'See you back at the car.'

Laura could see the attraction of Martin Christie, any woman could, not that she'd ever gone for the Greek god look herself. And when he finally stood in front of her, tanned and smiling, pushing his blond locks off his forehead as she introduced herself, the thought flashed through her head that Harriet Burns was a lucky woman – if being widowed while in the process of conducting an affair could be counted as luck.

But maybe they'd not become intimate until after the husband's death. That was what Harriet had said and Martin was sticking to that line too. He would do, of course, in the circumstances.

'I'll be honest with you, officer,' he said, 'I was attracted to Harriet the moment I met her. She's not like all the giggly girls I end up teaching. But, you know, she was older than me and married – absolutely off limits. I never even thought about asking her out.'

'And now?'

'Now, I love her to bits.' He gave Laura the benefit of his smile – such brilliant white teeth. 'Of course, it was terrible what happened to Andy. I think it helped that I didn't know him. She just needed to get away from his world of horses and everything.'

'So one thing led to another?'

'I know it looks indecently hasty but that's exactly what happened. I can assure you it's not frivolous. She needs support at this time and that's me. I'm going to make sure she gets through this in one piece.'

He made his conduct sound positively altruistic. On the other hand, he seemed genuinely committed to Harriet. Even if their romance had been underway before Andy's death, was that significant? Martin was doubtless the beneficiary of another person's bad deed.

'Do you know Joe Parkin?'

'You mean the guy who's up for Andy's murder? Never met him. I don't know any of those racing people.'

He seemed sincere. Laura would be asking Parkin if he knew Martin in due course but it was surely a very long shot that they had an association.

'Can you tell me your whereabouts on the evening of the twenty-eighth of June, Mr Christie?'

'You mean the night Andy died?'

She nodded.

He considered the question. 'I was on my way to Spain to see my parents. My father had just been taken ill. I got the call at lunchtime so I just dropped everything and ran.'

'You're sure that was the twenty-eighth?'

'Positive. It was a Wednesday, wasn't it? Dad had a heart attack. I'm not likely to forget that day.'

Laura caught sight of Pete emerging from the clubhouse door, come to hurry her up no doubt. She closed her notebook. 'How's your father now?'

'On the mend, thank God. It wasn't as serious as they first thought but you've just got to drop everything in those circumstances, haven't you?'

There was no arguing with that.

'Thanks for your time, Mr Christie.'

'Martin, please.' He gave her another of his megawatt smiles.

'If it's not too much trouble, could you look out the details of your itinerary that day?'

The smile wobbled at the edges. 'I got the last flight from Heathrow, round about eight. Just made it. But I'll look out the precise times for you.'

Pete was grinning as they made their way back to the car park. 'Just how many people do you aim to bang up for Andy's murder?'

'I'm just trying to be thorough. Someone else could have shoved Andy off the cliff after Joe Parkin had left – it's possible. You've got to look at the wife's lover in those circumstances.'

'Not if he's in an aeroplane at the time.' Pete yanked open the car door. 'I had a chat with Christie's boss while you were admiring his back-hand. He says Martin was really cut up when he got the call about his father. He came back after lunch in a real state and just tore off. Nice to know some kids still care about their old dads, eh?'

* * *

'I remember the tennis club at Spillbury,' Ursula Leopold said when Zoe asked her over the phone. 'Joel was a member. He left them twenty thousand pounds for some all-weather courts, which I hope they've made good use of. I've bought decent horses for that amount of money.'

But her involvement with the club had ceased on her husband's death and she had no knowledge of a schoolboy player called Martin Christie.

'Give me ten minutes,' she said. 'Let me see if I can track down someone who might be able to help you.'

That had been an hour and a half ago and Zoe's hopes had begun to fade.

She was mucking out Magnetic when her phone rang.

'Well,' said the voice down the line, 'I don't know what went on over there but it's a sensitive subject. You'd have thought I was asking if they had Nazi sympathies or something.'

Zoe's heart sank. If Ursula had failed to get anyone to talk then this line of inquiry was doomed. 'You had no luck then.'

'I didn't say that, my dear. I finally prevailed on a lady who was once Joel's mixed doubles partner. I was bloody awful at tennis but Rosemary was first-rate – still is, I expect. She says she still plays. Anyhow, you'll have to take down the address.'

'She'll talk to me?'

'As a personal favour, and because I blew your

trumpet pretty hard. But I think you ought to go as soon as possible, before she changes her mind.'

'I'm really grateful, Mrs Leopold. I don't know how to thank you.'

'That's easy enough. Just make sure you ride me plenty of winners.'

That went without saying.

It hurt Martin to be pleasant for the rest of the morning but he forced himself to smile at his pupils and to trade banter with Ken as he packed away his stuff at lunchtime. Not because he cared about any of them but because it was good discipline to conceal the fury that boiled inside him.

'Sorry to leave you in the lurch again, mate,' he said to Ken as he headed for the door. He'd arranged to knock off early for the weekend.

'No sweat,' Ken said with a grin. 'I'm getting used to it.'

He wouldn't look so damned cheerful if he knew his star coach wouldn't be back on Monday. Too bad. Martin wondered if he'd be a married man by then – as good as, anyway.

But there were things to do before he could think about the Promised Land ahead.

Top of the list was teaching a certain jockey a lesson. He'd heard from Harriet that Pat had suffered a nasty fall at Salisbury and wouldn't be riding for a few days.

Martin reckoned he'd be recovering at home. Well, it might take longer than he thought. The little shit had not heeded his warning to stop pestering Harriet about money. And he'd shopped them to the police, hence the visit this morning from that mumsy detective.

Can you tell me your whereabouts on the evening of the twenty-eighth of June, Mr Christie?

What kind of a question was that? It was insulting.

And she hadn't even had the decency to back off when he'd told her his father had had a heart attack.

'If it's not too much trouble, could you look out the details of your itinerary that day?'

Well, it was too much trouble, as it happened. He'd come up with some information for her if he had to, but he wouldn't be rushing to provide it. Let her ask him again. With any luck, he wouldn't be around – he'd be on his honeymoon. Try looking for me next week when I'm lying on a beach in Mexico, you soppy cow. It was amazing an ageing frump like her could find employment in the CID. Shouldn't she be a schoolteacher or a nurse or something?

It was a decent cycle ride to the coast but Martin wasn't daunted. He knew the journey there and back was well within his compass. And the dissatisfaction that pumped through his body made the miles fly by.

He'd promised Harriet he'd drop in on Pat. And where Harriet was concerned, he was a man of his word.

Zoe found the house in Spillbury without difficulty. A woman in baggy brown cord trousers and a bedraggled man's shirt was kneeling over a flower bed in the front garden. She looked up as Zoe opened the gate.

'Are you the jockey?' she demanded. Obviously this was Rosemary Dean. 'You don't look tough enough to control those big horses.'

Though the tone was peremptory, the tanned face beneath a neat grey bob was smiling. A day earlier and Zoe might have taken offence at her words, but victory over the long course at Salisbury was fresh in her memory.

'No jockeys are very big, Mrs Dean.'

'Of course not, I'm only teasing.' She got to her feet, standing a good six inches taller than Zoe. 'It's Miss, as it happens, but you'll call me Rosemary. Come inside.'

Zoe followed the woman indoors. The house was old, built of yellow stone. As Rosemary made coffee she explained it was a Somerset longhouse dating back to the seventeenth century. Zoe nodded politely. In other circumstances she might have found it of interest but not now.

Finally, Rosemary sat down. 'Why don't you tell me exactly what you're after?'

It was a blunt enough question.

'I'm trying to find out about a tennis player called Martin Christie. I understand he used to belong to the club here.'

'I remember him.' There were no smiles now. 'Why do you want to know?'

They were facing each other across the kitchen table. Rosemary sat back in her chair, her hands folded on the table top. The flint-grey eyes missed nothing. She was waiting.

'It's just that Martin has become involved with my sister.'

'In what way?'

'She says he's asked her to marry him. But she's only just become a widow and I'm worried she's rushing into something stupid.'

'Oh dear.' Rosemary's demeanour had softened. There was nothing flinty about her eyes now, they swam with sympathy. She reached across the table and patted Zoe's hand. 'Do you mind waiting a moment? I've got to fetch something from upstairs.'

It sounded ominous.

Pat was lost in thought, looking out of the bedroom window – which was fortunate. As a consequence he saw the cyclist coming down the lane and halting outside the house. There was something familiar about the figure in a silver crash helmet but it wasn't till the helmet came off that he realised who it was.

The arrival of the tennis coach wiped all other thoughts from his mind – thoughts that had absorbed him half the night and all morning.

Zoe thoughts.

He'd woken in the night and hoped to find her sleeping beside him. But the other side of the bed was empty. He'd stumbled slowly, painfully, to his feet, nursing a secret hope that she might be curled up on the sofa next door. But she wasn't there either.

As he walked into the kitchen he was perplexed to feel small stony things beneath his bare feet. He flicked on the light and peered at the floor. Grey pellets were scattered across the lino – he couldn't understand it.

Then he took in the table top. The bottle of pills, his riding gear – and his body protector. And the river of lead shot that covered the table top and flowed onto the floor.

Zoe had found his secret and she'd left him a message. Despite his accident and her concern, despite the fact that they'd patched things up and there was still – surely? – a connection between them, despite all that she plainly hadn't forgiven him for cheating.

It would have been too much to expect.

He'd gone back to bed with a heavy heart and lain awake, cursing his stupidity. Having Zoe by his side again for just a few hours had shown how much she mattered to him. She mattered a damn sight more than money.

There were Ronan and Bernie to consider, of course, but there had to be other ways of helping them without stopping horses. He could take out a loan. Scrimp and save like other people did. He'd think of something.

In the morning he emptied the body protector of all the shot and cut it into pieces. He dumped the remnants in the dustbin outside.

Facing facts, the damn thing hadn't done him much good. He'd ridden losers when he could have had winners. He'd only managed to get his hands on a small proportion of the money he'd won. And the extra weight around his chest had probably contributed to the severity of yesterday's fall. Not forgetting that he'd also lost the woman he loved.

It was while he was brooding on all this that his visitor arrived. He edged himself behind the curtain and watched. There'd been a call on the landline earlier and the caller had hung up when he had answered. Might that have been Martin, checking on his whereabouts?

Pat's stomach turned over.

He watched Martin consider his car for a moment, then the tennis coach strode to the front door. The doorbell echoed throughout the house.

Pat stayed where he was.

Harriet would have told Martin about their last conversation. And the police would have begun asking him questions about their relationship. It wouldn't take a genius to work out who had tipped them off.

There were no neighbours to come to his aid – Jayne, who lived next door, was out.

Pat was hurting, physically and mentally. He'd been no match for him before and now the tennis coach would play with him like a cat with a mouse. And he knew just how cruel Martin could be

The bell rang again. Insistently. Martin must know he was in. Apart from the phone call, he'd seen his car.

But Pat was not going to let him in.

He might not be the toughest guy in the world but he wasn't stupid.

The green leather book lay on the table between them. Zoe could tell it was a photograph album but Rosemary hadn't opened it yet.

'Martin was a junior member of our club. His mother was a keen player and she brought him along from when he was little. I can remember that boy from when he was not much bigger than his racquet. It's extraordinary to think about it now. He didn't stay little very long, though. By the time he won the under-fifteen competition he was bigger than most of the men at the club. Handsome, too, of course. I assume you've met him.'

'Yes. He's not my type though.' Her type was completely different. Her type was one of a kind – Pat.

But her feckless Irish boyfriend wasn't the issue right now.

Rosemary was explaining the set-up at the club. 'He used to play with the adults and did very well. He played with my ladies doubles partner in the mixed doubles championship. They came runners-up the year he won the under-fifteens. It's less than ten years ago.' Her face was sombre. 'Though it seems like a hundred.'

Zoe waited for her to go on but Rosemary seemed to have come to a standstill.

Zoe pointed to the book. 'Is there a photo of him in here?'

The other woman shot her a look of outrage. 'Certainly not.'

Zoe winced inside. She hadn't meant to insult her hostess, only to kickstart the conversation. Fortunately, it worked.

'He teamed up with my friend Gail Dixon and they really hit it off.' Rosemary didn't look happy about it. 'They were easily the best pair. Gail wasn't much of a singles player, she wasn't assertive enough. But when she played with a dominant partner she was inspired. She could read what you were going to do before you did it and she dovetailed her game around yours. She was the best doubles partner I ever had by miles. Not that summer though,' she added sourly.

'Why not?'

'Because of Martin.' It hurt Rosemary to say it,

Zoe could tell. 'She put everything into playing with this schoolboy. When she was on court with me she was no longer on my wavelength, she was on his. Off court as well as on it, as it turned out.'

Zoe had guessed as much but she waited, eager to hear what else Rosemary would say. She didn't think she'd enjoy hearing it but she had to know.

Rosemary sighed heavily. 'Gail was a lovely person. Honest, sweet-natured, intelligent. Married to the most charming man. But she threw everything away for a schoolboy. Would you like to see a picture of her?'

Rosemary wasn't waiting for Zoe's reply, she was already flipping through the pages of the album.

'There.' She swivelled the book round so Zoe could see. The photo took up the whole page – a young woman in tennis whites gravely regarding the camera.

'She was the adult,' Rosemary said, 'so she got the blame for what happened. But I know better.'

She said some other things too but Zoe couldn't take them in. She was mesmerised by the image in front of her.

Looking at Gail Dixon – the hair tones and skin colour, the way she held herself gracefully, like a dancer – Zoe could have been looking at a photograph of her sister.

Martin was convinced Pat was inside the house but he plainly wasn't going to open the door. He looked up at the first floor, where he thought he'd seen the curtains move when he'd first arrived. So the bastard had seen him.

He considered his options. He could simply leave – get back to Bridgwater and pack. He'd wasted enough time already on this excursion. And if Pat had spotted him then he'd know why he was after him. His very presence here was a message. He didn't have to lay a finger on the jockey to put the wind up him.

But it wasn't satisfactory. There were things he wanted to say – and do – to Pat. Like point out to him that if he carried on talking to the police then he, Martin, would be obliged to tell them that the jockey had been wagering on horses. Or he could go to the racing authorities. In either case, he was certain Pat would not like it.

The main point, however, was to terrify the little turd into submission. Make him realise that having made an agreement – and he had – it was not acceptable to break it.

The front door looked pretty flimsy, as if one good shoulder charge would bust it open. Or maybe he could simply put a boot through the front-room window and step over the sill.

He could imagine Pat cowering upstairs, shitting himself at the sound of breaking glass, knowing he would soon be on the wrong end of some serious pain.

Last time he'd threatened the jockey with

serious injury, enough to keep him out of the saddle for some while. It was the kind of promise he was duty bound to keep.

However, he was certain the jockey was keeping an eye on him from inside. It would be smarter to take him by surprise.

Pat watched the blond man turn away from the door and pick up his bike. The big bastard was giving up – thank God for that.

Below, Martin mounted his bike and rode lazily back in the direction he had come. Pat stared after him, even once the menacing figure had disappeared from sight round the bend in the road.

He was holding a poker in his sweat-slicked hand – he couldn't even remember picking it up.

He slumped on the bed, heart thumping, conscious of the aches and pains he'd picked up the day before. Not that they bothered him. Suddenly he felt much better.

Martin dragged the bike into a stand of trees behind the bus stop and hooked his helmet over the handlebars. There were no other houses between here and Pat's place and he didn't see why he shouldn't be able to cut back along the edge of the field behind him. It would surely be easy enough to get into Pat's garden from the farmland.

Then he'd be able to break in unobserved.

He vaulted the gate and strode purposefully along the hedgerow.

The field was bordered by a stand of hawthorn and holly, behind which he could see the wooden slats of a garden fence, a couple of metres high. Martin pushed himself through the undergrowth to the barrier. It was new and looked robust enough to keep out wildlife and casual intruders. But Martin wasn't casual.

He edged along the fence towards the road, looking for anything that might make his assault a bit simpler: a tree stump, a discarded oil drum or other rubbish which would give him a leg-up and an easier purchase on the top of the fence.

He found it at the point where new fencing joined the old right up by the side of the house. He wouldn't have to climb. The old wood was rotten and sagging, he could simply push the slats to one side and step onto the garden path.

Martin found himself grinning foolishly. He couldn't wait to see the look on that little shit's face when he found his visitor hadn't gone after all.

Then he heard a car coming up the lane and froze where he was. Being so close to the road he might be visible.

The car was stopping, damn it. Parking, he estimated, right next to Pat's vehicle.

He heard a car door slam and the echo of a doorbell. He knew that sound – he'd rung loud enough on Pat's bell himself.

Then came a woman's voice. 'I've got your shopping.'

'Thanks, Jayne.' That was the jockey.

'How are you feeling? Fancy a cup of tea?'

And he heard the sound of doors opening and closing and the two voices mingling before they were cut off by a final slam.

Martin stood rooted to the spot as he analysed the situation. Pat had gone into the house of his next-door neighbour.

He looked at his watch. He had no more time to waste.

As Martin headed back down the field he reflected that the little bastard didn't know how lucky he was.

Zoe drove a car like she did a horse – instinctively. Her hands and feet were in tune as she slipped up and down the gears, anticipating the manoeuvres of those around her, expertly judging gaps in the traffic. And, despite her many misgivings, instinct was taking her in one direction. To Pat. She had to digest what Rosemary Dean had just told her – debate and discuss it and then decide what to bloody well do about it. Jack was a rock, a shoulder to cry on and a man of substance. But Pat, for all his flaws, was the only man she could ask to put himself on the line for her.

Something was up with him, she could tell, when he finally opened the door to her. But whatever was troubling him could wait. At least he looked pleased to see her and hugged her close. But that could wait too.

They sat in the front room and she launched into a description of her encounter with Rosemary.

The landlady called out to Martin as he reached the top of the first flight of stairs. He suppressed his irritation and hoisted a smile onto his face as he turned back. Emily always did this to him, waited till he was almost out of sight and beyond the call of politeness before she hailed him. She claimed to be going deaf but she always knew when he came in. Maybe she sat behind the curtains watching the street or she was acutely aware of vibrations in the floorboards or something. It was a damned nuisance, whatever it was.

'So sorry to trouble you,' she said as he reached the bottom of the stairs, 'but I thought you'd like to know the police were asking for you.'

It took a second for him to process the information. Emily was staring up at him, an insubstantial figure in a multi-hued cardigan whose colours had long ago faded into a uniform dun. Her curranty black eyes surveyed him with interest.

He laughed. 'That's funny, because I was chatting to them at work today. I expect they came here first.'

'The lady said she was following up on your meeting this morning. They've only been gone an hour. A DC Hammond and a DC Pugh.' She read their names off a piece of paper.

'Fine.' It wasn't fine at all but Emily mustn't know that. 'They want some information in connection with an investigation. I'll dig it out and give them a call.'

'I helped them as much as I could.'

In the pause that followed, he heard some rubbish pop music blaring from the kitchen. Emily always had the radio on too loud – it had probably driven her deaf in the first place.

'And how was that?'

'I gave them the date you went to Spain, of course, after your poor father had his heart attack. The twenty-ninth of June – I looked it up on my calendar.'

He made an effort to keep smiling. 'I think you'll find it was the twenty-eighth.'

'Oh no. That was the Wednesday when you came back late and you were bleeding, remember?' She cast a glance at the rug on the hall floor, a mangy item in the same condition as her cardigan but which had sustained some bloodstains on the night in question. It had been a sore point between them, the rug having belonged to Emily's grandmother.

'You didn't go until the next morning,' she continued. 'That's when you told me about your father and I put it on my calendar so I would remember to say a special prayer for him at church.'

Emily was a regular member of the local congregation. It comprised the entirety of her social circle.

'How is your father?' she added. 'Is he still making progress?'

'He's as good as new.'

'Marvellous.' The creases of her leathery face aligned themselves into a grotesque beam. 'My prayers have worked, you see.'

It was tempting – and it would have been so simple – to grab and shake the old bag until her bones snapped like twigs and the breath of life in her lungs turned to dust. He'd be doing her a favour – she'd lived too damn long anyway.

But what would be the point? The damage was already done.

Instead he bowed his head in a gesture of humility. 'Thank you, Emily. I'm sure your prayers made all the difference.'

She patted his hand. 'I pray for you too, you know.'

Thank God somebody did.

At first Pat found it hard to take in all the details of Zoe's account of some tennis pal of Ursula's from years ago, when that thug Martin was underage. His near miss with the bastard loomed too large.

Then Zoe pulled a photograph from her bag and Pat was able to push his own situation to one side.

She gave it to him without comment. A woman

in tennis clothes, a little flushed from her exertions possibly, holding her hair off her face with one hand, reserve and amusement in her familiar green eyes.

'I didn't know your sister played tennis,' he said.

'That's not Harriet.'

He looked again. The facial similarity was not exact. Harriet's nose was longer and her jaw firmer than this woman. But everything else – the hair, the eyes, the cool stare – was the same.

'Crikey,' muttered Pat, 'she sure looks like Harriet. Who is it then?'

'Her name was Gail Dixon, happily married to Alex, an architect, until she got involved with Martin. The pair of them disappeared together for a fortnight in the summer of nineteen ninety-eight. Gail would ring in from time to time to say they were safe and well but would not reveal their whereabouts. Martin's parents wanted to call in the police but Alex managed to hold them off. Eventually he got Gail to admit where they were and he drove to Scotland and brought his wife back. Martin made his own way home by train. The whole thing was a red-hot local scandal though they hushed it up as best they could. Gail returned to Alex who must have been potty about her because he accepted that her fling was a crazy passion that had burned itself out. They moved to a big old house which Alex started to do up. Their plan was to have a family.'

Pat was listening now all right. 'This Rosemary woman knows all the gory details, doesn't she?'

'She was close to Gail – until Martin came along anyway. Then she stood up for Gail after they came back from Scotland. The thing is, Gail had put Martin behind her and was trying to get on with her life but Martin wouldn't let go. He was obsessed with her. He'd watch her house and follow her and he'd threaten Alex whenever he intervened. They complained to Martin's parents who did what they could but Martin was physically uncontrollable.'

'The architect should have taken his wife a long way away,' said Pat.

'They didn't realise that until they were in the middle of doing up their new place. There was a lot of building work, with scaffolding up the back of the house. One day Alex came home and found Martin on top of this scaffolding, threatening to jump off. It was a Sunday and there were no builders, just Alex. He called to the boy to come down but he wouldn't, so he went up the scaffold to try and talk some sense into him. When he got up close, Martin pushed him off. He fell twenty feet onto a stone-paved patio and was killed.'

Zoe paused for a moment.

'Go on.'

'It looked like an accident. There were no witnesses and Alex often went up the scaffolding to check on the builders' progress. The inquest found they'd cut a few corners with safety precautions.'

'But if there were no witnesses,' said Pat, 'how does Rosemary know Martin did it?'

'Because Martin confessed to Gail. He kept away from her for a while, till the drama had blown over, then he started coming round again. She'd put the house up for sale and had moved in with Rosemary while she worked out what to do with her life. First Martin tried to woo her – couldn't they just be friends and so on. Then he demanded that they get married – he was sixteen by now – but she turned him down. He said that she was destined to be with him and that was the reason he'd killed Alex. Then he'd told her how he'd done it, by threatening suicide and luring Alex up the scaffolding. He even described what Alex was wearing that day and told her about the plaster on Alex's hand – he'd cut himself in the kitchen the night before. Gail was convinced.'

'Why didn't she go to the police?'

'Because she couldn't prove anything. And Martin said if she did that he'd make a statement that she'd sexually abused him the previous summer. He said she'd never escape him so she ought to just give in. He didn't care if she didn't love him any more, she was his to do with as he wanted. That's what Gail told Rosemary.'

Pat said nothing, caught up in the tale.

'But she did escape him in the end. She drove her car into a brick wall and killed herself.'

'Jesus.' Pat could imagine it. It sounded just like

the work of the Martin who had twisted his arm in knots and come banging on his door. He tried to be objective. 'This is all according to one source, isn't it? Rosemary could be making it all up.'

Zoe shook her head firmly. 'This isn't a court of law, Pat. My gut feeling is that she was telling the truth. Anyway, Rosemary knows nothing about Harriet.'

'Or about Andy's death.'

Neither of them spoke and he wondered if the thought that had now taken root in his mind was also growing in her. It was far-fetched and frightening but the more he turned it over, the more likely it seemed.

Martin threw things into a holdall – essentials only: a change of clothes, shaving kit and toothbrush, passport. What else mattered?

He looked around his two rooms. Though they were all the space he had, they still looked sparse. There were books and CDs but they could be replaced, as could his clothes, even his tennis racquets.

There was one thing.

He took the framed photograph from the back of the drawer where he'd hidden it from Harriet. If she'd found it he would have explained that the woman was a relative, a second cousin who'd been good to him when he was a kid and who'd died tragically. It wasn't so far from the truth, after all.

And the physical resemblance was just a coincidence, though one that explained why he had immediately felt drawn to Harriet when he'd first caught sight of her.

He took the photo of Gail out of the frame and considered it closely, as he had done so many times over the years. Could he bear to part with it?

Yes.

He ripped that serious, beautiful face across the middle and then again, letting the pieces fall into the wastepaper basket. He'd been loyal to Gail far longer than she'd been true to him. He had a new Gail now and he'd put himself on the line to win her. Harriet deserved his total allegiance from this point on.

He'd considered getting her to drive round and pick him up but she might be caught up in her own packing and he wanted to get out of the house now. Just in case DC effing Hammond decided to return.

He was down the stairs and out of the door before old Emily could leap out on him again. In his haste he banged his arm against the newel post at the bottom of the stairs, turning the dull ache from his infected wound into a lancing dart of pain along his nerves. Jesus, that bloody dog had left its mark.

To think that he'd killed the man but the dog had turned out to be indestructible – it was laughable really.

Up on the cliff that night he'd not even thought about the dog. Hidden back from the path he'd watched as Andy was waylaid by some drunken fool – Joe Parkin, as it turned out. For one wonderful moment, while the pair rolled near the edge of the cliff, Martin thought the mystery assailant might do the job he'd set out to do himself. But life wasn't like that. In Martin's experience a man always had to do his own dirty work. Sure enough, Andy Burns had seen off his skinny attacker, who'd run away down the hillside steps.

After he'd gone, Andy had got to his feet, shaken the dirt from his clothes and stretched his limbs. Martin had watched him, silhouetted against the sky, facing out to sea. He didn't look like a man with much fight left in him – not that Martin gave him the opportunity.

Andy wouldn't have known what hit him. Martin thudded into his body and hurled him over the edge. It was like putting the shot except that, instead of a fifteen-pound weight, he was throwing a man whose scream of terror pierced the air as he sailed out into the void.

Martin got down on his knees cautiously. Thinking – a crazy thought – what if he looks up and sees me? But there was no movement from the white-shirted shape below and, thank God, no sound. It would have been dreadful if Andy had lain there screaming in pain or yelling for help. He might have been faced with the prospect of going down there and finishing the bastard off.

But there'd been nothing. He thought to himself

that it was a remarkably clean job. A shove, a split-second tumble through the air and lights out. Bye bye, Harriet's husband.

He'd forgotten the dog. In his planning, when he'd observed Andy walking along the cliff top, he'd decided simply to ignore the animal. It wasn't big or ferocious. Shove Andy off the cliff and scarper. The dog couldn't exactly bear witness, could it?

The creature had come flying out of the dusk, snapping at Martin's ankles. He'd tried shooing it away but it wouldn't leave him alone. And when he'd turned back to the steps, the stupid animal had followed, growling and barking.

'You've asked for it,' he muttered, grabbing it round the collar so he could swing it over the cliff. But in the process the bloody animal had sunk its teeth into his arm. The shock had been worse than the pain. In fact, it hardly hurt, not then.

He'd tried to shake it off but the little beast wouldn't let go. Trying to prise its jaws apart with one hand didn't work either. Only when he began to throttle the dog did the jaws relax their hold.

Finally, he'd picked up the snarling, squirming bundle of fur and hurled it far out into the void. But the repulsive creature had survived. Thank God it couldn't talk, but its beady little eyes followed Martin's every movement when he was around Harriet. It knew.

But it didn't know that soon Martin would have

Harriet all to himself. The pair of them would be off to their wedding in Las Vegas. Somehow Martin doubted that they'd ever come back.

Chapter Twenty

'Has it occurred to you,' Pat said finally, looking into Zoe's guileless face, 'that Martin might have killed Andy?'

Zoe blinked. 'What?' As if the idea was the most preposterous thing in the world when, the more Pat thought about it, the more possible it seemed.

'Look,' he said, 'Martin's obsessed with Harriet, obviously. She's the spitting image of this woman he was in love with when he was fifteen. If he killed Gail's husband and got away with it, why shouldn't he shove Andy over the cliff?'

She shook her head. 'There's nothing to suggest Martin was anywhere near Andy that night. Harriet said his father was taken ill and he was on his way to Spain.'

'But suppose he was lying? If I'd killed someone I'd scarper pretty quick and let the dust settle. Anyway, he could have been at Beach Head that night. He knows the way all right.'

'What do you mean?' she said.

'Martin was here a couple of hours ago. He came banging on the door but I wouldn't let him in.'

'Oh Pat.' She grasped his hand. 'Why didn't you tell me?'

'Because your story was more important. Anyhow, he hung around and I was worried he would try and break in, but then Jayne turned up and he scarpered. The thing is, if he cycled here now he could have cycled to Beach Head. How far are we here from there? Three or four miles, that's all. For all we know, he could have staked Andy out, watched him a few times up there with Jasper. Andy used to go up there every evening.'

She leapt to her feet, grabbing Gail's photograph. 'I've got to talk to Harriet. I'll show her this.'

'I'm coming with you.'

'No, Pat. She won't listen if you're with me. And God knows what Martin might do to you if he's there.'

He was on his feet too. 'I'm not letting you face up to Martin on your own, Zoe.' He couldn't. The bastard would probably break his neck but so what?

'No, Pat.'

'Look, we'll go in your car and I'll keep out of sight. You can go in on your own but I'll be there. Just in case.'

In case of what? He didn't like to think.

The burst of music took Harriet by surprise. She was in the kitchen, sorting out dog food for Zoe to take with her when she picked up Jasper.

The music trumpeted on from the hall, some classical stuff. Then she realised it was Martin's mobile. He was upstairs, having turned up hot and sweaty ten minutes ago.

'I'd have picked you up,' she scolded him after she'd disentangled herself from his musky embrace – not that she'd minded all that much. There was something animal and brutish about Martin that thrilled her.

He'd laughed and begun to peel off his clothes but she'd shooed him off to get a bath. There was too much to do, considering their intended departure time of seven thirty the next morning.

Now she picked up his phone and answered the call.

'Martin?' The plummy female voice was familiar.

'That's Mrs Christie, isn't it? This is Harriet.'

There was a pause. 'Oh yes, Martin's new girl-friend.'

More than that. Harriet felt a pang of disappointment that Martin hadn't told his mother that she was about to become his wife.

'He's in the bath at the moment. I'll get him to call you back.'

'Please do, my dear. I hate to nag but I'm still worried about his arm, he could develop rabies or something.'

'Why would he develop rabies?'

'From the dog bite, of course. It looked very

nasty that week he was here but he refused to see a doctor. He said because he was bitten by an English dog he'd be all right because there wasn't any rabies in England. I suppose that is right, isn't it?'

What on earth was the woman on about?

'But he hasn't got a dog bite.'

'Well, he had one when he arrived here.'

Harriet was slowly working it out. 'You mean on his arm.'

'Absolutely, his racquet arm. He hadn't even taken the time to get it properly dressed. Just jumped on the first plane home to his mother. He should have gone to the hospital and then travelled in the evening when it's cooler, like we do.'

'But I thought he did travel in the evening.'

'No. He pitched up here right in the middle of our siesta. Not that we mind of course, though some notice would have been nice.'

There was something wrong here. Harriet almost wished she hadn't troubled to answer the phone, it was like talking to someone in a foreign language.

'But there was an emergency,' she said. 'Martin just dropped everything when he heard about his father's illness.'

'He told you my husband was ill?' The woman sounded puzzled.

'Martin said he'd had a heart attack. I'm so sorry. I hope he's feeling better now he's out of hospital.'

There was a pause, followed by a heavy sigh. 'He

never was in hospital, young lady. Just get Martin to give me a call, will you? And if I were you,' she added, her voice heavy with resignation, 'I wouldn't believe everything my son tells you.'

Harriet put the phone down and walked blindly through the kitchen and out into the garden. She needed air.

She needed to think.

'Just so you know,' Pat said, 'I threw away that safety vest.'

Zoe said nothing, just concentrated on the road as she drove to Bridgwater.

'I cut it into bits and put it in the bin,' he added. 'I'm sorry.'

Zoe just put her foot down.

'Steady,' Pat said. 'It won't do Harriet any good if you kill us before we get there.'

So she slowed a fraction. She wanted to snap her fingers and be outside her sister's door at that very moment.

'They're going off early tomorrow,' she said.

'How do you know that?'

'Harriet asked me to look after Jasper. She gave me a key to get in, in case they'd already left.'

'Where are they going?'

'London. For the weekend.'

'Are you sure?'

'That's what she said.'

She touched ninety as she overtook a line of cars.

'There's another thing you don't know,' she added. 'Martin asked her to marry him.'

'When did she tell you that?'

'That night we went round there. She swore me to secrecy. I told her she couldn't possibly get married before the trial was over. At the time I thought she'd agreed with me.'

'And now?'

'I think she'll do whatever he wants her to do. But you can't just run off to London and get married, can you? It's hardly Gretna Green.'

'Oh Jesus.' Pat suddenly remembered the piece of paper Harriet had left in the café. 'They're not going to London. I bet they're getting married in Las Vegas.'

Harriet found Martin in the bedroom pulling a T-shirt over his head. Her eyes were drawn to the wound on his right forearm. It looked hideous. Red and angry and raw.

'How's your father getting on?' She tried to make the question sound casual.

'Dad's fine,' he said. 'Well on the road to recovery.'

'How long was he in hospital?'

'I told you before. Just under a week.'

'No, he wasn't.'

His head snapped back and he stared at her in surprise.

'Your mother phoned while you were in the bath.' Her voice was shaking with emotion and for a moment she feared she wouldn't get the words out. She forced herself to go on. 'She says your father never had a heart attack at all.'

For a second his face was without expression then it clouded with concern as he stepped towards her. 'Look at you, babe, you're upset. Come here.' He opened his arms but she stood her ground.

'Why did you lie to me, Martin?'

'Yeah, I'm sorry.' He shot her a rueful smile. 'The thing is, you'd just dumped me and I was really cut up. I had to get away for a while so I invented an excuse for Ken.'

'But you lied to me too, Martin. And you carried on lying about it, like just now. I made a terrible fool of myself with your mother.'

He hung his head, almost like a penitent child. Harriet rarely thought of the age difference between them but she did so now.

'I guess it was pride,' he said. 'You're such a fantastic woman and so mature. Sometimes I can hardly believe how lucky I am to have you in my life. I didn't want to seem, you know, like some lovesick kid.'

Her heart softened. She supposed it made sense. Except . . .

'So what happened after we talked in the park that day?'

'I'd had it – you'd done my head in. I told Ken I'd had an emergency call from Spain and I got the first flight out.'

'What, that afternoon?'

He looked puzzled. 'Sure. Well, by the time I'd got to Heathrow and checked in it was evening. I got a plane about seven.'

He was lying to her again. His mother said he'd turned up in the middle of their siesta – the early afternoon, in other words. Why would he lie about that? Maybe he hadn't gone straight home.

'Satisfied?' he said, smiling now. 'Now you've put me through the third degree, can we get on with the business of preparing to run off and get married?'

'I can't go through with it, Martin.'

'What?' The smile vanished. 'Just because I told some fib about my dad?'

'Not only that. Your mother says you arrived in the afternoon, so you couldn't have flown out when you said.'

'What the hell does it matter when I flew out, Harriet?' Storm clouds were gathering in his eyes.

'It matters because I want to know where you were the night Andy died.'

His face stretched into an incredulous grin. 'Very funny, Harriet. I was lurking in the bushes up on the cliff and I shoved him over the edge. After that bloke Joe had beaten him up, of course. We're a well-known hit team. We do jobs for the Mafia.'

'Martin, seriously, where were you?'

He shrugged. 'I can't remember. I went home and got pissed for once. You'd just chucked me for good.'

She'd also as good as told him that if her husband wasn't around she'd have stayed with him. And that very night, suddenly Andy wasn't around any more.

And there was something else.

'Why did you lie about your arm? You said you'd cut it on barbed wire but it's a dog bite, isn't it?'

'Look,' he was exasperated, 'the whole business of dogs was a sensitive subject. You were upset about Jasper going over the cliff, I didn't want to blame it on a dog. I know it was stupid of me, I'm sorry.'

She didn't know if that made sense or not. But it reminded her of how much Jasper didn't like Martin. The only human being on the planet Jasper didn't adore – didn't that say something about Martin?

The smile was back but his eyes were not smiling. 'Come off it, Harriet, do you seriously think I could kill someone?'

She remembered what he'd done to the farmer, how he'd knocked him down and offered to go back and hurt him some more. And what he'd said he'd do to Pat and how she'd believed him.

Actually, yes, she did think he could kill someone.

'I'm not catching that plane tomorrow, Martin.'

'Don't be ridiculous, babe.'

'I've got to think this through.'

'You're getting cold feet, it's only natural.'

'Maybe. But I think you should go.'
She turned for the door – which was a mistake.
She never reached it.

Laura rang the bell for the third time, aware of Pete
Pugh fidgeting at her elbow. It had been good of
him to agree they should call back this evening but
she'd spent most of the day conducting interviews
in a garage. Now it was her turn. But maybe Pete
was in luck – it didn't look like anyone was home.

As they were about to leave, the door suddenly
jerked open though she'd not heard any footsteps
from inside. Christie's landlady, Mrs Jenkins,
stared up at them.

'Hello again,' she said. She was beaming. Two
visits from the police must have made her day.
'Martin's not in, you know. But I told him about
your visit when he came back. He said he'd give
you a call but I told him there wasn't any point as
I'd already looked on my calendar.'

'Did he say where he was going, Mrs Jenkins?'

'No. He seemed in a bit of a rush and he had a
bag.'

'What sort of bag?' Pete asked, probably just to
demonstrate to Laura that he was onside with this
investigation even though he'd rather be hunting
stolen BMWs. She appreciated it.

'I suppose you'd call it an overnight bag.' Her
little face wrinkled into a mischievous grin. 'He's
probably gone to stay with his girlfriend. He's in

love with her, you know. A red-headed young lady.'

'Mrs Burns?'

'I didn't know she was a Mrs.' Emily looked less pleased with this state of affairs.

'She's a widow,' Laura added to make her feel better about it.

Pete, bored doubtless, had progressed a few feet into the hallway. 'Do you mind if we take a look at Mr Christie's rooms?'

Mrs Jenkins didn't but she excused herself from making the climb to the top of the house.

The two rooms occupied by Martin Christie appeared to have been abandoned in a hurry. The doors of the wardrobe hung open and the top drawer of a chest projected into the small room, still half full of underwear and T-shirts. There was little of much interest or value on view, in Laura's opinion.

'Do you think he's done a runner?' Pete was obviously thinking along the same lines as she was.

'Possibly.'

Her attention was caught by bits of discarded photograph in the wastepaper basket. She rescued them and pieced them into a rectangle on the table top.

'Is that the girlfriend?' asked Pete.

Laura peered at it closely. 'Maybe – I can't be sure.'

'Bloody funny to tear up a photo of the woman you love. Unless it's all gone wrong, of course.'

Laura thought so too.

'Let's get round to Harriet's sharpish,' she said.

She saw Pete swallow a groan. 'How about tomorrow first thing?'

But she was already heading for the stairs, knowing Pete would be right behind her.

Martin had always had trouble handling denial, that's what the child psychologists used to say. An assortment of tennis coaches used to put it more bluntly but it amounted to the same thing. When Martin didn't get his own way, he lost it. He'd broken a lot of racquets in his youth.

Maybe it would have been different if Harriet hadn't turned her back on him. After all, she'd said no to him before and he'd not reacted. Not this time though.

He punched her on the back of the neck, a classic axe-hand blow which he'd been taught by one of the guys in the gym. Of course, it was meant to be used on rabbits but back in the war, the guy said, the SOE were trained to kill the enemy with it. You could shatter the spine apparently.

He didn't think he'd killed Harriet but, frankly, he didn't care. She'd ruined everything. Why was it that there was never a perfect woman? Even the best – like Gail, like Harriet – they always let him down.

The bottom line was, despite their special beauty, neither of them was special enough inside.

They didn't believe in him, they'd both turned their backs on him. It had been more understandable with Gail. He'd been just a kid at the time and there was all that pressure on the pair of them from her husband and his parents. So her decision to leave him was explicable, if not exactly excusable.

Harriet had turned out to be a big disappointment, however. If he could have just got her on the plane, things would have worked out, he knew it. And once they were married he could have trained her, got her to commit to him body and soul. Together they would have forged a supreme bond. Even if that had meant being tough with her, he would have been prepared to do it.

But her wilfulness had spoiled everything. When it came down to it, women always spoiled it.

She must have banged herself against the door frame as she went down. There was blood but not much, easily wiped up. Her limbs sprawled awkwardly and her head hung at an angle. Maybe he had killed her after all. Too bad. She was rubbish to him now. Something to be shoved out of sight while he got away.

The effing dog was shut up in the kitchen but he had to go in there to get the masking tape. It barked and growled even worse than usual as he opened the door but it didn't dare get too close. It wasn't that stupid. If he got the chance he'd kill it before he left.

He was in the shit but he could escape if he acted quickly. The plane tickets were in Harriet's handbag, along with $10,000. He'd wanted her to get more but she'd objected to carrying even that much cash and he hadn't been able to budge her. That kind of thing should have told him that maybe she wasn't really the one for him. Where did you go to find a woman who just did what you told her?

On second thoughts, maybe he should forget the plane. It was too dangerous to risk. If Harriet was found in the next few hours the police would be waiting for him. His best bet was Holyhead to Ireland. From there he could find a ferry to Spain. He couldn't go back to his parents, though; they'd be after him there too.

I still fancy Mexico, he thought, as he pushed the body under the bed.

Then the doorbell rang.

He froze.

The bell rang again. It didn't matter, whoever it was would go away.

The situation was ironic really, considering what had gone on earlier at Pat's place. The boot was on the other foot.

Thirty seconds ticked by. Would whoever it was ring again or call it a day?

They did neither. Instead there was a clicking sound in the lock, like a key being turned.

Zoe's heart was in her mouth as she opened the

door. Harriet couldn't have left already, surely? Her car was outside. And she'd said she'd be in to hand over Jasper, though she'd insisted on Zoe having a key 'just in case'.

Just in case what? Suppose she'd left early, in a taxi.

That would be a disaster.

The hall was empty as Zoe stepped inside but she could hear Jasper barking and scrabbling on the other side of the kitchen door. She was about to open it when a voice spoke from behind her.

'Hi, Zoe.' It was Martin, he must have been in one of the rooms.

So they hadn't gone; that was a relief.

'Why didn't you answer the door?'

He shrugged. 'I was busy, sorry. I suppose you've come to get the dog.'

'Where's Harriet?'

'She's popped out.'

'I'll wait for her then.'

'Actually, I've got a lot to get on with. Why don't you take the dog and I'll get Harriet to call you when she returns?'

Zoe hesitated. There was something odd about this. Harriet hadn't said she was going out and, in any case, why couldn't she wait for her?

She pulled her mobile out of her pocket and hit Harriet's number.

'What are you doing?'

He seemed even bigger in the small hall and he

was horribly close. She brushed past him into the living room, expecting in some mad way to find Harriet sitting there. The room was empty but from elsewhere in the flat came the sound of a ringtone.

His bulk filled the doorway but she ducked under his arm and followed the sound – there were compensations for being small.

In the bedroom Harriet's bag sat on the bedside table, chirruping merrily. She grabbed it and shook the contents across the counterpane. Phone, lipstick, car keys, plane tickets . . .

'Where is she?' Zoe screamed at Martin, who had followed her.

He leaned casually against the door jamb. 'She just popped out, I told you.' She knew instinctively his nonchalance was phoney.

'Without her bag or her phone . . .?' Zoe's voice tailed off as she saw something on the faded cream wallpaper by his elbow. A streak of something red and liquid. It was dribbling slowly down the wall.

Was that her sister's blood?

'What have you done with her, you bastard?'

'Calm down, Zoe. Honestly, Harriet's—'

But she didn't let him finish. Without thought for the consequences, she leapt forward, fingers jabbing for those hideous sky-blue eyes.

She caught him once, snagging the skin of his cheek as he reared back, then he had her in his grasp, turning his big frame to pin her body against the wall.

'You should have gone while you had the chance,' he said.

Pat got out of the car. He'd waited, as agreed, and watched Zoe let herself in. Obviously Harriet wasn't in. Any moment now he expected Zoe to reappear, maybe with Jasper. He was surprised Zoe hadn't summoned him over before she'd used the keys but he knew how anxious she was. She obviously hadn't wanted to wait.

He hovered on the doorstep, unsure whether to ring the bell. Suppose something was wrong – he didn't like to speculate what exactly. Suppose Harriet had been in the shower or something and now Zoe was deep into her anti-Martin pitch – his turning up could ruin everything.

Or suppose Martin was there?

He could hear nothing from inside except the steady barking of Jasper.

So why was Jasper barking? He'd never bark at Zoe.

There was a door in the wooden fencing at the side of the house. Pat tried the handle – locked. But the fence wasn't that high.

He dragged the dustbin from its place behind the hedge that bordered the road and climbed up. In a second he was straddling the top of the fence. The paving on the other side didn't look that far down, not much further anyway than the ground from the back of a big horse, though harder. He winced as he landed on all fours. He wondered what the doctor who'd discharged him at Salisbury yesterday would say if he could see what he was up to now.

The fence, of course, was only the first obstacle. Now he had to get into the flat.

None of the windows along the side looked accessible.

He peered into the kitchen. There was no one there, only Jasper. He could just see the small brown body agitating by the door that led into the hall.

Pat moved swiftly down the side passage to the garden. He might be able to force the back door or break the pane so he could reach in and turn the key.

But as he rounded the corner of the house he saw the door was standing open.

As Zoe lay on her side, with Martin looming over her, tying her still tighter, she wondered if he was going to kill her. Their fight had been short, her speed and wiry strength no match for his weight. She'd got in a few blows, the gouges on his cheek dripped blood on the pair of them as he bound her, but they hadn't stopped him.

He'd trussed her with belts and scarves from Harriet's wardrobe and wound so much masking tape round her jaw that she could make no useful sound. Thank God, she could still breathe through her nose.

He was kneeling over her now, his sweat and blood dripping on her face. She glared at him, trying to summon all the hate and defiance that she possessed. But she suspected he looked into her eyes and read only abject fear. Because that was the top and bottom of what she felt. She was completely at his mercy and she could see from the madness in his expression that she meant nothing to him.

Please don't kill me!

He reached out a big hand and pinched her nostrils together. He was smiling.

It didn't take long. She had little air in her lungs anyway and already she could feel the pent-up fire in her throat and the panic rising as she thrashed her head against his iron grip.

The pressure broke. Suddenly she could breathe again. Why?

His gaze jerked away from her face beyond her prone body to the door.

She didn't know. She couldn't see. But as Martin rose to his feet she realised that Jasper had stopped barking.

When it came to the crunch, Pat knew he was a coward. People went on about jockeys being courageous but falling off some dumb four-legged beast was just a hazard of the trade. It was what you had to put up with if you wanted to ride for a living, and he'd never thought of doing anything else.

This was different. If Martin was beyond that kitchen door then all his instincts told him he'd be bloody stupid to go through it. But Zoe was out there. Harriet too.

Maybe it was just the pair of them having a sisterly heart-to-heart and Jasper, who was now licking his hand in welcome, had been barking for some reason beyond human comprehension.

Whatever the ins and outs, he had to go through that door. Right now.

He took a knife from the block by the chopping board. Not the biggest but the sharpest looking. And if he ended up looking a fool in front of the Burns sisters, he'd take the ridicule.

Ahead, the hall was empty. Pat took two cautious paces and turned into the sitting-room doorway. No one.

Behind him Jasper began to growl, a back-of-the-throat warning.

'Hello, Pat.'

He whirled round. Martin was standing in front of him, silhouetted against the evening sunlight that shone through the windowpanes of the front door. He looked huge.

'That's not very friendly,' Martin said.

Pat was holding the knife in front of him. He lifted his arm, pointing the blade at Martin's face. 'Where's Zoe?' he demanded.

'She's in here,' Martin pointed to the room on the other side of the corridor. 'See for yourself.'

'Zoe!' he shouted and stepped forward.

He saw a shock of blonde hair on the floor, a face half hidden by masking tape.

He didn't see Martin move but suddenly his legs had gone from beneath him and the weight of the other man was bearing down on his chest. Martin's right hand was clenched round the wrist that held the knife, forcing the blade to point harmlessly at the ceiling. Though an angry scarlet gash decorated the flesh of Martin's forearm, the grip was unbreakable.

'Drop the knife,' Martin hissed.

Pat hit him with his free hand but it was like punching a brick wall. Martin closed his fingers round Pat's fist and began to squeeze. The pain in his hand was intense, as if the bones and tendons were being crushed in a vice.

'Drop it.' His face was inches from Pat's. His eyes gleaming with spite and pleasure.

Is this how he was going to die?

Zoe tried to turn her body. Lying as she was, she could not see out into the hall but she could hear. There'd been Pat's voice and Martin's. And the sound of men scuffling and straining.

How had Pat got in?

Did it matter? There could only be one winner between the two of them. Martin would kill Pat and then come back to finish what he'd started before.

She heaved her hips, wriggling and rolling; she

had to see what was happening. But all she succeeded in doing was wedging herself half under the bed – where the skin of her cheek came to rest on something soft and silky. She twisted her head and suddenly she was looking through a copper curtain. A tangle of hair covered her face.

The hair moved and fell away. Then she was staring into the slack face of her sister. She, too, wore a brown gag or tape and her eyes were shut. Harriet was here, hidden beneath the bed – and Martin had killed her.

From out in the hall came a roar of pain.

Harriet's eyes opened.

Pat didn't think he could hold the knife any longer. He was losing all sensation in his wrist while his other hand was being squeezed to a pulp. But he hung on. These might be the last seconds of his life and he was fighting for every one of them.

A cry of agony rang through his head, expressing all he felt. But the cry was not his.

There, thrusting his brown head into Pat's field of vision, was Jasper. His jaws were clenched around Martin's forearm and the big man was screaming as the dog bit down into the old wound.

Suddenly Pat's knife hand was free.

He thrust without thinking into the target that presented itself, jabbing deep into the flesh of Martin's neck.

Blood fountained across the three of them as

they squirmed blindly on the floor. Martin's big hands scrabbled for the knife, even as he seemed to lose control of his jerking limbs. Then the hands fell away and the body that had been bearing down on Pat like an immovable rock seemed to turn to jelly.

Pat felt the life leak out of him. It seemed to take an age.

God forgive me, he thought, I've killed someone.

But he deserved it.

As Pat lay trapped beneath Martin's dead weight he heard the sound of a bell. Looking up he could see the shapes of figures on the other side of the front door.

'Open up,' called a voice. 'Police.'

Better late than never, he supposed.

Postscript

Newmarket on the last Saturday of October. It didn't seem right to Zoe that the season was almost at an end. For the past few months she'd barely been at a race meeting and she felt she'd been robbed of her chance to become champion apprentice. Still, it was good to stand in the parade ring beside Jack and Ursula while the familiar Golden Syrup-coloured form of Pipsqueak was led up for her to mount. Almost like old times.

'Good luck, lass,' Jack said as she settled into the saddle. He had no other instructions for her and his face was sombre. For him, this race could be more than the last of the season. As far as she knew, he was still undecided whether to call it a day for good. He'd spent a long time on the phone to his daughter recently and the pull of retirement was strong.

She tried to clear her mind of all distractions as she headed down to the starting gates. After all, this was a Group One race, the Dewhurst Stakes at Newmarket. If Pipsqueak won this, he would be favourite for next year's Two Thousand Guineas

Laura, the nice policewoman who'd been such a rock in the past few months – she'd be sitting in front of the TV at home with her new husband. Diane, too, had said she'd be putting some of her husband's money on Pipsqueak, but not to worry, because he wouldn't miss it. Even Harriet had said she'd try to catch it on the TV in the pub next door to the salon in Taunton where she was now working.

Physically, Harriet had made a full recovery though Zoe wasn't sure how she was coping with the mental hangover of her relationship with Martin. 'I feel like I've woken up from a bad dream,' she'd said to Zoe, 'the kind that dogs you all day.' Zoe had confidence that the therapist she was seeing would soon set her right. And she'd taken up playing tennis with Diane – that had to be a good sign, didn't it? Even better, she'd moved back to the coast where Zoe and Pat could keep in close touch.

It was a pity Pat wouldn't be watching the race today. He was in Ireland for a meeting with his brother Ronan and his new legal team. Harriet was paying for their services and for the maintenance of Ronan's family when the inevitable happened and Ronan went to jail. Though the relationship between Harriet and Pat wasn't yet plain sailing, the signs were good. The fact that Harriet had offered to pay Pat the money he'd claimed had helped. But Pat hadn't wanted it. 'Just make sure you spend it where it's needed,' he'd said and that was what Harriet was doing.

Zoe popped Pipsqueak into his starting stall where they waited for a reluctant animal to load right next to them.

Suddenly there was the rattle of kit and jockeys' shouts as the gates sprang open and they plunged down the course. She wasn't going to be champion apprentice this year, but she might well be riding the champion two-year-old colt. She'd know in just over a minute.

Ursula's voice cut into Jack's thoughts. 'What's going on in that old head of yours?'

'Nothing.'

'Rubbish. I know you well enough. There's something bothering you.'

As if there hadn't been enough to bother him recently.

'I'm thinking that this could be my last race as a working man. And that young Zoe would have walked away with apprentice jockey if she'd had the chance.'

'I thought as much.'

'Well, why did you ask then?'

He'd miss bickering with Ursula at race meetings in the future. But then, he'd miss a lot of things about this life.

'Have you definitely decided to retire?'

'Maybe.' He was reluctant to admit that his decision depended on one race – the one unfolding in front of them. If Zoe could pull off a victory that would be a sign.

On the track, two horses were heading the field into the last furlong. Pipsqueak was the second of them.

Jack held his breath. He couldn't help it.

It had been a while since Zoe had ridden Pipsqueak in a finish. He'd been off with a viral infection and she'd been out of commission too. She didn't think that either of them had the form they'd shown back in the early summer. But she was wrong. As they raced out of the dip, two lengths behind the leaders, Zoe flicked the whip and gave Pipsqueak the command to dig deep and suddenly they were flying, just as they had been at Nottingham all those months ago. He still had those afterburners – still had that will to win. How could she have doubted him?

It was close, but they won. She was back and it felt good. In fact everything felt good since she'd agreed to marry Pat.

'OK then,' Jack said. 'I'd better do one more season and help young Zoe land that apprentice championship.'

Ursula gave him a hearty thump on the back.

'Thank God for that. I wasn't looking forward to shifting my horses.'

The relief was intense. Now he could plan ahead. The first thing he'd do was ring Joe Parkin. Pat had brought the lad round to Beach Head as soon as he'd got out of prison and they'd cleared the air. Jack had been impressed how well Joe had taken his ordeal. 'I was a bit of a prat, guv,' he'd said. 'If I'd never whacked Andy with a whip, I'd never have ended up inside, would I?'

Jack would offer Joe his old job back. It felt like the right thing to do.

And maybe he should extend that gallop after all, as Andy had wanted.

On second thoughts, perhaps he wasn't planning for just one more season after all.